## OPE...

The Russian lieutenant had been told to expect chaos on the battlefield. But he had no idea it would be anything like this. Grenades were going off everywhere. Guns were being shot in all directions. He looked up and saw a third wave of paratroopers coming down. Half crazed with pain, he ordered his noncom to stop the soldiers shooting at their own men.

''No!'' the noncom shouted back.

The lieutenant, on the verge of passing out from loss of blood, gathered his strength. ''I command you to order these men to cease fire.''

''No, you fool!'' the noncom said. ''Those are not our men. The Americans have jumped onto the same airfield as we. The Americans are here! We're fighting the damn Americans!''

# CRADLE
## OF FIRE

*where the world's ultimate nightmare
can come true . . .*

# CRADLE
## OF FIRE

J. V. Smith, Jr.

AN ONYX BOOK

ONYX
Published by the Penguin Group
Penguin Books USA Inc., 375 Hudson Street,
New York, New York 10014, U. S. A.
Penguin Books Ltd, 27 Wrights Lane,
London W8 5TZ, England
Penguin Books Australia Ltd, Ringwood,
Victoria, Australia
Penguin Books Canada Ltd, 10 Alcorn Avenue, Toronto, Ontario, Canada
M4V 3B2
Penguin Books (N. Z.) Ltd, 182–190 Wairau Road,
Auckland 10, New Zealand

Penguin Books Ltd, Registered Offices:
Harmondsworth, Middlesex, England

First published by Onyx, an imprint of New American Library, a division of
Penguin Books USA Inc.

First Printing, February, 1992
10  9  8  7  6  5  4  3  2  1

**PUBLISHER'S NOTE**
This is a work of fiction. Names, characters, places, and incidents either are
the product of the author's imagination or are used fictitiously, and any
resemblance to actual persons, living or dead, events, or locales is entirely
coincidental.

In memory of Herbert Koliba and Ray Loftus for two. To all the men of D Company, First Squadron, Eleventh Armored Cavalry Regiment—Blackhorse, sir!

## ACKNOWLEDGMENTS

Thanks to Larry Hoeg, for photos and reminiscences of eastern Iran, to Deb and Ray Rowden for transcription and typing, and to John Silbersack for his tutoring. A special thanks to my friend Jerry Wilson.

# Prologue

**Mashhad, Iran**

His enemies called him Ferret. So did his friends. And
so did his subordinates when they thought he couldn't
hear them sniggering.

The light coming from the stairwell, filtered through
filmy, streaked door glass, fell on the nervous face that
gave him his nickname. His forehead and chin re-
ceded, accenting his pointed nose into long relief. His
flinty eyes cast black glances right, then left.

His real name was Major Abu al-Batt. He had never
served in army fighting units after his initial armor
training. Because of his ability to wheedle the safest
assignments, he'd always found staff positions. Tonight, though, that would change. Forever. He would
taste combat. Personal armed combat against the
Imam. His first and last battle.

Abu the Ferret dried his palms on his tunic, feeling
for the reassuring grips of his dagger and the taped
length of pipe stuck into the waistband of his trousers.
For the twentieth time, they were still there. His conspirator was not here, though. He cursed under his
breath. Where was the man who had been planted inside the shrine? He should have acted already. Had the
plan been betrayed? Of course, he only knew of the
plan by coincidence. Maybe it had been changed after
he fulfilled his miserable courier duties. Or maybe he'd
been carrying a counterfeit plan, a ruse. Would they
have risked sacrificing him that way?

His eyes darted to the glowing digits of his watch.
3:13. No matter if they hadn't invited him into the

assassination plan. He could do it himself. Do it. Or go slink back to bed like a coward. He pushed against the stairwell door. Locked. Where was the bastard with the key? Now was the moment to act. At no other time would the Imam's men be sleeping more soundly. In less than an hour, the first early risers would be up trying to outpray each other. Trying to impress the old Imam. A slit of a grin creased his face. Imagine the impression his pipe was going to make! Imagine . . .

Abu tensed. A distant scuffing. In two silent strides, he slipped across the hallway into a recessed doorway. The sounds were bare feet padding on tile. From an adjoining corridor. He saw a ghost of movement and pressed into the doorway's shadow. The figure approached.

The man would pass. Probably going to sneak into the pantry for a snack. He could not have been a conspirator, for he moved too boldly, hardly trying to muffle the noise of his leathery soles. He plodded like an ass to its fodder. Pass by, ass.

The figure did not pass by, however. He stopped on the spot where Abu had stood just seconds ago. He jerked a quick look both ways down the hallway and reached to the neckline of his tunic. Then Abu knew he must be a conspirator, one of his own. But how to approach him now without startling him?

He stood before the stairwell door, his heart pounding. All he had to do was open this door, dash up the stairs, and open a second door. On the way down, he was to unbolt the lightproof shutters on the stairwell landing. Then he could dash back to his room, throw the key into the sewer, and feign sleeping until the assassins accomplished their mission. He fished the master key from the loop around his neck and stepped up to the stairwell door. Suddenly his heart bashed against the inside of his ribs. Had he felt warm spots on the cold tiles? *Somebody had been standing here!* When he looked down, he saw the damp outlines of bare feet protruding from under his own soles. As he looked up, he felt a rush of acrid air filled with the scent of fear.

*Betrayed!*

"Quiet, ass!"

But he could not stifle a yelp of surprise. A smothering hand cut off his breath. He bit the hand and struggled, grasping backward to clamp on the genitals of his attacker. He uttered a groan as a stabbing agony pierced his chest, a sharp, hot poke of angina that took away his breath and electrified his heart and brain. He tried to suck air, but the hand clamped over his nose and mouth prevented it. Yet he felt his chest expanding. Air sucking through the wound. Killed. Damnation. He'd been murdered. He failed. He tried to see his killer, but caught only a glimpse of a pointed face. *A familiar face. That damned al-Batt!* He'd been at the evening's feasts. Angrily he reasoned, *there must have been an error!* He tried to utter the code words. "Praise Allah," he sputtered incoherently into the hand clasped on his face. The hand loosened. "What was that?" Before he could repeat it, a sharp poke into his heart stiffened his body. In seconds, he was dead.

Abu leaned over, knock-kneed, his testes throbbing. He cursed himself and the dead man at his feet as the muggy bouquet of the opened chest rose to his long, narrow nostrils. Leaning down carefully, he tore the string from the dead man's neck, producing a roughly hewn key. A second of panic set off a wave of adrenaline, making his hands tremble. What if this was not a conspirator after all? What if the key would not fit anything but the dead man's bedroom door? What if he was only sneaking into the pantry after all?

He lifted the key to its slot and wiggled it. Gently, at first. It would not turn. A shock wave of panic hit him. He wiggled it vigorously, angrily, prayerfully. He moaned, cursed. The key turned a fraction. He twisted as hard as he dared, feeling the scraping of brass against brass. The bolt withdrew into the lock. Abu stepped into the stairwell. He hung the loop over his own gown and panted raggedly, trying to control his breathing, waiting for the pain in his groin to slacken.

The key slid down on its loop, chilling a spot on his chest, and he caught his breath. He prayed for a chill on his heart as well, for any compassion now would only jeopardize his mission of vengeance.

The Ferret's bare feet padded up to the fourth-floor landing. Abu turned, grinning as he ascended, intending to disarm the guard with an absurd smile. His explanation would be that he was making a last-second security check and had found the door open below. For a small bribe, he would not report the sentry to the officer of the guard. His grin ached. He would have a second or two to draw near the sentry with his lie, near enough to . . .

Then he saw that a lie would not be necessary, and his grin dissolved into a tiny, wicked sneer.

The guard's straight-backed chair reclined backward against the wall, resting on its two back legs. His rifle lay across his lap. His stubbled chin thrust outward and upward, allowing the back of the head to cradle between the shoulders.

Offering the stubbled throat.

Abu positioned himself before the guard. His left hand grasped the head of oily, black hair. At the same instant, he sliced downward, cutting beneath the left ear. He drew the blade across the front of the throat, feeling the blade rasp on whiskers, sawing through cartilage, cleaving down to vertebrae. He waited for that rush of air meant to escape the mouth as a scream of warning, but which would come as a bubbling hiss. Nothing. The exhalation escaped through the neck as a normal breath.

"Drugged," murmured Abu in despair. His second unnecessary killing of the night. "The man has been drugged."

The guard's body did not even go rigid. The chair legs simply began slipping even before the blade had completed its slice. The Ferret held the man's weight by his hair. His left foot caught the chair before it could clatter against the concrete. He lowered the dying body to the floor. A little gush of blood swamped over his feet.

Abu's rabid grin darkened. Two errors in only a few seconds. How many more errors would he be allotted?

He tried the door to the fourth-floor hallway. Locked. Of course. His key would not work in this door—he just knew it wouldn't. They would follow his footprints of blood to his room. He'd be killed, a fragment of his body at a time. That didn't matter. What would matter would be the shame of failure. Again. Still.

He checked his watch.

Again he pulled the loop of string and dredged up the master key, wet and slippery from his body sweat. Maybe. Maybe he would not fail again. He turned the key. The lock yielded, and Abu prayed thanks.

To implicate the guard, the Ferret tied a pouch of silver coins to the man's belt and tucked it into the waistband.

He was back on a successful path. All was set.

He glanced at the guard, huddled in a bloody heap. He could stop here. To clear the way for the hired assassins, he merely had to unlock the windows and shutters at the landing and go back to his room. He could go downstairs and wash himself clean of the blood. When the alarm was raised, he could act like another of the sleeping occupants of the Shiite shrine. From this point, others would do the killing.

He checked his watch again. They should be here by now. Had the mission been scrubbed? Had they been discovered at a routine checkpoint or in a surprise traffic stop? Maybe they had simply experienced mechanical problems. Perhaps they'd gotten lost in the labyrinth of Mashhad's bewildering streets. This opportunity might be lost. Such a chance might never come again for the group of honorable men his father represented. Certainly, no such miracle as tonight would ever present itself again. Certainly . . . *wait!*

What was he debating himself about? What about his own needs? Forget his father. Forget the plan. What about his promise of vengeance? Would he betray the memory of his mother after coming this far?

He wrenched open the fourth-floor door and entered the hallway.

Abu the Ferret tried half a dozen rooms without success. All he had to do was push the door in and sniff the expelled puff of air. His nose would tell him. It wasn't a pretty nose, but it was an accurate one. Finally, he opened a door that released the musty, stale scent of the old man. He inhaled deeply, drawing the taste of the smell over his palate, too. He knew the right scent. This was the one.

He snorted the old man's reek from his nose and went in.

The starkness of the quarters surprised him. He'd expected secret luxuries. It disappointed the Ferret to find the old religious leader absent of hypocrisy among all the other reasons to hate him.

There, across the uncarpeted room, lay his victim, the Ayatollah Fahzi, object of Abu's lifetime of hatred.

Shaded candles cast a dim gloom on the cot. The old man lay naked and stiff on rumpled white sheets with heavy blankets tossed to the side. Abu padded across the room. He saw sweat glistened on the frail body. Then he saw the glint from the slit of one eye. *So the old devil lies awake!*

On the floor, stretched out on a mat, lay a young priest, one of the corps of novice priests who tended the old mullah twenty-four hours a day.

The old man's hand inched toward the side of the mattress, bony fingers pulling it along like pale, hairless tarantula legs yoked to the arm.

Abu didn't care. Not now. He gripped his knife and felt his little grin stretch. Too late for any kind of alarm. Too late even if a cannon went off . . . unless the cannon was aimed at him.

The tarantula hand flopped over the side of the bed onto the shoulder below.

Instantly, the young priest came up on his knees as if praying at the side of the cot. He smacked his lips. "What is it, Holy One?"

"It" was a knife at his Adam's apple. "It" sliced a ragged smile into the throat. This time the soundless scream hissed from the neck as it should have, carrying an odor more sickening than foul breath. Blood splattered the old priest before the body fell, quivering, back onto its mat on the floor.

Abu cursed the old man, one in an unbroken line of militant clerics dating from Khomeini who had paralyzed Iran since the 1970s with their despotic, medieval rule.

The Imam opened his mouth as if he would curse back. Only a croak, dry and meaningless, issued from his throat.

The Ferret saw the man sneer up at him. Such defiance! The old dried-up fig did not fear him! Instead, the eyes glinted with hatred the likes of which had killed thousands—if one included the human-wave tactics against Iraq, *millions*—of Iranians.

Abu glanced at his watch. No time for the lengthy ritual this assassination deserved. He withdrew his length of pipe, eighteen inches of iron, three-quarters of an inch in diameter, wrapped in cloth tape. He draped the woolen blanket and sheet over the skeleton of the old man to muffle the sounds, leaving the face uncovered so he could record the image of pain in his memory.

The body barely made a lump under the bulky covers. The Ferret raised the pipe and smashed it heavily on one foot, crushing the small tent it made of the blankets.

A surprisingly loud groan escaped the old lips.

Abu named his dead mother and wheeled, crashing the pipe down over the larynx, smashing it like leathery eggshells.

The old man gasped for air that could not be drawn through the crushed neck.

He would suffocate in minutes. Too quick. Too bad.

Abu grabbed the wispy beard and muttered the name of his mother into the old ear, insurance that the old man would die hearing the name of one of his victims.

In response, the Imam gagged on his own blood. The old fart was trying to spit blood on him!

Abu smashed the toothless mouth, then turned to the old man's other foot, then each lower leg, then the knees, naming a member of his family for each blow.

The blanket darkened, and the old man rose up to a sitting position. It was his last response, but Abu kept pounding until the pipe slipped from his grasp.

Exhausted, Abu stood gasping. His senses came back. He glanced at his watch and gasped.

Dear Allah, where had the time gone?

Abu dashed for the door and ran from the old man's room to the stairwell. On the landing, he unlocked the window, threw it up and unlatched the shutters. He shoved them out and heard the rasping of a rope over the top of one shutter. The assassins had come!

He wanted to greet them, to tell them their mission had been done. They could finish the lesser luminaries of the revolutionary government, but he had done the important work. He wanted to shout to them. He wanted to boast of his part in this. His father would be so proud. His mother must be smiling down on him.

He looked up to return the smile and saw a rope dangling outside. Time to go.

He whirled and felt a tiny slap on his chest.

The key! He scrambled back up to the top and hung it around the neck of the guard. It and the purse of coins would implicate the dead man as the accomplice from inside the shrine.

Then he ran pell-mell down the stairs, huffing and straining to drag the conspirator into the stairwell. He dried his bloody feet on the man's back and, stepping over the puddle of gore on the tiles, ran toward his room.

It hardly mattered, he realized.

He had broken the curse of his country. He had avenged his family. He had cut the continuous chain of one old man after another who had run the country into ruin since the revolution. He had opened the way for more moderate men to make overtures to the West.

Maybe the Americans would find somebody reasonable to deal with, perhaps his father. Maybe now his
final, suicidal act would redeem him as a soldier and
patriot. And a son. Surely his father would forgive him
for taking such a risk. Surely he would rise in his es-
timation now.

The knowledge that he could die happy slowed his
steps. Abu wanted to relish the feeling. In these first
seconds of the first real peace he had known in years,
he wondered if all he had meant to do in life had been
done in the fleeting minutes on the floor above. Now
if he died, even his worst enemies could not call him
a buffoon. He'd done what nobody had been able to
do for decades—not the Iraqis, not the rebels in exile,
not the generals before his father, not the Soviets, not
even the Americans. He'd broken the string of clerics!

The leader of the paid assassination team had found
great satisfaction in seeing the mission carried off so
smoothly. He and two Mongoloid-featured Turkomans, men as rough as the mountains they ushered
from, had scaled the outer walls of the shrine and
found the roof to the living quarters. As promised, and
on time, the shutters to the window at the landing had
been opened. The guard had been disposed of. The
doors had been unlocked. Always before, there had
been blunders. Never had a plan been so well executed.

That thought vanished the instant he opened the door
to the mullah's room and was struck in the face by the
scent of blood and gore overpowering even the fra-
grance of incense.

A body lay seeping into a mat on the floor.

On the cot lay a mass of bloodied covers.

The old man.

It could mean only one thing: a smoothly executed
betrayal.

The leader's eyes burned beneath his heavy brow.
He was slight and part Persian, a killer by training and
by the glory of his god. He wished he could kill now—
not the old man but the traitor.

From another part of the building, he heard shouting and the sounds of running feet.

He called to his men, who had already begun entering bedrooms and bestowing eternal punishment to other mullahs with their daggers.

They ran toward the stairwell landing, drawing pistols from their waistbands. Already they knew the stairway to the roof had been welded shut. Otherwise there would have been no need for the ropes and the accomplice . . . rather, the traitor.

The first assassin had already grasped the rope and swung out into the night when the doors below the landing burst open. A guard with an AK-50 assault rifle fired three quick rounds from the ground below, and the Mongol dropped three and a half stories to the walkway, screaming in defiance with his final breath.

Abu had decided to throw his military tunic over his sleeping gown. Wise to show his uniform. Even if the security detail panicked, they could not fail to recognize him as an overnight guest. He had to go out when the alarm was sounded. It would be cowardly—even suspicious—if he remained in his room during the murder of the Imam by assassins. He carried his dagger. No combat veteran would have rushed into danger without a weapon, he reasoned. Clever, Abu, he told himself. Very clever. He waited for the sounds of running feet. He mingled with the rush of stale bodies and breath streaming toward the stairwell. He didn't want to be in the lead, nor in the crowd of stragglers holding back from the sound of gunfire.

"Let me by," he demanded, shoving the men in front of him. "I'm a soldier . . . I'm an officer." He did not, however, shove anybody aside. He pushed them ahead like shields.

Ahead, the sergeant of the guards shouted, demanding a surrender. For an instant, the leader looked as if he might give up—already the second Turkoman had raised his hands.

Abu was close enough to lean around the doorway

to the stairwell. He looked over the shoulders he kept before him.

"You have a dagger," somebody behind him said.

"Yes, to defend the Imam with my life," Abu declared.

One man said. "Well, then he is up there."

Another said, "You must go." The crowd between Abu and the door parted.

Abu groped for a reasonable excuse not to. All at once, he felt not so clever. Next, he felt a shove in the back. He resisted. Another man pushed him. He skidded into the stairwell, stumbling over his first victim of the night, slipping in the very blood he had let, bellowing a curse, offering a threat to the bastards who had shoved him.

The leader of the assassins saw the weasel-faced man in an army tunic slide to a stop at the bottom step, brandishing a dagger. The murderous threats were bombast. The man looking both sheepish and fearful rather than angry or impassioned. He looked guilty, by Allah!

The leader knew he'd found the traitor.

He aimed his pistol and fired at the man with the weasel face . . . just as a complement of guards behind Abu opened up.

Abu saw the assassins jerk about on the stairwell and tumble toward him. He didn't care about them. His own visions of glory were kicked right out of him. Twice. One kick hit him in the thigh, a slug which stung and knocked him off balance. The second shot hit him in the chest, robbing him of breath. He forgot the trivial first blow. This was more like being stabbed with a heavy spear—a dull, blunt spear that drove the air out of his lungs and threw him off balance. He fell backward, crashing into the wall of the stairwell, spinning and tumbling down the lower stairs to the landing above the basement.

The pain! It drained him of enthusiasm for personal honor. Honor, hell. Clever? No. He was a buffoon

after all. *Look at the reward you have earned for yourself, you fool.*

He lay gasping for breath. He felt himself losing
consciousness. A wave of weakness swept him. Cold
. . . oh, so cold. He heard droning inside his head.

So this was death.

"Praise Allah!" he murmured. It was the code he
was to use when contacting his general to confirm he
had delivered the plan, to confirm that he had left
Mashhad.

Revolutionary Guards knelt to assist him. "Praise
Allah," they said.

Abu smiled through gritted teeth. The dumb bastards! They thought he'd been calling on his god. All
he'd done was repeat the code.

"Praise Allah," he murmured, he heard a whistling
of air sucked into his chest. Like the man he'd knifed
earlier, just meters away. He knew he was done. He
laughed, gurgling through his chest wound. When he
caught up with the man he'd knifed, there would be
hell to pay. Did they have buffoons in the afterlife? He
hoped not. "Praise Allah."

"Praise Allah," the soldiers chanted reverently on
his behalf.

# BOOK I

# SPARKS

# 1

Sundown came suddenly to the high desert. Standing in one of the jagged creases of the rumpled sandpaper of the Mojave, Lieutenant Colonel Nelson Miles felt more than saw the tidal wave of shadow race across the sands, engulfing him in chilly shade. A sudden shudder broke his reverie, brought him back to the here and now. He realized he'd been spacing, staring at the gravel at his feet. He looked up and saw that the sun had been sucked into the ragged, stony gullet of the Sierra Nevada range.

Miles snorted in disgust toward the beauty of the golden-orange halo left behind by the sun. *As if nature had any right to preen before him.* His nostrils flared. *Sonofabitch.* He raised his bulky chin and cursed the fiery display.

With darkness would come a full-scale test of the Osprey, and he would be doing no more than sitting behind a desk. He hated passivity. Always, he wanted to make things move, to see results. Leave the theory to the PhDs, he had always said. And to the staff weenies.

He spat the words: "Staff weenie." For chrissakes, now he was one of them. Make that *still one of them.*

He snatched the military baseball cap from his head and slapped it against the tree trunk of his thigh. He kept up an impatient, irregular tempo long after the impact stopped raising white billows of desert dust from his army flight suit.

* * *

A radio operator who had left the subcommand center found Miles by following the slapping sound. The buck sergeant approached warily. At the mouth of the gully, where the fissure opened into a rocky valley, stood his superior officer lashing his leg with his hat. The sergeant started to speak, then stopped, fearing he might startle Miles, still an unknown quantity among the enlisted staff. Miles looked mean as hell. Sure, he had not abused anybody, verbally or otherwise, since he joined the G3 operations section. Barracks rumor had it that Miles had been in charge of the Army Aviation School's pilot survival course. Pilots on the escape and evasion course called him Swamp Creature. The sergeant grimaced in the dark. He'd rather piss off crocodiles than the Creature. The grapevine further reported he'd been a football player at the Academy. A fullback who would rather run at people than by them. A hitter.

The grapevine had it right, the sergeant surmised. Nobody could have a body like that and *not* play football. Damn, he'd have hated to try to bang helmets with a guy built like stacks of boulders. Even under the baggy Nomex flight suit, he seemed to be wearing protective pads. His fists were like the broad, rounded stones found in stream bottoms. The lower half of his face was oversized, his chin protruding as if he would drive it into your forehead. Like he'd crunched a mouthful of stones down to pea-gravel and was about to spew them in your face. The man looked dangerous. Swamp Creature. Yeah.

The buck sergeant lost his nerve. Hell with sneaking up on the guy. Better find a more discreet approach to Miles if he was going to stand there looking pissed off. He'd backtrack, then make a lot of noise in a second trip. He lifted a foot. The slapping stopped.

"What do you want, Sergeant?"

*How could he tell a sergeant in this light?* "Uh, Lieutenant Colonel Miles . . . sir?"

"Yes?"

"Sir, yes, sir . . . we're about to make our final

operational checks before the test? The NCOIC said you wanted to be told?'' Each of his statements sounded like a question.

"Thank you, Sergeant. Say, were you sneaking up on me? You planning to scare me or something?" The tone in Miles' voice had softened. Still it did not reassure the sergeant.

"Honest to God, sir, I never . . . I was trying to sneak away . . . I mean—''

"Relax. Put that foot back on the ground and stop standing there like a flamingo." Miles smiled, turning his face aside to hide the grin in a shadow. "Forget it, Sergeant. I know what you mean. You didn't want to startle me. Instead, I startled you. Sorry. Tell the NCOIC I'll be there in a minute.''

The sergeant saluted awkwardly and tried to execute an about-face. The sandy soil caught his feet and spun him off-balance. He ducked under the IR-scattering camouflage netting and passed through the light traps into the sub-command center.

"Lighten up," Miles told himself. He slapped himself with the hat. Bad enough he was making himself crazy. Slap. *You'll get everybody else crazy, too, by running around mad as hell all the time. It's not these people's fault you're stuck on staff . . . not their fault you didn't get the assignment you wanted . . . not their fault you've been asked to kill the best goddamned weapons system the Army ever had.* Slap . . . slap. "SonofaBITCH."

"Colonel Miles, the general wants you on the horn.''

Miles raised an eyebrow at the bank of five handsets hanging before his face above a shelf full of six screens. Each handset panel was itself a virtual keyboard of buttons and lights. Most of the lights illuminated steadily or blinked continuously as the time for the test approached.

"Sir," the spec four pleaded, "the general—''

Miles turned deliberately toward the voice and saw

that this was one of the new kids who had been sent in when General Bayard Wilkerson demanded that every listening post and command post be double-manned—no matter that most of the extras would be underfoot. The kid wasn't to blame for not knowing the complexity of a sub-command post did not lend itself to such generalized statements. The "horn" the young man had referred to could have been any one of nearly two dozen preset frequencies to brigade and battalion headquarters, to aerial subposts, to satellite links and more. It might have meant one of several windows displaying electronic information on each of the screens, including low-light television. It might have even been a live television linkup that Wilkerson was so fond of using to send reprimands long distance. Or it could have been the SuperStarScreen, a receiver screen capable of tuning in to as many as four SuperStarlights, powerful night vision devices positioned with the cavalry screen and other night observation posts.

Miles cleared his throat to ask for clarification. He heard a familiar voice.

"Colonel Miles, the general's on FM tac-four. Sorry about the confusion." It was the buck sergeant he'd rattled in the encounter outside the command center.

A radio speaker squawked. "This is Ace Five. Goddammit, Miles, where've you been?" The scratchy, demanding, demeaning voice of the assistant division commander for maneuver perfectly matched the wiry, angular man himself, Miles thought. He was showing absolutely no concern for radio security, call signs, or common courtesy. Miles was grateful that every device in today's army used scramblers to encode information, making it unusable to enemy eavesdroppers. However, every American enlisted signalman tuned in to the frequency was hearing Wilkerson treat him like a buck-ass private AWOL from KP.

Miles clenched his teeth, scanning his status screens, trying to assimilate the more abstract numerical reports for the answer to the inevitable question.

"General, this station will be up and operational within . . ." He looked for a sign for his sergeant and saw the two fingers. ". . . two minutes."

Brigadier General Bayard Wilkerson barked, "Get after it, dammit, we've got us a chicken to choke. Are you ready?"

Miles cleared his throat. He glanced at the sergeant. One finger. Gain some time with a little gobblede-gook. "This is Seven-Seven. All status screens show we're completely on schedule—"

"Bullshit on the status screens." Wilkerson cut him off. "You're stalling me. I've got access to those, same as you. That data is always fifteen minutes behind, anyhow. Your sector's master screen hasn't come up yet. What the hell's going on?"

Damned frequency override! In the old days, Miles thought, a radio could either transmit or receive but not both at once.

"Seven-Seven here. That screen isn't even sched-uled to—"

"Don't give me that schedules shit, Miles. You have to monitor your sector. If the chicken gets through your section of wire mesh, you get the hatchet. That's the way the game's being played."

Miles cursed the frequency override again. He reached for his own override switch to suppress the general's tirade. The wonders of turn-of-the-century technology had spawned receivers with priority over-rides. That meant a higher headquarters could inter-rupt on a frequency at any time a lower command was transmitting. It had been designed for tactical emer-gencies, but Wilkerson and too many officers like him used it to chew ass any time he wanted. Which was most of the time, Miles had noted. Now was the time to draw the line with Wilkerson. If he let the general ridicule him now, he'd be forever seen as a weakling. He would establish himself. No need to be insubor-dinate, but . . .

He flipped the switch and cut off the general with his own overriding burst of power, which activated a series of cutout circuits in Wilkerson's transmitter-receiver. "Goddammit, General—" he began. Then he saw a movement in the corner of his vision. The buck sergeant waved a closed fist at him. Miles' face grew hot that some of his men had to hear this degrading conversation. But the sergeant was smiling, poking his thumb up from the bouncing fist. Miles's desktop screen flickered. He smiled back at the sergeant. So . . . that was how a smile was supposed to feel. He let up on the override.

Wilkerson sputtered at him. "What do you mean cutting me off, Colonel? You'd better have a goddamned good explanation for talking to me like that, or else I'll . . ."

Miles stopped listening. He scanned the desktop, an electronic tactical map with instant focus and a full range of magnification power of the terrain features and symbols. All checkpoints but one at 1:100,000 scale showed green. As he watched, the final red spot fluttered and went green. Miles skimmed the information in the margin windows of the screen. They checked out. Miles read the private message scrolling across the bottom of his personal screen: ALL SYSTEMS GREEN WITHIN THE LAST 00:30 SECS. ALL MARGINAL DATA ACCURATE TO WITHIN THE LAST 00:15. ALL VOICE COMMUNICATIONS SECURE (THANK GOODNESS!) TO THE LAST 00:00. ALL IMAGES READY FOR LINKUP TO HIGHER AT YOUR FINGERTIPS. SGT KOPMEYER.

Miles used an elaborate keyboard and an electronic mouse to wipe the (THANK GOODNESS!) from the screen. Using the four-key combination of the day's secure code, he authorized and executed the instantaneous linkup with the division command center, where Wilkerson still ranted over voice radio. Like all radios nowadays, this one was scrambled, secure from interception by enemy receivers. Small consolation, Miles thought. The only ones not listening to this asschewing were the Soviets. He wiped Kopmeyer's name off and put in his own. He lifted the spring-loaded cover and hit the SEND button. There. Off my ass, general.

Wilkerson had never stopped badgering him, had never let up for an answer. With a sadistic smile, Miles overrode him again. "General, take a look at your screen. I've been trying to tell you our screen is up, but you won't let me. This is Seven-Seven, out here."

By now Wilkerson could see for himself on the live screen display at his own station. Without another word for Miles, he began bitching at the commander of another subsector. For a second, Miles wondered how a man with that kind of disposition would cope with stress under combat. Instantly, that very thought scraped the scab off a personal wound. How the hell would he know how somebody else might act under fire? He had missed the last fighting himself. The very words, "desert" and "storm," no matter how they were used, made him angry.

"Sergeant Kopmeyer," he said, straining the words through his teeth.

"Sir?"

"Thanks for saving my butt with the ADC." Miles pointed a thumbprint at the buck sergeant. He felt a twinge of embarrassment that he'd not even learned the man's name until he read it on the screen. Cripes, he hoped he could operate this center more alertly than this when the "chicken" that Wilkerson referred to came down his sector.

"It was nothing—"

"Nothing, hell!" Miles caught himself growling. Composed himself. Continued. "What I mean is, you were first-rate. When you're first-rate, don't disparage yourself. Better to be tenth-rate than second-rate."

"Sir?"

"The distance between second-rate and tenth is a tiny stumble compared to the enormous drop from first-rate to second."

"Yessir."

Miles watched a look of awe dawning on the sergeant's face. "Don't be so impressed, Sergeant. It's not my line. It's a paraphrase. I stole it."

"Yessir." Kopmeyer grinned. "It's a first-rate line, sir."

Miles laughed. "Have you got a nickname I can use?"

"Call me Kop, sir . . . if you want."

"I want . . . Kop. What say we get down to cases here. We've got a mission."

"Choke that chicken, sir?"

Miles inhaled deeply, restraining the urge to admonish, to correct, to protect—as if the "chicken" required his protection. "No, Kop, we're running a tactical test against a sophisticated weapons system. You ever seen it?" Kopmeyer shook his head. "It's not a chicken. It's an eagle, a sea eagle, a goddamned killer. It's called Osprey, and it's the future of warfare, Kop."

"First-rate?"

"First-rate."

"Think we'll see it on the screens tonight, sir?"

Miles chewed on a lip before answering. "Would you like to see it in person?"

Kopmeyer answered with a gape. Not possible, the expression said.

Miles winked and nodded. "Better get back to work, Kop. I'll let you know when it's time." *Way to go, Miles. Not enough to be thought stupid. You've got to open your mouth and prove it.*

Major General Lawrence Wadsworth didn't even hang his coat before approaching Preston Brooks. He'd seen the bustling in the hallways. What could be so important that the Pentagon had caught fire at three o'clock in the morning? He hadn't seen anything like this since Desert Storm.

"Whaddya got, Preston?" he said to the back of the closely cropped head of the Marine major.

Brooks bolted to attention, a Marine reaction he'd never quite conquered in Washington, D.C., where everybody in uniform assumed a workable informality except for ceremonial necessity. "Good morning,

General Wadsworth. I have some things here you may want to pass up the line this morning.''

Wadsworth tossed his coat over a chair and sat, leaning back on it.

Brooks began his report.

''I've been following Iraqi troop movements for weeks . . . well, actually for the whole time I've been here. Like everybody else, I had been focusing on the disputed border between the Iras.''

Wadsworth nodded at ''Iras,'' intelligence shorthand for any term that included both Iran and Iraq. He also noticed the past tense, as in ''had been focusing on the disputed border.''

Brooks continued. ''As you know, sir, the Iras have been exchanging missiles and truces on and off for decades. It's been like a chess game, sometimes hot, sometimes stalemated for long periods. Every time one army moves into an attack position, the other reinforces the sector that is threatened.''

Wadsworth shrugged. ''History.''

Brooks said, ''I've noticed something completely out of character in the routine analyses from the central region in the last week. I've watched dozers building new defensive tank positions and improving old ones. I've seen new trenches, fighting positions, and overhead shelters being built. I've seen new TOCs being sited. The Iraqis are digging in, sir. They're preparing to defend against an attack on Baghdad.''

Wadsworth squinted. ''Do you mean to say the Iraqis are preparing to run an extensive defensive operation while the Iranians haven't even instigated anything offensive?''

''Exactly, sir. Yes, sir. The Iraqis are expecting something to happen.''

Wadsworth sat erect. This *was* significant. But he doubted it was the reason he'd been awakened. He could have had a routine briefing during normal duty hours for a scoop that had been developing over a week or two. Besides there might be other explanations for the digging in. He tried one out on the major.

"What about the new Iraqi command group at the Ira front? Another post-Kuwait purge? Couldn't this just be a new broom sweeping out the laxity?"

"I thought that at first, sir. But then I began seeing delay and defend positions being dug in depth from the front back toward Baghdad. And temporary tactical bridging has been dropped in place along several new routes toward the rear positions. This is way different from the static defenses we've seen in the eighties and nineties."

"And in the cities?"

"There we've seen evidence of stepped-up evacuation exercises and air-raid drills. The Iraqis are expecting to be hit."

Wadsworth stroked his chin. "No signs of an Iraqi offensive, though? They're not starting anything?"

"Nothing I can see, sir. Just the rallying of more mech and tank reserves around Baghdad. A mobile reserve. More defensive posturing, in my opinion."

"What the hell's going on, Preston?"

Brooks stiffened into an even more formal posture. Internally, Wadsworth followed suit, bracing himself for the punch line.

"I saw furious activity from the holy city of Mashhad in the northeast of Iran."

Wadsworth squinted. "Didn't I see something in the closing INTSUMS yesterday about the ayatollah visiting Mashhad?"

"Yes, sir. But this activity wasn't the type we've seen in any of his past visits. I think the Imam is dead—"

"Kee-rist! Another one of the old bastards? That's the third one in the last two years. Natural causes?"

"Judging from the chaos, no. This is no natural causes event. Maybe it's a coup . . . or he may have been assassinated. From the looks of things, civil war is imminent in Iran. I've already taken the liberty of calling in our entire staff. It may have to go straight to the president, sir."

"My God, do you suppose the Iraqis might have hit

Fahzi?'' Wadsworth whispered to himself more than Brooks, who shrugged in answer anyhow. ''What time is it in Iran?'' He glanced at his own watch to learn Washington time had reached 3:30 A.M. Rather than taking the trouble to figure the time difference of eight hours, thirty minutes between Washington and Tehran, an hour less when the nation was on Daylight time, he depended on his encyclopedic Marine to have the instant answer.

''1100 hours,'' said Brooks.

Wadsworth's mind raced ahead of the clock. So many details would have to be ironed out. For if Brooks's conclusions were true, major strategic implications for the United States lay before them.

Zero-zero-four-zero hours.

Forty minutes after midnight, Pacific Daylight Time.

Major General Steve Little noted the time as the hangar doors slid open. With the hangar illuminated only by red floodlights, outside actually seemed bright. Since Salyut-19 space station had passed over the horizon three minutes ago, the Soviets would be blind to events here for about six hours, until the Salyut-18 came by. With official Washington asleep on Eastern Time—Little glanced at his watch and calculated . . . zero-three-four-zero hours—hardly anybody on the Pentagon's Unified Defense Staff, successor to the Joint Chiefs of Staff, would even be aware that the first weapons system conceived under the new procurement procedure was now being born into the real world. The Osprey would be rolled out to take its last major test before the three dozen prototypes would be accepted into the army and full-scale manufacturing began.

This was a historic moment, and he knew it.

He glanced at the engineers and scientists and pilots and division staff officers assembled. They sure as hell acted as if they were engaged in something more consequential than spending another night at work launching a new military toy.

"I feel like I'm a part of history," said a reverent voice at Little's shoulder.

He turned to the assistant division commander for logistics, the officer responsible for shepherding the enormous administration and logistical support into shape for this test: Brigadier General Rita Bernadino.

She understood that conventional ground warfare could take a leap in an entirely new direction with this machine they were about to see in action. She knew that each major war on the globe had introduced new elements that made previous tactics obsolete. Only this one might drive into obsolescence some weapons and tactics that had been around for nearly a century.

"You know it, General," said Little.

Then they both watched as a ground-handling tractor towed the AV-33AA Osprey into the brisk night air. Electronics pods beneath the nose would become the craft eyes and ears in the night. Little thought he saw a hand wave from the upper canopy, where the pilot and copilot sat side by side. He waved back and whispered a silent "good luck." Then from the lower, larger canopy, he saw a momentary reflection that also looked like a wave. That couldn't be, for the lower canopy was filled with navigation and night-vision devices. For a second he felt sheepish. Then he inhaled and waved anyhow. "Good luck, Osprey," he said.

Osprey. From the Latin, it literally meant *the bone breaker.* A bird of prey that lives exclusively on fish. Black plumage on top, whitish underneath.

Exactly the paint scheme of this mechanical predator of the air.

It merged into the blackness of the tarmac, so dark and dull was its upper skin paint. When the tow bar had been disconnected, Little had to sweep his gaze back and forth to find the plane again. He kept losing the aircraft in the night.

"My god," he said. "I hope it's just as invisible to all the electronic eyes."

"Let's go, Osprey," said Bernadino in her soft Texan's drawl. "Let's go kick some butt."

The aircraft became visible on the tarmac when its navigation lights—the green and red markers required by the FAA for flight on the domestic airways—blinked on to signal all was well.

The Osprey's lights blinked three times, then went to black. The twin engines whined to a higher pitch, although it made little more noise than a household air conditioner.

Little heard a pitch change in the popping air being forced down onto the tarmac. Then he thought he saw the Osprey hovering. He swiveled his head, centering the sound between his ears as it moved.

There!

Out against the white fog bank that was the dried bed of Bicycle Lake, he saw the Osprey's dark form floating.

When the Osprey melted into the blackness of the desert, Little and Bernadino went inside to monitor the electronic gadgetry that would determine the bird's capability to live up to its promise of changing the way men conducted warfare.

Inside the Osprey's cockpit, Lieutenant Colonel Joel Parker had to pee. Again. Nothing he'd ever done had caused him so much anxiety. Not even combat. He'd flown AH-64 Apache attack helicopters in Desert Storm, accounting for thirteen kills and two probables himself on the road to Basra. Fifteen Soviet tanks, a dozen of them T-72s. Sure, the tanks were manned by Iraqis. But Parker liked to think of them as Soviet kills. It was a way of keeping his mind tuned to the potential of the next war. Don't be fighting the last war, he told his men and women. The next one, the next one—is what his mentor in the Persian Gulf kept telling him, even while he wanted to savor his kills.

Good advice that was, too. Considering that he was fighting a different kind of battle now. Now he was the leading fighter in the politico-military contest to bring Osprey into the inventory for a new kind of warfare. The Soviet military had been stung by the devastation of Iraq's 1991 army. Their advisors, their tactics, their machines. Devastated.

There'd been hell to pay. Two power changes in the Soviet Union—one of them a bloody coup. There was the potential for new warfare for a while—militants had begun diverting the economy to new tanks, new helicopters, new strategies of militaristic adventure. But, thankfully, moderates had taken control of the Kremlin and helped cool emotions heated to boiling by conservative militarists.

Still, things could change again. They had to be ready. For the next one.

"This mission scares the piss out of me, Jim," he said to his copilot. "Literally." To prove it to himself, he urinated into the tube clasped onto his crotch.

"If war is hell, this is worse than meeting your mother-in-law at a whorehouse," said Chief Warrant Officer Three Jim Longstreet.

They began coordinating the actions of their crew for their mission: to fly through the most intense electronic shield ever to blanket a patch of earth.

AV-33AA.

The "AV" stood for Attack Vehicle. "AA" was simply a model designation in the craft's evolution, but those who knew of the program called it the Ack-Ack, the age-old label for anti-aircraft platform. In truth, it was the nomenclature that best described the new Osprey mission: air-to-air combat against Soviet helicopters that might threaten American anti-tank helicopters. Because of dominance of the skies over the Gulf in Desert Storm, attack helicopters had complete freedom to shoot tanks like fish in a puddle. Not likely that would ever happen again. Thus, the Osprey development program.

The AV-33AA technology had evolved from the Army's XV programs in fits and starts from the 1940s. The idea had been the same all along, an airplane fuselage with oversized props that could be tilted upward like rotors, allowing the plane to hover like a helicopter. The Navy and Air Force developed similar V-22 technology into prototypes in the 1980s and production models in the early 1990s. The craft performed missions from mine-sweeping and anti-submarine warfare to medical evacuation and special operations, carrying up to twenty-four passengers in the cabin—at speeds in excess of three hundred knots.

The Osprey in the V-33 series, however, had evolved into a bird completely different from its predecessors.

Side by side, the craft hardly resembled its elder, smaller cousin. Wings originally placed level with the top of the fuselage now grew out near the bottom. Paired vertical tail fins had been canted and joined to form an inverted V. These two modifications in effect raised the cockpit so that periscopes and gunsights were the highest spots when the craft hovered. On most other fighting and reconnaissance helicopters, the rotor blades atop the mast and fuselage poked into enemy radar's line of sight well before the pilot had hovered high enough to see and fire to the front. Worse than that, in order to fire weapons slung below the fuselage or hanging from wing stores, the entire helicopter had to unmask to hover completely in the open. This had led to development of a new generation of anti-helicopter radar, which then allowed the unique design of the Osprey's rotors to emerge.

The tilt rotors of the Osprey at a hover described a plane level with the pilots' heads. Each propellor plane had been encircled by a "doughnut" ring fin that absorbed and scattered, rather than returned, radar signals. The loss in airspeed due to the drag was more than compensated by the increase in protection from radar detection.

The Osprey's most potent weapons, its Raptor missiles, didn't even have to be unmasked to be fired. The combat crews could acquire targets and engage them with minimal exposure of on-board equipment. In the case of remote sensors, the crew could acquire targets either by radar or thermal imagery and fire from complete defilade, hovering below line of fire.

But tonight's mission did not involve weapons drill.

Tonight, the idea was to defeat an enemy's detection devices. This was more important than weaponry, for if the Osprey couldn't escape detection, it wouldn't be able to avoid destruction.

Parker took the flight controls first, a collective stick for the left hand and a cyclic grip for the right. Thus, the AV-33AA flew like a helicopter, but better.

"Beginning dash," he said into the intercom. He would fly the first five kilometers at two hundred knots—less than half the craft's top airspeed—at fifty feet above the ground. The route, preprogrammed, could be flown by computer, but the idea was for him to get the feel of the controls, the navigation and weapons readouts and the terrain. The next five kilometers would be similarly done by Longstreet as his warmup. They'd be masked from the "enemy" by mountains for that distance. Then they'd have to slow down and begin their sneak tactics for the hundred-fifty-kilometer run. They'd have to be inside a hangar at China Lake within five hours, out of sight of Salyut-19. Average ground speed required a mere thirty kilometers an hour. The dash would give them some time in the bank for later when they might have to expose themselves to radar and fly more carefully.

The Osprey's fuselage had been covered with a second skin incorporating stealth technology, an in-between skin with folds like the bellows of a giant accordion. These forced radar signals that had passed through the nonreflective skin of the craft to be reflected into the valleys of each fold and scattered irregularly, reducing the aircraft's radar signature to practically nothing at ranges longer than half a kilometer. Within that distance, Osprey would have to resort to electronic ruses and masking itself behind terrain and foliage.

A second effect of the skin was to give the craft a shape neither like a helicopter nor an airplane. If anything, it seemed as if the old V-22 Osprey had been shrink-wrapped in a fiberglass composition skin. People who'd seen this craft fly almost universally reported the same reaction: it looked like a flying saucer, a spaceship out of an old sci-fi movie. It didn't seem to have wings when it sliced through the air, flitting around like a misshapen, motorized plaything.

But the Osprey was no toy. It was a virtually invisible killer, and tonight the mission was stealth.

To defeat it, captured Soviet-Iraqi weapons systems and radar sets had been linked with American detection equipment over the air route. Above that net of electronic mesh flew an EC-3H AWACS air battle direction center, adding a second complete umbrella of detection and guidance equipment for the exercise's "enemy." True, the AWACS stood off a hundred miles for realism's sake—no intelligence or command aircraft would ever survive long by loitering above the battlefield—but even a hundred miles was unrealistically close. The AWACS radar would be able to look down and receive the propellor returns from Osprey in any prolonged maneuver that tipped the path of the blades toward the airplane.

The "enemy" also enjoyed absolute air superiority. Four braces of fighters flew air cover. Sixteen US helicopters and four Soviet Hind-D attack gunships, captured at Nasiriyah, prowled the airspace between. On the ground, more than three hundred men crouched in listening and observation posts. The division headquarters had manned two field command posts, designating them sub-command posts. Each brigade pooled its command facilities, adding to the detection force's array.

All these had only one mission.

Under the direction of Brigadier General Bayard Wilkerson, they were to detect one Osprey and simulate killing it.

Wadsworth jabbed his felt-tipped marker at the flip chart as he addressed the Marine major. "OK, Preston, let's see what we've got. Everybody in this building, including the goddamned PX concessionaires, seems to think Ayatollah Fahzi is worm chow, assas-

sinated by persons unknown. We don't even get to savor the possibility, because it happened on our watch
at this desk. We have to assume it's true in case we
get called on for expert advice in somebody's briefing.
Ready?''

Brooks nodded.

"We'll set it up with a little history. Where we
gonna start?''

The major puffed up a little. "Sir, I recommend we
begin at the fighting and peacetime jockeying of the
eighties. I'll talk about the Iraqi invasion of Khuzestan, which has always been disputed. Both countries
claim it. The Iraqis call it Arabistan. They traded advantages for the first half of the decade, then settled
into a war of attrition. The mullahs refused the little
Western aid they might have gotten and burned up a
generation of Iranian youth in human-wave tactics
that—''

Wadsworth held up a hand. "Be brief about it,
though. Same with Desert Storm. We want to concentrate on developments in the last six months to a year.''
He waved his hand for the Marine to continue.

"Well, sir, since Desert Storm, Iraq has begun putting its military back together—they've been allowed
because of the constant pressure of the Iranians. There
has even been intelligence confirming a renewed
chemical manufacturing capability. It's almost certain
they've kept the means to deliver gas via jets, artillery,
and post-Scud generation rockets. Rumors suggest a
tactical nuclear capability, but nothing confirmed.''

His eyes narrowed, Wadsworth cocked his head.
"Has the Iranian army changed all that much?''

The major grimaced. "No, sir. Even though the Iranians helped get the release of all the Western hostages
in Lebanon and received parts and arms, they haven't
changed their dispositions much. Khuzestan is still
heavily defended. The Ira border is guarded everywhere, with most armor concentrated along the
Baghdad-Tehran highway. Either side could launch a
limited offensive on a moment's notice, but the de-

fenses would seem to make it too risky to try. Now
and then some division trades positions with another,
but nothing tipped the scales until . . ." Brooks
walked up to his map of the region and studied the
markings on units.

He turned to his boss and said, "You know, sir, I
can't figure this. The Iranian order of battle hasn't
swung an inch in any direction for years. It's the Iraqis
who have developed an offensive capability. The Iranians are ripe for an Iraqi attack, yet—"

Wadsworth finished his sentence. "Yet, it's the Iraqis
who are setting new defenses into position. That's what's
bothering the hell out of me, too. Why? Why the hell
are they doing it without a provocation?"

Wadsworth's secure telephone squawked at him.
They both stared at it, as it continued to demand attention. Gingerly, Wadsworth reached for it. "I hope
this isn't somebody asking the same questions we are
because I don't want to have to come up with the answers."

By the time Wadsworth had finished speaking,
Brooks knew they would, indeed, be answering those
questions. As the phone rattled into its cradle, he
asked, "Who wants the briefing, sir?"

Wadsworth's face had gone slack. "Preston, we'd
better start digging up some creative answers." He
studied his watch as if he did not believe the digits.
"We've got just a little more than three hours to brief
the chairman and—"

"Here? Our office?"

"Of course not, son. We're going over to the White
House Situation Room."

Nearly three hours had passed since the Osprey had
melded with the night beyond Bicycle Lake.

"Another hour. We're getting down to nut-busting
time," said Major General Steve Little. "We'll have
to bring in the bird and get it into a hangar."

"Crunch time," said Brigadier General Bernadino.
"What do you say, sir? Give them another hour to get

the hell on the move? They could be down for maintenance problems.''

Little didn't answer, but just brushed at the lighted spot on the electronic map display on the course, as if that would get the craft moving. Osprey had been watched from twenty thousand feet by the EC-3H for about ten kilometers after it had crossed the battle line of the Front Line of Troops, the FLOT, formerly the FEBA, Forward Edge of the Battle Area, universally called ''the shit'' by soldiers who had to be there. Then the AWACS had lost radar contact with the propellors pointed at the sky. Ten minutes later, it had reacquired, but the image hadn't moved since.

Osprey hadn't gotten as far as the Black Eagle scout helicopter on its failed practice run weeks before. The only other images had been the Apaches and Hinds as they patrolled the course.

Little had grown progressively more ill at ease. His division was to be the centerpiece of the Rapid Deployment Force. Now these Ospreys were to be the centerpiece of the division's anti-helicopter force, but this critical test had stalled. No way would Osprey get to China Lake now. Not undetected, anyhow, for now it would have to take off and fly at more than a hundred knots.

The general peeled himself out of his chair and ambled halfheartedly across the room for another cup of coffee. It seemed to him that was all he'd done. Would this be the state of modern warfare for major generals? he wondered. Drink a gallon of coffee, then piss two?

Before he'd even poured his first cup of the second gallon, a yelp came from the map display.

''General, come here,'' said Bernadino. Already she felt a sinking in her stomach. That damned Wilkerson! He was going to defeat the Osprey. Suddenly, her knees wanted to unhinge on her. She felt herself swaying in the surge of emotion. *Get hold of yourself, Rita. You can't become what they expect you to be, for crying out loud.*

Already a crowd of strained faces had begun to

gather over the electronic map. In half a dozen spots, electronic images sparkled. The radar transmitters painted each one from at least two directions, according to the master target acquisition readout.

The secure telephone rasped insistently, an enormous katydid in rut.

"What the hell's going on?" asked a handful of men and women at once.

The telephone handset was thrust at Little. He took it reluctantly. As the man in charge, he had to. "General Little."

The conversation in the command center died out as everybody eavesdropped on the grunts and monosyllabic responses from the division commander.

Little hung up. He looked around the room. The staff, enlisted and commissioned alike, averted his gaze. Their commanding officer wore a pained expression that could only mean one thing: The Osprey had tubed it.

"That was the assistant division commander for maneuver. General Wilkerson," he added as if somebody might have forgotten the name that had become synonymous with ass-chewing. "The ADC regretfully reports that no less than thirteen radar and infrared target acquisition devices have conclusively and repeatedly painted the Osprey in the last ten minutes. In effect, the bird has been shot down many times over."

Miles backed away from his master screen's depiction of flashing lights, the same array the general officers had been looking at the Bicycle Lake command center. The vacuum he left when he moved away was filled by a handful of staff officers pushing in to see the displayed electronic kill of the Osprey.

At six-four taller than most of the men in the center, Miles surveyed a circle with one turn of his body. Nearly everybody's attention focused either on the jabbering radio reports of the craft's demise or the master screen. For all intents, the test was over.

Miles connected with Kopmeyer. He winked at the

sergeant—again, a little too confidently. Maybe the Osprey wasn't as good as he thought. Maybe he wasn't as smart as he thought. All that talk about first-rate made him nervous.

Kopmeyer's eyebrows raised the question.

Miles flicked his head toward the nearest exit. Behind him, he heard the chatter rising. Then came the tapping of another set of boot heels following his own. He pushed aside the curtain into a dimly lit anteroom. An interior security guard and receptionist made a move to stand. Miles showed him a palm to let the man remain seated. Kopmeyer stepped into the room puffing. Together, they stepped into the circular compartment the size of a small washroom. Miles grasped an inner handle and pushed.

"Out of breath already, Kop?"

The interior wall of the cylinder spun, shutting off the dim light behind them, then opening on the opposite side to a dimmer light, that of the stars.

"No, sir . . . well, yes, I'm excited, I guess."

Miles stepped out into the night.

"All right, Kop, assuming I'm right, we have to hurry. So I'll talk as we go. We're the last command center along the route, right?"

"Right."

"And what's happening inside our command center and every other TOC in the division?"

"People are crowding around the master screens to see the killing . . . same as with the Black Eagle and the others as soon as the test was over."

"Bingo, Kop. Everybody's attention is fixed on the killing zone, which is about twenty klicks or so into the exercise route. And what do you suppose is happening with people on the ground."

Kopmeyer thought it over. They had circled the command center by now. Miles led the way up the gulch as if he had reconned it, and the sergeant wondered again whether the colonel could see in the dark. Finally, between huffs, he said, "I imagine guys are pretty much doing the same thing on the ground . . .

I guess all their attention is focused on that spot.''

"Pilots?"

"Flying to the kill zone."

"Radars?"

"Well, if they're in line of sight, I'd guess they're all trying to point at the same coordinates so they can say they been in on the kill all along."

"Exactly." Miles picked up the pace as they passed the spot where power generators had been dug in to muffle sound and minimize the heat signature. Now the two men jogged.

Kopmeyer's eyes had adjusted well enough so he could stumble along faster now. Of course, he reasoned, even a lieutenant colonel couldn't see in the dark. On the other hand, this guy *could* climb a hill. Gradually, the officer pulled away. Grunting and wheezing, the younger man struggle upward toward the shadowy figure that disappeared, then reappeared. He knew he couldn't call after for help or a slower pace, so he kept struggling upward for half an hour.

Then he ran into a rock. At least the impact felt like that. Then he realized the rock had a warm, cloth exterior. He'd run right into the colonel's back, smashing his own nose. For a second, he wondered whether he'd been punched.

"Jeez, I'm sorry, sir," he groaned, gasping for breath.

"Sorry, Kop. I thought you saw me. Listen."

Kopmeyer could do little else. He certainly couldn't see for the tears in his eyes after the knock on the nose.

"I can't be sure," Miles said, "but I think this is the spot. Remember the map?" Kopmeyer grunted as respectfully as he could. "Well, we have radar and surveillance on top of this ridge. They can look down directly on the valley floor. They could look pretty much down on the bird's rotoprops. Or, they could pretty much see any movement below with the SuperStars."

"Yessir." Kopmeyer had found his voice.

"We're standing in a dead spot. It's right below a place where the mountain bellies out for more than a mile of its length. There's no line of sight from up there. It's a dead spot from below too because of the little ridge we just climbed. It's really the only place the bird can fly masked and have absolute assurance it won't be seen. I figured out several routes to China Lake—good ones too—but this terrain offers the only certain passage through the last leg of any of those routes."

"But sir, what's the difference if the bird has already been painted and shot down."

"Well, you're right. *If* it's been painted, there's absolutely no . . . Listen . . ."

Kopmeyer froze. He studied Miles's face as best he could in the dimly silver light. He saw it rotate from left to right, back and forth, chin up and chin down, as if searching the sky with radar.

"Do you hear anything, Kop?" Miles whispered.

Kopmeyer, following the example, whispered in response. "What kind of sound am I lis . . ." He heard it! A faint noise like a tongue sputtering . . . no, more like somebody riffling a thumb over the edge of the book's pages. Kopmeyer stepped up onto a three-foot boulder and pivoted his head around as he'd seen Miles doing.

"Better get down off that rock, Kop."

"Sir?"

Suddenly, it seemed to Kopmeyer that the very air had spawned a shadow in his face. The shadow seethed at him, pounced at him, threatened to engulf him. He froze for a second. As his knees buckled into a crouch, he felt a hand on the back of his belt. Then he was jerked cleanly from his feet. He toppled backward. As he fell, he went spread-eagle. He saw the shadow turn from black to the color and shape of a cloud. A rush of air blasted his eyes shut with sand and peppered his face with stinging pebbles. He hit the ground flat on his back and lost his breath in a gush. The cloud of sound chattered at him in annoyance, then disappeared, leaving him in a cloud of lung-biting aircraft exhaust. His nose stung with the smell.

Again, Kopmeyer gasped for his breath. He was aware of another shadow over him and found breath to moan. But it was only the dark shape of Miles. He thought of the Swamp Creature hovering over him.

"You all right, Kop?"

In a few seconds, his breath came back and he answered belatedly. "Yes. What the hell was that?" He already knew, of course.

"That, my son, was the Osprey. Now that this test is a success, they're going to be bringing production models out. You'll be seeing a lot more of them."

"Yessir," Kopmeyer grunted. As they started down the hill, he kept shaking his head. His next look, he told himself, would be his first.

General Little finally called a halt to the exercise, half an hour before its official end, resigning from his chess game at the inevitability of checkmate. He gave an official time hack and ordered the word to go out that radio listening silence was lifted. He sounded like a doctor who'd just pronounced his own father dead. He scheduled a morning postmortem and assembled the command center staff for a final debriefing that amounted to a pat on the back for everyone. Nobody sitting around the conference table wanted that pat on the back, though. Not for killing Osprey.

Least of all, Bernadino. She felt thoroughly sick to her stomach.

The secure phone rasped in the conference room. Little stopped speaking and scowled at the instrument. "Why do we even have that thing still operational?" he asked nobody in particular.

The COMSEC operations officer, a captain, held out the phone. Little waved it away.

"General, sir, you'd better take this call."

"I'm talking to the group . . ." said Little. *Get that phone out of my face, you little cretin,* said his expression, although he was much too civilized to make such a remark to a subordinate officer.

"General, this is a landline call from Lieutenant Colonel Parker," insisted the captain.

"Well tell him to fly that thing to a hangar before the Soviet Salyut sat—" Little's expression went blank. He looked at Bernadino. Her expression showed she couldn't explain it, either. How the hell could the Osprey pilot in the middle of nowhere be making a landline call? Where would he get a telephone?

"This is General Little," he said into the mouthpiece.

He listened, his creased expression smoothing out second by second. He leaned over the electronic map.

"But I'm looking at the goddamned map. They've got you lit up in a handful of places in the last few minutes . . ."

He listened some more.

Then he said, "Joel, you are a damned lifesaver. Looks like you win the right for that battalion to exist, Colonel. I can't say I know anybody who's had to prove his command before he could even take over. Congratulations."

He hung up. Beaming reflections of the lighted map images from his teeth to the waiting staff, Little said, "That was . . . well, you know that was Parker. He and Longstreet and that lovely damned ship have been sitting down at China Lake since about thirty minutes ago. All those images now on the map are simulators and Javelin deception devices they dropped off on the course—timers set to make it look like . . . Dammit, people, they made it and nobody detected them. Not even our own AWACS, for crying out loud. Nobody at all! Not even airfield security guards. Not until they went into the snack bar and ordered coffee, for Pete's sake, did anybody even know they were down on the ground."

By now Little's exuberance had caught on with the others. They were slapping each other's backs and shaking hands as if they'd been riding shotgun aboard the Osprey. Little and Bernadino shook hands.

"General," he said, "that craft of ours may change ground warfare the way the tank ended static trench warfare."

# 2

Major Aleksandr Mendenyev felt a catch in his throat as he uttered the words: "Sixty meters." The armed elevator operator and his armed assistant examined Mendenyev's I.D., which also indicated the authorized level of his descent into the depths below. The two soldiers of the elite Kremlin guard knew, as he did, that the lower the depth, the more important the meeting, and the more exalted the participants.

Mendenyev had never been below forty meters—linear dimensions were used so as to obscure the true number of levels. The strategy worked, for *he* surely didn't know how many tunnels and shafts penetrated the earth here, though some wags had observed privately that the main elevator shaft terminated in hell, where the truly supreme party chief ruled with fire and damnation.

But this trip was no laughing matter. The elevator car plunged as if in free fall, the LED digits of the meter gauge blurring. Mendenyev, seeing the guards exchange secretive glances, felt his stomach rise into his chest, where it was pounded back down by his thumping heart. He carried the military and political assessments of his Middle Eastern division. This information was to be coupled with that of other sources: all terribly secret, mostly KGB. He knew his role today—bearer of bad news. He was the messenger expected to be sacrificed for the ill tidings he carried.

His superior had taken suddenly ill when notified of the joint intelligence meeting. He had ordered Mendenyev to carry the news on his behalf, wishing his subordinate well with such compassion, it appeared he thought he might never see him alive again. Wasn't that always the way? Mendenyev mused. The cowardly superiors threw their expendable subordinates to the lions when trouble began, but when plaudits were handed out, the same superiors crushed their own people in the stampede for personal aggrandizement. Mendenyev remembered an old parable from his native Georgia Republic: *The fox does not bark and complain at the grass fires that sweep the steppe clean periodically, nor does he run. He simply holes up in a burrow till the flames are past. Then he picks his way carefully through the ashes and feasts on the carrion of those less wise.*

Mendenyev worked for such foxes, Dudov and Zuyenko. Polomarchuk he regarded as less a fox than a dog—no, more a stubborn ass. The fervor of the new post-Warsaw Pact leadership had ground to a halt in the face of dampening bureaucracy. The foxes had surfaced to resume feeding.

The meter indicator slowed to readable. Mendenyev felt himself shrinking, growing heavier. Finally, the numerals read sixty. The doors swished open. Two more guards met him, examined his access papers and identification, and pointed down a sterile hallway.

As in the rooms above the surface, this one had been built to intimidate. The ceilings rose to five meters or higher—Mendenyev couldn't be sure for the dimness of the peripheral light. Spotlights illuminated the central meeting table, which rested on a raised platform. The luminaries sat around the table. Arrayed behind each of the key figures at this meeting sat clumps of aides and advisers ready to lunge forward to hand up a file or to answer a question each time his superior at the table glanced back over his shoulder.

Not wanting to align himself with any of the clumps, he found a spot at the edge of the room.

For about ten seconds.

"Aleksandr Mendenyev," bellowed a voice from the platform.

"Here, sir."

"Come forward," commanded Marshal Leonid Abramov, Chief of the General Staff. "Speak up for your division, Major. Your chief is ill, eh?"

"Yes, Comrade Marshal. He sends his sincere regrets—"

Abramov winked and smiled, his broad face cracking like weathered rubber.

Mendenyev welcomed the smile, a friendly face among all the stern expressions now fixed on him. Ironic, he thought, that the smiling Abramov didn't even know he had become the enemy to Mendenyev. He took the chair offered and sat with his folders before him.

"Your report?" asked a less friendly face, that of General Dimitrovich Polomarchuk, First Deputy of the General Staff. For the first time, Mendenyev glanced around the table. You didn't get much higher than these men—or in terms of descent beneath the Kremlin, you didn't get much lower, he thought ironically. These were members of the Kollegiya, the Main Military Council of the Ministry of Defense. Only the ancient Isryev himself, the Minister—

"Your report?" repeated Polomarchuk.

Mendenyev had already decided that he should neither lie nor shade the truth. No doubt, these men already knew most of the answers to any questions they would ask.

"Comrades," he said, hearing his voice sound much more confident than he felt. "We have witnessed events of significant importance in Iran in general and around the city of Mashhad in particular. We have indisputable intelligence the Imam has been killed in his bed in Mashhad."

He told of confirmation of the commotion in the living quarters of the shrine, the scrambled telephone messages that had been decoded and translated, telling of a suspected American assassination team hitting the Imam. Nobody had seen the body—although there were Iranian agents inside the shrine, they hadn't reported out yet.

"This is probably because everybody inside is likely to be suspected as a collaborator. Any attempt at outside contacts, any suspicious behavior will mean instant death."

"You said American participation?" asked Abramov.

"Respectfully, Comrade General, I said the Iranians accused the Great Satan America. They accuse the Americans for the greatest proportion of their ills. And us for the remainder," he added. "One possibility we must not overlook is that we too will be blamed for the death of the rabid ayatollah."

The general grunted. "The *latest* rabid ayatollah."

The room went silent, all eyes on Abramov. As the grizzled veteran nibbled his lower lip thoughtfully, Mendenyev barely breathed. He had said what he had been ordered to say. Left to his own devices, he would have offered a more plausible explanation. The foxes, clever or not, had erred by treating Abramov like a fool.

Abramov inhaled deeply, and his question came on the end of his exhalation, low and wheezy. "Why does our analysis section not suspect the Iraqis? I have been told of some military reposturing."

"Insignificant," muttered Polomarchuk.

Abramov's eyes locked on his first deputy. "Even so, my general, in the new light of the assassination"—he shrugged, raising his palms to the level of his shoulders—"why would we not consider the Iraqis suspect, say, for the sake of argument alone?"

"Preposterous," spat Polomarchuk. "It cannot possibly be the Iraqis."

"Oh?" Abramov's eyes narrowed. "And why do you doubt the possibility?"

Mendenyev tried not to squirm as he broke into the tense encounter between the senior officers: "Respectfully, Comrade Deputy Polomarchuk, it is indeed possible that the Iraqis were involved. At this moment, we have no evidence of Iraqi participation. On the other hand," he said, shifting his body to face Abramov and putting on his most professional expression, "we have directed maximum resources to find out the identity and sponsors of the liquidated assassination team. We expect a report within twenty-four hours. We have not yet ruled out an assassination from within Iran's military, either. But again, we have no evidence."

Abramov nodded thoughtfully. Feeling himself now the object of scrutiny, Mendenyev struggled to keep a neutral expression. Abramov's head began bobbing faster. Mendenyev resisted the tendency to release a sigh of relief.

"Fine," said Abramov. "But I want to hear that report sooner than twenty-four hours. Much sooner. Give me progress reports every four hours"—Mendenyev flinched involuntarily—"even if it is not polished. And you shall talk directly to me with these summaries."

"You ignorant bastard!" Ivan Ivanovich Dudov bellowed the instant the office door shut on Mendenyev and Polomarchuk.

Mendenyev cringed. But the explosion of wrath was not for him.

"You silly, imbecilic whoreson! I overheard everything, Polomarchuk. Everything!" As he spoke, Dudov's hands flew about him as if trying to escape the leashes of his arms. "You owe this junior officer your very life. A child could instruct you that it is a mistake to tell a parent not to look into this closet or under that bed. Any moron knows that to protest too much is to draw attention to the very thing you want to hide."

Polomarchuk squirmed, pained that he should be hearing this sort of admonishment in front of a junior.

Mendenyev fidgeted as well, and Dudov saw it. His color lightened from scarlet-blue to red. His hands gripped the edge of his desk as if to anchor themselves. When he spoke again, his voice had regained a more normal pitch, although Mendenyev could hear a rasp the strain of yelling had produced.

"Fine. I accept the blame for not specifying precisely what should be mentioned and what issues should be skirted.''

Mendenyev saw that Polomarchuk was still fuming at being disgraced. He knew he'd be the target of his wrath sooner of later. Polomarchuk would make hell of his life, maybe ruin his career. That's what bullies did. He shut out the thoughts of himself. He was of little concern here. There was the matter of the brief-ings Abramov had demanded. ''These detailed brief-ings that Marshal Abramov has called for—what shall I say or not say?''

Dudov smiled, now calm. ''The truth. Investigate deeply and report accurately. Feed him some choice de-tails—if you like, something that implicates the Iraqis. It matters very little now. Whoever assassinated the old Per-sian fart has put our timetable off, but not irretrievably so.''

''We might have to postpone our plans for months,'' Polomarchuk commiserated.

Dudov sniffed. ''On the contrary, comrade. We've just been handed the hammer. The Iranian iron is hot. We must strike or we might lose all. The Iraqis may choose to delay, but we will not. I have considered a much bolder plan as well, one that might restore the Fatherland to its former status as a preeminent power.''

Polomarchuk grimaced, trying to comprehend the reasoning for an accelerated timetable. Mendenyev understood the import at once. ''Shall I try to discover who really committed the murder of the Iranian cleric?''

Dudov shrugged. ''Why not? Someday we might have occasion to thank them. But for now I have more important concerns. Gordeyev has convened a meeting of the Troika.''

Polomarchuk nodded, his fat lips pursed with self-importance. ''I will be there.''

''No!'' Dudov barked. Polomarchuk's face dark-ened, and Dudov realized he must not make an enemy of this buffoon, for he would be most dangerous if he were to become devious as well as stupid. He said to the general, "I have only to reorder the political priorities with the Iraqi president. You, on the other hand, have significant military preparations to consider. Imagine the difficulty of moving our timetable up by weeks. Only you will be able to do the job."

Polomarchuk puffed up.

Dudov said, "Mendenyev will make his report on the assassination in Iran. That briefing will be the last any of us will ever attend. For any other meetings called by Gordeyev, you must both find an excuse to be absent."

Mendenyev nodded emphatically, hoping he would be told no more details. He did not want to be involved any further. Polomarchuk merely squinted hard, trying to decipher the reasoning behind the odd mandate.

Dudov was in no mood to explain. Instead, he added emphasis, "In no case, under penalty of death, must either of you attend Gordeyev's meeting. Do you understand?" Both men nodded this time—even the dullard, Polomarchuk, understood the meaning of "under penalty of death." Dudov dismissed both men with a wave of his hand.

As many times as he'd been in the White House Situation Room, Wadsworth knew he'd never get over being awed. He heard a commotion at the doorway. Men and women began rising in anticipation.

"Ladies, Gentlemen, the president of the United States."

President Kathryn Chase entered to the sound of scraping chairs. President Katy, as she was called by the country's less reverential newscasts and papers. Everybody sat back down when she flicked her hand. Wadsworth felt overawed in her presence. A woman she might be, but her stern gaze left the bravest of men feeling spiked by her eyes.

Wadsworth noticed that the four-star who directed Unified Defense Intelligence was staring hard at him in warning. *Don't mouth off, Wadsworth,* the look said. Wadsworth answered the glare with a preposterous smile.

The President formed a bipod with her forearms on the table and rested her chin on her knuckles.

"National security adviser?" Her question declared the meeting convened.

The NSA spoke briskly and forcefully. He said the meeting's purpose was to evaluate the analysis from Unified Defense Intelligence. He repeated the scenario suggested by Brooks. He revealed that NSA intercepts from Iran confirmed the general disorder and the conclusion that the Imam had died. He described the military posture of Iraq in great detail and summarized the generally inactive situation in all the other powers of the Gulf region.

When the NSA finished speaking, the president raised her eyebrows. "What about DCI?"

The director of Central Intelligence said, "Madam President, as you know, it's been decades since we've been able to penetrate the Revolutionary Government . . ."

"As I recall," said Chase, "we have never penetrated the Revolutionary Government beyond the level of janitorial contractors."

"I stand corrected, Madam President." The DCI reddened and began talking about CIA sources within the Iraqi military and political hierarchy, which *had* been penetrated, which had confirmed the correctness of UDI's Intsum.

"Our highest source within the Iraqi army is one General Alnasrawi, the commander of all artillery and relative of the president," said the DCI. "He did not alert us to such a possibility. But he is on reconnaissance near the front at this moment. We will have his report tonight."

Wadsworth recognized the maneuver—he was stalling about Iran by talking about Iraq. Wadsworth decided he'd like to know the essence of Alnasrawi's report to match against his and Preston Brooks's assumptions. Pretty damned hot, getting a source right next to the Iraqi leader. But the president wasn't buying into Iraq.

"Mister director," she said, "would you mind very much tabling this rehash of what we already know? I'd like to know who sent the holy man in Iran to his fiery reward, if you please. And if it's not too much trouble, what are the intentions of the responsible party—or parties?"

The secretary of state, seizing a chance at the limelight, noted that, although he had no military experience, the current Iraqi maneuvers pointed to a defense against an Iran offensive.

"Bull," interrupted Defense. "At worst, it's a military preparedness exercise." He laid the assassination to Iranian moderates. "If there is such a thing as moderates over there," he added gratuitously.

DCI pointed his finger at the Iraqis for killing the ayatollah. "I'd give even money the Soviets had something to do with it, though," he said. "The new Soviets are no different from the old ones."

As men and women began to argue about who might attack whom, Wadsworth relaxed. He welcomed this kind of chaos because it reduced the likelihood that the wrestling elephants would pay any attention to inconsequential insects like himself. He noticed the President, watching and listening, categorizing and sifting, taking the measure of every argument in the room.

Finally, she shifted in her chair, signalling she had had enough. "Ladies and gentlemen, enough brainstorming. Who's doing what to whom in the Persian Gulf?"

She looked at the four-star director of UDI, who steered her inquiry away by swiveling in the direction of Wadsworth and his group from the Persian Gulf division.

Wadsworth felt his gut galvanized as the president spoke gently, "Major General Wadsworth. How about it? Who killed the damnable Ayatollah Fahzi? What's going on in the region?"

Wadsworth rose to his feet. "Madame President, I agree with everyone who's given you an assessment."

She smiled for the first time since entering the room. "That's a rare position for you, General. Now, seriously. I'm simply not going to let you equivocate like this."

Wadsworth decided to cut through all the posturing. "It doesn't really matter who killed the ayatollah, now does it? After all, it's unlikely that anyone will demand an international tribunal to punish the perpetrators. The Iranians will blame us, the Soviets, and the Iraqis. Throw in the Israelis for good measure. My money is on either the Iraqis or a splinter within the Iranian army."

"Why?" demanded State.

"No evidence to back up my feeling. Purely gut reaction. More important is whether anybody contacts us within seventy-two hours. If we are contacted by moderates. Of course, as I say, it doesn't matter as much as restoring normal relations before—"

"Bull," interrupted State. "It matters, General. Anytime a head of state is assassinated and the United States is subject to the fallout, it matters." Murmurs of assent rose up.

"Let him finish," the President said in a low voice that silenced the room.

Wadsworth said, "Yes, mister secretary, it does matter. But in this case, not as much as what is about to happen in the region."

"And what is that?" said the secretary with a sneer.

"In my opinion, the Iraqis are in a defensive posture only inasmuch that such preparations are the precursors of an offensive operation."

"Come on, General, the Iraqis have already had their butts kicked out of Kuwait recently enough. What makes you think they'd do something equally stupid now?"

"The concentration of armor capable of striking from Baghdad toward either Khuzestan or Tehran, for one thing. By now, it's pretty apparent the Soviets have cheated by rearming the Iraqis with T-72s by at least half again as many as the UN approved. We've seen some T-80s too. They've rebuilt a lot of hulls salvaged from Desert Storm using spare parts alone.

"For another thing, their defensive preparations do not include any significant defensive improvements in the area adjacent to Khuzestan. That leads me to believe it is precisely there they will direct a main attack. Perhaps this is too circumstantial, I admit. If I'm wrong, no harm. If I'm right, the assassination will cause the attack to be launched very soon to take advantage of the confusion in Iran."

The President pursed her lips. "I buy it . . . if only because it's a worst-case scenario. We have to prepare for another round of Iraqi adventurism. Goddammit, I just knew we were being too harsh with peace terms when we wouldn't let up on them." She shook her head, a sign of impatience with herself for dwelling on the past.

Keeping her gaze riveted on Wadsworth, she continued. "For starters, I want a concerted effort to find out exactly who's behind the assassination. Let's open some contacts if there are any so-called Iranian moderates. Maybe this is an opportunity to regain some influence there."

Then, as casually as if she'd commanded strategic forces for an entire career, President Katy ordered an increased naval show of strength in the Gulf. She demanded a report on the progress of modernization of the Rapid Deployment Force. She asked for a briefing on all likely Gulf contingencies, especially ones that included either Soviet or American military intervention.

This time Mendenyev descended ninety-nine meters. This time the elevator guards didn't play any pranks on his stomach. This time he saw only a dozen people in the room as he was directed to a chair before the ruling Troika.

This time he was the focus of attention.

"We have the background, Aleksandr Ilyovich Mendenyev. What have you learned since the earlier briefing of the military staff? What of the assassins? What of the situation at Mashhad?''

His inquisitor smiled, clearly meaning to put him at ease. It didn't work, of course. Mendenyev gulped in the presence of Sergei Nikolaevich Gordeyev, Party Chairman, Premier, President, and Supreme Marshal of the Soviet, the political giant who'd succeeded the experiments with democracy in the post-Gulf war years, a confrontation commonly known as the War of Shame. For the Soviet client had lost it, even with massive military support from the hardliners who had ousted the architect of failed restructuring of the Soviet economy. Nobody forgot that. And nobody forgot that failed efforts in the ensuing peace process had signalled the end of their country as a superpower. Plenty of blame had passed around in the intervening years of coups and counter-coups. Until Gordeyev had come to power and restored some normalcy. Gordeyev was a charmer, but there was a dangerous man behind the smile.

Mendenyev wasn't fooled by any smiles. He referred to his notes, determined to stick to his script and avoid any ad-lib remarks like those of Polomarchuk earlier. ''The assassins have been traced to the province of Kurdestan in the east of Iran. Two Turkomans led by a Persian hothead trained in Syria by members of our own special instructional teams.''

Zuyenko, the KGB chief, stirred, and Dudov the third member of the ruling Troika, scowled.

Mendenyev wondered in an instant of panic whether Dudov was really angry or was making the face for Gordeyev's sake. He hastened to add, ''But there is no connection to us or to any major splinter group of activists we know of. This group is a splinter of a splinter, obviously for hire and, although well-trained for their mission, not politically aligned.''

''Hired by whom?'' asked Gordeyev.

''We are unsure, Comrade Marshal.''

''The possibilities, then?''

''Perhaps the Iraqis. The Americans. The Israelis. Even the Iranians themselves. There are groups of mil-

itary officers within the country who would benefit
from the death of the present clerics.''

"Yes, the so-called government in exile here in
Moscow, for example."

"Yes, Comrade Marshal. Any one of these parties
could make overtures to the West for aid and arms if
the religious fanatics could be neutralized politically.
But we don't know yet who is to blame."

"Of course." Gordeyev smiled too broadly. "But
*we* did not conduct the mission—we do know that,
don't we?" He paused and looked ominously around
the room before continuing. "And how do you explain
the Iraqi preparations for defensive operations?"

"We conclude the Iraqis are assuming a defensive
posture. They expected some sort of Iranian offensive
before there was any evidence to warrant such preparations. That would lead us to suspect them of the
assassination. But we do not yet know for certain."

Petr Koblov, the foreign minister, spoke up. "You
spoke of the Iranian government in exile here in Moscow. We owe them—"

"No. We owe them nothing," Gordeyev snapped.

"What shall I tell them?" Koblov whined. "They
are demanding to be seen, to be installed with our
assistance to the position they have rightfully—"

"Stall them."

Koblov opened his mouth, but Gordeyev's glare
froze his tongue.

Gordeyev smirked. "Thank you, Comrade Foreign
Minister." To the others he said, "We will argue later,
comrades. For now, we will hear from each of you
your status and your conclusions. Assure me, comrades, that we did not participate and have no knowledge of the participants in the murder of the holy man
in Mashhad."

Gordeyev had no interest in a military adventure. Of
that, everyone in the room was now certain. Mendenyev had learned of his reputation as a pragmatist, a
soldier who realized that a politician could slide a unit
~~rker~~ six inches across a tactical map to claim vic-
~~·ile~~ a general had to earn those victories one

kilometer at a time at the cost of men and machines. His only interest in Iran was to maintain the status quo.

As the silence was filled by grunts of the assurance Gordeyev demanded, Mendenyev mustered all his willpower to not look into the bland face of Ivan Ivanovich Dudov. He saw the turning of heads to show innocence of any plot, the narrowing of gazes trying to divine a guilty party.

Mendenyev could barely stifle a smile. Here a group of the most powerful men on earth, in charge of one of the most powerful military machines in the world were acting like a bunch of school kids when the teacher demands to know who farted.

To say General Amiri drove too fast, exceeding the safety margin of his headlights, was a vast understatement. Amiri's aide, Colonel Bakri al-Bakri, clung with one white-knuckled hand to the dashboard and the other to his seat back to brace himself in the careening Desert Rover. The windshield was down, strapped to the hood, and the canvas top had been rolled back. In the rear seat, the top three deputy field generals in the Iraqi army sat, knees crammed together like schoolgirls on a bus.

All wore goggles to keep the pinging dust and frigid wind off their eyes. All but Amiri grimaced, trying vainly to see the desert track ahead now that dusk had given way to full night. But they could see little, for Amiri had been running full throttle with only a hooded blackout light for more than an hour.

He seemed to be possessed of the instincts and night vision of a desert owl. He never lost the track a single time. Somehow he'd swerved to avoid the black hulk of a self-propelled artillery piece dead in the road. That encounter, once behind them, left the generals and aide trading glances of wonder. Not one of them had seen the tracked vehicle until Amiri swerved. They'd not even been given the chance to experience the closeness of death until it had passed behind them,

rendering their fearfulness a sweaty but harmless afterthought.

All at once Amiri lurched forward over the steering
wheel. His four terrified passengers reacted by reaching toward him, all thinking he'd suffered a heart attack. But when the glow flicked off ahead of the Rover,
they withdrew their gloved, clawed hands. He'd merely
shut off the last shred of light, completely blacking out
the Rover. Only when they were without that tiny shaft
of light did they appreciate how bright it had actually
been. Now they seemed trapped in a well of blackness. The only illumination came from the pinpoints
of stars above. How could this madman drive in this
darkness?

They knew why he must darken the lights, of course.
The Iranian border lay barely a kilometer ahead. This
close, they'd likely already passed one or more enemy
patrols, maybe more. More likely—and most dangerous—they'd might encourage more than one ambush
by a few friendly patrols, too.

Still, Amiri didn't slow down.

Al-Bakri, his aide, wondered at the man's stamina
in the last weeks. He'd been fueled by meals on the
run, canned and dried troop rations with tepid canteen
water as he'd inspected troop positions personally
across the breadth of the front facing Iran. He'd gone
down to the underground tactical centers of every division and then down to brigade level. He'd inspected
dozens of fighting bunkers and even individual fox-
holes, ordering another heaping of sandbags for overhead cover in one infantry company. Then on the way
out, he took the captain of the company aboard his
helicopter, relieving him of his duties—and of his life,
incidentally, for a summary court martial the same day
condemned the bewildered captain to death for incompetence endangering his command in the face of the
enemy.

From that day forward, not a foxhole in Iraq lacked
for depth of overhead cover.

''Colonel al-Bakri, one doesn't have to reprimand
very many captains before all captains imagine the

sting of your whip,'' Amiri had mused in private to his aide.

Without warning, Amiri cut the ignition and coasted to a stop atop an undistinguished rise, leaving just the bare crest of the hill between the Rover and exposure to the front. Before the generals could release the grasps on their knees, Amiri was striding toward the skyline.

The others caught up to him, stumbling into his back. They cursed, milling about on the gravelly soil.

Amiri inhaled deeply of the air, smelling of salty marshes to the southeast. ''Smell the air,'' he ordered them.

One general, Yusuf Alnasrawi, snorted to show his displeasure at the inconveniences of this night. He commanded the country's artillery from the ancient US 105-millimeter towed pieces used by militia and reserve units, to the modern Scarabs, which delivered multiple conventional warheads capable of blanketing nearly a square kilometer with bomblets or accurately delivering half a ton of explosives to an accuracy of within a hundred feet. Naturally, such delivery systems implied a tactical nuclear capability. That alone gave him a preeminent position among military men. More than that, however, as brother-in-law to the Iraqi president, Alnasrawi enjoyed an insider's position at the very seat of political power. He had even let it leak out among certain politicians in Baghdad that he was the heir-apparent to Amiri, if not the presidency itself.

''Inhale it deeply,'' Amiri said and drew his own lungs full. ''The smell of life, gentlemen.''

Alnasrawi held a finger to one nostril and blew the other clear of the mud formed from desert dust and nasal mucus. He switched nostrils and snorted again.

Amiri ignored him. ''This land is the very cradle of civilized society, even the very cradle of life. Here man was born. Here many have died. Many others will shed their blood as well.''

He remained silent a long time, then dropped to his knees as if to pray. The others shuffled around in uneasy embarrassment, grateful for the inky blackness that hid their puzzled expressions from the suddenly erratic commander of the Iraqi army.

"Come," he said, jumping to his feet and marching back to the Rover. Again he switched on the hooded light of the Rover's blackout drive. Beneath the vertically slitted cat-eyes of light, he spread a map.

Immediately, the generals forgot their discomfort with their commander's behavior. Of psychology they knew nothing. Maps they understood. They glanced down at the lines, the arrows, the unit dispositions, comprehending the hieroglyphic language of the soldier. Abdul Qubain, commander of all armored forces reconstituted after the Kuwait debacle, knelt on one knee and touched the markings on the map as if to read them in Braille because his eyes would not believe what they saw.

General Khadduri, commander of infantry forces, studied the symbols sternly over the shoulder of Qubain.

Alnasrawi crossed his arms after a bare glance. "What is this?" he demanded. "My dear general, is this a joke? Tell us this map is but a ruse we intend to drop into the hands of an enemy reconnaissance patrol." He laughed weakly when the others did not join him in protest. "Please," he added grudgingly, as if to paper over his insubordination.

Amiri pulled a pointer from his uniform pocket and telescoped it to a length of a meter.

"My dear generals, here is our plan to transport the Persian enemy to destruction and to return Khuzestan province to its rightful name and ownership—Arabistan and Iraq. And, if I may say, to restore honor to the army of Iraq."

When he had finished speaking, the commanders of armor and infantry were riveted to the map, stunned. The wholesale reorganization of the army in the last months now made sense to them. Now they understood why all the Iraqi Army tank forces had been gathered under a single giant command. Now they knew why the combined-arms concept had been apparently abandoned after decades of practice. If they'd had the vision of Amiri, they'd have seen that the teamwork combination of armor, artillery, and infantry hadn't been scrapped at all. It had been elevated to a grander scale.

"Genius," whispered Qubain. "My general, whose genius is this? And do we have the blessing of our president for such a bold endeavor?"

"But of course . . ."

"Madness," scoffed Alnasrawi. "These are the scratchings of a madman. What if you cannot entice the Iranians into battle on the Baghdad-Tehran highway? They will not give up Khuzestan until the last man and boy have sacrificed themselves . . . in any case, my brother-in-law will never approve such a risky undertaking. You have forgotten your history, Amiri. Once before we have taken that province. The Iranians loosed the waters of the dam above Dezful. We left dozens of tanks and thousands of good soldiers behind, trapped in the mud. Besides, who can believe the Soviets? They have become eunuchs. Bah!"

Amiri smiled tolerantly and shrugged.

His aide suddenly stiffened. He'd seen his general like this before. This demeanor was not in the least the sheepish behavior it seemed. Indeed, Amiri had become dangerously angry behind that foolish grin.

"As you can see, it is the first of our objectives once the invasion begins—"

"Madness," Alnasrawi blurted. He began fidgeting. "Let us return to base. I have more important matters to attend to than this." He took a step.

Amiri raised a hand and smiled more broadly than before, a gleaming show of teeth. Alnasrawi stopped between strides.

"But I have not told you of my secret weapon, dear Alnasrawi."

"Bah! Secret weapon, indeed." He hesitated. "What secret weapon?" he muttered.

"Al-Bakri, show the general our secret weapon."

The aide drew a tube from beneath his jacket, aimed it toward the Zagros Mountains of Iran and slapped one end against his thigh. The tube hissed angrily and sent a dim stream of sparks skyward.

A few seconds later a blue cluster exploded a hundred meters in the air.

Seconds after that, mortars and small-arms fire discharged, dropping explosives and stringing tracers toward the east. In answer, Iranians opened up.

"You are mad," Alnasrawi said, no longer disguising his contempt. "A signal cluster that, incidentally, endangers the most senior officers in our entire holy country to the extent they might be exterminated with a single stray round of mortar fire or a wild burst of bullets. You call that a secret weapon?"

"No, my heroic friend, I call *this* my secret weapon."

Alnasrawi looked down into the muzzle of a pearl-handled .45-caliber pistol, a relic given to Amiri by an American mercenary. Alnasrawi opened his mouth to protest, but he had no opportunity. The .45 barked, and the slug shattered his cheekbone like a blunt instrument, blowing out the liquid contents of his left eye, tunneling into his brain.

The other generals froze, only their eyes darting from the cyclops eye of the .45 to the sneer of Amiri to the narrowed eyes of his aide, who now covered them with a machine pistol.

"No need to worry, my generals. Your deaths, if they come, will come in heroic battles with the Persians. Tragically, Alnasrawi has died from the very stray bullet he predicted from that firefight below us. We will all mourn him, eh?"

The stunned generals nodded.

"But not for long," said Amiri, holstering his pistol. "For we must be prepared for battle. Not even our aching grief can be allowed to interfere with our resolve to restore the cradle of life to its glory. Al-Bakri."

"General Amiri?"

"You are no longer my aide."

"My general . . ."

"You are no longer a colonel of artillery."

Al-Bakri's eyes flicked a glance down to the pistol hand of Amiri to see if he would be experiencing the same fate as the recalcitrant Alnasrawi. No pistol. But he still couldn't find his voice.

Amiri continued, "You are general of all the artillery. You will execute this plan just as you helped me develop it."

Shocked, al-Bakri said, "My general. I'm honored. But to jump three ranks . . . to direct all the other artillery commanders . . ."

Amiri had already moved to the driver's side of the Rover. "You are refusing the command?"

"No!" barked al-Bakri.

"Do you object to the plan then?" Amiri waved a hand at the head of the former commander of artillery as it lay lifeless seeping fluids into the earth.

"No!" yelped the new commander of artillery.

Amiri smiled affectionately, and started the Rover's engine. al-Bakri looked over his shoulder at the form of the murdered Alnasrawi.

Amiri leaned over and whispered, "Forget him. He was a traitor to his own brother."

"The Soviets?" asked al-Bakri.

"No," said Amiri with a grimace, "they are our allies again. He"—he tossed his head—"was an agent for the damned heathen Americans."


By 0800 hours, Supreme Marshal Gordeyev had convened a meeting of his tight inner circle. Besides the minister of defense, the foreign minister, and the number-two man in the Troika, Yermakov, was present, but Dudov had not arrived.

The meeting could not start without him, the Politburo ministers knew. They might discuss and haggle over issues, but the Troika decided. In effect, that meant Gordeyev decided, for he controlled the military, all-important since the turmoil of democratic uprisings had been put down. Yerkamkov's main responsibility in the Troika was to oversee the revival of the still-stagnant economy. To this foundation, Dudov brought his strong grip on the restored Communist

Party, although it was rumored that as Gordeyev diminished the preeminent position of the party elite, Dudov's star would be eclipsed.

Gordeyev, with an impatient look at his watch, asked, "Comrades, where is Dudov? Has he been delayed by a tardy cook or wine steward?"

The foreign minister answered smoothly, "Comrade Marshal, Dudov is late because he wishes to perform a mission directed by no less a dignitary than yourself."

Gordeyev smirked at Koblov's toadying. "Pray, what mission did I order him to accomplish?"

"He is meeting with our comrades from the Iranian government in exile, obtaining a status report from them, inquiring of their possible influence on events in Iran and directing them to pursue a course of patience and diplomacy with us until events will permit them their rightful stations in Tehran."

Gordeyev's face reddened. "Allow me to set the record straight for you. I did not direct him to meet with the Iranians. I directed him to keep our comrades at a distance until the changing situation could be evaluated. In fact, I would have preferred that a member of this circle not meet with the Iranians. I would not have wanted even you to meet with them, to lend unnecessarily legitimacy to them by mere association with us—"

"Comrade Marshall—"

Gordeyev shouted. "Damn! Of all people, you diplomatic toads should see the impression such a meeting will convey to the Americans. If our comrades," he said sarcastically, "our Iranian comrades in exile now are shown to be responsible for the assassination—and knowing them for the fanatics they are, they'll probably claim responsibility for the murder—the blood of that damned Fahzi will be splashed on our hands as well."

The foreign minister squirmed as Gordeyev pounded his fist on the table.

"Koblov," Gordeyev continued, "have you called in the ambassadors? Have the Iraqis been warned not to start anything? The Iranian? What does he say for himself?"

"Comrade Dudov has called on the ambassador of Iraq to present himself this very evening. The Iranian has been recalled to Tehran, but a deputy ambassador will also be called for consultations—"

"So why is Dudov chasing around after that band of hotheads?"

Those seated at the table became edgy. Most had never seen such antics from the supreme marshal.

Loud as he shouted, Gordeyev heard a commotion even louder outside the conference room.

The foreign minister rushed out the door as the entire assemblage stood.

Gordeyev uttered yet another curse—in frustration that his righteous rage had been interrupted. He called after Koblov as the door slammed shut. "Come back here, you cowardly—"

Koblov obeyed, dashing back into the conference area breathless and disheveled.

"Comrades," he wailed. "Somebody has brought the Iraqi ambassador here. And the Iranian. *And* the government in exile, too. They are engaged in a brawl . . ."

Gordeyev roared for silence. "I will kill the man who did this. Where is Dudov? Did he order this? I thought only Polomarchuk was the only fucking idiot . . ."

"Comrade Marshal," whimpered the stunned Koblov. "They are each under official escort. Each is in possession of an invitation signed by you. Each . . ."

The door behind the foreign minister crashed into his back. The body of the Iraqi ambassador, bloodied and limp, was launched into the room clutching his bleeding side. Half a dozen Persians poured into the conference room after him. Three of the men held bloody daggers.

The two groups, one Soviet, the other Iranian, faced each other in a moment of stunned silence. Outside, the sounds of booted security men stampeded down the hallway toward the room.

At first Gordeyev put his hand to the butt of his pistol, thinking this was an assault. But no, the group made no effort to threaten, so he did not draw the pistol.

"You are all dead men," growled Gordeyev at the group.

A spokesman stepped forward. "But your excellency . . ." He brandished a briefcase. "We have instructions written by your own hand," he said in broken Russian.

Gordeyev shouted, "I did not—" The anger in his face subsided with the dawning of a new insight. Finally, he understood.

Too late, he realized this was no diplomatic faux pas, no bureaucratic accident, not even a piece of idiocy concocted by the fanatic Iranians in exile who were crazier still than those who governed in Tehran.

He recognized the briefcase.

He'd seen it yesterday. In Dudov's hands. Now it was here in the room. Dudov was not. He glanced around—neither was the KGB chief Zuyenko, nor Polomarchuk.

It could only mean one thing.

Dudov had won.

His knees buckled as he sought cover behind his desk, but he was too late.

The briefcase vaporized.

In the next instant flesh peeled from the very bones of all the men in the room, but they did not scream, for the bomb's concussion had already rendered them senseless. Pieces of their bodies were hurled against the walls.

In a stroke, the so-called moderate leadership of the Soviet Union had been eliminated.

# 3

Miles held the shot glass in the pincers of his thumb and forefinger, suspending the shooter of amber tequila over a mug of beer. "Depth charge ready," he said.

"Bearing, zero-six-niner. Range, dead zero. Depth, shallow. Enemy sub positively identified," growled Major Herman Blanks, the Osprey battalion operations officer. He spoke into his fist, a mock radio mike.

Major P.B. Keyes, the third in their party, said, "Enemy sub I.D.'d as Bare-ass Bayard Wilkerson, Asshole class."

Miles asked, "Permission to implant a charge in Wilkerson's ass?"

"Granted," said Blanks wistfully.

Miles released the shooter and snapped at the geyser of beer that spouted up when it splashed into the beer. He raised the mug and chugged the beer and the drink, rapping the heavier glass on the bar when he was done, then extracting the shooter from his mouth. He slid the glasses toward the bartender, who gave him refills in both. "This isn't as much fun as it was when I was a pilot," he said. "Now I'm a . . ." His own burp cut him off.

Grinning broadly and falsely at Keyes, Blanks finished his sentence for him: "A staff weenie."

Keyes winced. Miles, huddling over his newly refilled glasses. This time he sipped his shot and chased it with a moderate gulp of beer.

Miles glared at both of them. "Why the sour expression, P.B.?"

"Tequila," said Keyes lamely. "How can you drink that oily stuff?"

"Bullshit, P.B. You're being kind. Too kind. Don't patronize me. I missed out on Desert Storm because I was on the development staff for the damned Osprey. You two got to fly guns in combat. Now you're in guns again, for chrissakes, and Blanks is even in Ospreys. Jeez, the operations officer at that. Schedules himself if he wants to." He inhaled deeply through his nose. "I'm a goddamned weenie again."

"Stop feeling so sorry for yourself, Nelson," said Blanks, completely irreverent toward his senior in rank. "We've come up together. Hell, you and P.B. have been in the same outfits since flight school. You ain't the only officer that had to pull duty on staff, you know. What about me? You think ops isn't staff?"

"In an operational Osprey battalion? Hell no, it isn't staff. Staff is when you fly a desk. Like me. Your fucking office is inside your bird, Herman. Your desk is a kneeboard. You call that staff?"

Blanks half-stifled a belch, half-answered with it. "I gotta go. The old lady's gonna be steamed as it is. Me and the old man have a briefing tomorrow at division." He sighed. "I have to do the talking. To Wilkerson, no less. Shit. Sorry, Nelson, didn't mean to bring up old unpleasantries."

"No need to be sorry," he murmured to the back of the departing Blanks. Thinking of his own wife and toddling child, he downed another drink.

"Dead," he croaked through a belch. "I'm feeling dead."

"You're feeling sorry for yourself."

"How does it go? 'Being undead isn't being alive'?"

"Nelson," said Keyes, "you mind if I talk buddy-to-buddy?"

"No. We go too far back for you to even ask the question . . ."

Keyes smiled to show his relief.

". . . Major Keyes," said Miles, finishing with a grin.

They both chuckled, the moment of levity clearing the air. Keyes said, "You've got to lighten up, Nelson. If anybody should be concerned about career moves, it's us, not you. You're the one who's been promoted as a five-percenter all along. You're the tactical genius they called in to write the damned doctrine for the Osprey. Look at me. I'm a troop commander for a bunch of tank killers, but it's my third assignment in gunships. Sure, I'm happy with it, and yes, I'm good at it, but my career isn't being managed. I started out as a scout pilot in Kiowas. I moved up to scout platoon leader—in Kiowas again. Then I got promoted to a gunship troop commander—which I do in a Black Eagle instead of a Kiowa. Big deal, I'm in a different brand of scout now, but it's basically the same thing— flying a scout. I'm already as far up the ladder as I'm going to get, Nelson. You're not done going places."

Miles lowered his eyes to his drinks, then shoved them away as if he didn't want to look at them. "I'm sorry, Patrician," he said, using Keyes's first name, which hardly anybody outside of family knew. "I've been so wrapped up in my own problems, I haven't realized how badly I've acted toward my friends."

"Forget it, Nelson."

"I can't—it's poisoned me. When I saw Joel Parker's name on the change of command order to get that Osprey battalion, I nearly choked with envy. Joel should be a friend of mine. Instead, I practically hate him. Imagine that! I've never had more than a minute's personal conversation with the man." He grabbed his drink and slugged it down. "That's irrational."

"Look, Nelson, stop thinking about your problems for a minute. Think about the guys who respect you, think of your friends . . . for chrissakes, think of me. If you make it impossible to bring up the subjects of the Osprey and staff work and Joel Parker and fighting the Iraqis, what the hell are we going to have to talk about?"

Miles inhaled suddenly, straightening the slump in

his shoulders. "You're right, P.B. Absolutely correct." He put a hand on his friend's shoulder. "There is one thing we'll always be able to talk about, though."

One of Keyes's eyebrows formed a hook. "What's that?"

"Wilkerson."

Keyes cleared his throat and looked away.

"Come on, P.B., you're not going to try to tell me he isn't an asshole, are you? If I stop whining about not being in Ospreys, at least give me Wilkerson to bitch about."

Keyes wagged his head. "I've worked with the guy before, Nelson . . ." He paused a second, because they both knew this was another reference to the sensitive topic of the Gulf campaign that Miles had missed. Miles waved an impatient gesture to tell his friend he needn't tiptoe around the topic. Keyes continued, "I admit he's high-strung. He started off the same way with us in Saudi before the fighting started. I hear he's a screamer first time he goes into any unit. Maybe he uses that to establish his presence. I don't condone the way he flies off the rotor hub, but in time, he'll get the feel of this division. He'll fit in, you'll see."

Miles narrowed one eye at Keyes. "Did you hear about the way he chewed out me and half a dozen other people in public last night?"

Nodding, Keyes said, "Look, I know the feeling. I've had it both barrels from him, both overseas and here. Once in Saudi—this was before he got called back to the States—he chewed me out over the way I was leading my platoon in Desert Shield when the thing was still an exercise—I mean, he was a colonel then, and he took over the command of my damned platoon. Embarrassed the hell out of me. After that, I thought he was carrying a torch for me. I avoided him for months. Then one day in the officers club tent, he looked me up and apologized. He bought me a beer. Hell, he even wrote me a commendation letter for the same field exercise that he threatened to court-martial me over.''

Miles shrugged. ''I haven't seen that side of him. Maybe I've got the guy figured wrong.''

''Wait, there's more. So when he came to this division, I thought he would be my buddy or something. No way. First time he saw me, he chewed my ass. By name, if that's any consolation. I'm just going to stay out of his sight for a while now.''

''Until he looks you up and gives you a commendation letter,'' said Miles, an ironic note in his tone of voice.

Keyes nodded.

Miles giggled, the liquor now working to take the edge off his anger. ''I'll probably get a medal of honor,'' he said.

Keyes clapped him on the shoulder. ''It'll be a perfect companion to the purple heart for the bloody asschewing he gave you.''


She rolled over onto his back, pressing his face into his pillow. Miles grunted impatiently.

''Nel, the baby's still asleep.''

He grumped incoherently.

''What's that?''

''I said, 'not being dead isn't being alive.' ''

She corrected him. ''unbeingdead isn't beingalive' to be exact.''

She writhed on his cabled back, massaging him with her body. ''Now how's about coming alive.'' Instead of relaxing, he grew tense under her hands. She whispered into his ear. ''It's Saturday. You've been in the field for three weeks except to get fresh laundry. I haven't been made to feel like a woman for nearly a month. Today's the day, pal.''

He lifted his head. ''I gotta go in. Wilkerson is on the prowl, and the G3 is scared shitless. He thinks if everybody works around the clock, Wilkerson will get off his butt. Fat chance. What time is it?''

''Time for me, Nelson Miles.'' She grasped his ears and shoved him face-down into the pillow again. ''And time for you to prove you haven't gone sweet on some soldier boy out there in the desert. I'm going to check on Christian. When I get back, you better be ready or I'm going to start an investigation of the relationship between you and that Sergeant Kopmeyer you were raving about last night."

He laughed, forcing his head up easily, although she threw her shoulder into the back of his neck. "Jeez, look at the time, Julia. I haven't got time. Honest."

When she spoke again, there was an edge to her voice. "Nelson, you make the time. And I don't mean the minute or two it's going to take you to get off. I mean, either you take the time to make me happy or make me madder than hell. If you've got time for depth charges with the boys at the club last night, and a counseling session with P.B., you've got time for me this morning."

"Way to go, J-girl. How am I going to perform under pressure like that?"

"Quit whining. It doesn't become an army officer. I'm going to check on the kids. You get ready."

When she returned from the children's room, her mood had changed, however. "Guess what I saw on the television when I went into the kitchen?"

"The Smurfs have gone porno?"

"Fahzi—the ayatollah—has been killed. Assassinated. You think it will mean any trouble in the Middle East? Again?"

"Naw." No such luck.

"You won't have to go to war or nothing, will you, Nel?"

"Hell no, the ayatollah doesn't mean a thing to us." He studied the taut face, trying to hide the eagerness in his own expression. "Hey, you're serious."

He grabbed her, engulfing her slender body in an enormous hug, burying her beneath him. She groaned greedily and wrapped her lithe legs around the trunk of one of his thighs. In the next half hour, until their year-old son, Christian, toddled in, catching them nakedly engaged, he completely forgot about Wilkerson and the Osprey.

* * *

The newly installed, self-appointed leadership of the Soviet Union met in Lubyanka, headquarters of the KGB, as emergency repairs were being made to repair bomb damage to the Kremlin.

"The Troika has gone the way it came," announced Dudov to the Politburo. "Not by election, not by appointment, not by legitimate succession, but by the violence it inspired in seizing power from the interim government after the War of Shame."

Grunts of assent rose up in salute to his words. Nobody objected to Dudov's revisionist view of history, especially the part about his "interim government," which itself had achieved power via a bloodbath.

"And I humbly announce the results of your vote."

The outcome of Dudov's vote had hardly been in doubt. He, KGB Chairman Zuyenko, and Boris Fomenko, newly named foreign minister, had distributed ballots with only their names on it.

"And I humbly accept the leadership of the party and of the government—and with it the burden and responsibility to carry the titles of general secretary, president and premier."

He slammed a fist on the table. "No more will an elite minority of three rule the country like imperial czarists. From now on, all of you"—he swept his arms in an exaggerated breaststroke—"*all* of you share in the glory and the burden of governance of the greatest Socialist state the world has seen."

He sat down abruptly.

Marshal Dimitrovich Polomarchuk, who had been elevated to minister of defense, bolted to his feet to lead the applause. Zuyenko stood beside him, his narrowed eyes scrutinizing faces. Hastily, the remainder of the Politburo gained their feet and joined their hands in rhythmic clapping. Some of the expressions showed dismay at the similarity between the previous Troika and the current one. But, as usual, nobody dissented on such a matter. Everybody would wait for the shakeups, evaluate the fallouts, and analyze the balance of new alliances with old power bases.

After permitting a full minute of applause, Dudov stood. The others sat.

"The time for speeches has ended. Now it is time for actions to punish the perpetrators of the heinous crime against our former leaders. Your findings, Anatoli Petrovich."

Zuyenko nodded in acknowledgment and rose, casting a baleful gaze around the table. Several men stirred uneasily. The KGB had suddenly made a quantum leap from underling to usurper with unlimited power—power at the level it held before the end of the War of Shame, when a client state using Soviet weapons and advisers was soundly defeated by American clients and weapons. The dreaded East-West confrontation had materialized only as a "pocket war," but the West had won it decisively.

The KGB chief said, "The killing was obviously the work of a terrorist element from among the Iranians—perhaps the same group responsible for the death of their own mullah, Fahzi. We suspect either the deputy ambassador or a traitor hidden in the midst of the government-in-exile." He sat down, then remembered something and popped back up to add, "With CIA support."

For the benefit of all the assembled members, Dudov repeated the essence of the KGB report and embellished it. "The Iranians are to blame. We have incontrovertible proof that the maniacs blamed us for the death of the ayatollah. We will issue a statement to that effect within the hour. We will share our evidence with the world that the CIA perpetrated the death of the Persian leadership—in league with Turks and relatives of the Shah."

Men around the table pursed their lips, memorizing the proper verbiage to recount this story down the line within their own chains of commands. Nobody asked questions and nobody challenged conclusions, for it was obvious that Dudov would not be issuing an invitation to debate the declarations of dogma now being stated.

"Now," Dudov said, "what must we do to ensure the longevity of the Fatherland? Minister of defense?"

Polomarchuk, still flushed by his succession to a position he never expected to hold, ejaculated, "We must mobilize even further to defend against attack by those crazy bastard Persians and the puppeteer Americans." He glared at Abramov, daring him to dispute his conclusion.

Major Mendenyev, sitting at the periphery of the assembly, watched Abramov fight his own emotions, refusing to be baited. The general even manufactured a tug in the muscles on half his face, imitating a bemused grin with this particular array of weathered wrinkles.

In the Gordeyev regime, Abramov had been the odds-on favorite to become minister of defense. Mendenyev knew from his detailed examination of the man's file that he had earned his reputation as a competent soldier, the kind of general he would want to serve in combat with, if he should ever be posted to a battle theater.

Abramov was no yes-man. He never lacked an acerbic word in giving counsel, and this had created antagonism, if not dangerous enemies. That he endured at all owed to the fact his style was marked by a total absence of either flamboyance or political motivation. Abramov remained a rock of common sense, always forcing his superiors to factor in a consideration to the ordinary soldier when making political decisions that affected the army. He was the rare officer who weighed a battle, not in the currency of glory to the Fatherland but in bloodshed to the sons of the Fatherland. He never backed away from a military threat to his country. But he had never been pushed into a military adventure that was strategically unwise, either. These qualities had made him a court favorite of Gordeyev, another soldier's soldier.

Now Gordeyev was gone. How would he ever survive under Dudov's leadership? Mendenyev wondered. Abramov's brand of dissent would never be tolerated. A more pliant military would be needed. Thus Polo-

marchuk. Surely Abramov understood such realities.
Surely he would retire to a drafty apartment in a republic far from the intrigues of Moscow.

Mendenyev wondered what he would have done
faced with Dudov's decisions. He would never have
chosen the incompetent Polomarchuk, of course. But,
considering Dudov's position, he wouldn't have chosen that Turk, Abramov, either.

He watched the other assembled Soviets cautiously
nodding at the party line. He realized they must be
unsure of the reasons being given for the country to
mobilize. Thanks to Desert Storm—the War of
Shame—Iran was again the most powerful of the Gulf
states, yes. However, against the Soviet Union it
amounted to no more than a troublesome gnat. *Mobilize a superpower against a country of gnats? To defend against what?* their expressions asked. Gradually,
the faces of the more insightful members of the assembly began to harden as they grasped the message between the lines. Mendenyev had understood for a long
time—the dogma did not have to be rational to be
swallowed, only consistent. Of course, everybody
must swallow the same line.

Emboldened, Polomarchuk added, "We must also
shore up the southern border with Turkey in case those
NATO warmongers get any ideas. We mustn't forget
how the Turks piled onto the helpless Iraqis once they
were certain of a victory by the bullying Americans."

"True," said Dudov.

Heads turned to Dudov at the declaration of support
for this new truth. The looks seemed to concede that
Polomarchuk really wasn't either so dumb or so smart
as anybody had supposed, but that he was merely re-
hashing words given him by somebody else. As men
squinted with the effort of memorizing new truths, the
concentration was broken by a voice tinged with skepticism.

"Surely the general secretary knows nothing of a
threat on our southern flank," Abramov said to Dudov, bypassing Polomarchuk.

"We have no direct intelligence of an overt threat

against the Fatherland,'' interjected Polomarchuk, reasserting himself with his former superior officer. ''But even you can deduce from this imagery''—he slapped an enlarged photograph showing a purported Iranian invasion preparations intended against Baghdad—''that Iraq, one of our valued allies, will soon be attacked.''

Abramov bridled, but bit back a retort. It ought to seem obvious to a first-year cadet that defensive preparations by one military force did not lead to the absolute conclusion the other side would attack.

Polomarchuk paused an unnecessarily long time to let Abramov writhe. Dudov, too, seemed content to let the moment linger.

Dudov spoke, ''Comrade Zuyenko and I have labored over a general strategy we wish to present at this time. You will have twenty-four hours to examine the plan. Then you will be given time to address the assembly here and brief us of your capability to support it.'' He ignored the eyebrows around the table raising imperceptibly as he continued, ''In short, we have decided to stand behind our Iraqi brothers. Under this new leadership, we will do so with decisiveness this time.''

Abramov's forehead turned into a washboard of tight wrinkles as he smirked and asked, ''Do they know of our intentions to save their hides?''

Polomarchuk snorted. ''We have been in constant contact since—''

''Since this morning,'' Dudov barked loud enough to override Polomarchuk. Silence fell awkwardly in the room.

Abramov had caught the slip. So, the assassination of Gordeyev had been preceded by unauthorized Iraqi contact. Of course! The succession of power had been only one aim of the killing of Gordeyev.

Dudov grimaced before recovering his original bluster. ''We will not ignore the Iranian madmen who would stir up trouble among Muslims in the Soviet Union and upset the balance in the Middle East by conquest of a neighbor.''

Abramov shook his head at the illogic in that.

Dudov didn't see the headshake. He unveiled a wall map of the region and turned to face it.

"There are two strategic objectives in the region that will accomplish both our aims," he said, spreading the palm of his left hand over a spot on it while he talked to his audience over his shoulder. "Comrades, this will be one objective in the hostilities that are sure to follow the provocations of the Iranians."

His announcement was met by blank faces. For the hand covered Tehran. They were declaring war on Iran? the expressions asked. All but Abramov, whose face twisted into a smirk. This was a plan that had been concocted long before this morning.

Dudov gave them all a look of disdain. He moved his other hand lower on the map. Abramov saw the objective and swallowed with difficulty. He examined Dudov's face. The man was serious, deadly serious. He meant to get them into war with the Americans.

When the UH-60D Blackhawk landed at Edwards Air Force Base, General Rita Bernadino dismounted and strode across the concrete aircraft parking area before the pilots had even cut back the helicopter's RPM. A half mile of hangar space had been dedicated to the Osprey program, for Fort Irwin did not contain enough hangars to keep the aircraft out of sight of the probing eyes of Soviet satellites. So these hangars, left over from experimental aircraft and the scrapped space shuttle, had been modified and extended. Some new structures had been added, but not too many, for even the addition of new buildings might cause the Soviets to change their patterns of stratospheric surveillance. For all the Soviets knew, this new division was merely another collection of helicopters designed for anti-tank purposes. Even the maintenance facilities and troops for the Osprey were required to be kept out of sight. This caused a great deal of complaining among the soldiers and mechanics. Because the rule had been applied so strictly, they could not even leave their barracks while off-duty to play ball or to sunbathe during the day. It was one of the few policy areas where Bernadino and Wilkerson concurred.

The sun at this altitude baked her body right through her clothing, but the heat's effects and her own fatigue vanished. Because there in the huge rectangular shadow of an open aircraft hangar door stood Major General Steve Little with his legs spread, hands on hips, a smile playing on his lips. God, didn't he ever grow tired? she wondered. Everywhere he went among the thousands of divisional men and women, officers and soldiers perked up. She had seen it before. Now she felt it herself.

"Rita."

"Sir." She shot him a salute.

He pointed into the darkness of the hangar. "Come," he said. "We'll chat as we walk to the briefing area. Soon as we get there, it will be all business. It seems like it's been months since we've just chatted."

She made small talk as best she could, but was distracted. Inside the hangar, she saw things she didn't like, electronics equipment exposed to drifting dust and sand. She made a mental note to get on the avionics technicians. She saw stacks of EMI shields piled up like crushed car bodies. General Little directed her around a temporary partition to an impromptu briefing area.

As she rounded the corner of the partition, she saw Wilkerson. She felt her jaws tighten. She felt the cold glare of Wilkerson's eyes, even as he said, "Well, well, well, if it isn't the best logistics officer in the division."

*For a woman,* she added mentally to finish his sentence for him. Always a put-down. Why didn't this guy ever lighten up?

The briefing was mostly routine. The reports of the training maneuver, and intelligence side of the division's operations—under the control of Wilkerson—indicated that everything was on schedule. Suddenly, however, Little stirred in his chair. Wilkerson held up a hand to silence his briefer.

"I know you all have a full plate already," Little said. "But I want the G4 to start contingency planning to prepare to deploy by air, possibly to the Middle East."

The men and women in the room held their collective breath. Little looked around the room to reassure himself that everybody present had security clearance. "I'm not in possession of any orders to deploy, mind you. But as you know, the Rapid Deployment Force has been alerted to step up planning for such a deployment contingency. We're a part of that. That's all."

He paused. His staff examined his face as if trying to determine whether the division had deployment alert orders or not. "Look, I'm not handling this very well, I know. I assure you, we've not been alerted. We do not have a timetable. We've maintained deployment contingency plans for all regions of the world. We would be negligent if we didn't dust off the Desert Shield OPLAN for movement to the Middle East. If there is ever going to be a deployment, I assure you, we'll be part of it."

The staff all seemed to exhale at once.

Except for Rita. She knew her half of the briefing was going to cause difficulties. As the briefers for the maneuver side finished up, Wilkerson himself stood up to put the capper on their words. "About all there is left," he said offhandedly, "is to give us an enemy we can kill." With a flourish, he sat down. "What's it gonna be this time? The damned Eye-rainians?"

*What a pompous S.O.B,* she thought, biting her lip to stifle a spiteful glare.

Little nodded at Bernadino. In turn, she nodded at the G4, the division's logistical staff officer. He began briefing.

In contrast to the polished maneuver story, the logistics report clanked off the ear. Maintenance availability figures on all models of helicopters pointed to a steady decline. The continual wear on the helicopters' moving parts escalated as maintenance and flying went to a round-the-clock schedule. Worst of all, the

G4 said, Osprey's availability was taking the steepest nose dive. The alternating six-hour intervals of operation and maintenance just were not enough time to sustain upkeep on the sophisticated craft. Just the problems of sand and the harsh environment and strictly night-flying missions at low level had taken a toll. There had been blade strikes. There was excessive turbine fan wear in the engines. The rotor strikes had been caused by rotor wash lifting up loose debris, then sucking it down through the blades. Several helicopter bellies had scraped rocks or snagged on uneven ground while flying at a low level. But those problems could be anticipated in any maneuver situation. Now, it seemed that instead of requiring two to three hours of maintenance for every flight hour, not uncommon among helicopters, the Osprey would be requiring two to three times that. With the one-to-one ratio now employed, the Ospreys just couldn't stay in the air safely.

It was a bleak picture. Little glanced uneasily at Bernadino. She met his glance and nodded soberly. On the other hand, Wilkerson practically smiled at the misfortune of Osprey.

Little uncharacteristically interrupted the briefing.

"What does this mean to us? How do we deal with this situation here, and how does this situation limit us should we be required to go into combat?" The G4 officer stammered.

Bernadino rescued him. "General Little," she said, "the Osprey is a good aircraft. It can do what it was designed for. But we've been flying those birds more than would be required in combat. In combat they would have a mission, they would launch and execute it by night and put down for maintenance by day—we would have up to twelve hours at a time to rest crews and repair ships. Now it seems we are spending too much time being out for the sake of flying, just because the Soviet satellites give us a six-hour window of opportunity. I don't think we need to press the men and the machines quite so hard. So far every field exercise that the Osprey has been tested on has been a success. I don't see that we are having extraordinary maintenance problems with our people or equipment when you examine the hours flown. But we're not giving ourselves enough continuous down-time for maintenance.''

"We have to train." This interruption came from Wilkerson.

She saw the movement of his body stiffening from the corner of her eye, but she refused to condescend even to look at him. So she answered a spot on the wall of the hangar over General Little's head, trying to suppress a scowl.

"I know that, General Wilkerson, but we don't have to ride these horses into the ground. There are no replacements until the production line starts up. That's months away.''

"We're not going to have an opportunity to train after we deploy and have to face the Russians. It has to be *now*.''

"General, we're already at the mercy of the Russian satellite schedule. It would not hurt our pilots in those units to get twelve hours of sleep in a row. It would not hurt for the aircraft to get twenty-four hours of stand-down time to get put back into shape.''

"Is that what you recommend?" asked Little.

"Yes.''

"No," snapped Wilkerson. "We need the training time.''

Little spoke. "How many missions have you got scheduled in advance?''

"An indefinite number. We intend to train, train, train our men and fly those birds every six hours until I say when. We expect to get support.'' he stared baldly at Bernadino and finished. "I'm sure our top divisional logistics officer is going to support us.''

Little thought for a moment before speaking. "All right, the pilots for the next mission are probably ready to go. Let them go the first flying period after dark. Then I want a forty-eight-hour stand-down. The three of us will get together at the end of those forty-eight hours to see where we are.''

It was Rita Bernadino's turn to smile.

Abramov's jaws hurt from biting back one retort after another, retorts that launched from his throat into his mouth like projectile vomit after a drinking binge. *What idiots!* They had learned nothing from the post-Perestroika experience. First, unrest in the republics, then impatience with the unending economic stagnation led to the ouster of Gorbachev by hard-liners. Then the country had been impoverished by their heavy-handed attempts to put all Gorbachev's genies back into the bottle. There were the embarrassments of the War of Shame, the destruction of Iraq. On the heels of independence in the Baltic states had come uprisings in the republics and a virtual civil war. For a while, hard-liners restored their brutal brand of order, but soon even wider revolts took place. The hard-liners were ousted, fleeing into oblivion. Into the power vacuum left by the hard-liners came the moderate Troika. It had barely begun to make a comeback under the rigorous tutelage of Gordeyev and Yermakov, who favored economic stability over military growth.

The military men should know better. But Abramov watched as they nodded. *Sheep,* he thought. *Lambs in fucking wolves' clothing!*

Suddenly he felt the eyes of all the men in the room. *Oh hell!* Had he actually disparaged them aloud?

No.

Somebody had asked a question.

"Forgive me, comrades," he said. "I was studying this master plan so intently, I failed to hear the question."

Polomarchuk, his new superior, spoke. "I asked you, Comrade Marshal, for your opinion of this strategy of punishing the Iranians."

Abramov smiled. He chose his words carefully, for he knew he must sound neither too pleased nor too soured on the proposal. The imperious ministers in this gathering would believe neither.

"At first inspection, the plan is brilliant in its boldness. It will succeed—not easily—but certainly. If, as you say, we have agreed to attack Tehran to draw pressure from the Iraqi drive on Khuzestan Province, I have no doubt we will succeed. The Iranians will send every soldier who can walk against us. The Iraqis expect to have a holiday march to Khuzestan.''

He took another deep breath. Time enough for their incredulity to sharpen. They would never swallow such glib flattery. It showed in the exchange of dubious glances between Dudov and Zuyenko.

''But,'' said Abramov. He waited. They studied him. He studied them. Now he had them. He stood up and walked closer to the map.

''Look here,'' he said, pointing to Tehran. ''Their capital will not be taken so easily as you might think.''

''We will occupy it in less than a week's fighting,'' sputtered Polomarchuk, preening.

You boastful, ignorant bastard. Heaven help our armies if you direct them, Abramov thought.

Instead he said, ''Of that there can be no doubt. But we have some experiences already about occupying cities, and at any rate, there is a simpler way to accomplish the same aims.''

''What aims?'' Polomarchuk demanded, completely missing the reference to the debacle of Afghanistan.

''Why, the strategic aims, of course, Comrade Marshal.'' Abramov smiled broadly. He felt everyone in the room lean forward expectantly.

''We simply take our own holiday drive across the border to cut off Tabriz from the rest of the country. We will have access to the Tabriz oilfields just the same as if we made the longer attack to threaten Tehran. It will be an easier objective to hold against counterattacks.''

''Nonsense!'' Polomarchuk dismissed his former boss with a toss of a hand. ''What effect would that have? The Iranians would not know we had crossed their border if we went only that distance.''

''Ah, but what is the harm in that? They will have their hands full with the Iraqis, don't you see?''

"But, we agreed with the Iraqis—" Polomarchuk's protest froze in his throat at the stare from Dudov.

At that moment, Abramov knew indisputably from the "we" in that gleaming fragment that Dudov's group and the Iraqis had ordained this attack long ago. The bombing in Gordeyev's office had removed the last obstacle to the treachery concocted between Iraq and Dudov. He wondered whether the assassination of the Iranian Imam was tied to the timetable of the Gordeyev killing.

His pondering was interrupted by Dudov, who regarded him through squinted eyes. "Marshal Abramov, please spell out this idea of yours for us."

"Certainly, comrade. The very aims you specified as essential in the attack on Tehran will be met at Tabriz. We simply isolate the city and its surrounding oilfields, stores of crude oil, and refined products. Thus, we have immediate access to tons of petroleum stocks at very little cost. We avoid the enormous mountains before Tehran and mountain fighting . . ." He paused to let the as yet unmentioned lesson of Afghanistan sink in yet again. "We maintain perfectly safe lines of communication to the Fatherland in the Azerbaijan Republic. We do not threaten the capital, which would arouse masses of fanatical Iranians against us. We do not even occupy Tabriz. We simply slice it off"—he sketched an imaginary crescent south of the city—"thereby avoiding any chance of being surrounded by the crazy Iranians. This strike will not be enough to provoke the Western alliance. We stand toe to toe with the Turks—they will blink without American soldiers at their shoulders. The Europeans . . . Bah! Do you think they would mobilize against a frontier so remote?"

Dudov's eyes bored into him. He, practiced in deceit, was trying to detect it in Abramov. "The Iraqis will regard our diminished attack as treachery, won't they?"

"Perhaps, but why should our soldiers take on the bulk of the burden? Why should we draw all the wrath of the Iranian madmen? Let the Iraqis shoulder their fair share of the fighting. Besides, you could tell them our intent is a two-stage attack." Dudov started nodding. Abramov continued, not wanting to lose his momentum, "Later, you can stall them off by saying our army has met unexpected resistance and cannot continue the campaign toward Tehran. You could put them off indefinitely with that argument."

Abramov lowered his head in humility as he sat in his chair. He let his shoulders slump. He wore one of his intentionally blank expressions, expectant not arrogant. Slowly he looked around the room, counting votes in the expressions on the faces of the others.

By the time he'd reached the thoughtfully narrowed eyes of Dudov, he knew he had won the day. He never could have talked the group into postponing an invasion altogether. He would have been posted to Siberia, not necessarily in command. So instead he had tried to overwhelm the men with strategic reason.

Dudov tossed a scant nod to Zuyenko, who blinked rapidly in response. Even Polomarchuk, with his sycophant's innate ability to read body language of men more powerful, began nodding. Soon the room was in total silent agreement.

"Give your staff the task of arriving at the details of a plan," Dudov said to Polomarchuk.

"I will do it," said Polomarchuk.

Abramov smiled pleasantly.

"Now," Dudov said, regaining his imperious tone, "What do you suggest we do with our primary objective, the Strait of Hormuz? How should we execute that part of the plan?"

Abramov looked up and said mildly, "Since we have been discussing your . . . our agreement with the Iraqis, one has to ask whether the attack on Bandar Abbas was coordinated with them in advance."

Dudov chuckled, amused at Abramov's delicacy in accusing him of treachery. "No, this is an independent Soviet adventure. We don't coordinate such things with insects like Iraq."

"Well then . . . we should send that idiotic plan back to the school playground where it was hatched."

Dudov barked his astonishment. Polomarchuk squealed. Zuyenko stiffened for battle. The argument, thus launched, continued vehemently into the night. All against one, all against Abramov.

"The EMI test? Are you sure?"

Bernadino was stunned by the report from the G4. EMI, electromagnetic interference. In areas where every conceivable sort of airborne transmissions—from microwave to FM to UHF to VHF to HF to lasers communications—was in effect, EMI sometimes did strange things to computers and sophisticated electronic circuitry. The Blackhawk and Cobra fleets had to be grounded in the 1980s until shields could be installed to modify the craft—after more than a dozen deaths. The Ospreys out there tonight were running several sequences of EMI tests. That alone was no cause for alarm. However, she remembered something from this afternoon in the hangar. *That* recollection scared the hell out of her.

When she had been walking in with Major General Little, she had noticed stacks of technical equipment lying around. Still, this was not unusual in aircraft operations. When Ospreys or any other kind of aircraft were in maintenance, it was common practice to remove cowlings and doors and hatches to get at the components for repair. But what she had made a mental note of, and what she had intended to make a written note of, was a corner of the hangar that had an excessive number of EMI shields. It took her about three seconds to calculate that there were twice as many shields lying about than Ospreys. Did it mean that these were being replaced? Or in the hustle to get Ospreys flying, were there birds out there now without EMI shields? Were there any aircraft going through that test? Surely, nobody would be stupid enough to send aircraft out into EMI tests without EMI shields. But then, the people who took care of EMI shields were maintenance people. The people who flew combat missions and combat training missions were tactical people. The two camps didn't always talk.

Were there any Ospreys going through tests without EMI shields? She fired the question at the G4.

All he could answer was to say he would check. She would, too. She hollered for her aide.

"Yes, ma'am?"

"Get my driver."

When he brought her car, she yanked open the driver's door. "Move over so I can drive."

She sped toward the maintenance hangar to get some answers from the night shift on duty. As she careened toward the flight line, she prayed for herself. God, just this one time, let me get away with a lapse. Such a little one. I deserve it, God. Just one.

Parker's Osprey passed over the start line a few seconds after the test bird. The first report from the Osprey crew wending its way toward the simulated battlefields was a summary of the emissions they could detect with their sensors and receivers.

Within a minute, the pilot reported they had gone through the zone of normal communications without problems. Parker looked at the navigation map electronically drawn for him on the console between his position and the copilot. Its scale was adjustable. Now the scale was 1 to 50,000. It could be adjusted up to 250,000 or even as high as 1 to a million, as the aircraft accelerated to maximum speed.

A hill rose up ahead of the test aircraft, blocking most of the emissions from the densest part of the test area. The pilot reported through the jamming again before cresting the hill. "All systems normal. Entering ground zero."

Parker waited a few seconds after the Osprey disappeared from sight. "Take her back, Jim. Let's go back and pick up another pair of newbies and take them through. Then let's call it a night. The rest of the people are much more experienced at this, so—"

A shriek pierced his headset.

"What . . ."

An immense flash lit up the cockpit.

"Crash!" yelled Longstreet.

"I've got it," Parker commanded. Instinctively, Longstreet relinquished the controls to the battalion commander, who picked up the aircraft at about thirty feet in altitude, spun it around on its central vertical axis, and accelerated to one hundred-fifty knots in seconds toward the spot where they'd seen the Osprey enter the high intensity jamming course.

At once, they both realized it was a mistake. Parker lowered the collective again just as Longstreet grabbed the controls to wrest them away. No time now for cockpit protocol, and there wouldn't have been seconds ago, either, if he hadn't been so fatigued.

The mistake was to have unmasked the Osprey from behind the hill mass, exposing it to the electronic briar patch that might have snatched the other bird from the air.

The men lost control of their Osprey.

Parker thought it felt a lot like a helicopter losing its tail rotor or having a fluctuation in power. He reached for his intercom button and shouted, "What the hell?"

Longstreet's face reflected desperation in the glow of the projected images off the windscreen, the billowing fire of the other craft burning on the ground.

The controls jerked right and left, tearing at the shoulders of both men. The trim pedals began shoving against their feet. The nose began to lift, and both men laid their combined weights into the cyclic stick. But it kept shoving back at them. Parker heard the warrant officer scream. He looked over and saw Longstreet had wedged his knee between the cyclic and the seat, trying to hold off the stick. But it kept shoving backward. Unbelieving, Parker watched the man's thigh bow upward in the middle. Then a snap sounded in the cockpit and the spear of the warrant officer's broken femur pierced through flesh and flight suit and impaled him in the chest with a spear of bone.

Horrified, Parker heard the screams from inside the cockpit and from back in the cabin where a minimal combat control crew of two men worked the communications.

The aircraft jerked again wildly to the left and kept bucking backward.

*"Goddamn!"* Parker shouted, *"What the fuck . . ."* The image on the windscreen had gone black as the noise pointed skyward. Then it became gray and pebbly.

The Osprey had reared over on its back. It began accelerating toward the earth upside down. The pebbles grew into stones and in less than three seconds into boulders that joined the men in the cockpit.

When the craft struck the earth, it pancaked on its top and exploded as engines, rotors, and flue mingled. The impact killed the men on board, but the Osprey's destruction was prolonged as forward momentum skipped it across the desert like a fiery Frisbee. It spun fifty feet into the air, whirling, tossing off flaming debris, slowly arcing over on its side. The tail hit first, and the aircraft cartwheeled on one wing and the nose. The tail collapsed. One wing broke off and skidded away like a sled, leaving a burning track of fuel. The Osprey stood on its nose for a second, a burning pillar, then toppled into its own pyre, the metals and fuel burning with the roar of an enormous blowtorch.

At the maintenance office inside the hangar, Bernadino repeated the question. "How many of those goddamned aircraft are out there without EMI shields?"

The battalion maintenance officer stammered. There was no chart for aircraft flying without EMI shields. He turned to her, "Ma'am, they are all supposed to have them."

"I know *that,* goddammit"—a thought occurred to her—"then it *is* possible that the aircraft flying all have the shields?" She was hoping out loud that was the case.

Her driver sat in a chair by the door, intensely interested in watching the army captain get chewed out by the army general. Until she whirled on him, too. "Get the command center on the radio."

He looked at her, startled, unable to believe that she

was talking to him like a private when there was a captain's ass available to chew on.''

''Goddammit, soldier, get the command center on the radio.''

He did. She took the radio mike and informed the command center to call an immediate halt to the operation in the field. There was a logistics emergency that she would have to look into before allowing them to continue. There was hesitation in the voice of the radio operator answering her. So she began cursing at him. ''Goddammit, soldier, this is an emergency.''

The radio receiver began whirring. A hiccup of static snapped across the air. A hesitant voice disregarded any semblance of radiotelephone procedure or security. ''General . . . there's an emergency here . . . two of our Ospreys have gone down . . . there's been a crash . . . two Ospreys.''

Rita Bernadino felt a kick in the belly. It hit her so hard she had to grasp for the edge of the table to steady herself.

# BOOK II

# SMOKE

# 4

Abu the Ferret felt the shifting of night air currents, then smelled the rancid odor of a man.

He cracked one eyelid open a slit. A ghostly figure glided toward him.

He remembered his own approach to the old man on the cot. *Just like the old Imam!* Only this time he was the victim. He struggled against the idea formed in his half-conscious state. It couldn't be true, unless . . . Unless he were already dead! Unless this was the afterlife. Unless he was condemned to relive and redie the murder he'd committed . . . as the victim. His attacker reached for him! He jerked away. A pain in the chest nailed him back to the spot on the mattress.

A cool hand stroked his forehead.

"Praise Allah," intoned the voice of a young man.

Abu whimpered. "Don't kill me."

"Of course not, Colonel." The voice reassured him. "I am here to care for you. Do you desire water?"

Abu hissed a dry "Yes."

"I am Mansour. I will be your servant until you have recovered from your wounds."

"My wounds . . ." He moved, letting the pains in his chest and leg jab him to assure him he was alive. "I am not dreaming them?"

"No, my colonel, they are real. Praise God, they are not serious. A clean shot through the skin of the thigh—a scratch. A glancing bullet against one rib. Probably a cracked rib."

He wanted to ask for assurance that he was not dead.

But that would be absurd. So he said. "I can hardly breathe."

"The rib. And your fall down the stairs has bruised your back and chest. You will be on your feet in a day and back at the war front inside a week."

"But—"

"I will bring you water." Mansour swept from the room, leaving swirls of his body odor in the air.

So. He was alive. What had happened since the night of the assassination? The Imam! The creases of pain in his angular face softened into a nostalgic smile. What a triumph killing him had been. He had been so lucky. So reckless, yet so lucky. He might yet be caught and tortured and killed for his heinous act against the Revolutionary Government. Then again, though, the real assassination team had tried to kill him. That was the truly lucky part. What better proof did he need of his innocence? Only he and his . . .

His thoughts darkened as he remembered his father. He would guess from the injuries that Abu had been involved. He would be furious. Not for fear for his son's safety, but for the risk Abu had taken. Getting caught would implicate the moderates in the assassination plot. They certainly had motive. The country had been left in shambles by the succession of old clerics who had held power since the late 1970s. The way to progress lay through the pragmatism of a younger generation of nonclergy, a generation not obsessed with the blindly intense hatred of the West. Abu had been lectured on this principle for years.

But Abu's motivations had been personal. His mother had been stoned to death before his very eyes. She'd been killed because she had been so immodest as to first neglect to cover her face in public, then so unrepentant as to berate her accusers and so insolent as to denigrate the Revolution and the memory of the Khomeini, who had wrought it. Because she had railed against the more or less continual war against Iraq.

Abu snorted in hatred. On the next inhalation, he picked up the freshly rancid odor of Mansour.

"Your water, Colonel."

"Major," Abu corrected. He took the glass, wincing as the movement stuck another dagger of pain into his ribs. He studied Mansour's face. The unkempt young man smiled stupidly down upon him. He felt a twinge of guilt in the aftermath of the pain. Did this fool know?

"What's wrong, priest? Why are you staring at me?"

"You are a hero, Colonel."

"Major. I told you I am a major."

Mansour's face broke into an absurd grin. "No, a hero and a colonel. They have promoted you."

"What? Why?"

"You sacrificed yourself in the name of Allah and the Imam. You volunteered for martyrdom."

Abu almost laughed. He inhaled a trickle of water and coughed, the spasms shooting fresh pains into his chest. When he finally got his breath back raggedly, he wheezed, "What is the Revolutionary Council doing?"

Mansour's hands, shoulders, eyebrows, and lips sagged. "Now they are rounding up the incompetents responsible for allowing the assassination to occur."

Abu nodded thoughtfully. A purge, he reflected. "And?"

"They ordered a strike at Baghdad to punish those behind the assassination of our beloved Imam."

"Leave me," Abu ordered. When he was alone, he struggled to his feet. It took a full twenty minutes. He began pacing, cautiously at first. He had to rehabilitate the leg. He would be needed at the front. He must get back his strength, and he must report to his general— that is what he would tell them. He smiled wolfishly through the grimace that accompanied his pain. *A hero. Indeed.* Imagine how much more heroic he would seem tomorrow when he demanded a return to the new front to fight the bastard Iraqis. The sooner, the better, he would insist. The farther from the inquisition into the death of the Imam, the better. Fact was, Abu the Ferret would rather battle the Iraqis any day. The Americans had revealed the hollowness of

their army. Better to fight them than face the clerics of
a Revolutionary Court seeking to place blame for the
bastard Imam.

General Amiri sat in the outer office of the Iraqi
president, his stomach clenching, his lungs drawing
breath erratically. This was not the personal fear of
being killed in battle he'd occasionally felt as a soldier. This was not the professional fear he'd felt as
commander of the only tank regiment to distinguish
itself against the Americans. No, this was the fear of
failure, of disaster he could not control. He'd not found
many things in his life he could not master. But he
was about to face one thing that would almost certainly not bend to his will. He was about to face the
inner circle of the Revolutionary Command Council
of his country.

His summons to appear before them could mean
several things, all of them bad. Somebody in the Ba'ath
party, the ruling elite, wanted to second-guess his
plan. Or change it. Or had suddenly gotten fearful
enough to scrap the plan altogether. This latter point
worried him most of all, for he had begun to doubt the
ability of the plan to succeed. So much had gone
against it in the last days.

The sound of a door latch stole his breath for a moment.

"The president wishes to see you now."

The soft-spoken announcement startled Amiri more
than if it had been shouted in his ear. The president?
Not the executive council? Before he could ask, the
owner of the voice, a short, slender man in a charcoal
suit presented his back for the general to follow.

The office was small, private, and personalized with
the dignified clutter of books and papers. Amiri immediately realized he had been called in for a private
discussion.

The man behind the desk gestured at a comfortable
winged chair. The man slouched carelessly in his own
oversized executive chair behind the desk. Amiri shuddered. The president, silvered at the temples and with

speckles of gray in his mustache, wore the trace of a smile but drilled him with his eyes.

"My dear General Amiri," he declared, almost as if surprised to see him. But Amiri knew better than that. Nobody had ever controlled this country more calculatingly than the president. Now more than ever, he knew, he must set aside that half-mad image of his. That kind of demeanor worked with subordinates or peers who could be cowed. This president would not be intimidated. More incredible than surviving the dangers of warfare, this man had overcome the intrigues of violent, subversive politics.

Amiri looked around. The man in the gray suit had soundlessly vanished.

"General, we meet alone for the first time."

"Yes, your excellency. We have not spoken since the council approved the plan."

"Your plan," corrected the president. "You developed the genius in that plan. You have been meticulously supervising it, according to the reports I hear."

"Yes, your excellency."

"I was unshakable." A long pause. "But now I am bothered, Amiri."

"Excellency?"

"My faith has been shaken—not in you, of course, but in the plan."

"Yes, your excellency." Amiri could never remember being so at a loss for words, so unwilling to speak. The more the president protested he had not lost faith in him, the more likely he had. He didn't understand the ways of politics well, but he understood doublespeak when he heard it.

The president continued in a low voice. "But . . . now the Imam has been killed. Now the Iranians have grown more threatening, more irrational than ever, wouldn't you say?"

Amiri grimaced. There was only one answer. "Yes, your excellency."

"Now, in retrospect . . . the timing, I mean . . . it seems a brilliant addition to the plan—your plan—because it gives us a chance for decisive political victory as well as the military victory because the enemy is in such disarray.'' The president twisted the upper half of his body to look back at Amiri. ''It is most fortuitous that the Imam has been assassinated, wouldn't you say?''

Amiri dared not keep his tongue any longer. ''No, your excellency, the murder is a disaster. The assassination has come at the worst possible time because it will focus hatred and attention on Iraq and the military border situation. Already the Iranians are on highest alert. Already we've seen a two-fold increase in reconnaissance efforts against us. Our preparations were weeks away from readiness to launch a counterfeit attack in the central border region, to be followed up with the actual thrust toward Dezful in the south. They may attack us before we are ready—''

The president held up a hand. ''Don't babble, Amiri. You needn't protest so much. I know you would never execute an assassination in this region . . .'' The president's hand drew a rising spiral in the air, and he shrugged offhandedly. ''. . . unless I had been informed.''

''No, your excellency, even more emphatically than that, I would never even *support* an assassination that you had not personally authorized—''

''Which I would never do.''

Amiri nodded emphatically.

The president chuckled nonchalantly. ''I know. I had had your background thoroughly rechecked in the light of this. You are beyond suspicion, Amiri.''

Amiri knew the man was telling him he knew everything. Nevertheless, he relaxed. Nothing in his background would incriminate him.

''Speaking of new light, Amiri, what are your intentions regarding attack preparations?''

''I believe we should proceed with the plan to attack Iran despite the assassination.'' For a moment, Amiri stumbled. ''Ah, forgive me, excellency. Do not think me presumptuous but well prepared. I ordered my staff to complete an accelerated timetable for an offensive.''

"So then, do you counsel the abandonment of defensive preparations and a swing to the offensive?"

"No, excellency. If anything, we have to expect the worst from the Iranians because of the untimely assassination. It's very possible they will act unpredictably. If the Iranians should attack, we can hold them well enough. If they attack in the proper place—in the central region—we will have just the excuse we need to counterattack. But if they attack in the southern border region, I'm afraid . . ."

"You're telling me the offensive has been jeopardized."

"Yes, excellency."

"Yet you wish to proceed with your original plan for the attack? And on an accelerated timetable?"

"I do."

"So do I. That is why I have taken precautions against failure. I have made a pact with the devil."

"Excellency, I do not understand." Amiri was beginning to understand all too well, though. There were devils and there was *the* devil.

"I'm sorry, I am not making myself clear. Let me say the pact was not with the devil exactly, but with somebody worse—the Soviets."

Amiri nodded, feeling like a very small pawn in these political games.

The president smiled genuinely for the first time. "So," he said, leaning deeply into his chair. "Tell me how you have solved the dilemma of your new timetable."

Amiri did. With animation and enthusiasm.

When he'd finished, the president leaned forward and said, "My dear Ali Salaam Amiri, you have reassured me. I must assure you, I have never lost my complete confidence in you."

Amiri, welcoming the dismissal in the tone, stood. "Thank you, excellency."

The president accompanied him to the door, placing a warm hand on Amiri's shoulder. The touch, despite its warmth, renewed a chill in Amiri's gut.

"Two final things, my general."

"Excellency?" Amiri's throat almost hitched on the last syllable. He felt the presence of people behind him, perhaps a security squad of secret police to arrest him.

"My brother-in-law. Alnasrawi. You were with him when he died?"

All Amiri could think of was that squad waiting to arrest him. Had he so misjudged his generals out there that night? Had one of them been a traitor? For himself, he knew he must not lie about a single detail of that night—except for the part about pulling the trigger.

"I was with him, your excellency."

"Then tell me . . . this is such a hard time for my wife and her family still . . . did Alnasrawi have any words of love for her and for his children?"

The ice block felt as if it might expand into an iceberg. "No, your excellency. His last words were an expression of his disapproval of my plan against the Iranians. I had hoped to dissuade him of his opposition. But then the bullets began flying . . ." Amiri's voice trailed off. "He was killed instantly, but perhaps I could fabricate a few such last words in a letter to his family."

The president smiled shrewdly, as if in admiration at Amiri's audacity. "No. I have already done that. He was a pig. I guessed he would scoff at a plan of such boldness. He died without ever drawing a creative breath. I have even heard nasty whispers that he was working for a foreign power—perhaps the Americans, or even the Israelis." He shook his head, dismissing Alnasrawi from it. "These warmongering Iranians, Amiri? We'll soon begin opening the gates of hell for them?"

"Soon, excellency." He turned and was relieved to see nobody behind him. He opened the door and stepped out of the office.

The door shut him out. No security squad waited outside, either. Just the man in the charcoal gray suit who led him from the palace, restored in the years since the American bomb damage. Does he know?

Amiri wondered. Does he know I killed his wife's brother? Could he still be so cold?

Major General Mohammed Bani-Sadr led the commander of tank forces of the Iranian Army out of earshot of his superior officer's retinue. When they had walked nearly a quarter-mile away from the field headquarters at Karand, the senior officer removed his cap and lifted his narrow face to the sun. "This is far enough, Bani-Sadr. I am exhausted by too little sleep in the last few days."

Bani-Sadr didn't care about his commander's lack of sleep. "You ask the impossible. I won't do it."

Unperturbed, General Abolhassen Saddeq replaced his cap. "You do not wish to lead the advance on Iraq?"

"Bah! You know me better, Saddeq. We have soldiered together, fought side by side. I have commanded you. Now you command me. I am still a soldier, and I will attack the Iraqis and raze their capital worse than the American bombers, if you give me the resources. You know that is not the problem."

"I have given you your promotion and the command of an armored corps."

"Bah! I cannot be bought."

"Then what is the problem?"

"Do I have to say things that will insult you, my friend?"

"Say only the truth, Bani-Sadr." Saddeq's long face grew even longer and sharper, belying his words. He clearly did not want to hear the truth at all.

Bani-Sadr gave it to him anyhow. "The problem is that you are no longer content to be a soldier. You have strayed into the realm of politicians. You have gotten yourself involved in intrigues, this assassination . . . these things are not the domain of the soldier. I fear the results have proven it. The damned Fahzi is dead but nothing has happened. Where are the so-called moderates? They are cowards, no? All have gone into hiding, eh?"

"So you think it immoderate for the Revolutionary Council to try to punish the Iraqis?"

Bani-Sadr's face wizened into a maniacal grin. "Hah! the Iraqis did not kill the Imam."

"Come, Bani-Sadr, what would you have them do? Attack the Soviet Union? Threaten the 'Great Satan' America? Do nothing? Wait for a confession from me and the others responsible? Be realistic. Something must be done to galvanize public support behind the new council. You know that. What better to do than strike out at the weakened Iraqi military machine."

"Surely you don't expect yet another decade-long war will salvage our country from the fanatic clerics?"

Saddeq smiled indulgently. "We are the soldiers who must execute the war. We have some control of many factors that influence a battle. We can set the pace of our attack. We can ameliorate the rate of casualties. We can press the Iraqis until they resist too strongly, and then we can return to our present defensive positions. We simply have to give the moderates in government a bit of time to consolidate."

"To play politics."

"Call it what you will. We have only to measure our attack so that it will minimize casualties, yet be seen as nothing less than the steadfast obedience to orders. They don't expect us to conquer the Iraqis, only to kill a few of them."

"You have seen the intelligence. They are preparing stronger defenses. They are not as weak as they were in the nineties."

Saddeq shrugged. "What does it matter? We attack. We run into resistance. We withdraw. All you have to do is sustain a combat of three or four days and kill a few thousand Iraqis in retribution for the assassination of the beloved Imam."

Bani-Sadr's face warped in frustration, but he held back a retort. Saddeq put a hand on his friend's shoulder. Bani-Sadr pulled away. "Do not patronize me, Saddeq. I will conduct the main attack. I will press as far as reasonable toward Baghdad. When the Iraqi resistance becomes dangerous, I will conduct a delay back to defensive positions. I do so under a personal protest to you, for that is not the way soldiers fight; it is the way politicians fight."

"And the other?"

"That is the impossible part. I must protest strenuously against taking Major Abu al-Batt into my division to command a tank battalion."

"Lieutenant Colonel," Saddeq corrected him with a wry expression. "He has been promoted. He has even been declared a hero. He will serve you faithfully."

Bani-Sadr snorted, his face bending out of shape again as if he'd encountered a foul odor. "As well as he served you in Mashhad? Leave him in Mashhad."

"I cannot. Already I hear rumors of suspicions about his involvement in the assassination. We dare not let a trail lead from him to me . . . that would taint every general with whom I've had contact in the army."

Bani-Sadr choked off an indignant squeal in his throat. "Fine for you, but what about me? If you put him on my staff, the trail leads to me. Take him onto your staff, Saddeq. Keep him out of further trouble."

"You know I can't, Bani-Sadr." With a sigh of resignation, he added, "I am sorry to unload my problem on you, but he is yours. I have already given instructions for the official orders to be posted. I cannot keep my son directly under my own command."

Resting his elbows on the hood of his desert command post—a Land Rover—Iraq's General Amiri knew he'd have the fight of his life on his hands, not because of the odds of success but because of the need to convince the Iranians this was his main attack.

The Iranian armor division's intentions could not be misinterpreted. The unit had marched directly from the foothills of the Zagros Mountains, where it had guarded the main highway toward Bakhtaran to the border, where the road turned to the southwest, toward Baghdad just a hundred kilometers away. The tanks had been kept well hidden, traveling at night. There had been other armor movements all along the front, but this division would lead the main attack. Of that, Amiri was certain.

He knew the Iranian army facing him reflected its commanding officer, General Mohammed Bani-Sadr. Bani-Sadr was tough. He'd held his ground year after year, attack after attack from ground and air. Even forces three times the size of his own hadn't caused his forces to budge from defensive positions in those foothills.

"Bani-Sadr," he said to his aide. "The man's rabid. How in heaven does a madman think?"

Amiri's aide looked at his superior as if to say the general ought to know. Amiri clapped the major on the shoulder and laughed. His laugh was too hearty, hollow even to Amiri. Ever since his former aide, Bakri, had assumed command of artillery, he hadn't had anyone close enough who understood him.

He refocused his field glasses in the direction of the battle at the border ten miles away. "From here," he said, "the action seems so remote. You can barely hear the sounds of cannon fire because the wind is carrying it off to the southeast toward the Gulf."

Amiri's aide cleared his throat and shuffled his feet, searching for an answer to his commander.

Amiri changed subjects. "I want to be closer to the battle."

Finally, here was a topic the aide could address. "General, your staff is correct in persuading you to stay back. Nobody else can execute your plan as well as you."

Amiri grunted his reluctant assent. He knew how this battle must unfold. The Iranians would have to achieve initial successes. His army would have to give up ground grudgingly. He, the general of the army, would have to make his presence and his grave concern known in the region. He couldn't risk getting killed, though. Later, when the Iranians had been completely sucked in, he would unleash his main attack in the south, toward Dezful.

"The plan is simplicity itself," Amiri whispered.

"We entice them to attack with small forays. Our forces here respond by acting as if they have been caught off guard. They are hampered by a shortage of manpower and difficulties in resupply of ammunition. This will be magnified by a series of disasters designed to encourage the attackers. The best the border defenders will be able to manage will be to delay the attacking forces for eighteen to twenty-four hours. They will be overrun, forced a short ways back toward Baghdad."

As Amiri forecast the timetable of the battle, his aide's face went slack in the night. He murmured, "Baghdad? The Iranians will attack Baghdad?"

Amiri wagged his head. "No. They will not come within sight of the capital. They will be halted soon after they commit themselves to battle."

The aide sighed in relief.

Amiri continued. "But not until their successes have developed into a bloodlust. Bani-Sadr will be unable to resist the breakthrough and pursuit phases of the armored attack. Every armor officer in the world dreams of it. He will try to do . . ." His voice trailed off without completing the sentence. There was no need to complete it. Every military man in the world knew the sentence ended, ". . . what the Seventh Armored Corps did to the Republican Guard in Desert Storm."

Amiri said, "We will give him what he expects."

The aide's face darkened. "No," he said. "You don't mean—"

Amiri nodded. "Yes. These border units will display total surprise because they have not been informed of our intelligence about the Iranian assault. They will die cursing the feebleness of artillery support. They will perish in anger because our tactical air has been committed to striking the Iranians where the enemy ruses are being played out. They will fire their weapons until their ammunition is exhausted—their resupply having been held up by bureaucratic bungling."

"These men are being sacrificed, my general?" the aide asked breathlessly.

"Yes, that is the word exactly. Sacrificed. The Iraqi soldiers on the border tonight are being sacrificed so the mistakes of our predecessors will not be made again. These men will die Islamic heroes. Yet, they will not even be aware of their heroism or sacrifice. They will believe they have been abandoned by their commander and a staff in disarray. All so our weaknesses will seem convincingly overwhelming to the Iranians. All so the attack in the south can succeed."

The aide put his hands to his ears and clenched his eyes shut in a grimace. "You should not be telling me these things, my general. If these facts ever become known . . ."

Amiri smiled wearily and clapped a hand on the shoulder of his aide. Beneath the caves of his eyebrows, his eyes twinkled in the light of distant flares. "No matter, my friend. You have had time enough to make peace with your family and God. This . . . treachery of mine will not be my undoing, even if it is discovered. No, it is the attack in the south that will enshrine us as heroes or condemn us as knaves. You and I will leave that battlefield as victors . . . or we will not leave it at all."

Abu lay on his belly beside Bani-Sadr as both observed through night-vision binoculars. Abu's thigh and chest still hurt. He grunted with the effort of trying to suspend his weight on toes and elbows.

"Sit still, old woman," Bani-Sadr commanded without lowering his glasses.

Abu collapsed, biting his mouth shut so he would not groan. Hot beads of sweat collected all over his body, wetting his clothes, exposing him to the night's chill. He tasted blood where he had bitten down on the inside of his mouth. But he did not utter a sound, except for his breathing.

"Must you breathe like a cow?" The general stood up and slapped his clothing impatiently. "Stay here.

I'm moving farther down the line." Then Bani-Sadr
was gone.

Ostracized. That was what they had done to him.
His own father had refused to see him after his return
from Mashhad. Bani-Sadr acted as he were chained to
a leper. "I tried to refuse you a spot in my command," he had said by way of introduction. "But I
have orders to take you anyhow. So I will. I cannot
foist you off onto a serious commander. So I will take
you with me like my lap dog. If you disappoint me, I
will beat you like a cur. Is that clear?"

Abu could find no words to reply. It was all he could
do to nod. Was this how a hero of the Revolution was
to be treated? True to his word, Bani-Sadr had treated
him like a cur from the first.

Abu lowered his forehead to rest on his arm. Re-
buked by his father. Reduced to the status of an animal. Hero, indeed! He felt like weeping. But he would
not. He jammed the goggles against his eyes and re-
sumed searching the field where the battle would begin, although he could not see well at first through his
watery eyes.

The night sky magnified sight and sound. Perhaps
it was the relative blackness, the almost total useless-
ness of human eyes that enlarged the brightness of
stars, the midnight blue of the atmosphere, and the
noises of the desert night.

Abu had memorized the maps and studied the terrain on night reconnaissances—daylight patrols had
been prohibited for fear of tipping off the enemy. He
had prepared himself for war—if only for his personal
survival—but he now knew Bani-Sadr would never let
him do more than watch. He felt sorry for himself for
his inability to succeed even at posturing as a soldier.
All he had for his personal honor was the knowledge
that he'd killed the bastard Imam. That, he had to keep
to himself. Nobody could know. His father, through
Bani-Sadr, had forever banned the subject from discussion. Still, he had done the deed. Nobody could
take that away from him. His eyes cleared. He re-
solved not to let the others bother him.

He knew where, about two miles away, the most remote Iraqi outposts were situated on the forward slope of a gentle knoll. This very moment, Iranian commandos slithered like snakes toward the outposts. Abu tried to pick out the small groups of killers, but could not. It reassured him that all he could see at that distance was the general lay of the land.

Characteristic of many places along the front, the ground dictated where defensive positions could be occupied. Here the Iranians had superior and so far impregnable defenses in the foothills. The mountains offered superior cover, and the defenders could shoot down the attackers. The Iraqis had positioned themselves out of range of direct-fire weapons and had dug in against artillery. Their defensive resources consisted of terrain that permitted maneuver against an attacking force from those mountains. The Iraqis thought themselves safe enough and they couldn't project their power any farther than they could shoot. So the war here had been a flexible standoff for decades.

Abu knew the history of warfare in this region. He had seen Bani-Sadr's plan. This time, there would be no such mistake as in 1982 in Operation Muslim Ibn Aqil. Then, armor forces had trailed along after the slow-moving infantry in the attack made at eighteen points on a twenty-two-mile front. Today, tanks would punch through Iraqi lines on a narrow front and drive toward the capital of Iraq. Bani-Sadr might be cruel, Abu reflected, but he was also a clever commander. He would open the gates of Baghdad with tank fire.

Abu heard a noise nearby. For a full fifteen seconds he stopped breathing, fearful that an Iraqi patrol might be stalking him as well. Finally, he decided the noise had come from an animal, perhaps a despised ferret like himself.

He cursed himself for his momentary cowardice and traded the night-vision binoculars for an infrared receiver to watch for the signals that would trigger the battle.

In about ten minutes, Abu saw an infrared signal twinkle green in the eyepiece of his receiver. One after another along a five mile front, IR flashlights flickered in the direction of his spot on the ridge. He felt the anticipation of battle building in him. Such a powerful flow of adrenaline excited him so he barely thought of his wounds.

He pushed himself on his knees and peered around the mid-distance between him and the outposts that had been occupied. The first skirmishers, knots of ten or twelve soldiers and engineers, had begun to materialize. Behind them a quarter mile or so, swarms of soldiers moved forward along streambeds and dry gullies. The engineers began clearing paths through the minefields and wire, creating avenues to give the Iranian tanks a running start against the main Iraqi defenses.

Soon would come an artillery barrage, intermittent at first, as if it were simple harassment. Tanks would begin moving. Iraqi ground surveillance radar and radio bands would be bombarded with jamming signals. The Iraqis at the front would of course realize an attack had begun and begin polling the listening posts, which by then would be neutralized. The surprise would not be the indicators of an attack but the disguise of its exact location. Points up and down the border would be receiving even more intense artillery preparation. More sounds of armor movement would be heard there because of radio transmissions and radar emissions and the busy rumbling of tanks driven back and forth to make enough noise to emulate two or three times their actual number.

Then, by the time the actual column of attackers had been established, Bani-Sadr's lead brigade should already be punching into the first real defenses, should be getting full artillery priority.

The artillery barrage came as a shrieking eruption of the fire rolling across the landscape on a twenty-mile front. It lit and contorted Abu's ferret face in a series of wicked, surrealistic expressions caught by the strobing explosions. No longer restrained by the requirements for surprise, and entirely forgetful of his wounds, Abu leaped to his feet and let out a throaty cheer. "Die, you bastards," he yelled. So this was combat! He shook a fist toward the west. "I'm coming for you bastards. I'm coming!"

"Silence, cow."

In the blue-white flicker of a flare, he saw Bani-Sadr. He'd come back and caught him unawares. How long had he been there? Humiliated again, Abu hung his head and waited for the tirade to come.

This time Bani-Sadr did not yell at Abu. He did worse. He turned to his aide and other staff members and said, "Come, soldiers," before striding away toward the field headquarters.

Abu's throat hurt worse than his chest and thigh, although he had suddenly become aware of their pain, too. He looked down at his bedraggled body and saw blood had been seeping through his bandages and staining his uniform. He nearly gave in to the tears. But he did not. Not this time.

# 5

When the telephone rang after midnight, Miles automatically reached for it, but she grabbed his massive hand and put it back on her breast. "Let the machine have it," Julie whispered. "You're busy with your wife."

"Right, besides, you're moaning so much, it would embarrass me." He moved beneath her, and they both moaned.

She whispered in his ear, and Miles tried to ignore the interruption of his answering machine message, but the instant he heard the tone in the caller's voice, he knew something bad had happened.

"Shush," he said.

"Don't shush—" Then she heard it, too, the division aviation officer identifying himself and using the words she had dreaded her whole marriage to an army pilot: "aircraft accident."

He lifted her clear, rolled over, and picked up the phone. She hugged him from behind.

"Disregard the recording, this is Colonel Miles . . . What accident? . . . What for? . . . sure . . . Who? . . . Oh, God."

"Anybody we know?" she murmured in his ear.

He put out his hand, reaching around his shoulder, touching her lips tenderly with cold fingertips. "No," he whispered past the phone. "Yes," he said firmly into it. "I'll be right there."

He hung up and walked across the bedroom, dropping heavily into a chair. She padded across the carpet and touched his shoulder.

"I have to go in. They couldn't tell me all the details over the phone. But I've been appointed to investigate an aircraft accident."

"I heard that part. You're shaking all over. There's something else, isn't there? Something worse?" It was more a statement than a question.

"They couldn't tell me the kind of aircraft—"

"Then it has to be an Osprey," she whispered.

He was nodding. "Worse than that. It's . . . it's Joel . . ." His throat clutched up, and he couldn't get the last name out.

"My God, Joel Parker? Joel Parker killed in an Osprey crash?"

He made a little choking sound and flapped a hand in a gesture of both futility and affirmation.

She murmured a prayer and hugged him until he gripped her waist to free himself. He began dressing, and she left him with his grief.

On the way out, he found her bent over a cup of coffee studying the kitchen tile. He stepped up to her, putting the tips of his polished ebony boots within her line of vision.

"I'm going to do a good job on this investigation, no matter how emotionally involved I am. I'll gut out the situation. I'll be all right."

She looked up into his face, his expression softer than she had seen it in weeks. "Is that all?"

"No."

"What else?"

"I love you." He reached for her shoulders and lifted her to her feet.

She pressed toward him, and they hugged each other tightly for a full ten seconds before he slipped from her grasp, detoured to his son's bedroom, kissed the bundle of a boy huddled inside flannel sleeping pajamas in a corner of his crib, and hurried to his car.

Miles was cleared onto the fort and directed to park at the gate by the Air Cavalry Combat Division's staff duty officer, another lieutenant colonel. The duty officer led him from the cooling, ticking Corvette to a waiting Blackhawk helicopter and handed him a thick binder labeled "DIVISIONAL SOP-AIRCRAFT MISHAP INVESTIGATION." Aircraft Mishap, Miles thought as the Blackhawk roared up to operating RPM. Helluva euphemism for a crash.

The SDO briefed him about the pertinent details that had been relayed from the Osprey battalion team at the crash site. He listened absently at first, but then his attention perked up at the preliminary report that the EMI shields might have been missing from both of the downed craft. His mind wouldn't let him focus completely on the here and now. He kept thinking about later, about the inevitable viewing of bodies and parts of bodies.

Miles felt a stab of guilt slide off its shelf into his consciousness. How many times had he hated Parker for getting the command he had coveted? How often had he cursed both Parker and General Little, who had dropped his career in the dust? And Wilkerson, who had ground it there as if putting out a cigarette beneath his heel? Suddenly he felt dirty and small. No wonder the general had passed him over. He was nothing but a venal little louse. Maybe the general had seen that quality in him. Maybe he'd gotten what he'd deserved, after all. Maybe he was born to be a staff weenie. Maybe Wilkerson was the good guy, and he was the shithead.

At the crash site, Miles saw Lifesaver medical evacuation teams already at work. They had arrived on the scene within minutes after the accidents, but they found no living bodies to evacuate. Doctors had made the death pronouncements already. Medics had been detailed to the grisly task of collecting body parts and their severe distress showed in the eyes that peered over surgical masks. Looking into those eyes, Miles suddenly felt the severity of the night chill and shuddered in sympathy with them.

Within minutes, two CH-47 Chinook cargo helicopters were hovering a hundred feet above the desert at the two crash sites. Miles watched them drop their separate cargoes. Slung beneath each Chinook was the wreckage of one or more helicopters from the Graveyard, the post salvage dump. He thought he recognized parts of a Huey and a scout in the glare of the cargo chopper's landing light.

He knew the first priority here. Now that it had been established that nobody had survived, the parts of the Osprey took precedence over human parts. The metallic remains would be collected into cargo nets and hauled away to be dropped outside hangars at Edwards Air Force Base. Work details of mechanics and other soldiers would drag the pieces under cover. After the sun rose later in the day, when the Soviet Salyut satellite flew over, it would photograph conventional aircraft parts and piece together a phony story.

After the investigating team had a roof over their heads, the work parties would start sorting the remaining human parts from the wreckage.

Miles watched and took notes. Busying himself with writing down mechanical details helped. Anything was better than preoccupying himself with the gore and destruction. In time, he became absorbed in it, insulating himself from the thoughts of all the wives and children who had to be notified tonight.

"Sir?" It was Sergeant Kopmeyer, his confidant at the Osprey detection command center.

Miles smiled as warmly as his taut face muscles would permit. "Kop. Glad to see you again. What are you doing here?"

"The G3 NCO detailed me to be your right-hand man as long as you need me."

"Oh?" Miles frowned. "Do I hear something between the lines in that?"

Kopmeyer sniggered. "Sir, meaning no disrespect, can I ask you something?"

"Kop, anytime somebody says 'meaning no disrespect,' that just what they're about to do. Just ask your question or make your comment."

"Fine, sir. What the hell did you do to get the division staff down on your ass? All I ever did was defend you when the G3 NCO was poor-mouthing you. 'Fine,' he says. 'You wanna take Miles's side, you go on and be his permanent sidekick.' Then he boots my ass out of the building. Here I am.'' He pinched his nose at the smell of burning wreckage. ''I think I'm gonna be sick.''

''If you think this is bad, wait until tomorrow.''

Miles worked throughout the night and into the next evening before he stopped for a nap and a meal. Seeing the bodies in the field and poring over the wreckage in the hangar had kept him continually queasy. Despite the inferno of the crashes, work parties kept finding pieces of human flesh and bones, which had to be placed in plastic sacks and accumulated in ice chests. When the chests filled up, some lucky private made a morgue run, getting away from the devastation for a while. As the day heated up, the hangar air became thick with the stench. Miles wore a surgical mask scented with a few drops of shaving lotion to stifle the smell. He was sprinkling it for the third time in an hour when he heard a commotion at the door of the hangar.

The military police had blocked the path of somebody who didn't belong. They were trying to herd the man out, and he was refusing to be herded. Miles recognized Keyes and shouted, ''Hey, let that man in here.''

''Sir, he isn't even a member of the Osprey battalion. He's just a scout pilot—''

''Goddammit, Major Keyes is a material witness to this investigation and I ordered him to come here. Now let him through.''

Keyes slipped through the space the MPs created in their lines and strode toward Miles, extending his hand. With a grim smile, he mumbled, ''Just a scout pilot, my ass. P.B. Keyes, commander of the best gunship troop in the goddamned army is all. Just because I do my job from the front seat of a scout . . .'' He wrinkled his nose at the smell in the hangar.

Miles shook his hand gratefully and handed him a

freshly scented surgical mask. "What's up, P.B.? Don't tell me I've got more problems."

Keyes sucked a partial breath through the mask and gagged. "Let's get some fresh air," he wheezed.

Outside, he said, "Nelson, I came by as quickly as I could get away from the troop. I know this must be devastating for you." His eyes narrowed at his friend. "You don't suppose Wilkerson gave this investigation to you on purpose, do you?"

Miles gave him a scant smile. "You're the one who turned around my thinking about the man. Don't tell me you're going against your own advice about giving him the benefit of doubt."

"Right. Forget him. How are you doing?"

"Okay. But I can't help being struck by the irony of these events. Remember when the Desert Storm thing came up, I was in the Osprey development group? Well, I wasn't allowed into combat because I was too important to the group. Then when the command of the new Osprey battalion came up, I was turned down. Know why?"

Keyes wagged his head.

"General Little wanted somebody who'd been in combat with him. He didn't want somebody who'd stayed Stateside in combat research and development. Ironic, huh? So Joe Parker gets the command. I got a nice note from Little. I wasted years of anger about that. I hated Parker, and he never did anything wrong. Now Parker is dead, and the big irony is that I'll never get the chance to apologize to him. God, P.B., why do I have to learn all my lessons the hard way?"

"Listen, Nelson, this is not a lesson. It's not punishment. It's no more than an accident. Parker is dead. It might have been you. You're general officer material, for chrissakes, Miles. If you weren't so damned intent on that Osprey, you'd see it. It's plain to Blanks and the rest of us. You're being groomed for bigger things, boy."

Miles stared at the tarmac. "Thanks, P.B. Even if you're wrong, I feel better. There is one thing, though. I want you to understand this about me."

Keyes cocked his head. "What?"

"I don't want to be groomed. I want to be like you. I want to be in command of troops, not machines or reports. I don't want to be a general as much as a commander—one as good as you."

Keyes clucked his tongue. "There's the real irony, my friend. Nine of ten officers who know you, envy you. And you envy me. I'm just glad you're my friend." He clapped Miles on the shoulder. "Good luck, my friend."

"That's it? You just came by to say that?" Miles's voice quavered with the realization.

Keyes winked at him.

They parted with a firm, lingering handshake, and Miles reentered the gloomy hangar with its scent of death. A medic handed Parker's wallet to him. He made a quick inventory of currency and credit cards for the record. He couldn't help but see the pictures of Parker's wife and daughter. The sight of a pie-faced, wide-eyed toddler put an exclamation point on his feelings as he remembered his own son, Christian. For a moment, he was silent, fighting back a new wave of emotion.

Then he collected himself and got back to business. He ordered the division surgeon to evaluate the health hazard to those piecing aircraft together and then directed a disinfectant to be sprayed on the wreckage to keep out the flies and to minimize the chance of disease spreading. He encouraged the men in their gruesome tasks, offering them hope they could be done by day's end if they kept at it.

By evening, Miles was ready to move his investigation into a conference room in the battalion's main hangar. The team had collected all the available oil samples to send off to crash labs for analysis. Medical teams had begun autopsies. Miles and two other investigators began building a list of all the men and women they'd have to interview. Miles released one shift of investigators and began briefing a second. After they had been dispatched to their duties, he rounded up the tireless Kopmeyer.

Kopmeyer had already proved himself invaluable to Miles. As a signal specialist and electronic warfare technician, he understood computers and the potential for interference from high-intensity radiation environments. He translated the technical jargon into everyday language for Miles.

Miles scratched his head. "I know we're not supposed to focus on any single cause or contributing factor at this stage of the investigation. But things seem to be narrowing down to a single factor. Since there were two accidents almost simultaneously, yet half a kilometer apart, it seems unlikely that coincidental pilot error occurred."

Kopmeyer smirked. "I don't know about all those twenty-five cent words, Colonel. But if you're trying to say the lack of EMI shields caused two crashes, I think you're onto something."

"Way to cut through the crap, Kop. That's exactly what I'm trying to say. We have to examine everything, but my personality resists that kind of inquiry. I need a crap cutter."

"Crap cutter is my middle name, Colonel. What do you need?"

"I know those Ospreys crashed because the EWI shields were left off. Sooner or later, we'll be asking why. We'll get some rational explanations. Meanwhile, I want you to snoop around with the avionics guys at the battalion maintenance hangar. I'd be interested in what the grunts are saying about those shields."

Polomarchuk breezed into Dudov's inner sanctum. The exhilaration of his rise to the top ranks still had him puffed up with self-importance. So he did not see the extra man until after he fanned a stack of papers before Dudov and Zuyenko. He had lowered himself halfway into his seat before he stopped short.

"Mendenyev?" he croaked at the intelligence officer standing at attention to the side. "What are you doing here?"

"I invited him," said Dudov dryly.

"But why?"

"You shall see."

Polomarchuk twitched, and Zuyenko unveiled a small, sarcastic smile at the pompous minister's discomfort. Mendenyev stared down at his shoes.

Polomarchuk lowered himself into his chair. "Well," he said, "the subject is Abramov . . . Do you want to discuss this before a junior officer?"

Dudov ignored the question. "First, I invite you to sit down, Comrade Mendenyev." He tossed an annoyed glance at Polomarchuk. "You, Comrade, are incorrect. The subject is not Abramov. It is the battle plan. Abramov has made some sense to me."

Polomarchuk cleared his throat.

"But not to you?" Dudov asked, challenging him.

Polomarchuk opened his mouth. Then, as his eyes met and read Dudov's, he hesitated. In the next instant, he suffered a coughing fit, which he stifled in a crusty handkerchief, a semi-starched white flag of surrender.

Dudov accepted the capitulation without gloating. "I agree with his reasoning to cut off Tabriz instead of occupying Tehran." He paused, allowing the KGB chief and the defense minister to cast their votes with nods. Mendenyev was not consulted. "The only difficulty is with the Iraqis. They have insisted from the first that we take Tehran. They will view this change with resentment."

"I have reason to believe," said the KGB chief, pausing dramatically to let it sink in that he had spies everywhere, including Baghdad, "that they fully expect us to become engaged in another Afghanistan. Naturally, they want us to get deeply involved in combat with the Persians so they might achieve their own ends without sacrifice. But they are realists. They will understand if we take a safer course."

Dudov nodded thoughtfully. Polomarchuk aped Dudov.

Zuyenko shrugged. "Besides, we have never told them we intended to attack toward Bandar Abbas. What is one more surprise to them?"

Dudov slapped a palm on the table, indicating his decision. "Done then. We cut off Tabriz. Now for Bandar Abbas. That is next. Is Abramov correct again? Will this bring the West into a war? Will they attack in Europe? Will they land troops in the Gulf and try to stop us from reaching the warm water? This will not be the same situation as the so-called Desert Storm. They will not have a safe haven from which to launch their tanks this time. What do you think?"

"I think," Polomarchuk began in a small voice, "that if we are afraid of what the West will do, we should avoid taking that action altogether. If we have the strength and the will, attack. If we lack either the strength or the will, stay home. Tabriz is the safer course. But there is no victory in stealing the lunch from a child. Now Bandar Abbas . . . that is a bold stroke. There is a plan with balls."

Dudov and Zuyenko stared at Polomarchuk for a long time. Polomarchuk squirmed, then dropped his shoulders in apology, withdrawing his words with body language.

"Comrade!" barked Dudov. "Brilliant. You have stated the case simply and eloquently."

Polomarchuk hesitated to see if he were being mocked. When he saw Dudov was genuine, he puffed up again and permitted himself the exaggerated smile of a clown.

"Now all that is left is to decide on who must command this 'bold stroke,' as you call it. It must be a military officer with stature, somebody like—"

Polomarchuk opened his mouth and raised a finger, but Dudov was not to be interrupted.

"—somebody like you or Abramov. If this is to be an important military action, it must be commanded by an important military officer."

Polomarchuk's mouth worked dryly for a moment longer. "Abramov," he finally said. "In addition to the qualifications you specify, it would be better to have this Caesar out of Rome, so to speak."

Dudov and Zuyenko shared a smile. "Again, you show a brilliant insight, Comrade. Abramov it is."

The clown smile returned to Polomarchuk's face for a second. Then he sobered. "But we must have a means of putting a leash on that old fox so he does not sabotage the effort either by neglect or by design."

"Exactly!"

Polomarchuk looked confused. He hadn't ever experienced such positive reinforcement from Dudov before, and it made him wary.

Dudov inclined his head toward Mendenyev. "What do you think of assigning Major Aleksandr Mendenyev to be Abramov's aide? It is the perfect way for us to keep in touch with the marshal's execution of our military effort?"

"Yes . . . excellent." Now Polomarchuk knew why the major had been invited to the meeting. The conclusion reached had been foregone. He had ratified it as surely as if he'd read a script prepared by them. Dudov smiled and dismissed Mendenyev.

"We have some details of intelligence to tidy up about the Americans as well." Dudov waved an open palm at Zuyenko.

"Preliminary, of course," said the KGB chief, shifting in his chair.

Polomarchuk fired a quick shot of derision into the opening created by the momentary silence. "You have rumors you cannot confirm."

Zuyenko's facial skin tightened like a wrinkled sheet yanked across a lumpy bed. But he did not fire back a retort. Instead, he spoke in measured, flat fragments.

"Activity in the American west," he said. "At their National Training Site. Weeks of unnaturally strong and frequent electronic emissions. Patterns that suggest testing of new equipment. Perhaps new computers. Perhaps even new weapons systems. Last night an abrupt halt. Today satellite views of a pair of aircraft mishaps. Conventional craft, to be sure. Helicopters. We are monitoring the situation. It is suspicious, to say the least."

"Human source intelligence?" asked Polomarchuk

Zuyenko's face hardened again. "We are seeking it.

Rumors, as you say. Rumors are all we have. Suggestions of an entirely new weapons system."

Polomarchuk snorted.

Zuyenko leaned forward as if he would leap from his chair. "You have something to say, Comrade?" he growled.

"If you haven't read about it in the American press—which delivers information superior to the work of your agents, I doubt whether there could possibly be a new weapons system."

Zuyenko coiled into an even tighter crouch. The two glared at each other.

"Well," interrupted Dudov, dampening the tension. "I suppose the point of this . . . exchange of information should be clarified for the both of you."

The pair released each other from their stares.

"I want all possible relevant information passed to you, Marshal Polomarchuk. From Comrade Zuyenko. Then I want Abramov to have the pertinent details. All of them. It might be essential to his part of this military plan. Do you understand the need for open lines of communication?"

Neither man responded.

"Both of you," snapped Dudov.

"Yes," they answered in unison.

Dudov sighed in exaggerated self-satisfaction. "Now all that remains is to justify the intervention. The 1921 treaty permits us to intervene in the interest of national security and peace in the region. I recommend we coordinate our timetable with the Iraqis. As soon as they launch their counter-invasion, we condemn them publicly."

"Yes," said Zuyenko. "We are already justified by treaty in entering Iran."

Dudov's face creased in a vicious smile. "We must subdue them to save them."

Polomarchuk's face twisted in confusion. "We have condemned the Iranians for rattling sabers at Iraq. Now we condemn the Iraqis?"

Dudov smiled. "Marvelous, isn't it?" He stood up and led the stalking Zuyenko from the meeting room, leaving the dismayed Polomarchuk staring emptily at the wall.

Kopmeyer's "crap cutter" assignment produced immediate results.

Miles was chairing one of the countless investigation team briefings in the hangar conference room barely three hours after he'd sent the sergeant off to avionics. He heard a commotion at the door and saw Kopmeyer trying to make eye contact around the bulk of a master sergeant blocking the doorway. Miles turned the briefing over to his assistant and shoved by the hefty noncom.

"Back so soon, Kop?"

"Let me get right to it, Colonel. Those EMI shields weren't left off."

"Not so, Kop. We know they were. We've got the wreckage from the crash sites—no shields. The hangar crew found extras stacked—"

Kopmeyer waved a hand in his face. "I mean they were left off. On purpose. But not at first. They were on before the flight. They were on during the daytime preflight. They were taken off and thrown onto the stacks of shields of the Ospreys that were down for maintenance just before the crew piled on board."

Miles's complexion suddenly turned ashen. "That would mean sabotage—"

"Naw, Colonel, more like gross neglect."

Miles shook his head to clear the cobwebs. "Who said so? Who could do such a thing?"

"One of the maintenance techs did it. A private two."

"Why? Who said so? What in the hell—?"

"Easy, Colonel. One thing at a time. The guy's name was Thompson. Somebody saw him throwing the shields around the hangar after the Ospreys were off. He said he was on cleanup detail. No more was said."

"Where is he now?"

"He disappeared. He was supposed to be off the next day, so nobody thought nothing of it. But now they're looking for him all over the barracks. Not because they think he did anything but because he's AWOL.''

''Why hasn't anybody come forward?''

''They're about to. Like I said, nobody thought much of it at first. When I started asking questions, the guys acted like they all had these suspicions but were afraid to speak up. Once one got going, they all unloaded.''

''What do the soldiers think he did it for?''

''No reason. Just screwed up. The guy's a constant screwup. When the birds crashed, he probably realized he was to blame after people started talking about the shields. He's hiding out. He'll turn up, you'll see. He's just a common turd. He used to be a crew chief with the scouts in First Brigade. Couldn't cut it. His platoon leader fired his ass. Got him busted from spec four.''

''So they put him into maintenance? What kind of sense is that?''

Kopmeyer's face twisted up quizzically. ''You have no idea how often the company dud gets busted down into maintenance. Broke this guy's heart. All he ever wanted to be was a scout. All he ever talked about. You should talk to the lieutenant if you want to know about him. L.T.'s name is Barlow.''

Miles shook his head. ''Not now, Kop. For now we have to find the guy.''

''I'm on the way.''

''Not you. It's time for the MP's and criminal investigators to get into it. This is way more than just an accident now.''

Next day, just as the FBI entered the manhunt, Private E-2 Erwin Thompson turned up in a Barstow motel. Housekeeping services saw that Thompson's room was to have been vacated. So the maid removed the *Do Not Disturb* sign and used her master keys to open both the dead bolt and the knob lock. As she cracked an opening into the room, a rush of foul air met her. She turned and ran to the manager without entering

Thompson's room. He called police even before investigating.

They found Thompson hanging naked on the inside of the bathroom door. The tools of his profession lay on the bathroom counter—a spool of heavy-gauge stainless steel safety wire, a pair of side-cutters, a pair or duckbill pliers. A full hundred feet of the wire had been unspooled and twisted into a thin steel cable looped at both ends. One end had been square-knotted around the doorknob on the outside of the door. The cable had been draped over the door. A sliding loop had been formed.

Police investigators found half a bottle of whiskey and an empty vial of barbiturates. The television blared out mid-morning cartoons still.

The police reconstructed events. Thompson had set up his makeshift gallows. He had washed down the pills with bourbon. He had undressed and stood on the toilet lid, his back to the door. He had slipped the noose around his neck and shoved against the door, falling off the seat. The cable had cut into his throat, spraying the interior of the room with blood. He had soiled the floor. The coroner fixed the time of death as sometime during the night of the crash. Everything fit.

On the mirror, printed in large block letters with the complimentary soap, were his final words: I'm sorry for the Osprey crashes. E. Thompson.

At the Pentagon, Major General Wadsworth sat with Major Preston Brooks looking over imagery and photographs from the Iraqi battlefield. The Marine finished his evaluation of the battle's progress.

"Okay, Preston, you see the attack faltering as Amiri keeps putting resistance in Bani-Sadr's way. Let's play suppose."

Brooks nodded.

"Suppose we're right in assuming Amiri is going to counterattack. Where will he attack into Iran?"

"General Wadsworth, Iran is a country built only for communication from northwest to southeast. Anybody who wants to go in that direction can find a road, a river, a valley to travel. What's difficult is if you want to cross all the mountain ranges and deserts to travel in any other direction. It's part of the reason Iraq's aims have always been so limited. The terrain is so forbidding to military operations.''

"Except for one region," corrected Wadsworth. "Khuzestan. All that oil. And the fact it's the only province that lies in Mesopotamia, in the valley of the Tigris and Euphrates Rivers.''

"Yessir. Historically, Iran has been carved around the edges like a picnic ham. Much of what's left from what the Russians and Arabs and Afghanis have taken over the centuries is bone and gristle—with notable exceptions, Khuzestan for one. It's rich in oil and arable land. It extends the border of Iran toward Kuwait until the only Iraqi outlet to the sea is a lousy twenty-five kilometers of coastline.''

Wadsworth agreed with a grunt. "Sure. They tried to extend their outlet to the Gulf in the annexation of Kuwait in 1990. When that doesn't work, they rebuild their army and make a move in the other direction. So how does Amiri turn a battle more than two hundred-fifty miles away into an opportunity to strike at Khuzestan?''

Brooks didn't hesitate. "He already has. I mean, I think he's waited until the Iranians have committed reserves. He's let them react to limited successes. Now he's in the process of pinning them down. Next he counterattacks.''

Wadsworth shook his head suddenly, as if rearranging thoughts. Then he changed subjects abruptly. "Have we seen anything worthwhile from the Soviet desk?''

Brooks brightened. "I've been watching all the activity, the tank shuttling that's going on in the western Soviet Union. I can't put my finger on it, but something is odd about all the tank maintenance and retrofitting activity.''

Wadsworth squinted. "Western Soviet Union? What about it?''

"Well, sir, they've been shuttling tanks back and forth between the former Warsaw Pact countries and depots in the interior. The activity has been sudden. It seems inspired by the war in the Mideast—in fact, I first thought they'd be relocating hundreds of tanks from the depots to the southern military districts. But no, they just turn them around after a couple days and sent retro-fitted tanks back to the west."

Wadsworth grew suddenly dour. "Nothing? The Soviets are doing nothing in the southern military districts? I can't believe that. If they're doing nothing, I'm *very* suspicious."

Brooks waved a hand in front of his face. "No, sir, I don't mean nothing. I mean nothing effective has been seen in the southern districts. I mean, the reserve units have been mobilizing but that's no more than a circus. Those troops couldn't fight their way out of a crowded room. They've been doing a lot of defensive preparation . . . digging in tank-fighting positions, alternate positions, fortifications for the infantry improving lines of communications, stuff like that. Strictly defensive."

Wadsworth started again. "Lines of communication?"

"Sir? Yessir. Roads . . ."

"Railroads?"

"Yessir. The reserve troops have been repairing track, firming up roadbeds, fixing up transshipment points, improving railheads. Strictly busywork, I think, or maybe civic action kinds of projects. Under the facade of getting ready to defend against a very unlikely threat from Iran by just having places to drop supplies off the rails and stuff like . . ."

"Holy shit!" said Wadsworth. "The goddamned railroads. Which side of the Caspian?"

Brooks looked puzzled. "Both sides, sir."

"Chrissakes, that's it!"

Wadsworth put Brooks on the task of keeping tabs on every mechanized unit within three hundred miles of being able to reinforce Bani-Sadr's attack.

He grabbed for a secure phone and tapped out the

number to Scott Hancock, his friend at Central Intelligence.

"Scott," he said into the buzzing tunnel of the voice-scrambling equipment. "What's the latest from your contact in Iraq?" He waited a second, a frown crossing his face. "Killed by a stray bullet? I'll bet it was a stray. New subject . . . you know all that crap we've been getting on the T-80s and T-88s in Eastern Europe? Well, what's the latest on them?"

Hancock's reply came back tinged with uncertainty. "The analysts can practically get life-size pictures with detail that'd make you piss your pants. It's genuine, Nelson. Those tanks have been going in for retrofit and coming back as T-88s. Funny."

"Bet your ass it's funny. Any other sign of a mobilization? POL tankers, railbed maintenance, camouflage, troops? Anything?"

"Nothing. There hasn't even been an increase in the tanker fleet or rail tankers capable of supporting the increased numbers of battle tanks. For all the world to see, it looks like they're just stockpiling the somebitches and guarding them."

"Where?"

"Just tank parks. Heavily guarded field sites . . ."

"More security than normal?"

"Yes."

"But less field activity than before, right? I mean, they have more tanks but less training, I'll bet."

"Yes. By God, how did you know that?"

"Lucky guess."

"Well, that's one of the funny parts I was referring to. You know, if they were planning some funny stuff in Eastern Europe, they'd sure as hell have to get out in the field with the new equipment. They'd be training all over hell, getting ready with maneuvers, firing ranges, the works."

"Bet your ass, buddy. One more thing."

"Name it . . . but then you have to let me in on your brilliant deductions."

"We've been looking at snapshots your guys sent over. We've all been trying to prove by examination that somehow those tanks aren't what they seem, right?''

''Yeah.''

''Well, forget that for now. I want to see train schedules. I want somebody to give me a reading on the timetable the damned Soviets have been using.''

''Sure. But I can already tell you it's messed up.''

''How's that, Scott?''

''Well, they've been moving tanks eastward so fast they're piled up at the railheads. They can't get them moved back for retrofit as fast as they're getting them back out the field . . . I should say field storage.''

''Bingo! We've just caught the Russians up to their old shit.''

''Lay it on me, General.''

''They're going into Iran, buddy.''


It was in the evening that Miles delivered his report to the division commander and Wilkerson. When he finished the oral summary, he placed a four-inch-thick folder on Major General Little's desk. He glanced at Wilkerson, who responded with a scowl.

''That's the abbreviated report, sir. As lab analysis and medical reports filter down, they'll be added. Before it's done, the complete file will take up a filing cabinet. You wanted something in a hurry, though.'' He shrugged and pointed at the file, feeling slightly stupid for acting so nonchalant about a project that had kept him up for three solid days.

''Thank you, Colonel Miles. We were faced with grounding the whole Osprey fleet until you found the negligence factor instead of mechanical failure. Now we can get back to training. Thanks to you.''

''Actually, I had a sergeant named Kopmeyer who ran down the Thompson story for me.''

Little smiled and inspected Miles from boots to close-cropped haircut. Miles felt he was being pitied for the awful slackness in his face and the redness of his eyes.

The general said, ''The Ospreys will be flying tonight. Now all I need is a battalion commander.''

Miles took it as a dismissal. He stood erect and snapped a salute to the corner of his eyebrow. Then his vision clouded for a second, and he staggered. He heard a snicker from behind. General Little did not return his salute.

"When can you go to work?" Little asked.

"We'll be back at G3 in an hour, won't we, Colonel?" said Wilkerson.

Miles smiled weakly. "Right away, sir."

"Wrong," said Little.

"Sir?" he croaked.

"Wrong on both counts. You take the day off, Nelson. Get some sleep. Forget G3. Report to the Osprey battalion in the morning."

"What?" Wilkerson and Miles spoke in unison, the brigadier general in anger, Miles in astonishment.

Little answered them both at once. "You're my Osprey battalion commander, Nelson. I don't want any ceremony. And I don't want any delays, mister. Your battalion is already a full month behind the deployment status of the rest of the division. If we have to go tomorrow, your birds wouldn't be able to go over on the first wave. Fix that situation, hear?"

Miles was too stunned to answer coherently. He said the first thing that came to his mind. "Can I take Kopmeyer with me, sir?" Somehow, he associated the sergeant with his change in luck. Because of Kopmeyer, he had gotten the battalion. The sergeant was his charm now.

Little shrugged. "I don't see why not."

This time when Miles saluted, the general returned it. Miles spun, totally ignoring Wilkerson's scowl, intent on getting out the door. He visualized the parking lot where he'd left his car. He knew that when he got outside, he'd never be able to suppress a victory howl, no matter how tired he was, no matter how grief-stricken he was supposed to be over the death of Parker.

He had grasped the handle to Little's office door when he heard Wilkerson's voice. "Colonel, come back here a minute."

Miles stiffened, then forced himself to relax as he turned to face the one-star. He knew that sometimes his height and bulk made him look belligerent. He didn't want trouble. Not now. Now he had what he'd dreamed of having. Besides, he reasoned, Wilkerson was not such a bad-ass. Keyes had told him that. Wilkerson wanted to congratulate him. Sure, he wanted to add his commendation to Little's. Just as Keyes had said.

The sneer on Wilkerson's face told him before the words. "Just for the record, Colonel, it's only fair to tell you I was against the decision to give you that command, and up until a minute ago, I had expected my nominee would be appointed. I had one of the gunship officers in mind. I wanted somebody with combat experience. Nothing against you personally, but you're just a . . . ." The general flapped his hand as he searched for the word.

*Don't say it, asshole! Don't say it*, Miles thought, tensing his belly muscles.

". . . just a staff weenie." Wilkerson smirked at him, showing his teeth.

There it was in that smile, almost a dare for Miles to say something to jeopardize his command within the very minute it was given to him. Miles let his face go slack. He clamped his teeth together, fighting against the urge to speak. His knotted jaw muscles bulged as if he had stashed walnuts in his mouth. He glared into Wilkerson's sarcastic gaze and decided he would not be cowed. He knew what he looked like, with his size and the feeling of his angry expression— he looked threatening. He didn't care. He said, "Just for the record, General, I'm going to prove you wrong. *Again.* You were wrong about the Osprey being vulnerable to detection in its EW tests and you're wrong about me. You don't know anybody that could command that battalion better than I can. There isn't—"

"Don't you sass me, Colonel," Wilkerson snapped, jutting erect in his chair. "I'll have your ass—"

"Knock it off," said Little. "Both of you know this division has serious business ahead of it in the Middle

East. There's no room for bickering between two senior officers.''

Wilkerson flinched at being described as a peer of
Miles, but said nothing.

''As long as we're going on record here, I'll put in
my two-cents' worth. Colonel, you very nearly had the
job the first time it came up. The only factor that made
a difference was, in fact, the combat experience of Joel
Parker. Meanwhile, you've proven yourself in other
ways. I've kept an eye on you for years. General Bernadino has watched the way you handled this investigation. Both of us concur in the choice of you for the
Ospreys.''

Again Wilkerson winced, this time at the mention
of Bernadino's name and at the suggestion two of the
division's generals had conspired against him.

''Congratulations again, Colonel. Now you're dismissed once and for all,'' said Little, throwing a hard
glance toward Wilkerson to punctuate the remark.

Miles's celebration of his new command consisted
of a party of two in his home, with Julie Miles opening
a chilled bottle of wine.

''It's indecent to be partying,'' he said, even while
gulping the cold, dry wine. ''They just buried those
guys yesterday.''

''I'll tell you indecent,'' she said. ''Indecent is
staying away three days and nights straight. Indecent
is feeling guilty about getting the command you've
worked years to get. Indecent is not knowing when to
just say thanks and enjoying life.'' She gulped on a
catch in her throat. ''It's also going off to the Persian
Gulf. Oh, Nels, will you have to go?''

''Yes.''

''When?''

In answer, he crushed her to his chest.

Overcome by a crazy mixture of feelings that vac-
illated between desperation and joy and gloom, they
made love. Afterward, narcotized by the aftermath of
wine, passion, grief, and fatigue, Miles fell into an
uneasy unconsciousness.

Julie Miles propped herself on one elbow and rubbed his expansive back. Every few minutes he would awaken and look around his bedroom in confusion. Finally, she said, "Yes, Nelson, you're still the battalion commander of the Ospreys."

He grinned and murmured an incoherent expression of gratitude, then dropped into a sound sleep.

# 6

Bani-Sadr scrambled expertly up the front slope of the tank and scaled the exterior of the turret. Lowering himself into the commander's hatch, he leaned over and spoke in a low voice to the loader. As the soldier stood on the hinged seat and pulled the earpieces of the communications helmet out, he barked down at the skinny lieutenant colonel with the face of a ferret. "Quit shuffling about and climb aboard. My crew won't be holding your hand. If they treat me like a sergeant when I command this tank, you surely can't expect to be treated like one of the Imams."

The loader jumped down from the front of the tank, scowling at Abu, the interloper, as he strode in the direction of headquarters.

Abu clambered awkwardly up until he stood beside Bani-Sadr outside the turret and murmured. "I don't understand. You said I would have a job."

"You do, cow. You are my loader." He keyed a lever beneath the earpiece of his helmet and spoke into the boom mike. "Driver, move out."

The purring tank issued a throaty roar and belched a black cloud of diesel fumes. The rear of the tank crouched as the drive sprockets yanked down on the track end-connectors. Then the sixty-ton vehicle leaped forward, throwing Abu off-balance. He fell sideways on the sponson boxes on the fenders. The barely healed wound in his thigh stung him sharply as he scraped the tender scab on the edge of a spare parts compartment. The screeching, growling, clattering tank noises masked his yelping curses at the driver and Bani-Sadr.

Moments later, Abu dropped into the loader's hatch and yanked the too-small loader's helmet unceremoniously down over his hatchet face.

"General Bani-Sadr, what is this . . . this—"

"This is an M60A3 tank, built in the United States and once a main battle tank in the Iranian army. It is a relic of a bygone era of warfare. It was captured by the Iraqis in the eighties and won back by one captain Bani-Sadr when—"

"General Bani-Sadr, you know that's not what I mean. You are a general and I am merely a lieutenant colonel, true. But you have no right to disgrace me in this way. I—"

The driver, able to eavesdrop on the intercom, had let the tank slow to a crawl.

"Driver, speed up before I cut off your big ears," Bani-Sadr barked. The threat, though, was for Abu. Bani-Sadr scowled across the three-foot distance that separated their faces. He said nothing.

Cowed, Abu faced forward into the damp, marshy wind and stared into the night.

Gradually, light seeped into the edge of the sky. As Bani-Sadr's tank neared the forward battle areas, streaks of tracers skipped off the ground into the murky dawn. The general consulted his map. He updated the advances of his forward units by listening in to radio progress reports. Already, two breakthroughs had been exploited sufficiently to consider the gap one enormous chasm in the Iraqi defenses. Lead scout patrols reported being ten miles into the Iraqi rear, where support troops of the defenders were fleeing headlong, leaving tons of equipment.

Bani-Sadr ordered more light infantry forward to secure and widen the shoulders of the penetration by rolling up the Iraqi defenders. He demanded that units in contact elsewhere keep pressure on the Iraqis while rerouting units not engaged to the breakthrough.

By this time, Abu's anger had dissipated. He watched in fascination as Bani-Sadr put the pieces of his battle together. He saw the implications of these early successes and could not help saying reverently, "The road to Baghdad is open, General."

Bani-Sadr bit his lip. "It would seem so, Colonel."

"The Iraqis will close it off before the day is out if we . . . if you do not exploit this success."

"Yes, I suppose." Bani-Sadr bit his lip. Opposing forces tore at him. This was a battle he had been ordered to conduct, yes. The father of this weasel-faced cow had told him to be prepared to withdraw back to within Iranian borders once a "point" had been reached. Nobody had expected success. Nobody, including Bani-Sadr, had planned beyond a couple days' stalemate. Should he press the attack vigorously and seize victory? Wouldn't that stun the cowardly politicians and political generals behind this harebrained scheme? Could he do what the Americans had done on the road to Basra in 1991?

Bani-Sadr scowled fiercely. The attack had been too successful too early and too easily. He knew little of his adversary, Amiri. The general consensus was that the latest chief of the Iraqi army had demonstrated boldness and creativity in lesser commands, especially during Desert Storm, when his was one of the few units to distinguish itself. His chief deficiency was said to be his inexperience as a senior commander—his rise had been so fast in the years since the Iraqi army had been disgraced.

On the other hand, he'd seen the intelligence showing increased defensive preparations in depth all the way toward Baghdad. Had they been a contingency for the predictable aftermath of the Imam's assassination? Or were they a ruse of some kind? Or was this a lapse in the strategic defense of Baghdad?

The unknown quantity, he decided, was Amiri. Perhaps he'd underestimated the Iraqi. Maybe he was facing the first creative general he'd seen across the lines in decades of war. In fact, maybe he'd met a man to match his own generalship.

Bani-Sadr directed his M60A3 to the crown of a low hill. Beneath the crest on the far side, a line formation of thirteen Iranian T-72s stretched out over a kilometer. The general found the company commander's tank and pulled alongside. He directed Abu to step across and tell the captain to come up to his tactical radio frequency. When Abu returned, he replaced his helmet reluctantly because he saw a red-faced Bani-Sadr screaming into his microphone.

"I demand to know why your unit is cringing behind this hilltop while brave Iranian soldiers are dying on the other side."

The captain stammered his answer. "As I told you, General, we are gathering our strength for a new advance—"

"You fool. You gather nits while your brothers are dying below."

"General, I will move forward—"

"You will move now or I will have you shot."

Abu could not help flashing a self-satisfied smile.

Bani-Sadr's voice came across the intercom. "It delights you that somebody else has become the target of my rage?"

The startled Abu found himself pinned by Bani-Sadr's glare. "No."

"Liar." A sardonic smile softened Bani-Sadr's face.

Abu fought back a laugh. "Yes, then, I admit it."

Bani-Sadr rewarded the ferret-face lieutenant colonel with a brief smile. Then he grew serious and ordered his driver forward. "We will sweep back and forth across the front about a quarter mile behind these tanks. They will inevitably feel pushed from behind."

Abu snickered.

"The other commanders will be inspired by the bravery of this captain and his platoons. They will be moved by my motivating speeches. In no time—"

A radio call interrupted Bani-Sadr's snide commentary. The tank commander, gesticulating wildly with arm signals, waved the line of T-72s over the crest of the hill.

Abu heard the call sign of the reserve division's commander reporting a troublesome flank attack toward the rear of the Iranian advance. This news sobered Bani-Sadr instantly.

"Where are you?" Bani-Sadr demanded.

"Right behind you," the division commander reported.

Abu and Bani-Sadr whirled in their hatches. On final approach behind them was a UH-1N helicopter sending billows of dust blossoming into the sky. Bani-Sadr extracted himself from the tank commander's hatch.

He stood outside the turret and thrust his commander's helmet at Abu. "Take the helmet, cow," Bani-Sadr hollered.

Abu's mouth gaped open as he accepted the helmet. "What shall I do?"

"Follow the tank company. Wave your arms wildly. Scream unintelligibly into the radio. They will think it is I. Do something useful with your life for once, you son of a general—even if it is no more than to convince these fighting men that you are me."

"But—"

Bani-Sadr put on his steel helmet and skied down the front slope of the M60A3. The moment he stepped up into the division commander's Huey, the rotor wash generated a mushroom of dust. Then the helicopter turned tail and slid away, following the slope of the hill.

Abu stood dazed. He had been left alone—Bani-Sadr vanishing into the air, the tanks disappearing over the ridge.

"Move, cow!" Bani-Sadr's voice sounded even more threatening over the radio.

"But who shall be my loader?" Abu muttered to himself. In answer, he felt a grip on one ankle. He looked down into the face of the gunner who had peeled himself out of the cramped fighting station below and forward of the tank commander's feet. Obviously, he had seen Bani-Sadr pull this kind of switch before. The gunner pointed, indicating Abu should move into the commander's hatch.

Once Abu had assumed the command of the tank, he ordered into the intercom, "Driver, move ahead."

The engine belched smoke, but before the transmission caught, the RPM hesitated, then ebbed back to idle.

The gunner said, "Colonel you will have to fight the tank from your position in the cupola."

Abu scowled at the enlisted man. "I know that."

The gunner squinted. "Have you ever fought an M60 tank from there?"

Abu lied without flinching. "Of course I have, you cow. Driver, move out before I come forward and kick you in the teeth."

The tank lunged over the crest of the hill and descended on the enemy behind the attacking Iranian formation. Abu screamed, ignoring the pain it brought to his mending chest wound. To his delight, he found the scream sounded just like Bani-Sadr's.


"General Wadsworth," the president said, "The reason I've called you for this private meeting is that, instead of being the most informed person in the world, I often feel as if I've been placed in a nursing home. People near me want to shield me all the time."

Wadsworth noticed President Chase seemed excessively tired. And small. She had allowed the gray in her hair to remain untouched and, without makeup, the wrinkles in her face bunched the skin around the mouth and eyes. Her gray eyes, although cool and penetrating, showed red tinges.

"Sit down," she said. "First, let me apologize to you. It's beginning to look like you were right about the Iraqis planning an offensive."

Wadsworth nodded, accepting the apology.

"Let's be frank with each other, General. I want the bottom line. Will that be all right with you?"

"Yes ma'am."

"Don't give me that yes-ma'am crap, okay?"

No point in pussyfooting around with this woman, Wadsworth realized. Better to be very blunt. "I have some important information on Soviet involvement in the Middle East."

"What about the Soviets?"

"Tanks. It seems certain the Soviets and Iraqis co-ordinated the invasion of Iran long ago. The Soviets have been shifting hundreds of tanks for weeks."

The president stiffened. "Why hasn't anybody told me?"

"It's a well-disguised ruse. Freight cars carry T-80 tanks westward to depot facilities for retrofit to T-88 configuration. It looks innocent enough. But it also takes about fifty percent longer to get to the depot than it does for the return trip. So the returning freight cars are piling up at railheads before unloading. You see—"

The president frowned. "I don't see at all," she said quietly. "Tell me what it means."

"Ma'am," said Wadsworth soberly. "It means the Soviets are shifting combat tanks to another front, one where we've seen no build-up of fuel stocks. No POL activity is necessary, for crying out loud, because they'll leave all they want, where they're going. We've been looking just where they want us to. Now, I can't be certain, but I've asked for a detailed report on the rail maintenance activity in the Southern Soviet Military Districts. Seems the troops down there haven't really been engaged so much in mobilization as in the repair of lines of communications. We've been reading defensive intentions into that activity. But the shifting of tanks creates an entirely different possibility. My guess at this point would be the Soviets are planning an offensive operation."

"Into Iran?" The president's question came out as an uneasy declaration.

"Into Iran."

"By God, we've got to stop them."

She said it so matter-of-factly. He might have said the same words over a beer in the backyard, meaning "somebody ought to stop them." But in the silence, he realized that her statement was a declaration, the stuff of history. This was on a par with "Don't give up the ship" or "Nuts!"

"If we don't make them hesitate, if we don't put some pressure on that region by ourselves, they'll do it. Then we won't ever get them out without . . ." She pounded a feminine fist on the desk top. "By God, we've got to stop them. What do you think we should do?"

Wadsworth gulped. Why ask me? he thought. Chrissakes, I'm not the UDS commander.

"General, I asked you a question. Surely you have an opinion about how to stop the Soviets."

Wadsworth stammered for an instant. He cleared his throat and began again. "Naturally, ground forces would be the best way. But that would take—"

"Get to the point, General."

"The fastest, most effective way to counter those tanks when they invade is going to be our anti-tank helicopters. They and the Ospreys might buy us some time to get our own troops and tanks in."

"How much time could they buy us?"

"The larger question is how much would we need."

She drummed her fingers on her chin. "I wonder if there are really any moderates in Iran now that the latest hard-line ayatollah is out of the picture. Tell me a little more about this Osprey, General. I've alerted the Air Cavalry Combat Division already. They'll be among the first units into combat, and now I have to believe that's exactly what will happen."

Abu found himself shadowing the deepest Iranian penetration toward Baghdad his army had ever enjoyed.

In a day-long battle across the rugged, rolling hills, the regiment had fought to within sight of the Baghdad-Tehran highway. Enemy armor and mechanized infantry had fallen back along a series of parallel valleys. By late afternoon, though, the assault had bogged down against dug-in infantry fighting from a maze of trenches in an abandoned oilfield.

Abu ordered his driver to drive back and forth behind the leading elements of the battalions in heaviest contact. This maneuver inspired both combatant armies. When he rode along behind the Iranians, pumping a clenched fist in the direction of the Iraqis, the

lines surged forward. Every time he showed the profile
of his tank to the Iraqis, the intensity of return fire
increased. Because of this, his driver kept a good kilometer away behind the battle lines.

Despite Abu's doggedness, the advance stalled just
before the sun kissed the horizon. In the lengthening
shadows, Abu saw defeat. His army slackened its
fighting intensity like factory workers at day's end.
With nightfall, the Iraqis would be able to reinforce
and dig in. He might never again get them to capitalize
on the day's momentum, to press on toward Baghdad.
In the morning they would be sluggish. Both the men's
adrenaline and courage would be in deficit. This was
it. Bani-Sadr would come back and try to humiliate
him, although he felt sure he'd disgraced himself
enough.

As his tank lurched along behind a tank company,
he looked down the muzzle of the gun. What he saw
wrenched something inside his chest, leaving him
pained more than his wound alone could have done.
His subordinate leaders were staring at him. They were
looking for some sign that they should either go on or
give in to the day's fatigue and rest. To quit or to go.
It depended on him.

How to inspire them? Maybe he could fire his gun
into one of his subordinate officer's tank. Kill one and
make the others move. Would that work? Or would
they turn on him? The gun tube pointed beyond one
tank after another. Finally, he saw his chance for the
inspiration he needed.

"Driver, halt!" Abu shouted.

The driver slammed the brakes and left the tank
rocking, its 100-millimeter main gun pointed toward
the enemy. There was a little battle going on out there.
A tank company was sweeping the oil field with gunfire on the flanks of Iraqi trenches. A tiny maneuver,
almost insignificant on the huge static battlefield, was
developing. The company had kept inching forward,
probing a weakness in the defenses while more senior
commanders were yet looking for permission to stand
down for the day. That inspired Abu. Now how could

he spread the contagion to the rest of the army Bani-
Sadr had left him?

Abu dropped down into the cupola and grasped the
commander's override handle, which controlled the
turret and firing trigger. He slewed the turret, lowering the tube in the same motion. The driver protested
into the intercom, "A warning, please. You nearly
took off my head."

Abu grimaced. Already he'd proven himself an am-
ateur at fighting this tank. He'd been trained on the
Soviet T-62 and the British Chieftain, both now di-
nosaurs. His familiarity with this American antique
had been limited to an orientation course. He released
the override control and put his forehead to the rangefinder optics. He ranged on the dusty battlefield, then
slewed the turret again to find something to shoot at.
No definitive target presented itself, so he selected a
segment of the trenches where several lines joined. He
twirled the rangefinder wheel until the ghost image
joined up with the real image. He struggled to remember the next command.

"Troops entrenched," he said. He looked at the
range indicator. "Nine hundred fifty meters."

"Troops at nine hundred fifty," the gunner repeated
dryly.

Only then did Abu remember that the gunner had
left his fighting position to become the loader. He,
Abu, was fighting the tank alone now. He looked
sheepishly to his left. The gunner, wearing a forced
neutral expression, stood clear of the breech, bracing
himself with his left hand, reaching across the gun
with his right to switch off the safety on command.

Abu felt a hot flush of embarrassment. He clutched
the override angrily. "High explosive," he yelled into
the intercom, pressing his forehead into the headrest.

"High explosive ready, gun ready," the gunner replied.

Abu looked left to see how it had been done so
quickly.

The gunner braced himself, a wry smile playing on
his lips, and flipped the safety.

The tank bucked, catching Abu on the side of the helmet with the rangefinder. He was thrown back toward the radios as a blast first slapped him and vacuumed the tank and his lungs of air.

He was vaguely aware of the breech slamming back and forth, the enormous gate of the breech block sliding open, the expended shell extracting and clattering on the floor.

Shame and anger hit him at once. He had been clutching the firing trigger when the gunner had flipped off the safety. The gunner had seen it, too. He'd embarrassed his officer on purpose.

Abu nearly choked on his wrath. Before he could curse the man, though, the driver let loose a victorious screech.

"What a shot! Look at it explode!"

Abu focused through the rangefinder optics. The intersection of the trenches had erupted in orange blossoms of flame. As he watched, several distant explosions ruptured the earth. More important, dozens of panicked Iraqi infantrymen staggered from their trenches and ran about the naked battleground.

Abu fired three more quick rounds of high-explosive plastic. The other tanks, closer to the conflagration, opened up with machinegun fire. On a five hundred meter front, the resistance suddenly collapsed. Abu saw why. The digging of the trenches had exposed underground pipelines. Rivers of flame had begun flowing out from the original fire. He'd shot through a pressurized pipeline.

The tank company needed no encouragement from Abu, whom they didn't yet know as Bani-Sadr's alter ego. Their captain took the lead tanks on a sweep toward the south and back towards the west to a position that allowed him to enfilade the remaining infantry with flanking fire. The tank cannons began roaring in rapid fire at the Iraqis.

Abu, more hopefully than expectantly, said into his intercom, "Let's see if he could induce more explosions and turn this battle. What's in the breech?"

"Armor-piercing up," his gunner-turned-loader declared.

Abu fired the sabot-shot round—a titanium alloy bullet—through one of the oilfield tanks. Although it was nearly empty, the tank burst, spewing its dregs in a black, fiery wave outwards. Liquid fire poured into the trenches and cut off the Iraqi infantry fighting positions from each other, isolating them between parallel walls of fire.

"Praise Allah," his driver shouted reverently, more a cheer than a prayer.

Abu shouted into his radio for a renewal in the bombardment of the oilfield. Other tank commanders followed suit and in minutes half a dozen reservoirs had been set afire.

That was enough to shake the remaining Iraqis. At least a hundred soldiers were gunned down by machinegun fire or run down by Iraqi tanks as they panicked.

"They're running!" Abu shouted, spraying the battlefield with machinegun fire. "Forward!" he commanded his tank force.

The tiny victory inspired the Iranian tank company even further, spurring it into a rush to burst through the Iraqi lines. Other tank units that had seen this dramatic, fiery success took heart and pressed through Iraqi lines at several other points. Abu's raving and ranting over the radio net caused the tank company's success to be magnified. A full battalion of armor rolled into the oil field and continued to enlarge the attack, adding to the Iraqi panic.

Sensing that he had enormous potential in this seemingly insignificant segment of the battlefield, Abu shouted the map coordinates into his radio. "Give us a concentration of all artillery within range," he demanded. He personally directed the bombardment, not at any specific target but to lay down a barrage of lethal shrapnel to add to the growing panic. Then Abu sensed victory as the Iranian tank battalion picked its way through the burning oil field and began to exploit in earnest. What he realized suddenly was that this infantry dug in for the defense out here in the relatively open range had been the last depth in the defense in this part of the battlefield. By accident or by the will of God, he had been given the key to the weakest area of Iraqi defense.

In minutes, he was on the radio shouting to Bani-Sadr's staff to redirect more units as reinforcements. At the same time, he directed some of his own infantry commanders on his flanks to hold back the armor there and to see if this solitary success could be exploited to achieve a complete rout. Perhaps he could even turn the flank on the Iraqis and pour enough tanks through to make a meaningful thrust against Baghdad.

He hollered into his radio and directed more artillery, pouring it down on his own tanks as well as Iraqi infantry—if they were brave enough to press this attack, he knew they certainly must be smart enough to button up their tank hatches against artillery shrapnel.

The noise deafened him and the battle smoke suffocated him every time the breezes carried huge clouds over his tank. The roar and confusion of combat at once filled him with excitement and drained him of energy.

Through his rangefinder sight, he watched with awe as more and more of his tanks poured through the gap in Iraqi lines. As darkness fell, Abu stopped to drink water and to force down a can of sweet preserved fruit. He was not hungry. He was too excited to eat, but he knew he had to keep up his energy, for this might be an extended battle of two or three days. If so, he intended to be awake for all of it.

The airfield at Dezful, Iran, was destroyed in the first ten minutes of the invasion. Follow-on waves of Iraqi fighters and attack bombers swept northward toward the Davriaresh Dam. Their mission there was to soften the infantry positions dug in around the dam so air transports could deliver their parachute troops. The Iranians had to be prevented from emptying the lake behind the dam, or else the plains in Khuzestan Province would be flooded for weeks, impassable to Iraqi tanks. The purpose of the parachute assault was to capture the Davriaresh Dam intact.

The Iraqis controlled the Davriaresh Dam after only three hours of fighting. Intact. The door was now open for total Iraqi victory in Khuzestan Province—or, as the Iraqis had always called it, Arabistan. All that remained for General Amiri's army was to bloody the nose of Bani-Sadr's penetration and launch an armored counterattack at Khuzestan. Except now there was a new complication. Amiri studied reports of a breakthrough developing on the road to Baghdad. That news dampened everything. What would be gained by winning Arabistan at the cost of the capital city? Just the threat of it might cost him his life. He needed drastic measures to blunt the Iranian penetration. He needed them now.

# 7

Miles baked in the early morning sun as he stood on the tarmac parking area outside the Osprey hangar, his baggage at his feet. He felt dwarfed by the huge C5-B and C5-C Hercules aircraft inhaling one attack helicopter after another into their fuselages, enormous ribbed tunnels formed by the dropped tail decks and raised chins as men and women continued deployment preparations. Then there were the hangars, enormous enough to dwarf even the C5s. Not to mention Edwards Air Force Base itself, a flat expanse extending seemingly forever to mountains in the distance. And the sky, an enormous, misty-white expanse above. One element after another seeming to swallow the next smaller element, like the feeding links in an enormous food chain. With Miles at the bottom of the chain. Feeling like some microscopic organism in the pond scum. A sudden, incongruent shiver shook him out of the feeling of self-degradation.

"Jeez, get off it, Miles," he told himself aloud. Silent, he chanted the only line of poetry he knew, from e. e. cummings: *Only The Game Fish Swims Upstream . . . Only The Game Fish Swims Upstream . . .*

He picked up his duffel and his flight bag and began walking toward the flight hangar, avoiding the harried men and women loading the division's helicopter onto a C5. From inside the hangar, he heard the clanking of metal, the pounding of hammers, the scream of drills and other machines: the sounds of maintenance. In the distance, he heard the competition among rock, soul, and country radio stations. He smelled the pungent smells of dissected flying machines, their oils spilling into drip pans and onto the concrete floor. He inhaled deeply, absorbing with all his senses the feeling of being on the line with troops again. Unlike the stale air conditioning and superficial reality of inside staff work, this sounded and smelled down-to-earth. He knew he was going to love it.

As he crossed the threshold of the sunlight into the darkness of the hangar, his welcoming committee materialized as a bitter voice.

"Miles?"

Miles dropped his bags. He couldn't see much looking into the darkness of the hangar, but he knew the voice. He threw up a blind salute.

"Lieutenant Colonel Miles reporting, sir."

After an awkward silence, the general said, "As you were, Colonel. It's about time you got here. This unit has been without a commander for days. We're shipping off to war. Don't you want to go?"

Miles stood there stunned as his eyes began to adjust to the darkness, and the angry face of Brigadier General Bayard Wilkerson began to take form.

"I came as soon as I could get my gear together, sir—"

"Stow it, Miles. I don't want any of your excuses. I want you to know I haven't changed my mind about you. I argued against your getting this command even after you left the old man's office the other day. If you screw up, I'm going to see your ass relieved and shipped out of the division. If I ever get command of it—"

Wilkerson clammed up and looked around to make sure he hadn't been overheard. "I know what it is to command an aviation unit in combat. From what I've seen, you don't have the right stuff."

Miles knew about Wilkerson's reputation from Vietnam. The general had been a major as the war wound down, had commanded an air cavalry troop. There had been too damn little time to make a reputation and too little war. That had been his aviation experience in combat. His peacetime career had been a slow, deliberate rise to bird colonel. Then, just before Desert Storm, he'd been called back to the States and stuck in the Pentagon. Since then, he had risen only one grade to brigadier general. He'd been scheduled to be shipped to Saudi Arabia to join a combat division, where he might have earned a second star and by now have earned even a third star, but the ground battle had lasted only a hundred hours. The truce had come so soon and Brigadier General Wilkerson had stayed a brigadier general for much too long. Miles thought of his own situation. Pretty similar circumstances, he mused. They ought to be allies instead of enemies.

"I have to accept your being put in command. You don't have a hell of a lot of time to get acquainted with what's going on. I know you were working with the Osprey in its experimental stages. That doesn't mean shit around here now. We've been combat testing this unit for weeks. A lot of the doctrine you developed hasn't been worth much. You're going to have to set aside all your know-it-all attitudes and relearn the fighting doctrine from the bottom up. Got that?"

"Yes, sir." Miles looked around him, hoping the enlisted men weren't able to hear Wilkerson dress him down. Again.

"Then get to work." The general wheeled and was gone, receding into the shadows, leaving Miles standing in the sun wondering when the reconciliation predicted by Keyes would come.

Welcome to the Osprey battalion, he told himself. *Only The Game Fish Swims Upstream . . . Only The Game Fish Swims Upstream . . .* He bent over to pick up his bags again.

"Welcome."

Miles dropped his bags and threw up another salute before he'd even straightened up.

General Rita Bernadino stepped out of the darkness toward him. "You are very welcome here. Lieutenant Colonel Parker spoke of you a lot. I saw your accident report. First-rate. I'm impressed with your thoroughness . . . what are you smiling about?"

"Nothing, General. I'm just so glad to be here, I can't contain myself."

Miles struck his salute and shook the hand she offered. Miles knew of her reputation as well. She possessed one of the finest logistics minds, especially on nuts and bolts matters, and her cordial welcome was enough to claim Miles's loyalty forever. She'd been one of the miracle makers in the preparation for the Desert Storm offensive. She'd learned her trade literally under fire and in a desert environment. For the first time today, he felt like the future might be positive. Already General Bernadino had been able to mention Joel Parker's name without making him feel guilty about taking Joel's battalion.

She motioned to the shade of the hangar beside the door, then squatted down and picked up a twig. Miles knelt on one knee.

"Let me give you a quick brief, Nelson. The Osprey battalion doesn't get a lot of respect around here from anybody but the commanding general and me and my staff."

"Seems as if that ought to be enough," Miles murmured.

"In most ways, it is enough. But I don't want you to be deceived. I sometimes think this is more than just ordinary jealousies and unit prides that conflict in a friendly, competitive way. Some people have been intent on seeing the Osprey fail its trials."

Miles mouth fell open.

The general gathered a hitch in her voice and continued. "I don't mean they would rejoice at the deaths in those crashes. It's just that the rivalry for attention and resources is intense. The Osprey consumes a ton of both. We've practically had to double and sometimes even triple the maintenance support since the accidents. Depending on the month, we're gobbling up thirty to forty percent of the operations budget on less than four percent of the division's aircraft. My God, Nelson, there are only thirty-four aircraft—only thirty-two now—and no more are due out of the pipeline for months. Every other bird is combat-proven against the Iraqis. Osprey has yet to fire a shot in anger. Besides, the prevailing debate is whether it's even a plane or a helicopter. The Air Force has been agitating to get it switched to them, and not a few of our own purist colonels and generals would be only too happy to see it go to the boys in blue.''

''But one bird has the firepower of a whole battalion of gunships . . . good grief, General Bernadino, the weaponry of those thirty-two birds is capable of as much devastation as the whole rest of the division. And the mission! Christ, the mission of Apaches and Cobras is to kill tanks. The Osprey is out there to kill Russian helicopters and fixed-wing craft . . . even MiGs. There's no conflict in mission. There shouldn't be any. The Ospreys protect the tank killers.''

The general smiled and stood erect. ''I'm glad to see you're so passionate about the Osprey. Don't worry, though, you don't have to sell the commanding general and you don't have to sell me. The support is there, and so is the money. But it's an expensive craft. It eats up spare parts like some kind of mechanical carnivore. It has to prove itself, Colonel. It just has to.''

Miles purposely kept the send-off party for P. B. Keyes to a close-knit group. None of his friends liked ceremony, so only Blanks and Keyes and their families were invited. Typical of his low-key nature, Keyes tried to turn the party into a celebration of Miles's new command.

Just as typically, the three men huddled in a shady corner of the backyard upwind of the smoking barbecue and away from the chatter of children and wives.

''In case we don't get the chance to say it before you board up, P. B., good luck over there,'' said Miles.

Blanks chimed in, ''Yeah, save some work for us.''

The understated Keyes replied with a change of subject. ''How's it been the first couple days in command, Nelson?''

''Herm could tell you this job would be imposing

for George Patton himself. Joel Parker was a hell of an officer. I had no idea one man could command such devotion from his people. Remember how I felt guilty about stepping into a dead man's shoes?"

Keyes nodded.

Miles said, "Well, it's worse than that. It isn't the dead man's shoes I have to worry about, because Parker isn't dead. He was so damned competent and so much a presence, his men and women won't let him go."

Keyes shook his head in disbelief. "It couldn't be that bad. Maybe the morale is just shot . . . you know, temporarily." He looked to Blanks for confirmation.

Miles nodded to his operations officer. "Tell him, Herm."

"Morale is fine as fucking frog's hair. The battalion's tighter'n hell. Only trouble is—"

"I'm being shut out."

Blanks shook his head. "No, Nelson, it's not really that serious. They're just not used to you yet. The battalion is still in a state of shock. It's a collective thing, you know, like denial that Joel is gone. They'll get over it. Hell, I'm talking you up all the time. The maintenance crew is in hog heaven since you came along with your direct logistics line to General Bernadino's desk. The rest will fall in line. You've only had three days, for chrissakes. Give it some time."

Keyes laughed and shook his head. "Damn, Nelson, I thought for a second there you were having problems. As usual, they're only in your head. You've got to learn to be patient, man. You make peace with Wilkerson yet?"

Miles had already decided he would not get into a discussion about Wilkerson and ruin the evening. "We're asshole buddies," he said and joined in their laughter, letting himself be buffeted around by their kidding and backslapping. They were right, of course. He probably never would get over his impatience, but as he got older he at least could recognize it rearing its ugly head. It was just that the timetable didn't allow a lot of time with this battalion. Keyes would be leaving in the last group of Apaches and Black Eagles being deployed. Then, in a couple weeks at best, the Ospreys would be lifting off. Patience, hell.

The Salyut satellite evidence lay before them, thermal imagery from just hours before, evidence of the blunting of Bani-Sadr's thrust into Iraq. Amiri had begun his counter-invasion of Iran.

Polomarchuk had regained his haughtiness. Standing before the group, he crowed, "There we have it. All the reason we need. A traditional ally of the Soviet Union is being invaded by the mad Iraqis." He laughed as though he were revealing a delicious irony for the first time.

Dudov, ignoring Polomarchuk's bombast, looked at the junior officer in the room. "Comrade Mendenyev, does the intelligence analysis service interpret this action as an invasion? Is the situation unfolding as the *field* marshal suggests?" Dudov had adopted Abramov's practice of emphasizing "field" in field marshal, throwing into relief the fact that Polomarchuk had little actual field experience and no combat action behind him. Polomarchuk didn't catch on to the irony, giving it added flavor.

"Comrade secretary, I agree fully with Comrade Polomarchuk's portrayal of the situation. Amiri's lead divisions are rolling, not to punish Bani-Sadr, but toward Khuzestan Province. As of now, air forces have attacked. Airborne soldiers have landed on the dam north of Dezful. Thus, technically, it is indeed an invasion. When the armor punches into Iran, it will be the most significant fighting between the two countries since 1980."

Dudov asked Polomarchuk, "How quickly will we be prepared with our own operation?"

"A week. We'll be ready to launch operations in a week."

Abramov snorted behind a handkerchief to hide an expression of disdain. He didn't want to nullify his influence with this group by precipitating his own dismissal.

Polomarchuk faced him, his own insecurity with military matters now shaded by hostility at the disrespect of this subordinate. "You disagree?"

"My dear comrade marshal, I agree fully with your estimate in our ability to shorten preparation time to a week against Tabriz. But such an effort will drain our combat troops to the point of exhaustion. I suggest we use two weeks to prepare. The deeper thrust toward Bandar Abbas will require much more time."

All eyes seemed to narrow at once. Nobody seemed willing to take anything he said at face value anymore, he noticed.

"I would suggest a full month to ready the operation against the Gulf port. The call-up of reserve units in that area is already proving cumbersome. They are so poorly prepared, so inadequately equipped, that the operation might be endangered. We will require crack fighting units to be moved in. And more of the modern equipment, the T-80's and T-88's."

Dudov nodded in understanding, avoiding the step of placing blame for inadequate training and preparation, although readiness reports had been falsely sparkling for years. "The operation against Tabriz will go as planned. You will have an extra week. You will personally oversee that operation in every detail. You will be responsible to me for its success." Dudov inhaled deeply. His eyes narrowed at Abramov, warning him not to dispute the orders just given him. "You will lead the offensive to capture Bandar Abbas."

Abramov kept a straight face. "Yes," he said. "I will capture Bandar Abbas. All I ask is for a shifting in priority of air forces and surplus motorized infantry after you have consolidated your defenses around Tabriz."

Polomarchuk's face showed disappointment. Abramov hadn't flinched in the least at being sent to the most distant front.

Dudov nodded his assent to Abramov's request.

"You must . . . excuse me for putting it that way, it would be most beneficial if you insist the Iraqis keep up their pressure on the Iranian army along their southern border.'' He shrugged, ''It doesn't matter whether they fight to the death on the road to Baghdad or in Khuzestan Province. All that matters is that they occupy the Iranian army. I'm concerned that if they should ever declare a cease-fire for any reason, the Iranians would break loose and try to cut us off at Bandar Abbas.''

Dudov nodded again. ''I have the Iraqis in my pocket,'' he said. ''They will do as I ask.''

Abramov smiled. ''Then I will deliver Bandar Abbas to you.''

Dudov flashed a modest smile. ''Not to me,'' he said. ''To the Fatherland.'' Then he delivered his punch line, ''You will take Major Aleksandr Mendenyev here onto your staff.''

Abramov winced, but he recovered quickly. ''Yes, I could use an analyst as sharp as the major.''

''No, he will join the staff as your personal aide.''

As Abramov's jaw muscles knotted, it was Polomarchuk's turn to smile. Soon two irritants would be out of Moscow. If blame ever needed to be placed for failures in that part of the operation, who better than this hardhead?

A messenger interrupted the meeting and handed a sheet of paper to Dudov. As he read it, his face broadened into a bemused grin. ''This American housewife. She demands that we reveal our purpose in shifting tanks from the Warsaw Pact countries toward the southern military districts. She demands we cease threatening the Gulf and Iran by our . . . rhetoric, she calls it.''

Zuyenko, the KGB chief, asked, ''How could she have discovered the movement of decoys? I personally challenged our own intelligence satellite analysis to detect those movements. They still have not caught on that fakes are being shipped west, while the real tanks are moving southeastward.''

Dudov shrugged. ''It does not matter. She may not actually know at all but may merely be bluffing.''

''Won't the Iranians invite the Americans in?''

Dudov shrugged. ''Probably, but no matter. It will

take them months to assemble adequate invasion
forces. That is the one lesson we learned in watching
them in Saudia Arabia. Except for airborne units, it
will take months. By that time, we will be basking on
the beaches of the Gulf.''

General Amiri's ground attack into Iran amounted
to a hard smash on a single narrow front. Four tank
division and six motorized rifle divisions plunged into
the battle already waging along a twenty-mile front on
the road towards Dezful. Avoiding forces in contact,
he continued directing his lead divisions to plunge past
every bit of resistance. It was natural for his division
commanders to resist driving on. They wanted to stop
and finish to the last man every Iranian contingent they
encountered. Amiri knew the imperative of securing
his hold on that dam by pushing his armored forces
deep into Iran. Every time he overheard a report of
enemy contact, he intervened, directing that any resistance either be wiped out immediately or contained
and bypassed. He wanted his forces entrenched
quickly.

After three days of fighting, the Iraqis penetrated
Iran more than a hundred miles. The city of Dezful
had been bombarded and bypassed. Now Iraqi tanks
rumbled down the road eastward from Dezful racing
as fast as they could go across the plains between the
mountains and the marshes in Khuzestan Province.
The race was now to reach the Persian Gulf where the
marshes, the Gulf, and the mountains came together
near the border of the province. That achieved, the
Iranians would be encircled. Reinforcements would
have to come up the narrow coastline from the south.
Or they would have to filter down from the north where
Bani-Sadr was engaged. There would be little chance
that any forces would come directly across the mountains from the east, for his force at the Davriaresh
Dam had also demolished the railroad lines. Only
commando forces could infiltrate from that direction.

Amiri felt fairly smug. Because he was keeping
pressure on around Abadan and Shatt Al Arab, Iran's

all-important oil ports on the gulf, the Iranians in contact there could hardly pull away to fight. He had kept open the shoulders of his penetration by dropping off two infantry divisions. One mechanized division after another poured through. Soon he would have advanced far enough to truck more infantry through the breach. Now his only danger was that the circle would be too thinly manned to withstand any concentrated and coordinated attack at a single point on the circumference of the circle. For that reason, he had to finish up on those troublesome Iranians to the north around Baghdad. Then he could bring other troops and strengthen what was going to be a fatal entrapment down here.

But Amiri knew he could not feel too smug for too long. Bani-Sadr, the Iranian commander, simply would not roll over and give up. In the early part of the central battle, Iraqi tank regiments had been pressuring Bani-Sadr's strung-out divisions along the Baghdad highway. Amiri had insisted that the pressure remain constant and heavy on the Iranians. Bani-Sadr could not be released from battle to freely infiltrate southward where they might reinforce the defense of Khuzestan Province. Yet, as fighting grew fiercer and fiercer, Amiri realized his grip might not be on the throat of the Iranian but the tail of a tiger. He called for an updated battle report.

"The news is not good," his aide reported.

"Tell it, anyhow."

"General, your plan to invite the Iranians to attack toward Baghdad has proven all too successful. They are on the verge of breaking through our final defenses."

"What?"

The aide shrugged. "They have an open road to Baghdad."

"Get me the air force commander," he said grimly.

The aide shuffled about for a second. "My general, respectfully—"

"Now!" Amiri snapped. "It must be done."

"The Soviets," he muttered accusingly when he was alone. Their inactivity was forcing him to do this.

Where are the Soviets? he wondered. They had promised an assault against Tehran to keep the pressure off his own maneuvers. Where are the goddamned Soviets?

Bani-Sadr followed the battle in the oilfield by keeping abreast of radio reports as he directed events at the original breakthrough point. The Iraqis had displaced a regiment of tanks from farther north. Mechanized infantry of at least a reinforced division had materialized from Baghdad. Bani-Sadr's units had managed to cut off these counterattacking forces, but any Iraqi follow-on units threatened to cut off his own leading units before long. The victory for the moment hinged on the battle between his reserve tank regiment and the Iraqi reinforcements.

With the pressure growing on the Baghdad highway, Bani-Sadr believed he could do no worse than keep all that he had gained. If he stopped now and wheeled his lead units back toward Iran, they would sweep around the Iraqi stragglers, entrapping them and defeating a significant Iraqi army. Then he could dash toward Khuzestan and try to undo the damage already done there by the capture of that dam and the armored thrust.

The breakout at the oilfield, though, gave him pause. Suddenly, they were winning here. It would be a mistake to disengage now. If defenses that deep inside Iraq could be breached, there might be a clear path open toward Baghdad, after all. *What irony!* Saddeq's demonstration of sound and fury had turned into a genuine success. What if he should win this battle? Would Saddeq be embarrassed or pleased?

He decided. He spoke to his deputy, directing him to assume responsibility for the battle in the rear. Then he ordered his leading regiment to wheel toward Baghdad. He called for a helicopter to take him back to his tank.

In the noise, confusion and dust, Abu was starting to see a pattern to the chaotic battlefield. He sensed a pulse, a rhythm to things. He almost believed he could divine an order in all the confusion.

His chest pounded, for he knew what such a feeling meant. His father had told him that only certain men could find order in battle chaos. It was what made Bani-Sadr an effective commander. He knew that Bani-Sadr's temperament, his chaotic thinking, his turbulent emotions, his irascible nature were all finely tuned to exactly those same elements that occurred on a battlefield. Bani-Sadr's was the kind of chaotic harmony that he had never understood. So few men experienced the feeling, let alone comprehended it. So few men ever knew enough to *want* to understand it. Abu did. His first battle had made him want to understand everything that made Bani-Sadr the general he was.

Suddenly his gunner screeched into the intercom, interrupting his reverie.

"Aircraft!"

Abu followed the pointing hand and saw waves of MiG-29s coming from the south. He reached for his radio microphone to give reports, but then realized, of course, that Iranian radar had already picked out these if he could see them with the naked eye. Even as he spoke, pillars of smoke rose into the sky, surface-to-air missiles streaking to meet the oncoming waves of the Iraqi aircraft. Immediately, the aircraft adopted their characteristic pattern of avoidance. White-hot flares sparked in the daylight to try to draw away infrared-seeking missiles. Anti-SAM missiles were fired from the aircraft.

He felt a tug on his sleeve. The gunner was pointing and screaming. Abu saw a wave of MiG-19s coming in low and fast about five miles away.

Why would the Iraqis use such obsolete fighters? he wondered.

"Protective gear!" his gunner shouted.

Abu's heart stopped. The gunner knew what was to happen next. The Iraqis had used these sorts of tactics before. He had read about the results. Quickly, Abu dropped inside his tank. He ordered his gunner to switch frequencies through every battalion frequency, beginning with the lead units that had just passed through the Iraqi defenses.

The gunner began shouting the warning over one radio frequency after another, dispersing over the radio net to all subordinate commanders. It became a litany that rolled upward to the Iranian high command: "Chemical weapons! Gas! Gas! Gas!"

The MiG-19s swept in low on line, dispersing converging, billowing lines of smoky vapors behind.

But it was not smoke spewing from beneath the MiG-19s. Jets of liquid misted in the high-speed airstream flowing over the wings of the MiGs. A misty yellow rain—a combination of mustard gas and blister agent—descended on the clumps of tanks filing down the road toward Baghdad.

Abu had read combat reports from earlier wars. In this climate, where the body pores opened up to release heat and sweat, the blister gas would have an immediate and devastating effect.

Inside his protective mask, Abu had stuck scraps of bandages between the edges of the helmet and his collar. He had pulled on gloves handed to him by the gunner. He had buttoned his sleeves. Those precautions might save his life and others', but the yellow rain would jeopardize the momentum of the attack.

Already his vision was misted over as droplets of liquid clung to the lenses of his mask, forming greasy mud. When he tried to wipe it away, it smeared, scratching the lenses, blurring the vision further. He knew what would be happening down in the individual tanks now. Drivers barely would be able to see. Loaders would fumble around, barely keeping ammunition flowing to the breeches of their cannons. Gunners would be firing virtually blinded as their optics were misted over. Tank commanders would be unable to see their reticles—even the lighted reticles—in the range finders and sights of the tanks. The external surfaces of the tanks had become slick with the oily poisons.

Bani-Sadr's voice inside his headset startled Abu.

"What is happening at the battle front, you cow? Answer me."

Abu knew he was no cow, that he had influenced the success of this battle, that he had shown bravery and ingenuity under fire. He paused another moment to get control of his voice before answering. He reported the chemical attack.

"The ground war, cow. What is happening there?"

"The lead Iranian tank company commander launched a counterattack against the enemy. His unit had run into the stiff defenses of the Iraqi infantry dug in at the oil fields—"

"Save it for the history of the war. What is happening now?" Despite his words, the tone in Bani-Sadr's voice had flattened out, matching Abu's.

Abu continued, "Many tank crews have begun to move again. The road is open ahead of us."

Bani-Sadr's voice rose an octave. "Then take it. Lead the attack. Go! Attack! If you hesitate, all will be lost."

"Affirmative. Driver, move out," Abu said, in his excitement giving a crew command over the radio.

In the helicopter, Bani-Sadr smiled to himself. Maybe this son of a general would prove himself after all. Yes, he was a lieutenant colonel making the mistakes of a lieutenant. But he didn't lack for courage.

Abu's M60A3 navigated around other tanks stalled on or near the road. Soon he was the third tank in the column headed toward Baghdad. Behind him, he counted nearly twenty tanks on the move. But as many as that showed no inclination to advance. In the next minute, he saw why.

They overtook a Chieftain sitting at idle on the roadway. As they drove by, a pair of arms snaked out of the turret, followed by a bloodied face. An Iranian sergeant hauled himself to the top of the turret and writhed atop the tank before rolling off, bouncing on the fender and falling beneath the tracks of Abu's tank.

The M60A3 rolled over the pelvis of the sergeant, who lay face up. Abu opened his mouth to scream into his mask. Too late, he knew. He held his voice, shocked by the image of a man bursting. But even greater than that astonishment was the terror of realizing the man had no protective gear against the yellow mist. He had scratched his own face bloody. The other crews on the stopped tanks must have been similarly paralyzed.

"What do you want, Colonel?" It was the driver's muffled voice.

Abu realized he had keyed the intercom and gagged into it. He swallowed hard. "Nothing. Speed up. Get us out of here."

Abu looked back only once. He saw two dozen Iranian tanks following him. He saw more vehicles abandoned by crazed crewmen. He saw men dive from their hatches, falling at the side of the tanks. He saw them jump to the ground and roll, scrubbing their bodies in the sand and the dirt. Others ran around blindly, tearing at their faces. He saw several pouring water out of the water containers strapped to the outside of their tank turrets. Abu nearly vomited, but fought back the sickness. Vomit inside the mask would clog the filters. He knew he might not be able to clear it. If he should get those agents in his lungs, he would be joining the men on the ground.

He keyed his radio mike and reported the situation to Bani-Sadr. "I will go on if you command it," he finished.

As the sky darkened, so did Bani-Sadr's outlook. He realized that the ferret's bravery no longer mattered. With his tank numbers reduced to little more than a battalion, he had no choice but to consolidate and withdraw toward Iran. The drive to Baghdad—if successful, it could have negated the damage done at Dezful—was finished. Amiri had fooled him, and now had a head start in his own attack. Worst of all, he'd taken that dam. If he couldn't recover in the next two days, Khuzestan would be lost. He'd been against inviting Americans in to solve Iranian problems. Now he knew his country would need help and soon.

Abu heard Bani-Sadr's voice. It alarmed him that the general sounded so tired—even defeated.

Abu croaked into his microphone, "Turn about? Retreat?"

"Return immediately, my son. It is not a retreat."

Abu cursed into the radio. "Call it what you will, General. It is a retreat. Have you lost your stomach for battle?"

"Come back. Your father will be proud his son led the attack against Baghdad."

"To hell with him," Abu said without conviction.

"Come back. You will do your country no good if you kill yourself and your command. I . . . need you to help save Khuzestan Province from the damned Iraqi army. Every second we argue is a second lost to the defense of the region."

Abu choked on the sudden emotion that struck him. For the first time in his life, somebody had told him he was valued. His chest felt as if it would expand and burst. "They need me," he said over the tank's intercom so he could hear the words again.

"Huh?" asked his puzzled driver.

"I said turn this tank around so we can return to recover our country from the bastard Iraqis," bellowed Abu. "Now move, you cow."

Mount Kopuzhakh in the Soviet Union rose nearly thirteen thousand feet, poking into the clouds. It was not the largest mountain in Azerbaijan, the state east of the Caspian Sea, but its foothills crossed the border between the Soviet Union and Iran. This morning its ground control radar was directed at the clouds over Iran, searching up to a distance of two hundred nautical miles, all the distance that was needed to support the air-superiority umbrella over the ground attack. Once that attack had been successful, the Soviet plan called for a mobile ground radar to be placed atop the peak of Kuhhaye Sabalan, east of the vital capital of the oil-rich region, Tabriz. From this mountain, more than three miles high, the Soviets planned to keep an electronic eye over the airspace maintaining radar surveillance to Tehran.

The battle for air superiority over northern Iran was over almost from the moment the radar atop Kopuzhakh was turned on. Three waves of attack fighters rushed into Iran along three different axes. The first attack, on the central axis, was launched against the airfield just north of Tabriz only fifty miles from the Soviet border. Two flights of four Tupolev Tu-26 bombers did all the damage required, destroying the runway and setting afire six F-4 Phantoms on the tarmac parking area. The Tabriz airfield and the small contingent of Iranian aircraft were neutralized within six minutes from the time the attack began.

On the east axis, attack fighters swept down the coast of the Caspian at Ar Babil before coming inland, where Tabriz sits in the center of a bowl formed by mountains. This flight swept outside the edge of the bowl toward Mianeh, astride the main roads between Tehran and Tabriz. Their attack took out bridges on the two roads and cut off Tabriz.

The third wave of attackers came down fifty miles inside the western border of Iran across Lake Urmia and dropped its load of ordnance where the lake pressed up against the mountain, cutting off the last direct line of communication between Tabriz and the rest of Iran.

The Soviets avoided the strip of land between the lake and the Turkish border. Well before the attack had begun, the Turks had been warned of this defensive maneuver against Iranian "provocations" and were told not to react.

The attack was completed within twenty minutes. Soviet MiG-29 and the latest MiG-31 fighters loitered south of the bowl waiting for resistance from the Iranian Air Force from the direction of Tehran, but nothing came.

The Turks did send up fighters, but finding no provocation at the border, their fighters simply flew in giant oval tracks staying a hundred miles from the border. Likewise, the US Air Force based at Incirlik launched alert fighters, but in the air above Turkey as well as on the ground in Ankara, everybody seemed to be waiting for instructions.

Meanwhile, the Soviets launched the ground phase of the attack.

Elite paratrooper forces dropped to secure the airfields near the cities of Ardabil, Mianeh, and Maragheh. Within an hour after the first bombs had fallen on the airport at Tabriz, the Soviets had cut off the northernmost one hundred miles of Iran, except for that strip nearest Turkey.

By day's end, the western invasion of Iran had amounted to little more than a roadmarch for Marshal Polomarchuk's motorized forces. Through history, the border of the Soviet Union has crept south along the shores of the Caspian Sea, penetrating deeper and deeper into Persia. This time Soviet motorized infantry and elite mountain troops poured into the country. Two divisions of the mountain troops took up positions east of Tabriz meeting only minimal resistance and shut off access to the Soviet Union from that direction. Two more divisions south, shutting off access between the Caspian and the mountains. Between those four divisions poured seven motorized rifle divisions and two more mountain divisions. There was hardly any impediment to their attack. Iranian units stationed in the province, some six divisions, were scattered in defensive positions in the mountains near Iraq and around Tabriz. They were no match whatever for the Soviets that had intended to fight them, but didn't. The Soviets simply surrounded them as they cut off the province from the rest of Iran.

The lead elements of the Soviet forces raced down the road as fast as the tracks would allow within the first half day, the lead element had covered the roughest, most critical hundred miles, through the mountains. Victory was more or less assured by the time the second and third divisions had raced across the relatively open area in the central parts of the province and sealed off the roads and the mountain paths between Tehran and Tabriz. Two mountain divisions wheeled southward to meet the first threat that might come from the direction of Tehran. The remaining six divisions pressed onward toward Lake Urmia.

By nightfall, the lead elements of the first Soviet division had reached the airborne troops at Maragheh and relieved them of defenses there. The encirclement was complete. Within twenty-four hours, the Soviets were so well entrenched it would take a major organized counterattacking force to push them out of the region.

General Abramov had been correct in his assessment of this campaign. He could draw little comfort from being right. For he had the mission to make the far more difficult thrust toward the narrow strait on the Persian Gulf. Long before he boarded the plane ferrying him over the Caspian Sea, he knew what he would soon be facing: the Americans. They'd proven their willingness to fight. They'd showed their superiority in technology against the Iraqis with their Soviet weaponry. In the so-called War of Shame. And what would the next fight be called?

# 8

East of the Caspian Sea, the second Soviet invasion of Afghanistan in two decades progressed for nearly an hour without fanfare nearly thirty miles into the country. It too was less an invasion than a road march.

The sun still had not burned off the early morning chill as Mendenyev shifted his weight from one foot to the other and flexed his arms stiffly, trying to warm his body without calling attention to himself. Now and then he would glance from the corner of one eye to see how the stolid Abramov was bearing the cold.

Abramov caught him. "You need not peek at me like that. I won't have a voyeur for an aide."

"Comrade Marshal, I was not—"

"But you were. Let us face it together, Major. You do not want to be here spying on me. I do not want you here. But neither of us has a choice. So let's bear it without animosity toward each other. If you want to look at me, face me straight on. If you must know something, ask me straight on. If you dissent from my generalship, speak up. I will tell you anything you want to know."

Mendenyev's face darkened with embarrassment. He shrugged his shoulders up to his ears and spoke in a tone professing innocence. "But, Comrade Marshal, I am merely an aide—"

"Enough!" Abramov's heavy brow bunched and lowered like a thick, wrinkled awning above his eyes. "I thought I saw something in you, Mendenyev. I thought I detected a backbone. Don't whine at me. I despise it. Don't profess innocence. It disgusts me. If you cannot even discourse with me as an honorable soldier—face-to-face and man-to-man—then follow me around like a jackal and pick up whatever droppings you wish to send back to those other jackals in Moscow.''

Mendenyev drew a deep, cold, sobering breath. ''Marshal Abramov, you seem very confident about a lack of resistance from the Afghans. I would not have expected the invasion's leader to stay here at the railhead. I would have expected to be up front where the fighting will begin.''

Abramov wheeled, and Mendenyev flinched until he saw the smile creasing the general's face.

''That's better,'' Abramov said. ''I admire men who speak their minds. And now for an honest answer. It's far more important that I see that tanks and other combat vehicles are off-loaded and rolling, that the trains get turned around and back toward Mary to reload the flatcars. I have generals who can shove aside what little Afghan resistance is expected. I have nobody in this inexperienced staff who can operate a railhead with a commander's urgency.''

Mendenyev looked skyward. ''Other than reconnaissance aircraft, you have no aviation support.''

''I do not want general air strikes to announce the beginning of this attack. I have given orders that air forces will maintain cover for the operation as needed. Rest assured, Major, we have frontal aviation support standing by on several airfields within ten minutes of our lead reconnaissance units. The less resistance we stir up within this country, the better off we will be.''

''The object is to avoid confronting the Afghans then?''

Abramov nodded. ''I won't put my soldiers back into the same position as in the 1980s, with guerrillas constantly knocking out bridges and attacking convoys.''

Mendenyev had seen the maps. Abramov had directed the attack to pour into Iran at the point of the funnel where the borders of Pakistan and Afghanistan pointed into Iran at a virtually unknown spot on the globe.

"Zahedan," Mendenyev said, testing the word on his tongue.

"The most important airfield in the world for us, Major. Once we attack it, there will be no need to maintain a pretense about invading Iran. Once we occupy it, the invasion will be over. The Americans will not be able to project air forces deep enough into Iran to make a difference. They won't have the safe haven like Saudi Arabia when they smashed the Iraqis before. We will be the army with the clear lines of communication."

Mendenyev knew Highway A78, which ran all the way from the Soviet border in the north through Iran to the Gulf of Oman in the south, could be opened up for resupply from the Soviet Union. Then the route through Afghanistan would no longer have to be protected. Abramov had told his staff that traveling through Afghanistan was merely an expedient move to prolong doubt about the real target of the invasion. As it was, he had deployed little more than a regiment of motorized infantry with beefed-up artillery support to guard the flank against an incursion from the Iranians at Mashhad to the west. This was a calculated risk for the moment, but Abramov did not want to tie up entire divisions with flank security missions in the north. He wanted all his fighting forces well forward, in effect, bypassing harassment from Iranians and Afghanis. In the end, he would withdraw even his reinforced regiment and abandon the supply line temporarily. The southern part of the present route was protected by two hundred miles of desert, an effective barrier against Iranian sabotage. When he had captured Zahedan and after Polomarchuk released the surplus divisions from the Tabriz offensive, he would use those forces to reestablish a supply route inside Iran from Mashhad southward. Now if only Polomarchuk would live up to his part of the bargain.

Three tank divisions and four motorized rifle divisions led his attack. Still transshipping at Mary were four more divisions. Three more were still travelling by train from the Caspian. Across that sea were plenty more forces that probably wouldn't be needed around Tabriz—already that battleground was becoming congested by the overcommitment of forces. Abramov believed that, once Polomarchuk had assured himself of tranquility in what had become his own pet objective area, he would release the extra divisions.

"What are your plans for the regiment of airborne troops and two brigades of air mobile troops in bivouac here?"

Abramov snickered. "You are a graduate of enough military schools to guess. What do you speculate?"

The major pursed his lips. "Once resistance is encountered and forward airfields are needed, those troops will secure the airfields. Then they can leapfrog deeper into Iran, perhaps even to the port that has been selected as an objective."

"Straight from the book."

"Which port?"

You know as well as I that Polomarchuk and Dudov want Bandar Abbas on the Strait of Hormuz. So there really isn't a choice, is there?"

Mendenyev's back arched lazily. Inside, though, he felt anything but lazy. He had tensed until he thought his spine might snap. "Marshal Abramov. You order me to be direct with you. But you aren't being straightforward with me, are you?"

Abramov's coloring darkened again. "True. I have trouble trusting you, Major. Even though we both acknowledge you are reporting on me to your benefactors in Moscow, I cannot be sure there are other reasons for your being here."

"What other reasons could I have—"

"Don't make me answer that, Major. You might not even know all the reasons yourself. Remember that. You may one day be asked about me in ways you cannot avoid answering. You may be ordered to new missions in ways you cannot refuse."

Mendenyev wagged his head imperceptibly.

Abramov's mood lightened. "I will answer your

question. Saying you want to take Bandar Abbas is wholly different from actually acquiring it. Between the idea and the reality stand hundreds of miles of mountains and desert. Almost as rugged a trip but with fewer than half the mountains, is Chah Bahar on the Gulf of Oman, directly south of our entry point into Iran. If things prove too costly, I may have to propose an alternative warm-water port, Chah Bahar."

"I understand."

Abramov shrugged. "No need to understand. Not now. For now, the problem is neither combat with Afghanistan nor a decision on the final objective. The problem is how to get these tanks moving as fast as they can. For the Americans have already begun mobilizing soldiers and tanks and helicopters."

Mendenyev snorted derisively. "It will be months before the first tank can land here. If our navy allows it to land at all. What can the Americans do?"

"Good question, Major. Here is my answer, a prediction, if you will. It will not be more than a few weeks before the armies of the superpowers will be in combat for the first time."

Miles felt stiff and awkward with excitement as he stepped inside a cockpit for his first time as a battalion commander. Although it was not even his first time ever at the Osprey's controls, he was discovering that General Wilkerson was right—this Osprey was different from the prototype models he had learned to fly. This Osprey was better. As he had graduated from Hueys into Blackhawks, then Cobras and Apaches, the requirements of instrument flying and combat flying increased, but the actual flying had become easier and easier. In this Osprey, this Bentley of birds, flying was easiest of all. He couldn't even imagine what they could do with the next generation of rotary-wing aircraft to make them safer. Maybe they would be unmanned, remotely powered vehicles. As it was, this one practically flew itself, anyhow.

Of course, it didn't fly itself. Its crew consisted of pilot and copilot, who sat side by side in the elevated cockpit. Miles would act as pilot on this flight. His copilot was an instructor pilot who sat in the gunner's station below their feet in the Osprey's nose.

Behind them a narrow stairway led down to the combat command center, the Weapons and Electronic Warfare compartment. Beyond the stairway, a wall separated the pilot and copilot from the rest of the crew. Through a low, narrow doorway, the fuselage widened into a compartment that housed three more crew members—a weapons officer, a communications specialist, and an electronic-warfare specialist. These three crew members stayed glued to banks of radios, instruments, radar, navigation scopes, and, at times, television screens. All three had access to each other's scopes, and the pilot and copilot could also monitor weapons-firing status from the cockpit. Although the cabin space was spacious, it had been crammed with electronics, making it difficult for the three members of the WEW crew to move about.

Ar the rear of the WEW, another low doorway housed the heart of Osprey's fighting capacity, an innocuous-looking tunnel, cramped and narrow. Five double-wide locker doors lined each side of that passageway. Inside those doors, pairs of Raptor missiles stood upright in vertical tubes from which they'd be launched against enemy aircraft, making twenty missiles that could be fired without reloading. Aft of the Raptor compartment, the passage narrowed like the mouth of a funnel, fuselage sides angling inward, forming Osprey's short tail section. At the very rear, in the tiny triangular space created between the funnel sides, four narrow, horizontal locker doors held eight spare launcher tubes for reloads. In all, the Osprey carried twenty-eight missiles.

A hydraulic reloader folded into the roof of the tunnel. An operator could release one end and direct the reloader to a spare missile locker on its motorized track. The automated sequence opened a door to a pair of reloads, presented the two fresh missiles, transferred them to the reload arm, and backtracked the arm down the tunnel to replenish a fired pair of Raptors. The locker door opened and ejected a used firing-contact plate on the floor of the tunnel. The fresh tubes, mounted on a new plate as a module, went into the tube. Once again automated machinery hooked up the necessary air lines, electrical contacts, and firing computer connections. When the apparatus worked properly, a pair of missiles could be reloaded in forty-five seconds. Few crews needed more than a minute. Human hands were required only to pick up the used firing contact plate and to stow it for later rebuilding.

An enlisted crew chief occupied a station just out of the path of the reloader as it operated. When he first met his crew chief, Miles had winced at the power of the grip of Sergeant Joyce Bachman. ''Sorry,'' she had said. ''Been turning too many wrenches, Colonel.'' By the twitch of a grin at the corners of her mouth, Miles knew it hadn't been an accident. Bachman performed double duties. She was the on-board mechanic who kept records for the engine and airframe, and in combat, she operated the tail-mounted 20-mm cannon, firing to the rear with the aid of rear-looking optics capable of day or night acquisition. When required, she would monitor the operation of the automated reloader. Design engineers had equipped her station with a fold-down seat that let her operate a computer screen that helped her monitor normal operations of half a dozen major systems of the Osprey. Except for takeoffs and landings, she rarely had time to belt herself into the seat. If such a thing as a spare moment presented itself, she had to run from one end of the plane to another to inspect gauges or make minor repairs as needed. During Raptor firing and reloading, she had to monitor the operation of the hydraulic reloader and the disposal of the empty missile baseplates. Had not every available inch of the Osprey been used, her duties would have been necessarily divided between herself and an added crew member.

Miles felt a hand on his shoulder as he completed the run-up checklist with his copilot and the instructor, who would be grading his performance tonight. He glanced at his shoulder and saw a thumbs-up sign perched there.

"Crew chief reports station ready for flight," said Bachman, waggling her thumb.

"Thanks, Joyce. Buckle in for flight."

This was to be a dry crew run through a navigation exercise and a target acquisition course. Miles had been through his individual pilot refresher already. Although his performance had not been entirely smooth, he pressed his instructor and himself into the crew phase of flying.

"You sure you're ready, Colonel?" his instructor had asked.

"I'm sure." Miles saw the look of skepticism and answered it. "I'm sure I'm not a hundred percent. But I don't have the luxury of achieving perfection in one stage of my flying before I move into something else. I've got to get through this phase so I can have my combat copilot in that seat, so you can look over our shoulders and grade us. This bird is a crew-oriented ship. If one of us has imperfections, the others have to carry more of the burden. It will work . . . it has to work. If this battalion is going to make a difference, every single Osprey pilot, including the battalion commander, is going to have to go into combat."

The instructor smirked.

"Right," said Miles, smiling sheepishly. "Sorry for the damned Gipper speech."

The other stations reported.

"Weapons station ready for takeoff."

"Communications and Electronic Warfare up." Miles smiled at the sound of Kopmeyer's voice. He'd taken Kop to the battalion with him and the young sergeant had found a quicker transfer of his communications proficiency into Ospreys than even Miles had achieved.

"Weapons officer."

Miles saw the instructor writing already. He spoke into his mike. "From now on, weapons officer, take the report from the others in your compartment and minimize chatter on the intercom.''

"Roger,'' said Warrant Officer Roger Tryon.

Miles knew it was a good discipline to minimize talk. There were too many radios to monitor as it was. When they began flying in combat teams of paired Ospreys, things would be confusing enough. Besides, with the Soviet satellites appearing periodically, every second of flight time and training counted.

He scanned his instrument master panel. This was a collection of light beads that required no interpretation if all operations remained normal. A string of steady green beads lighted meant all thirty-six systems monitored—from transmission temperature to engine RPM to fuel level—were operating normally, or as preset. No further checks were needed. A blinking green meant normal operation but outside preset parameters. An illuminated LED readout next to the light described the deviation. An orange bead signalled caution for the deviation. A red bead indicated a danger condition, and coupled with an audio alarm, it became an emergency condition. An emergency panel described the details of the emergency and suggested a course of action.

"Green beads,'' he murmured into the intercom. Then he cross-checked his flight instruments for insurance, released the Osprey's brakes, and prepared to taxi. The tower cleared him for a vertical takeoff spot.

Osprey could take off and land on a prepared strip like an airplane, but combat training seldom required it. Only if one of the engines failed was an airplane landing needed.

Tonight's exercise required a helicopter takeoff. Miles rolled the Osprey down the taxi lane to a huge asphalt pad with an encircled capital "H.'' The Osprey looked like a squat, bulky cargo plane lumbering to its spot.

He feathered the prop blades and ordered the copilot to rotate the Osprey's wings and propellers to vertical. A pair of motors whined as the wings swiveled. Miles pulled up on the collective pitch lever at his left side, a control exactly like that of a helicopter for adding power to the engine and pitch to the rotor blades simultaneously.

"Release the engine gimbals," he said.

"Released," said the instructor.

The verbal reply was redundant to the response Miles immediately felt in the cyclic control, the vertical stick between his legs. When set up as an airplane, the wings were kept in the horizontal, and the props and engines were fixed at right angles. The AV-33AA Osprey had also been given the agility of a helicopter when its wings rotated skyward and its gimbals were released.

Each gimbal was one concentric band of alloyed steel mounted inside another. The two rings in the gimbal permitted the propellers to be tilted in any direction of the compass.

This feature gave an extraordinary stability to Osprey flight, surpassing both the helicopter and the airplane. Osprey could hover right or left without tilting its wings—this prevented the dipping toward the ground as in a helicopter and also avoided raising the wing into radar line of sight. When the craft had to turn while hovering, one prop tilted forward as the other tilted to the rear, allowing the pilot to swap ends in seconds without requiring clearance beyond the wingspan.

Miles pulled power and felt the shock-absorbing landing struts extend as the weight of the craft was lifted. He shoved the cyclic forward and pulled takeoff power for a twenty-degree angle of climb. Unlike a helicopter, the Osprey lifted off without dipping its nose. As he climbed, Miles added the control input to accelerate to two hundred knots for the dash to the start of the training course. On-board computers adjusted the wing rotation to achieve the needed airspeed and lift.

As Osprey flew, Miles adjusted controls to maneuver as he wished. Computers determined what corrections to make in blade pitch, gimbal angles, wing rotation, and aerodynamic surfaces like flaps and elevators. In the gimbal-free configuration, Miles flew the Osprey as he would a helicopter. The computers interpreted the requirements needed to meet the demands of control inputs and made the aircraft fly as a combination airplane and helicopter, choosing the best combination of capabilities. The pilot never knew— and never needed to know—the choices being made for him.

Miles was happy when his flight ended. Not because he'd done well—he hadn't.

"Colonel, you were a bit behind the aircraft tonight," his instructor pilot said by way of opening remarks in the cockpit debriefing. "I found you relying too much on the computer to keep oriented on the instruments. I disabled the voice-audio warning system and the caution light segment, and you went nearly a minute without discovering the zero-reading on the left engine oil pressure. You failed to pick up two warnings from the combat command center about bandits at twenty miles. We overflew a SAM site because I cut off the report from the Weapons and Electronic Warfare deck . . . you didn't catch the audio signal in your own headset."

"Jesus, I could have killed us three times over if this had been for real."

"Four times over, sir," corrected his IP, not softening his contradiction with a smile.

Why shouldn't he be stern? Miles thought. This was no normal training situation. This instructor had others to teach. Everybody in the crew had to absorb mountains of information just to become adequate in this aircraft. War would not be forgiving. Why should any of the men and women in leadership positions cut any slack to any member of the team?

Especially to the supposed leader of the battalion. Supposed leader, indeed, he thought. How would he ever measure up? he wondered.

# 9

Washington responded shrilly to events in the Middle East.

The White House spokesman condemned the Soviet and Iraqi invasions. On Capitol Hill, legislators on both sides of the aisle hurled accusations back and forth. Much of this was done for the benefit of television. Before the news broadcasts were even over, however, the blame shifted to the White House. The underlying unspoken theme developed that the electorate of the United States had erred in putting a woman in the presidency. A woman might be thoroughly competent in managing the country at peace, but what now that war was imminent?

In the Oval Office, President Kathryn Chase barely held her temper. "Weakness?" she snarled. "The Europeans are great fighters against the invading Huns. But anywhere else in the world? Hah. At least we had the foresight to pre-position most of that Air Cavalry Combat Division in the region. We'll use the damned thing, too, if the Soviets don't back off."

The men in the room sat silently. There was nothing to say. To reassure her that she was not weak would be taken as patronizing. In her mood, nobody dared take such a risk.

Her press secretary had just returned from the White House briefing room. "Ma'am, nobody is saying it out loud—"

"But what? *What?*"

"It wouldn't hurt to get out front and put your face on camera and reassure them. Tell them—"

"Tell them what? You want me to look in the camera's eye and say, 'I'm tough'? What will that prove? Will that make the Soviets withdraw from Tabriz? If you tell me it will do any good, I'll do it. Otherwise, I won't let style get in the way of substance."

The press secretary breathed in and held his breath.

"What's happening in Europe?" the President asked.

The secretary of state shrugged. "They're doing about what you'd expect. They're condemning the Soviets. They're alerting their armies and air forces. They're preparing to mobilize reserves, but it's all defensive."

The secretary of defense said, "We've got people on alert everywhere in Europe, the Indian Ocean, and the Middle East."

"The Rapid Deployment Force?"

"It's been alerted all along. The trouble is—"

"Forget what the trouble is. Get the RDF within striking range of the Soviets. Saudi Arabia. Iran. I want to be asked into Iran. When are we supposed to hear from Tehran? I want to burn the Soviets' fingers if they don't turn back to their own borders."

The men in the room stared at the President.

She looked back at them, taking on each one of them eye-to-eye until each one blinked and either bowed his head or glanced away.

"I'll tell you what this means, gentlemen. This means war, and you'd better be prepared for it in all areas, on all fronts—diplomatically, militarily, politically, economically, and otherwise. You'd better be prepared for it personally, too. It's part of the fabric of every one of your personalities now, whether you like it or not. I can't say whether Congress will demand or approve a formal declaration, but you can bet your asses this is war. You can—" An aide interrupted the meeting and handed her a note.

The men and women in the room watched her face

for a clue to the contents of the note. She gave them nothing until she spoke.

"Ladies and gentlemen, I've received this word from the Revolutionary Government of Iran. We're invited." She waited for her words to sink in. "I want to go public with a new briefing every couple hours or so loudly condemning both the Iraqis and the Soviets. Even if there's no news, I want the condemnations. We have been invited in by the Iranians."

Exclamations of surprise and dismay met her announcement. She waited until the room grew silent. She motioned to the aide and handed him the note. "Read the statement that will be released to the nation within the hour."

He stood and read without emotion. "General Abolhassen Saddeq, a representative of Iran's Revolutionary Government, has arrived in Canada to present the United States with appeals for aid to counter the Soviet invasion of his country on two fronts. Those appeals include request for military intervention on behalf of the host country. Those requests have been taken under advisement."

"Add this," she said. "The President will respond to them personally and address the nation later."

If any of the men in this room had had any doubts about the strength of this President before this meeting began, there were none now.

"Gentlemen, my response, when I finally do address the nation, is that we're going to grant Iran's request for assistance. We're going into Iran. You know what you have to do."

Abramov ordered a halt for his armies to rest and refuel as the tail of his columns passed Shindand, more than two hundred kilometers inside Afghanistan. He turned to his "aide," who stood beside him with face as dusty as the dirt tracks they had traveled over.

Mendenyev grinned awkwardly in return.

Abramov had surprised him early that morning when only straggler units remained to be off-loaded from rail cars.

"When last did you travel with real soldiers, share their rations and road dust, Major?" he had asked.

The sleepy major struggled to his feet and squinted at the field marshal, trying to make sense of this unexpected question.

"I thought as much," Abramov bellowed. "You have forgotten. The remedy is to come now. I will be flying an inspection tour of the military districts to encourage the commanders trying to mobilize follow-on units. You will be my presence in the armored column. I have arranged for you join a tank battalion."

Mendenyev's head cleared instantly. "Respectfully, sir. Am I not to stay with you? The . . . our superiors in Moscow expect me to—"

"They expect you to report on my operations. You will have a firsthand experience. You will have a taste of a soldier's point of view."

"Sir—"

"Hurry. Those engines you hear are from the very regiment you are to join for the road march."

"But—"

"I will pick you up later. Somewhere near Zahedan."

Abramov had left him stumbling around in the before dawn chill and darkness. Mendenyev had barely caught up with the regiment's last tank company as it rolled out of the railhead. During the day, when the column halted, he worked his way forward, finding the platoon commander's tank, getting directions to the company commander's vehicle. Finally, he found the regimental commander, who barely tolerated his presence.

All day long, Mendenyev fumed at the mistreatment. He thought he'd won an understanding with Abramov—they both had nasty feelings about being thrown together, but neither would make the other unnecessarily uncomfortable. Abramov had violated that unspoken agreement. Mendenyev mentally began composing his first report to Moscow. The hotter the day became, the thicker the coating of dust on his skin and clothing, the more difficult it became to breathe—the more savage did the report become.

Ten minutes after the afternoon halt, Mendenyev finally found a water trailer from which to fill his canteen. He scrubbed his face, rinsing three times before the muck began to run thin. He gargled with water that tasted of iodine.

As he swallowed one mouthful and spat a second, he heard the approach of a helicopter and knew it must be Abramov. The rotor wash raised a dust storm that blasted him all over again. Even before the cloud settled, Abramov found him. As he drew close, the general's face creased into a broad grin. Mendenyev wrote another disparaging phrase into his half-composed report to Moscow.

Abramov clapped a thick hand on the major's shoulder. "Put away the scowl, Major. This has not been punishment, or even a prank."

Mendenyev lifted his mud-streaked face, freshly dusted by the powder stirred up by the general's helicopter, to see whether Abramov was mocking him. He was not. Still, he demanded, "What was it then, Marshal Abramov?"

"A reminder of things long forgotten by those in Moscow . . . if they ever knew them. The macho politicians are this very moment moving markers around on a table. But markers never eat dust, nor endure a day like yours on the march. Markers never bleed. Perhaps they should. A marker should be invented to shed red ink or even animal blood on the strategic maps every time it is committed to combat."

Abramov removed four small vials from his jacket pocket, one scarlet, one black, two empty. He tossed the empty ones to Mendenyev. "Here. Fill one now. Scrape the mud from your skin into it. Blow your nose free of the snotty filth you've been breathing all day. Spit the dust into it. Keep the vial with you long after you've filled it. When you return to a desk to direct the movement of troops, keep this vial in sight. Remember this day. Armies do not move by scratching lines on maps. Armies move a soldier at a time, a truck at a time, a tank at a time. They endure much more shit than you have in a single day. But you don't have to drink an ocean to learn the taste of sea water. The vial will remind you well enough of this day. You'll be a better officer for it."

Mendenyev glanced down at the empty vials in his muddy palm.

"Do you need to ask about what to put into the other vial?"

Mendenyev shook his head without looking up.

"Come. Bring your gear to my helicopter. We leave as soon as I talk to the regimental commander. Do you have any report to make to me about him?"

Mendenyev looked up, again to read the marshal's face, again to see if he was being mocked. Abramov was serious. Mendenyev remembered the regimental commander's rudeness.

"Yes, I have a report," he said. "The commander is one of your best. His unit did not lose a tank during the entire march, except for two that he did not abandon, but ordered towed. I would move this regiment forward to lead any attack."

Abramov clapped another dust cloud from Menenyev's clothes. "And you thought you did not have anything to learn."

Mendenyev traipsed back along the column until he found the tank he'd leaped aboard first thing this morning. He tossed down his baggage into six inches of road dust as the crew watched with disinterest. He realized he'd never spoken a civil word to these men, who had yet to wash their faces. Mud streaks from their sweat ran in red-orange rivulets from hairlines to jawlines as they labored over post-march maintenance of their fighting vehicle.

Mendenyev picked up his bags and began to walk away. Suddenly, he returned and ordered the tank commander to assemble his men at attention. He stepped up to each of them to utter a word of thanks, looking sharply into the eyes that peered out from mud masks as if to memorize the faces. Finally, with each man flinching away, he drew the mouth of his open vial down a cheek, scraping dust and sweaty mud into the glass.

Then he left the puzzled crew standing as he trudged toward Abramov's helicopter.

In Karachi, Pakistan, Major General Steve Little watched his divisional helicopters issue from the birth canals of C5-Ds. Beside him stood Rita Bernadino.

"For the third time in my life, I'm going to be part of combat in a foreign country," he murmured. "If armies only exist to maintain the peace, we don't seem to be getting anywhere."

Rita Bernadino nodded but did not speak. This would be her first experience. The ACCD would be unable to avoid combat. The Soviets were pushing into southern Afghanistan. The RDF commander, General Calder Pickett aboard the *J.B. Bremner,* just now steaming from Diego Garcia, wanted to catch the enemy before they actually entered Iran. It sounded fine to her. But the thing that bothered her was that the Ospreys had not yet been deployed.

"Of course, the RDF commander has assured me of first priority in air cover—all the air cover we could need," Little said. "We'll need a lot."

"No tanks for a month," she reminded him.

"The ACCD is expected to play the anti-tank role in stopping the Soviets. I'm certain the division can do it. Except . . ."

She turned toward him, realizing they were no longer merely passing time of day. She knew about the exception on his mind but asked anyhow. "Except for what?"

"The Russian helicopters. Intelligence shows one hell of a lot of helicopters assigned to the Soviet divisions. Rita, that's a practice they have only experimented with in the past. Now it seems as if Mi-24 and the Mi-26, Mi-8, and Mi-6s are going to be integrated at all levels—the buggers are borrowing from our book."

"We'll do fine."

She didn't feel as reassured as she sounded. Apache

and Cobra helicopters had yet to be reassembled and armed. They had to be flown across Pakistan and re-fueled. The crews might have to go into combat with-out rest.

She had made her own map study and was thinking about Zahedan, within spitting distance of the borders of Afghanistan, Pakistan, and Iran. It was a traditional crossroads dating back to the desert trade caravans.

As if reading her thoughts, Little said, "The joint task force staff says the Soviets will have to take Za-hedan no matter what other Iranian objective they need."

She nodded. "I've built my logistics support plan around the area." She paused. "But . . ."

He shook his head. "But what can we do to stop them? I tell you, Rita, I don't know if we can do any-thing effective, but we have to try something. That's why the RDF commander approved an airborne drop. He's hoping to deny it from Soviet parachute divisions. Our job will be to hold off their tanks for as long as we can."

"How much time can we be expected to buy?"

He shrugged. "The diplomats need time to per-suade the Iraqis to back off. Then they can persuade them to break loose Iranian divisions and turn them toward Zahedan. If the Iranians could help, we might hold the airfield, and that would shut off any other gambit toward the Strait of Hormuz. The RDF needs time to get pre-positioned tanks shipped from Diego Garcia, Egypt, and Saudi Arabia—thank goodness the Arabs relented against storing them there in the last year."

"We need time for ourselves," she added.

"For the Ospreys. If we could just stall the Soviet tanks for a week, they could be on station. They could neutralize their attack helicopters. We might stand a chance. General, this whole damned operation is hanging by a thread."

"We'll do it, sir. We'll hold them off."

* * *

General Abramov trembled in sympathetic resonance with the quaking earth as his tank column rolling by. Ghostly clouds rose into the night sky, blacking out the setting moon. Combat was so close. He was no stranger to it, but he never could become hardened to the fear that engulfed him every time it drew nigh. He was not afraid of his fear, though. Fear kept him on edge, reduced his need for sleep and food. He used it to his advantage. He realized he had missed feeling this way. He felt sorry for men like Polomarchuk who would never experience it as they fattened in luxury as part of the Moscow elite.

Here the road weaved indecisively into Iran, then back into Afghanistan before storming back into Iran toward Zahedan. Abramov knew there would no longer be any doubt about the intended invasion. He needed Zahedan. The Americans needed to prevent him from taking it. With the Zahedan airfield, Soviet fighters and attack aircraft could extend their ranges to protect his armies in the battles on the coastline of Iran. As it was now, he had practically outrun the ability of the MiGs to provide air cover.

At that moment, he saw Mendenyev striding toward him. He saw the look and knew there would be bad news even before the major said, "Comrade Marshal, about our divisional helicopters and central aviation assets—"

Abramov's face darkened. "The bastards back in Moscow. What have they done now?"

"They have decided that it was necessary to protect the flank you left uncovered by withdrawing the last regiment to become your rear guard," Mendenyev said guardedly.

Abramov spat. "I suppose they have expedited a crossing of the Caspian with a division or two to accomplish this flank protection?"

"No, Comrade. They have detailed your divisional helicopters. They are more mobile in any case—"

"Don't defend them, Major. Just make your damned report without embellishment. What else have they done?"

"They have devised a plan to capture the Iranian government at Mashhad."

"So they have decided that the war needs yet another front. How is Polomarchuk planning to snatch the Iranians with a helicopter force?"

"I don't know. I assume special forces. Polomarchuk accuses you of under-utilizing the helicopters."

"You think that is true, Major?"

Mendenyev sensed the challenge in the question. Abramov was asking whether the spy in the field would be confirming an instance of incompetence to the foxes in Moscow. "No. You're keeping them at full operational flying ability until it becomes necessary to meet the Americans. In my opinion. I told them so."

Abramov nodded. "Don't defend me, either, Major. I don't require it." He sighed heavily. "I did not want to meet the American Cobras and Apaches without helicopter gunships of my own. But now it looks as if we might have to. The damned idiots in Moscow have committed both of my airmobile brigades and nearly all of my helicopter assets to the insignificant city of Mashhad, which I bypassed, which they might take anytime they want to anyway. Five surplus motorized rifle divisions are scratching each other's asses around Tabriz for lack of any better mission there."

Mendenyev scuffed at the dirt. It made him uncomfortable to be addressed like this. He continually felt his loyalties divided.

Abramov obviously didn't care. "It is a horrible misuse of military forces," he said. "It is a dilution of the most important part of the operation, the drive through Afghanistan into Iran. What is needed down here is going to be speed, firepower, and shock action, pushing deep into Iran before the Americans can react, before the Iranians could do more than squawk. They demand I take a seaport, then they withdraw the means for success. Is it any wonder we saw a War of Shame?"

Mendenyev bit his lip and kept silent.

It would be light in an hour. Fifty miles away, the first airborne troops would be getting ready to drop in to defeat whatever Iranian security forces might be at

Zahedan, and then secure it for later use by Soviet air forces.

"What else?" Abramov asked.

"Moscow keeps demanding reports of action, dispatches indicating victories."

"Not Moscow, eh? Polomarchuk, you mean. Tabriz was such a picnic, he wants to rub my nose in it by bringing up the subject continually."

"How shall I respond?"

Abramov spat. "Ignore the demands for victory. First we must fight. Keep agitating for the Mi-28 helicopter promised to me."

"Comrade Dudov sends a reply to that." Mendenyev waved a dispatch.

"Read it."

The major held a penlight to the paper. "The Mi-28 prototypes are undergoing their last tactical combat trials, even as the first production models are being assembled. Should these trials prove satisfactory in the next weeks, you will be allotted a number of the aircraft for combat testing. Yours is the only theater likely to involve engagements with American helicopters, the most stringent testing circumstances possible. But first you must make contact with the Americans. First you must draw the U.S. helicopters into such engagements. We await your first combat results. No further word regarding the subject Marshal Polomarchuk has been briefing you about."

"What is that? What has that fool been briefing me about?"

"I don't know."

"Find out."

Mendenyev saluted and stumbled across the rubbled surface of Afghanistan toward the field headquarters.

Except for that last item, Abramov felt the slightest bit of encouragement in the report from Dudov. After all the nonsense and braggadocio he'd suffered from Polomarchuk, it nearly generated a spark of respect in him for Dudov.

Without those armed helicopters, though, he felt apprehensive about making his first contact with the

Americans. If his army had learned anything at all from the experience of the Iraqis in Desert Storm, it was that U.S. attack helicopters could annihilate unprotected tanks. A second lesson was that helicopters had proved to be a most effective anti-helicopter weapon. Now, unless his own armed aircraft were returned to him soon, he would be relearning lesson number one within hours, when the assault on Zahedan kicked off.

# BOOK III

## FIRE

# 10

The Iranian security force for Zahedan's airfield consisted mainly of reservists, those too old or handicapped by war wounds from the western front. Guards walked their posts, because most vehicles had long ago been requisitioned for the western front. The few automobiles in the force had been dredged out of junk yards and patched together or were civilian vehicles converted to military uses.

The commander of the security company was driving himself around the airfield perimeter in just such a vehicle, a broken-down taxi that rumbled along on seven of eight cylinders with three of four shocks broken. Like a hermit crab, the vehicle sidled spasmodically down the road, stopping and starting as the engines sputtered and coughed. At each guard post, the commander would stop and shut it off even before it died on its own, then step out and have a word or two with his guards.

The guard at the northwest side of the field held up a hand as the captain began speaking, and then he heard it, too.

"Aircraft!" He turned around and around on the spot, but was unable to determine the direction from which the sound came. "From where?"

The captain muttered, "It sounds like . . . from everywhere . . . from every direction . . ."

High above, jets screamed, swooping overhead, then looping toward the south. More distant was the droning of heavier transport aircraft. Suddenly, the horizon began to light up as the fighters fired missiles. The captain and his guards jumped into the bunker, but after a tense minute of waiting for the missiles to explode on the ground, the captain stuck his head back out. The jets were not firing at the airfield. They were firing at other aircraft.

Soviet aircraft had arrived over Zahedan first, but from fifty miles away American fighters had initiated air-to-air combat. Because their ground control stations were too distant to be able to provide cover this far from the Soviet border, these Soviet planes were MiG-29s, which had their own look-down, shoot-down capability. They picked up the Americans at about the time the Americans began firing. From then on, it was a long-distance battle as opposing fighters maneuvered in the dark skies, getting closer and closer to each other as the rising sun began lightening up the battlefields one to five miles above the earth.

The leader of the Soviet MiG-29 flight needed to press the battle to the Americans, for behind him were air transports filled with parachute forces.

The lead Soviet transport pilot to arrive over Zahedan signaled to the cargo area. When lights flashed in the troop compartment, paratroopers dived out into the night. A brighter flash outside and the turbulence of an explosion told him before the radio call that one craft in the formation had been struck by the American fighters. He fought the controls and held his course as his paratrooper cargo departed.

The first jumper, a Russian lieutenant, launched out into the night, feeling the blast of the air and the shock of his parachute as it blossomed, breaking his short free-fall. Then he began skidding downward. Below, he could see some explosions and fire. Up above, the noise of the aircraft flying overhead and the sound of rushing air were deafening, and the explosions on the ground were little more than indistinct pops. The lieutenant struggled around in his harness, trying to pick out the silhouettes of his men in the skies around him. His platoon was responsible for attacking the security posts on the northwest side of the airfield, either from outside the airfield or inside, depending on where the vagaries of the wind would land them. He counted roughly twelve parachutes strung out behind him in the sky, before his canopy blocked his vision. He made a last check of the sky, looking for the following flight that would drop roughly along the same path as his platoon. Those were the ones they would have to be careful of. Once they got on the ground and became preoccupied with the Iranian security forces, they'd be in danger of other paratroopers landing on their heads.

Then he turned his attention to the ground rushing up to meet him quickly. It gave him a certain amount of confidence to know the landing zone was an airfield, which meant flat ground and a scarcity of vertical obstacles that might ram up his crotch. Every time he participated in one of these massive night jumps, a handful of soldiers seemed to find a way to castrate themselves by straddling the spikes of a tree, posts, or concertina wire.

The touchdown came within seconds, and he cushioned the blow by bending his knees, slumping his body, and rolling over. He felt his groin and found all his parts in order—a good landing. He shucked his harness and extended the shoulder stock of his submachine gun to carry it. Next, he tried to get his bearings, to see where his men were touching down, to ensure that none touched down on top of him. He began moving about, whispering loudly to collect his soldiers as a mother duck gathers ducklings. So far there had been no gunfire.

When he looked up into the sky at the second wave of aircraft, he realized he must have gotten turned around, because the aircraft seemed to be coming in from the south. Trying to orient himself, he dug into his jacket pocket, pulled out his wrist compass, and strapped it on.

He heard sporadic gunfire two hundred yards away. He listened hard to the character of the firing. These were individual rifle shots. That meant security forces, for his troops had been instructed to fire short bursts of automatic fire.

He began to orient himself in the direction of fire, checking it against the pointer on his compass. Damn! The needle must be broken, because the firing came from the wrong direction. He crept toward a low bunker from which the firing was coming. He looked left and right and determined the line of his defenses. He was quite sure that he was inside the airfield fence. Things seemed backward. He wondered if maybe the military mapmakers had gotten it wrong. After all, they had been intentionally making incorrect maps inside the Soviet Union for decades. Why wouldn't they get the topographical information wrong in Iran?

He began to hear intermittent gunfire from other directions as other units and soldiers began making contact with the security forces. Ahead, he saw the bunker quite clearly now. A broken-down civilian vehicle painted haphazardly in military colors was parked beside it. He loosed a burst of gunfire at the vehicle and saw it further hunker down toward the earth as he punctured two tires.

Angry gunfire in response. He directed several of the men closest to him to return fire, then he shouted for three other men to flank the bunker. Since they were attacking from the back, they should be able to take it safely.

"Use grenades!" he hollered at the maneuvering fire team. Then he squatted down and fired a burst at the bunker himself.

The lieutenant wasn't worried about this bunker. He was more concerned about reinforcing the troops. What if the garrison at this installation was larger than anticipated? He began shouting up and down the line, asking for the location of the machine guns and the anti-tank rockets. As men began shouting back and forth with him, as he began to assemble a mental idea of the outcome of the jump, he became more and more comfortable with his circumstances. It looked as though almost everybody had been accounted for. Before long, he would have his sector of the perimeter completely under control.

Now, if only the bastards in the second wave didn't

start jumping on his head. The lieutenant looked around and noted that the second wave of paratroopers had begun. Above them he heard the drone of other aircraft and saw a third wave of jumpers streaming out into the sky.

A third wave? Why the hell hadn't somebody told him there was going to be a third wave?

He shook his head, clucking at himself. This was none of his business. Maybe later when he made captain he'd understand the confusion in jump operations. Or he'd just add to the confusion.

Gradually, the intensity of gunfire and shouting began to increase. As other paratroopers hit the ground, he realized the firing was growing closer to his own position.

"Goddamn," he cursed. This area was becoming hotter. As the gunfire increased, he felt a stinging in his right knee and fell on his face. Stunned, he tried to get up but he found that his leg wouldn't work. Then he saw why. The stinging knee had developed a bend in the wrong direction. Then he saw that the leg was no longer even connected to the body except by a few strands of cloth and tendons. Then he saw his blood was gushing. Finally, he realized that he had not stumbled but that the leg had been shot off. Suddenly, he was afraid of dying.

The lieutenant screamed for some of his men to assist him, to bring a medic. As he lay there the gunfire around him grew louder and louder. Half crazed now in pain and anguish at seeing his leg blown off, the lieutenant began shrieking, asking the heavens why it had been him shot and who had done it? Three of his men rushed to him. One began vomiting at the sight of blood spurting out onto the earth. One just seemed frozen: he was a youngster barely out of training. The lieutenant grabbed him and demanded that he do something.

"What can I do, Lieutenant?"

The third man, a noncommissioned officer, took out his field bandage and used its ribbons of tie-down cloth to fashion a hasty tourniquet to cut off the flow of blood from the lieutenant's leg. The noncom looked around them, surveyed the battle situation, and shouted at the lieutenant.

The lieutenant shouted back that he could not hear. The lieutenant had been told to expect chaos on the battlefield. He had no idea it would by anything like this. Hand grenades arced in lazy trajectories all around him. Tracer fire crisscrossed the sky above him, and bullets raised geysers of dirt all around him. He looked up in the sky and saw a third wave of paratroopers preparing to touch down. He realized that Soviet soldiers on the ground might be shooting at each other. Half-crazed with pain, and feeling faint and thirsty, he ordered the noncom to make the soldiers stop shooting at their own men.

"No!" the noncom shouted at his officer.

The Russian lieutenant, on the verge of unconsciousness from loss of blood, gathered his strength. "I command you to order these men to cease fire."

"No, you fool! I said, the second wave of paratroopers were not our soldiers. The Americans have jumped onto the same airfield we did. The Americans are here! We're fighting goddamned Americans!"

Second Lieutenant Thomas Edwards of Savannah, Georgia, thought he had jumped into hell.

As he hit the silk, he realized that somehow some of his troops had already hit the ground ahead of him. How was that possible? Not until he came close to the ground did he realize that the dim figures shifting around in the darkness were not Americans at all. The goddamned Russians and the 82nd Airborne had made a combat jump onto the same objective at exactly the same time.

Edwards had been told about the number of tanks and the motorized rifle divisions headed his way. He'd been told that he was going to be dropped in to prevent an airmobile assault, to destroy the runway if necessary to keep Russian transports out, and to do their best just to hold out. So he knew he was in for a hell of a fight because he believed his superiors about all those things. He sure as hell didn't know that he was going to be in for this kind of fight. After Desert Storm there had been all those lessons learned about friendly fire. The between-war planners had dreamed up worst-case scenarios to teach in the military schools. Nobody had imagined anything like this, though.

Once on the ground, he fought free of his parachute rigging and began shouting for his men. All around, he heard Russians shouting in reply . . . no, they weren't answering him. They were simply experiencing the same confusion, trying to call to each other and to get organized as they too began to realize the second wave of paratroopers was their enemy. Edwards looked back up into the sky to pray for some help. In answer, he saw yet another wave of jumpers. He knew damned well those were not his own troops. So much for being in the glorious lead wave. He was going to be a Georgia boy caught like a piece of fatback between two pieces of Russian black bread. Along with about fifteen hundred others of his brigade.

The battle on the ground at Zahedan evolved into hundreds of individual battles as soldiers groped and called in the darkness for each other and then began moving through the smoke and dust clinging to the earth toward friendly replies. The men were forced to belly crawl, for anybody who presented more of a target was liable to get either his head or his butt shot off. Edwards tried to keep his shouts from pitching into screams. Sonofabitch. Technology. Radios that could reach the Pentagon through satellite linkups. Yet there seemed to be no better way than to shout back and forth to try to get organized. George Custer had better than this. He had bugle calls and pennant signals.

Edwards finally caught up to Specialist Four Greg Beach, his radio operator, yammering incoherently into the radio mike. Edwards grabbed the radio handset and began talking into it. What he heard back was no consolation. His captain company commander told him to get the hell off the air and get his platoon organized. Before Edwards could answer, the captain was shouting the same command at somebody else. Seconds later, he was hearing a call from the battalion commander using the company radio net, meaning that the battalion commander wasn't getting any answers to his questions either so he had tuned to the company radio net.

Somebody then got the idea to begin firing mortars. Explosions dotted the airfield randomly, spiking the confusion in the spots near where the rounds went off. Edwards wondered how anybody could see to fire a rifle, let alone an area-fire weapon. For himself, he had practically been within a flinch of shooting two of his own men. One was Terry Umbreit, a corporal fire-team leader who had sprained an ankle on landing. The other was Platoon Sergeant Jose Quintana, a squat, bowlegged noncom who wore a perpetual grin. Quintana dodged like a fullback cutting through the offensive line and lunged into the gathering that Edwards had established. "Don't shoot, Lieutenant, don't shoot," he shouted as he dived. He hit hard and rolled twice, coming to rest splayed out on his belly.

"Sergeant Quintana, you hit?"

Quintana raised his face and gave his answer in a huge smile. "Is this all we got?" he shouted, raising his voice over the growing racket of rifle fire.

"So far," Edwards said, trying to control the squeakiness in his throat. "Let's tighten it up and get a defense going." He gawked at the grinning Quintana. Edwards marveled at the man's coolness until he saw the look in the eyes and realized the goofy smile was an expression of terror. The men shifted until the four of them lay facing outwards, their feet touching as they formed a tiny perimeter.

All over the airfield, other men began trimming the numbers of battles down as they formed pockets of soldiers.

Edwards ordered Beach to begin digging in. "The rest of us will keep watch and take turns." A soldier ten yards away stood up to run. Edwards shouted, "Hey, soldier!"

The figure stopped running and turned, lifting an AKM assault rifle to his shoulder. Edwards loosed a burst of three from his M16 and cut the Soviet down.

Edwards cursed and said, "I'm glad the son of a bitch wasn't from Mississippi or some damned thing."

Umbreit shouted back over his shoulder, "Damn, Lieutenant! Ah'm from Mississip."

Edwards shouted again, "The bastard was probably just a Yankee, anyhow." Another figure darted by and Edwards hollered again, "Hey, soldier!"

"Yo," came the response.

Edwards recognized him as one of his squad leaders, Staff Sergeant Ray Kluth. "Get your ass over here," he commanded.

Using this technique, in the ensuing minutes Edwards was able to scrounge up half a dozen more men who were able to scratch divots in the earth and raise up an eight-inch barrier of dirt around a shallow fighting position. As the sun began to lighten the sky, the process of identifying friend and foe grew easier.

It was still dark enough for Umbreit to dash out from the hole and grab an RPG.

"Don't you fire that sonofabitch, Umbreit," Edwards commanded. "The sonofabitch has a backblast on it."

"Well, what the hell did I run out there and risk my butt for, L.T.?"

"Just stupid, I guess." As a burst of laughter inside the American crater vaporized the tension for a moment, Edwards was surprised at his own ability to remain calm, if that's what it was. He had created a semblance of order here in the dust amid the screaming, the firing, and the explosions. True, with daylight, the fighting and killing would go on in earnest, rather than haphazardly as it had gone on so far, but still, he didn't feel all that intimidated. "Maybe you can pound that thing up some Russian asshole," he shouted over the din. More in hysteria than humor, his remark was met by raucous laughter from the men in the scooped-out place on the hottest battlefield on earth.

The sun came up on a haphazard assortment of friendlies and foes. Soldiers from both armies had formed into clusters, and the clusters were enlarged by digging out small shovels full of dirt at a time, throwing up an embankment to protect themselves against direct-fire weapons. The Soviets had landed roughly the same numbers on the airfield as the Americans before the airdrop had been called off by both sides. One regiment of Soviet paratroopers and one brigade of the 82nd Airborne. Both units had suffered about twenty-percent casualties, with nearly as many of the injuries on both sides inflicted by friendly weapons as by the enemy.

As Lieutenant Edwards's group kept growing, their perimeter widened to accommodate all the men, and the depressions were dredged to a depth of three feet so the men could actually crawl on hands and knees rather than on their bellies. They kept extending outward, picking up more of their numbers. Before the sun was fully exposed over the horizon, Edwards had gathered about thirty of his platoon of forty-nine men. Outside his perimeter lay some corpses. Though he heard the shouts now and then from a wounded man whose name he recognized, he would not permit his only medic to leave the perimeter. With all the chaos, any man leaving cover drew fire. Already he'd seen half a dozen soldiers shot down by gunfire from both sides.

Although he should have been elated at having recovered so many men, he'd grown increasingly concerned. He'd lost most of his leadership. The only senior noncoms were Quintana, his platoon sergeant, and the one squad leader, Kluth. He couldn't get a fix on any of his other squad leaders or fire-team leaders.

The communications with the company headquarters indicated that nobody up the line knew any better than he did about what to do to extricate themselves from the Soviets. All that he could be thankful for was that the Russians didn't seem to be any better organized than themselves.

At mid-morning, Quintana grunted and pointed at the horizon. A propeller-driven Iranian commercial airbus circled the airstrip three times. Someone among the undisciplined troops—he hoped they weren't from the 82nd—fired at the airliner. Undaunted, it stretched its downwind leg and turned to final approach. As it came down towards the main runway, small-arms fire rose up from dozens of positions on the ground, and the aircraft broke off its approach.

"What a dumbass," muttered Beach. "Don't they see all the damned soldiers down here?"

"What bothers me about that is the idea that maybe they can't see us very well," offered Quintana.

Edwards grunted his assent and added, "Sooner or later, some general on one side or the other is going to bring helicopters or fighters down here to see if the other side can be blasted off this field. When that happens, a lot of people are going to get hurt."

"So what do we do, L.T.?"

Edwards looked into Umbreit's face. The man expected him to know how to get out of this one. He looked around at the others. Didn't they realize, he thought, that officer training didn't cover the instance of two armies jumping onto the same damned battlefield at once?

Apparently not. They looked at him as if he should know what to do. So he decided he'd better concoct a plan to at least get his platoon assembled with the rest of the company.

"Here goes. Umbreit, you throw smoke outside the entrenchment. Then I'll get on the radio and try to get a bearing to the company commander."

The grenade canister popped innocently and began hissing its yellow plume into the stuffy air. Edwards kept cajoling the company commander's radio operator to help him get a bearing. Finally, the sergeant told him that the smoke was a hundred yards east of the command position.

A little cheer went up in Edwards's pathetic perimeter.

"Nice work, L.T.," Quintana said.

"For all the good it does us." Still, Edwards puffed up a little and suggested the radio operator ask the other platoons to identify themselves in the same way. It worked at first, with lazy clouds sprouting up here and there. Before long, though, the Soviets soon followed suit and smoke grenades began popping all over the airfield.

The ACCD, minus the Ospreys, launched its first attack on the Soviets by leading with its best punch: the first brigade, equipped with AH-64 Apache gunships and Black Eagle armed scouts. At 1100 hours it moved to make contact, reconning along two axes toward the spot satellite data predicted for intercepting the advancing Soviets. One battalion of attack helicopters entered Iran near Ladiz, south of Zahedan. A second began filtering into Afghanistan near Cardan. The third followed the first prepared to respond to the need of either of the lead units.

About 1130, the lead scout team of Black Eagles from the second battalion reported rising columns of dust some twenty to thirty miles ahead as they crossed into Afghanistan. Later an advance scout saw the Soviets closing on Zahedan, leading with tanks. The scout reported the cloud of dust extended fifty miles or more into the interior of Afghanistan.

Rather than remain at the ground headquarters, Wilkerson opted to fly in his divisional aircraft, a forward airborne command post, one of three UH-60C Blackhawks especially outfitted with communications equipment. The command group in each bird consisted of staff officers to do the map plotting, mathematics, and handling of radio work, and a senior officer to make decisions. Wilkerson had designed and trained these command groups and had three aircraft specially outfitted, one for the division commander, one for the assistant division commander for maneuver, and one for the G3, the division operations officer. His configuration had proved so successful at Fort Irwin in training, especially with the widely dispersed Ospreys, that it had been adapted to each brigade commander's aircraft as well. The setup's beauty was the ability of its division commander to keep tabs on a far-flung battlefield, either personally or through one of his trusted staff officers. Thus, the brigade commander and his staff could make fewer reports and devote more attention to fighting. In his contributions to battlefield management of mobile units, Wilkerson had proved himself a genius, demonstrating and teaching a mastery of the mechanics and doctrine.

The down side of the setup, however, resulted from its very advantages. A higher command wanting to interfere in the affairs of a subordinate unit could usually have somebody within easy reach of meddling.

Wilkerson found some high ground about fifty kilometers southeast of Zahedan and ordered his helicopter put down so he could maintain communications. From there, he planned to monitor the battle, tracking the activities of all combat aviation units, preparing to take over the fighting at any time the brigade commander needed, and it didn't take long for Wilkerson to see a need to get himself involved.

The brigade commander's two lead battalions were separated by more than a hundred miles. Wilkerson eavesdropped on the brigade command net long enough to formulate a picture, then interjected, "Pacer Six, this is Ace Five. You'd better shadow that lead unit before it gets into contact and gets away from you, over."

"Negative, Ace. My Three is following that part of the attack. I'm staying centrally located, over."

"Negative, Pacer." Wilkerson insisted. "There's no way you'll be able to keep up with battle status with such extreme distances, and your operations bird doesn't have the commo package."

The strained voice of the brigade commander came back at him. "Ace Five, does the boss—"

Wilkerson overrode the brigade commander's transmission, electronically stepping on his protest. Of course, Little wouldn't know about this, because he wouldn't deign to lower himself to talking on a brigade net, Wilkerson thought. "Pacer Six, this is Ace Five, and I insist you tag along with the second battalion, for chrissakes. They've spotted the enemy. You're wasting precious time arguing here. I'll stand by as a relay station to higher headquarters until your ops bird comes back and takes over this part of the battle. Do you roger?"

"Roger," came the nearly hostile reply. "Be advised, I'm going to report this interference to Ace Six. He isn't going to—"

Wilkerson overrode again. "Save it, Colonel, dammit. Your own troops are practically fighting the goddamned Soviets already—haven't you been listening? You're missing the war by arguing with me. Tell that to General Little while you're at it. Be sure to mention that this is a new ball game, not the battlefield of the eighties, not even another Desert Storm. I'm sure you know who wrote the book on mobile battlefield management, so if you want to argue, save it for the post-mortem. Now get your ass moving, Colonel."

After the brigade commander had rogered, Wilkerson waited a decent interval and then ordered the near attack battalion to reposition, joining him on the high ground southeast of Zahedan. From there it could be launched against any tank units that might break through the initial attack. Then too, he had to be prepared for the possibility that other armored columns might threaten the airfield from a different direction than those already spotted in Afghanistan.

An hour later, the brigade commander he'd sent off requested the reserve battalion be released to him. Wilkerson demanded to know why.

"Ace Five, there are more tanks here than we can handle. Now are you going to let my reserve battalion join me or do I have to go over your head to Ace Six?"

Wilkerson relented. Soon he felt left out of the action, so he ordered the second brigade, that of the older OH-58 Kiowa scouts and the AH-1 Cobra gunships, to move into central Pakistan and shut down, waiting for orders to join the battle as it developed. Now he had his hands on the controls of more than half the division's firepower. If only he had those damned Ospreys, he thought. Miles and that bunch was sitting back in California, drinking wine, while the rest of the division was in combat.

Above central Afghanistan, an air battle continued to rage between the fighters of the United States and Soviet Union, ebbing and flowing like the tide. At first it shifted toward the Soviet border, but as the Soviets drew closer to their own border and could rearm, refuel, and reinforce, the air battle began to flow back toward the Arabian Sea, where the carrier fleets were stationed.

On takeday, the fragment of order Edwards had achieved in the morning had evaporated by mid-day. The airfield had become a graveyard of the living. The wounded had to lay screaming all day long until their voices weakened, until finally their cries no longer rose up. The flies and other insects feasted on the gore that oozed everywhere on the battlefield. Soldiers tried to keep their senses about them as they looked over the edges of their fighting positions and occasionally fired at other heads looking over other firing positions toward them. Gradually the battle had ground down into a stalemate, and both sides saw no option but to wait for the night to allow them to reorganize and somehow resume the struggle.

# 11

Miles issued instructions to the Weapons and Electronic Warfare crew and directed everybody to help conduct internal and external preparations for his first weapons exercise.

As the preflight inspection progressed, he marveled for the hundredth time at the weaponry of this bird.

The fuselage housed nine fixed twenty-millimeter cannon mounted above the right wing, and another bristled from the array of nose pods. These fired forward, controlled by either the pilot or copilot using a trigger on the cyclic stick control between the thighs. The pull of the trigger was followed by an instant's hesitation as a door in the stealth skin slid open to expose the muzzles of the gun above the right wing.

Underneath the Osprey's belly, two clamshell bombbay doors could open to sow mines, sensors, and even time-delayed bombs and bomblets. However, the most useful device below was a hydraulic arm irreverently called the "horsecock." In flight or while hovering, the arm swung downward, pivoting from the rear. It truly looked like a horse's penis unsheathing and lowering to the vertical. The arm was a powerfully pressurized rail using compressed gas and which fired a Javelin into the ground the way an aircraft carrier catapult uses steam to launch planes.

The Javelin was a thick spear that concealed several electronic devices used to enhance the Osprey's stealth mission. First was a deceptive emitter that issued counterfeit thermal and radar impulses. The thermal device generated heat in a frequency that could simulate a tank or an airplane or a helicopter on the ground. That was used to decoy infrared sensors. It also accepted radar signals and generated a signal simulating whirling helicopter rotor blades. By drawing fire this way, Javelin would expose the enemy at best and at least deceive him by drawing attention from the Osprey.

Another Javelin device acted like a Navy sonobuoy. It radiated strong radar signals that painted enemy aircraft. If an enemy aircraft were flying overhead, for example, the signal would be reflected back to earth, and receivers aboard the Osprey could pinpoint the direction to the plane. If two Javelin radar buoys were out, the computers aboard the Osprey could triangulate from their known locations to calculate the range to the aircraft.

Since signals emanated by a radar device give away the position of the transmitter, the enemy might fire upon the transmitter, but the passive receivers aboard the Osprey would have by then computed the data and thus not be directly endangered. Moreover, explosive charges in the Javelins would automatically destroy the devices either on a signal, if the enemy tried to tamper with them, or after it had been left for a preset period.

Along the walls of the Osprey fuselage on either side of the fighting compartment were the ten vertical tubes like missile silos aboard a Navy submarine. Within those tubes were pairs of Raptor missiles in their own launch tubes. These were the most potent weapons of the Osprey. They could be fired up to a range of twenty miles against aircraft of all types. They could also be used against air defenses, such as against anti-aircraft radar weapons, and had even been effective against lightly armored ground vehicles. The firing control of the Raptor could even be turned over to the Osprey's computer to identify targets and fire automatically, engaging as many as half a dozen targets at once. When friendly aircraft "squawked" the proper code, they would not be engaged by the discriminating computer.

At the rear of the Osprey, Miles inspected the tail

gun. Almost as an afterthought, somebody had decided that an aircraft operating behind enemy lines ought to have the capability to fire a gun to the rear to protect against enemy infantry. Forming an extension of the line of the fuselage, beneath the inverted $V$ of the tail, the twenty-millimeter cannon was shrouded in stealth skin and directed by a television camera that sighted down the barrel of the gun. Still, its capacity had been limited to a mere fifteen hundred rounds—about six seconds of firing time—and the gun could only swivel about twenty-five degrees in any direction from the center line of the craft. Inside the Osprey, each crew station could tune its auxiliary television screen to view out the rear, but hardly anybody did in normal operations. The pilots were too busy checking forward, and the WEW crew's attention was absorbed by the more important navigation and target acquisition displays. That left the primary responsibility for firing with the crew chief, but tonight, everybody but the crew chief would be tested on it. Since they would be firing Raptors for the first time as a crew, Bachman would have her hands full with reloading duties.

As the crew assembled under the nose of the Osprey, squatting on the tarmac outside the hangar, Miles reflected that it had always been this way, the leader assembling his troops, all of them squatting over his map for a briefing. Sometimes the plan was scratched into the dust. Other times, the grease pencil marks indicated dispositions and units. Flag officers used elaborate magnetic three-dimensional symbols. Had he wanted to, he could have pressed the entire group into the WEW compartment and given his briefing on a computer display terminal.

"Who wants to take first on tail gun?" said Barger. Nobody volunteered. Other crew duties demanded so much concentration, nobody really had time to become proficient. Barger smirked at Miles and turned his head before raising his eyebrows in exasperation so the check pilot would not see. The check pilot stood over the crew, listening and watching. Already the Osprey crew was being evaluated on crew duties and pre-flight performance.

"Tryon, assign somebody," Barger ordered.

"Kop, you first. Then Rush. Then Joyce. Then me."

Miles took in the crew as their names were mentioned. Roger Tryon, a thin, nervous whip of a warrant officer, commanded the WEW. He directed and coordinated the actions of the enlisted men in the fighting compartment. More important than that, though, Tryon was the first human in the automated acquisition and firing link. In battle, he followed the almost instantaneous sequence of target selection and firing. The more adept he was at keeping up with the computers, the faster the weapons could fire. Of course, he was the first human override to the Osprey's computer systems when they were in automatic mode.

Kopmeyer handled half a dozen radios and receivers, concentrating mostly on radar signals when combat was imminent. He never became excited, even when he carried on three to four conversations over radio and intercom nets and kept track of radar alert warnings. He had adapted so quickly to the Osprey that Miles often envied him.

Gordon Rush was a corporal who could do any function aboard the Osprey, including fly it. Rumor had it, he had more stick time than any other enlisted man, none of whom was permitted to fly. He deployed the Javelins, fired Raptors on command, and assisted with electronic-warfare duties and communications.

Sergeant Joyce Bachman, the crew chief, had already proven herself in Miles's shakedown flights, when he'd refamiliarized himself with the craft. She performed routine maintenance and kept the craft's logbook. During combat, she would be responsible for ensuring the automatic reloading system for Raptor missiles did its job. If her other duties permitted, she became the tail gunner.

Miles relayed the tactical briefing he'd been given, describing the expected threat along the battle course. Then they were off.

* * *

The check pilot rode in a portable jump seat behind the pilot and copilot so he could monitor the mission. By the time the Osprey had traveled a mile into the course, Miles and the crew had forgotten about him, too busy performing crew duties to be distracted.

The Osprey took on five Soviet attack "helicopters" in the fourth mile of the sweep. These were pop-up targets that suddenly poked up through slots in the tops of ground-level bunkers. Because the targets represented parked helicopters, they gave off no radar or thermal signature and had to be picked up visually.

"Five sleeping Hineys at two-o'clock," said Barger in his clear, controlled voice, even as he designated the target position by punching an electronic crosshair onto his video screen for the weapons officer to use as reference.

Miles felt a second of disappointment at not speaking faster, for he'd seen the Hind targets at the same moment, but realized he was being silly. Parked helicopters were no threat as such. They were to be engaged instantly, even if manually, by the crew in the WEW. His job was to avoid overflying the site and to look for SAM sites or infantry security that almost certainly would be emplaced near a temporary helicopter parking site.

He jinked the Osprey left and accelerated. Automatically, the firing computer continued to keep tabs on the designated target.

Ten seconds into the sequence, he heard Tryon bark the prefiring alert, "Raptor up."

"Fire," Barger ordered.

The Osprey rattled, then thumped as a firing port slid open and a blast of compressed air blew out the tube housing a single missile, sending it fifty feet into a gentle arc toward the target. Outside the craft, the only sound that would be heard was a hiss, like the agitated squawk of some night animal.

The designated missile's on-board computer had continually updated the firing solution as it was computed. At the firing command, the electrical and computer links had disconnected, leaving the remaining firing and detonating sequence for the missile to handle. The air blast blew the missile clear of the Osprey.

A long second later, the rocket motor ignited with a crack, and the missile covered a quarter mile in less than two seconds, detonating a hundred feet above the target, scattering a supersonic hailstorm of titanium pellets over an area the size of a football field. The blast shredded the targets to ribbons, although they'd been dispersed twenty meters apart, and the flash lit up the sky like a strobe light.

The blast of the Raptor would temporarily ruin the night vision of anybody within half a mile of it and anybody who looked at it for twice again the distance. What was more, the sensitive screens of most night-vision devices would have been whitewashed for up to a minute. But the Osprey's vision devices possessed automatic irises that reacted to changes of light intensity instantaneously to maintain a nearly constant night vision. The Osprey's eyes had been designed like those of a dragonfly, with more than ten thousand smaller eyes coordinated to shut down or open up, depending on light intensity. All ten thousand images could be coordinated to give a single image or to divide their effort to look in half a dozen directions at once and send the results to the different video screens of the crew.

Miles aimed the bird for a ridge line. "Prepare to deploy a Javelin radar buoy," he ordered. "On my command. Set to half a minute's delay—shit! Got a Grail gunner, twelve o'clock," he announced suddenly, jinking left to avoid overflying the human silhouette of a man holding a surface-to-air missile on the ridge line a hundred meters away.

"IR signature topside," said Barger, poking a button on his console.

"Javelin jettisoned," said Tryon's voice. "IR signature on command."

"Flashbulb out," added Rush.

Within seconds they'd completed the procedures that would have deflected a Grail SA-7 heat-seeking missile. Normally, the exhaust of the Osprey was ducted downward on low-level missions, so IR sensors could not pick up the craft from above. Barger had redirected the hot gases upward, shutting off any possibility the gunner could acquire or that the missile could home. Tryon had jettisoned a Javelin on the ridge line. Although its deployment was intended as a radar emitter, it could, on command, radiate a strong imitation of an IR signature and overpower any nearby sensor trying to lock on the Osprey. The flash bulb ejected simply was a canister of magnesium set to flash and burn white-hot and perform the same function. Osprey could evade the Grail gunner without the need to engage him.

By mile twenty-five, Osprey had encountered fourteen more Hinds in small formations, represented by radar emissions sent out from target antennae.

In the next ten miles, Barger identified a SAM array, including a radar van, and Miles engaged it with cannon fire and splattered the ground two miles ahead. For good measure, Tryon launched a Raptor that set off secondary fires the crew identified as mock fuel storage sites.

Miles began to feel a little smug. They'd killed everything within the time envelope that the computer weapons system had defined as standard. The computer itself would have shaved seconds off each engagement, but their manual coordination had been spectacular. After each engagement, each crew member had spent a second's worth of cannon fire through the tail gun for familiarization. Next was Miles's turn, and he was trying to think of something more constructive to do with the five hundred or so rounds left for him to fire.

"Bandit at nine o'clock," reported Rush. "Fast-mover closing at four hundred knots, ten miles."

Miles knew what the fast-mover was. Each exercise run had been allocated a drone craft to buzz the target area. The drone was no threat to acquire the Osprey—it simply flew by, intermittently transmitting a signal that would identify it as either enemy or friendly. The crew had to identify and prepare to engage. The test measured the decisiveness and accuracy of the crew.

"Raptor up," reported Tryon.

Miles noted the time elapsed as five seconds. He waited for either Tryon, Kop, or Rush to report the drone as either friendly or hostile. Another five seconds ticked by.

Miles grew impatient. He should have the ID by now. In combat, they'd be sitting ducks at this range if the enemy had acquired them. He felt Barger's eyes on him. For the first time in the course of the acquisitions, he remembered the check pilot grading their performance.

"Check fire," Miles ordered. If they couldn't determine the identity of the craft, they shouldn't fire on it, he knew. Unless it engaged them.

Miles turned and flew at the fast-moving drone. If it was enemy, the sooner he passed under it, the less effective it would be at attacking him.

"The drone transponder is malfunctioning," said a strange voice. At first Miles couldn't make the new voice. Then he realized the check pilot had spoken.

"Obviously," said Miles flipping his tail video screen on to watch the drone recede into the night.

"No, actually malfunctioning," said the check pilot. "I just got a call over the control net. Too bad. It was supposed to be enemy. I'd like to have seen how you handled it . . ."

On impulse, Miles clutched the tail gun toggle switch on his weapons panel and swung the crosshair over the disappearing exhaust of the drone. He held the firing trigger down and watched in the video rear view as two seconds' worth of firing sent a speckled pattern of tracers off into the night. The pattern blanketed the area where the drone had flown out of sight. Two seconds later, the sky lit up with an explosion. In another second the intercom erupted with exclamations of dismay.

"Shit-fire, Colonel!"

"And they call me a hot dog!" Bachman exclaimed.

Barger took the controls and flew the Osprey off the

weapons course. "Nice job, boss. I think we got us a crew here."

For the first time since he'd been in the battalion, Miles felt as if he belonged.

Major General Steve Little had assented to Brigadier General Wilkerson's desire to oversee the attacks on the tank columns in Afghanistan, but he warned him that the brigade commander deserved to conduct the battle and not be treated like an incompetent. Wilkerson acknowledged this order begrudgingly.

For himself, Little decided to follow the older model gunships and scout helicopters to Zahedan and study the dicey situation there. Unlike Wilkerson, who dropped down to talk on subordinate radio nets, he kept abreast of both fronts on the division command net as his brigades reported their progress.

At Zahedan, he was appalled by the situation. A lot of finesse was needed fighting here, where friendly soldiers were intermingled with the enemy. He was glad he had come instead of sending his ADC. Wilkerson's steamroller tactics didn't lend themselves to this delicate situation, where American soldiers could get shot up by American helicopters—especially when those helicopters belonged to his division.

Wilkerson obeyed Little's directive for all of ten minutes. By the time he had arrived at the lake bed to observe the battlefield, he decided the attack against the Soviets wasn't being pressed aggressively enough.

The brigade commander resisted Wilkerson's attempt to take over the battle. "General, if you want to do us some good, check out the resources to up FARRPS. We're going to be into the fight of our lives here and we could use a little help on the logistic side."

Wilkerson balked at that. He wasn't having anything to do with logistics, let alone checking out Forward Aviation Refueling and Rearming Points. That was for Rita Bernadino and people like her.

"I'll give the orders, Colonel," he retorted. "Get

that group on the right to swing over to the river and head north. Maybe you can get behind the bastards and start rolling them up from the rear.''

"We've lost the element of surprise here, General. Now we're getting into a fight. We're going to move and shoot. We could do a hell of a lot better if you just keep your nose out of it.''

"Don't you get insubordinate with me, mister. You might find yourself out of a job . . .''

"I *am* out of a job if I let you take over this brigade.''

Anyone less aggressive than Wilkerson would have been overjoyed with his commander, for the initial attack of the front line attack helicopters had rained destruction on the Soviet tanks. Each Apache was armed with the four Hellfire anti-tank missiles, seventy-two high-explosive rockets, and a 20-millimeter cannon in the nose turret. The attack was launched when each gunship loosed a Hellfire—that scouts could control by designating tanks with their own on-board lasers. Then the Apaches fired a second Hellfire and designated these missiles with their own laser sights. In that way, the firepower of the helicopters was doubled. Nearly two hundred helicopter missiles were on the way toward Soviet tanks in the first three minutes of the battle.

Abramov ordered his helicopter down so he could watch the first of his tanks rumble through the tiny border town and continue into Iran. He had already heard reports that Mashhad had surrendered to his divisions there after only the lightest resistance. This news cheered him only slightly. That trivial campaign had diverted not only five divisions but two airmobile brigades and virtually all his helicopter gunships.

Now he was driving full throttle toward Zahedan to relieve his troops there, but his tanks were running naked into the American helicopters.

Nothing seemed to be going Abramov's way. The air battle over Afghanistan was a standoff, and even at that, some of the American fighters had broken through the air cover and loosed bombs against his tanks. Fortunately, this area of Afghanistan was one giant, dried-up lake bed, so no matter how much the Americans destroyed the roads, his tanks could always bypass the destruction. Now he had ordered his commanders to begin dispersing their vehicles at even greater intervals, insisting at least one hundred meters be maintained between tanks and personnel carriers and artillery pieces. That way, the strikes from the air could be minimized.

Just then, he heard a crackle of radios and the jumble of voices. He couldn't distinguish the words, but he knew the tone, high-pitched and excited. He felt a burst of his own adrenaline. Somebody had made contact with the Americans. The battle was on. Even before his radio operators could summon him, he strode to the receivers. The first reports were of attack helicopters—the Americans called them Apaches and Black Eagles—hitting his column. Abramov's first reaction came as a momentary stab of fear for Mendenyev, whom he'd directed into the middle of the tank column for the day. Then a more important concern absorbed his attention: he had no way of fighting back effectively against helicopter attacks. "Damn those idiots in Moscow," he barked. The radio operator offered him a radio mike. He took it, but did not speak into it. Instead he listened, his eyes squinted as he began to visualize the picture of battle from the content and tone of the reports. The picture forming in his mind's eye discouraged him.

The Soviet alarm went up at about the same time as the first missile exploded on target.

For Mendenyev, the attack helicopters materialized out of the desert like dozens of mirages.

Rising up out of a depression in the lake bed and hovering in the southeast on a wide front, the scouts and first wave of attack helicopters hit the column in three places at once. Then the follow-on attack helicopters hit at three different places. In moments, virtually the whole column stalled at the same time, although they were strung out on the open desert. Everybody seemed mesmerized, even when the first wave of anti-tank missiles began striking, exploding, and burning.

Mendenyev, riding a BRDM reconnaissance-and-command car, had seen this picture before. He'd seen it in the combat footage from Iraq during Desert Storm. The Iraqis had done the unthinkable, leaving themselves broadside and bunched up so the Americans could kill them. Now the same was about to happen to the best of the Soviet fighting machine. Goddammit! His own people were no better than the half-wit Iraqis under Saddam. He shouted at the commanding officer, "Have them face the helicopters and fire." The stunned officer just watched the flight of missiles snaking across the desert. "Driver, move!" Mendenyev yelled, as he saw an anti-tank missile homing to the car broadside.

The driver floored it, and the missile struck a hundred meters beyond. Just as Mendenyev thought he might have to take command, the officer suddenly awakened and began maneuvering his other vehicles. Finally, the remaining vehicles in the killing zone responded with return machinegun and cannon fire.

Mendenyev watched one tank after another erupt in flames. He'd been told of double plates of reactive armor that would defeat any American missile, even a strike on the turret top. Yes, even after the Iraqi debacle, there was nothing to fear. The Iraqis had the early generations of equipment and inferior fighters. Soviets would never suffer the same indignities, the shameful disaster. Evidently, the Americans hadn't been persuaded by the same propaganda.

Mendenyev used a portable tactical radio to tune in on battle reports. In the first onslaught, forty-six Soviet tanks were destroyed. Another twenty-three were disabled, about half of those burning. Dozens more had been unaccounted for, either because the crews had abandoned them in panic or they were too frightened to report over the radios. Bastards! They were no better than cowards.

The first reaction of the Soviet tankers was to disperse and turn off the road, which meant that about half of them had turned their tails toward the attack helicopters rather than pointing their frontal armor and guns as they should have. In another minute, a couple hundred more missiles were on the way.

This time, the results were nearly as devastating, although the Soviet tanks had opportunity to turn a smaller profile.

Frontal armor on the T80 and T88 model tanks included reactive plates. On impact from any sort of round, whether it was a high explosive anti-tank weapon—one that directed a charge, focusing it into a small point, liquefying tank armor and punching a fiery hole into the vehicle—or inertia rounds, dense metallic bullets that punched into armored metal, the armored plating exploded and misdirected the projectiles, making it more difficult for them to penetrate.

The first Hellfires had been directed into the hulls around the suspension and the engine compartments of the tanks, since the sides of the hull were relatively thin. So those tanks that faced the helicopters and began firing immediately were the ones with the greatest opportunity for survival. All the same, they could not direct their tank rounds once they fired, and the Apaches and Black Eagles shifted continually and erratically even as they continued to laser-designate the Soviet targets. So the tank fire had little effect on the helicopters.

Those tanks that had turned their grills toward the attacking American force also had turned the rear of the turrets the wrong way. The second wave of Hellfire took out nearly sixty of those tanks, making more than one hundred twenty tanks out of commission in the first ten minutes of battle. A like number of mechanized vehicles, many filled with soldiers, had also suffered destruction from the missiles.

Mendenyev broke in on the command frequency and gave Abramov word of the disaster. Abramov in turn commanded his infantry troops to be dismounted so the vehicles, even if they were destroyed, would not burn with his soldiers inside. Then he ordered the commanders to continue moving and to fire while on the run. Dismounted soldiers were to lie down and shoot their rifles in the directions of American helicopters. Abramov decided that if he was able to raise enough dust and provide difficult enough targets, he might be able to get some help from the Soviet air forces.

P.B. Keyes's troop of Apaches, preceded by Black Eagle scouts, was the last of the American helicopters departing the battle sites to refuel and rearm. Flying his own Black Eagle, Keyes reported that the Russians had fanned out two motorized infantry divisions in a defensive perimeter to cover their remaining tanks, which now raced toward Zahedan.

"We can't return to FARRPs along the same route," he told his gunships along the way. "Detour to the north and swing around on the left flank of the Ivans."

When his platoon leaders had rogered, he directed platoon scouts, "Fly ahead to look for SAM radar vans and ZSU-23s and ZSU-30s. Since there was no Hiney threat from the air, we'd better keep our eyes on the ground."

Keyes had been puzzled by the lack of Hind gunships but more worried about the threat from the deadly track-mounted 23-millimeter and 30-millimeter anti-aircraft guns, mounted on tracked platforms and directed by radar.

Keyes caught the first battery of SAMs unprepared. A dozen men were scrambling to get to their vans and gun stations when he came up over the rise.

"Fire!" was all he had time to yell, as he began sweeping the site with cannon fire. Before he'd even heard the first yelping of his radar detection alarm, three of the SA-6 missiles were exploding on their launchers.

Keyes dropped his Black Eagle into a depression and observed the site through a periscope. "Keep moving," he ordered his Apaches. By strafing the

SAM site with cannons, the Black Eagles alone destroyed four air-defense positions. The Apaches passed by unimpeded, and were able to replenish fuel and ammunition for the anti-tank battle.

Meanwhile, Keyes deployed his scouts in pairs as SAM killers. By designating targets with their lasers and calling for fire from the Hellfires, they rained destruction on the positions without drawing fire from more than three missiles.

"No friendly losses," Keyes reported ebulliently. He estimated that half of all air defenses deployed to Afghanistan had been wiped out. "Ivan tried to concentrate his ZSU-23s and ZSU-30s with the SAMs. They're close enough to share radar and protect each other from the air force, but they're sitting ducks for helicopters."

Why had Ivan done that? Keyes wondered. The ZSUs could have been set up to operate automatically with their own radars. They had not. They must have expected help from the Hinds. Or at least they expected their own helicopters to be flying around—that would be a reason to keep the guns off automatic acquisition and firing mode. They hadn't gotten that, either. Where were the Hinds? Because they weren't around, most of the ZSUs sat melting in their own fires. Rather than being overjoyed, though, Keyes kept worrying about those Hinds.

Abramov's forces near Robat had been rendered virtually defenseless against aerial attack. The second wave of American attackers swooped down from the northeast on the motorized rifle divisions digging in east of Robat. The lighter armor skins of the BRDMs and BMPs were riddled with 20-millimeter cannon fire interspersed with armor-piercing rounds and high explosives. Each attack helicopter's fire power was equivalent to about three and a half Soviet tanks, and the mobility on this part of the battlefield was unmatched by anything that the Soviets had. In the second hour of battle, the Soviets did manage to break loose a flight of MIG-25s, but they were unable to acquire the helicopters flitting around on the ground, and their gunfire did as much damage to the Soviet positions as anything else. In the exchange of fire with the MiGs, only one American helicopter, a scout, was downed in that attack. In all, only six American helicopters had been lost.

Bernadino was amazed at how fast the shuttling aircraft were consuming ammunition and jet fuel. It had become almost a race between combat aircraft consumption and the Blackhawk helicopters and heavy-lift helicopters bringing forward fuel and ammunition. Crews would hardly break up the supplies for distribution to individual aircraft before the helicopters returned to gobble it up. She only wished that she could see its effect on the enemy.

Another issue bothered her as well. She ordered the logistics officer to establish three new resupply sites twenty miles closer to Iran directly west of the present position. "And disperse them," she ordered.

The man looked incredulous. Three new sites?

"The Soviets won't find it hard to identify this spot," she said, "what with every helicopter in the U.S. Army pinpointing their resupply site. "I want an alternate set up so we won't have to deal with the surprises the Soviets will be tossing this way at night."

She gave orders for contingents of men to position three dummy refueling and rearming points. "Set them up within five miles of here. Burn some fuel to leave a definite thermal signature for the Soviets to find."

After surveying Zahedan, General Little knew that not much could be done at the airfield today. The Americans and the Soviets were so intermingled there that helicopters were useless. An idea was forming in his head, but he knew it wouldn't work except at night. That's why the report of the advancing Soviet tanks filled him with uneasiness. He had to do something to forestall the Soviet tanks from arriving there before dark.

Little ordered the second brigade commander, with

his aged Cobra fleet and his modified OH-58s, to move some forces into blocking positions toward the northeast. If any Soviet tanks got through from that direction, he wanted them stopped in their tracks. They didn't have far to go. Soon they spotted the Soviet Union's depleted invading forces, the total of which now amounted to a reinforced tank battalion climbing the gentle slopes to the plateau on which Zahedan was situated.

As with the first brigade earlier, this was hardly a battle. The Kiowa Scouts took on the Soviets head-on with machinegun fire and some rocket fire. One company of attack helicopters loosed a dozen Hellfire and TOW missiles at the lead tanks in the column. The explosions on the reactive armor of the Soviet tanks didn't knock them all out, but it certainly stunned the surviving crews for a while and stopped the tanks in their tracks. As the Soviets began maneuvering and firing, the remainder of the attacking battalion closed in from the southern flank. The Soviets were strung out along the ascending road with little maneuver room. In fact, as some of the tanks drove off the road, their cant of the earth offered their turret tops and engine decks to the missiles. The Cobras loosed their wire-guided TOWs and continued to guide them as they traveled toward their destination. Those equipped with Hellfire missiles generally designated their own targets with on-board laser equipment. In short order, the Soviet tank battalion was literally stopped in its tracks, leaving the road blocked with wreckage. Before any other units could advance along this way, it would have to be cleared.

Naturally, the pilots of the second brigade were elated because they had met the enemy and had stopped them. Their victory was not nearly as dramatic as that carried out by the first brigade in their more modern aircraft, but both brigades had bloodied their enemies decisively. Commanders from both brigades felt they were actually ending the invasion of Iran in these two skirmishes, one minor and one major. Most important of all, Soviet relief forces would not be attacking American paratroopers on Zahedan this day. Major General Steve Little was not so confident. Like P.B. Keyes, he kept asking himself, Where are those goddamn Soviet attack helicopters?

# 12

Abramov shouted into the radio, "Where are those goddamn helicopters?"

His aviation officer reported that they had departed from Shindand within the past hour, and should be arriving on station within another hour, he promised.

"In another hour it'll be dark, damn you!" Abramov shouted, throwing down his radio transmitter. What was the point? The idiots weren't going to have an effect on this day's battle no matter what. Even if they got here when there was a little light left, he wouldn't dare send them out against American helicopters without an orientation to the terrain. Already, he'd lost too many tanks and too much equipment. His men had shed too much blood. Tomorrow, he promised himself, tomorrow he would make the Americans pay for his superiors' incompetence.

An hour after twilight, the sky had darkened to deep purple. General Little ordered his people to put the plan into effect to take that airfield. What he was proposing was going to work—it *had* to work. Otherwise, those infantrymen down there were going to be finished by tomorrow.

First, he sent a company of attack helicopters and scouts off to the south. Then he talked over secure voice radio to the officer in command of the Americans on the airfield.

The word was passed down the line quickly.

Lieutenant Edwards passed on the scheme from

higher, and started digging with his bayonet. He encouraged his skeptical men. "We have to dig a complete circle of divots around us."

"Every other platoon is doing the same, right?"

"Right, Beach."

"There's going to be a million perimeters on the airfield."

Edwards huffed, "Not a million. But a lot."

"L.T., I don't like this."

Quintana butted in. "You heard the L.T. Dig each hole the size of a steel pot. Get a can of Sterno or fuel pellets. If you don't have those, I've got some C-4."

Quintana, who had collected a pile of thumb-sized pinches of the plastic explosives, began to distribute the white chunks to his men, crawling around the perimeter to inspect preparations. "Put another hole here," he ordered. "Make it two—no more than ten feet apart."

They didn't have long to wait. In a half hour, a company of attack helicopters reported its birds were in position, and General Little gave the command. The helicopters flew toward the airfield, climbing at a thousand feet a minute in order to end up at the edge of the airfield some two thousand feet in the air. When they reached that altitude, they were instructed to look down on the airfield using infrared sighting systems and to arm their anti-tank missiles. It was to be a high-angle, precision operation.

Soon Edwards heard the slapping sound of rotor blades and, as the helicopters rose, the noise grew louder and louder. This was modern warfare. He remembered the video-gamelike pictures out of Iraq, the "smart" bombs flying down the airshafts of buildings. Shouldn't they be getting even smarter? Surely they didn't really intend to pull this stunt from their asses. In the distance, he heard the sound of approaching helicopters and shuddered.

"Get your butts down, men," he said. "Get your butts down and pray."

* * *

From two thousand feet, the attack helicopter pilots and their gunners looked down toward the dark airfield through thermal sights. As they watched, five hundred lighters and matches were lit simultaneously by the American infantry in a spectacular, low-light ceremony. Each of the helicopters went through the arming sequence. The airfield grew brighter with an eerie green daylight as hundreds of men lying on their bellies became visible.

On the ground, the American paratroopers put their matches and lighters into helmet-size divots they had dug. In each of the potholes were either chunks of C-4 explosive, a can of Sterno, or a tab of chemical fluid. At ground level, the blue light of the cooking fuels and even the orange light from the burning explosive compound were invisible. They gave a distinctive thermal image to the gunners above. There were enough divots around each position to clearly describe a circle. The helicopters above had been instructed to fire into groups of soldiers not protected by the lighted circles.

Captain Elliott, the scout platoon leader, directed the gunships. It gave him no particular thrill to know that he would be directing fire at helpless men who had landed in an untenable fighting position mixed up with the American soldiers. This wasn't a battle, it was a slaughter. He gave the command anyway: "Guns roll!"

In answer, six attack helicopters peeled off and fired. Then each fired a second missile and began pulling out, remaining in the firing run for only moments. By then, a second wave of six had begun to roll and a third had begun unwinding from a holding orbit farther away from the airfield.

After the first wave peeled off and began climbing away from the airfield, a barrage of rifle fire answered from below, and there were a few hits. Cobra helicopters had been given additional armor protection in the years since Vietnam—around the engine compartment and on the sides of the fuselage next to the crewmen were thin sheets of armor against small arms—but there were plenty of other vulnerable places. Two of the first wave of helicopters reported hits. Even so, they were able to fly off the airfield and land outside the range of Soviet fire.

When the second wave of helicopters rolled in, the Soviet troops still had not realized that the firing was not indiscriminate, but pinpoint fire. The second wave of attack helicopters was able to punch off another dozen anti-tank missiles and nearly every one was a bull's-eye inside a collection of Soviet troops.

As the third wave of helicopters began rolling, though, the Soviets began to panic. Groups of men scattered from their defensive positions.

The American airborne troops were ready for an instantaneous response. Elliott shouted over his FM radio when the first Soviets bolted, and before the third wave of helicopters had even fired their missiles, the infantrymen rose up high enough to begin shooting across the airfield.

The third wave of helicopters dove into steep attack angles, fired, and pulled out. In all, thirty positions of Soviet soldiers had been struck by the anti-tank missiles. Blast and percussion and shrapnel devastated the positions. There were also brave Soviet soldiers who no longer bothered ducking their heads. These got to their knees and began firing their SA-7 shoulder-fired missiles after the third wave of helicopters. The missiles took off in a shower of sparks and a plume of smoke trailing up in the sky, seeking the hot exhaust ovals that were the most vulnerable point on the Cobras. In the third wave, three Cobras disintegrated in the air.

Elliott screamed over the radio for the infantry to open fire on Grail gunners. The resultant surge in small-arms fire from American soldiers firing over the edge of their short revetments brought down a half dozen of these gunners and picked off more and more as each successive chopper wave rolled in. By the time a tenth wave had expended the last of their anti-tank missiles on the Soviet positions, the Red Army was badly depleted. White flags began waving at the end of rifle barrels. The battle for Zahedan had been shoved from its stalemate toward a conclusion.

Lieutenant Edwards had found that he could really call himself a platoon leader again. Nearly eighty percent of his soldiers had been regrouped under his command. The leadership problem had not improved, though. An inordinate number of noncoms had been killed in the first hours after landing. So Edwards redistributed what little seniority he had. He gave Corporal Umbreit the third squad. Kluth had the first, and Quintana agreed to help the most senior specialist fourth class get his feet on the ground in the second. Edwards decided to position himself with the weapons squad, making his radio operator, Beach, the squad leader.

Bad as his situation was with the loss of noncoms, other platoon leaders had lost more than half of all their men. Still, in all, the first brigade of the division had suffered only fifteen-percent casualties. Considering the closeness of the quarters and the ferocity of the fighting the day before, it was a remarkably low number.

On the flip side, the helicopters firing from altitude had brought Soviet losses of killed or wounded to more than sixty percent of the Soviet soldiers. Most of the remainder were now under guard in a concertina-wire enclosure on the side of one of the hangars. Their weapons had been stacked up into piles. Work details had been allotted to the digging of mass graves before any further decomposition took place.

Already, the second airborne assault had been called off. Instead, the planes were ordered to land on the airfield rather than scattering soldiers to the winds. By midday, elements of the 7th Infantry Division would be landed. By the end of the day tomorrow, all of the 7th would be on the ground plus the majority of the 82nd Airborne. Edwards was beginning to feel pretty confident about this first combat assignment of his. It had been bleak all right in the previous twenty-four hours. Now it looked like they would have things under control.

He couldn't have been more wrong. General Little received news from a scout two hundred miles north of the airfield: convoys of Soviet attack helicopters had been spotted flying toward Zahedan. Immediately, Little felt ill. The Soviets were within hours of engagement. He needed every minute of time to marshal his forces for a credible defense.

He directed his Cobra attack helicopters to take over the bulk of the fighting in the sands due east of Zahedan, where three divisions of Soviets were still tied down. The Apache gunships and Black Eagle scouts he ordered back for refueling and rearming. Their mission would be dedicated to air-to-air gun fighting against the Soviet Hinds.

This cheered Wilkerson a great deal. He had always been an ambitious "fast riser" who wanted to command a division of his own—indeed, this very division, and a victory over the Soviets would go a long way toward ensuring that. For Little was himself a fast riser who would be due to assume higher command at corps level before very long. When that happened, Wilkerson fully intended to take command of the ACCD. A good combat record as the assistant division commander for maneuver would almost guarantee his succession. Thus, he was buoyant as he briefed Little on the contact during the night.

Little, though, shared none of his excitement, for, according to reports from his other general, Bernadino, nearly half of the basic combat load of ammunition had been expended. She told him that resupply later today would bring the division's basic load of anti-tank Hellfire missiles and TOWs back up to eighty percent and that within three days they could be at one hundred percent, but only if they expended nothing more until then.

"Fat chance of that," Little muttered. An updated report told him that fifty miles to the north were the lead elements of another six Soviet motorized rifle divisions.

"It might take the remainder of our basic load just to deal with the three divisions coming from the north-west," Bernadino continued. "I don't know what we're going to do when those other six divisions get here. Don't even mention Soviet helicopters."

A glum intelligence officer interrupted the meeting to hand Little a message. Little, already solemn, turned grim.

"Another eleven or twelve divisions have been reported by a lone scout up north. They're within two hundred miles right now, two to three days' travel at most. To counter, the RDF commander has two divisions on the ground and he's preparing to airlift in two more. Ladies and gentlemen, have you got any ideas for this division to recommend to the joint task force commander?"

"Tell him he'd better get his butt in gear and get more combat troops," Wilkerson advised brashly, still brimming with the successes enjoyed over the Soviet tanks in the past twenty-four hours of fighting.

"And how do you suppose he'll react to such an ultimatum?"

Wilkerson sobered up.

Little spoke in grave, measured tones. "I'm going to suggest to the RDF commander we forget trying to defend Zahedan and lift those troops into the mountains. There's no way those forces can hold the airfield against that many divisions. But we might be able to prevent the Soviets from staging out of Zahedan if we're able to maintain a threat in the mountains. Up there, their mechanized and motorized advantage is going to be diminished. In effect, we'll become something like the mountain fighters in Afghanistan."

"I don't know," said Wilkerson. "Our troops are not mountain fighters, they're infantrymen. Let them take a stand at Zahedan and hold out there until they're able to be reinforced. If we project out the ratio of kills that we had against the Soviets in the last day or so, they don't have enough tanks in the entire country to last against the kind of damage we're inflicting. If we keep this up, they're going to quit."

"We don't have the damned ammunition to sustain a static defense against tanks!" said Bernadino. "We haven't even met their full surface-to-air missile capability. We were lucky on the first day. We were able to hit them first. It's still a standoff between our air force and theirs."

"What's more," Little added, "we haven't seen the first Soviet attack helicopter. If our intelligence is right, we're going to have one hell of a lot of trouble in a helicopter fight, that and protecting two infantry divisions."

Bernadino said, "We should lift out the troops and destroy the airfield. We could ask the Air Force to crater it and deny its use to the Soviets. Even a standoff could be considered a victory for us."

"Bullshit!" Wilkerson said, barely disguising his disgust at this . . . this *woman*. "I don't want a standoff. I want a victory. We can beat these Soviets. We can teach the bastards a lesson once and for all about their running around this part of the world invading countries and taking what they want."

Bernadino continued as if he hadn't spoken.

"Once we get those troops into the mountains, they'll have a better than even chance against armor. If those tanks get up here on this plain, it won't matter how well dug in our troops are. We cannot afford to sacrifice two or more infantry divisions here. We sure as hell aren't going to be able to sustain an airlift to resupply them even if they were to hold the Soviets to a stalemate. Plus, there's no question in my mind that only a small force is going to attempt to hold this airfield, anyhow. They're not sending fifteen or sixteen divisions down here merely to secure an airfield. A small force is going to hold it and prepare it to receive strike and resupply aircraft while the remainder of those tanks are going to head straight south toward the Gulf."

"It could buy us some time. Until we get tanks landed from Saudi Arabia." Little brightened the most he had the entire morning. "Yes," he said. "And if we drove them toward the interior of Iran, the damned

Iranians might be able to make some kind of contribution to this effort.''

"Does that mean then, that I have your approval to begin shifting the major effort from resupply of the attack helicopters to evacuation of troops on the airfield?''

Little nodded. "Yes. Do it.''

Wilkerson, seeing the discussion going against him, opened his mouth to protest but then clamped shut on it. He wasn't going to out-argue the two of them. The best he could do was get back out there and direct the choppers he had left.

By mid-morning, the first reports of helicopter sightings reached Wilkerson's battle command center, and he immediately sent out attack helicopters to meet up with the scouts who had reported the sightings. Within an hour, he was beginning to hear of imminent engagements. He told himself he didn't dare leave such an important battle in the hands of people less tactically proficient.

P.B. Keyes had hidden his Black Eagle in a ravine with another pair of scouts when the first Soviet formation of Hind-D gunships, flying a narrow formation of three abreast, poured over the ridgeline. At five-hundred-foot intervals, following waves of three appeared. At first Keyes reported his intention to call his gunships forward to engage the exposed column when a break presented itself, but soon it became apparent there would be no break. "Twenty-four Hinds and counting,'' he reported back to his platoon leaders, "stand by.''

"Stand by for what?'' asked a stranger. Keyes thought he recognized the voice from his distant past, but knew it did not belong on his radio net.

"Unknown station on Buckskin's frequency, this is Buckskin Six, get off my net.''

"This is Ace Five, I say again, stand by for what?''

Ace Five? The assistant division commander? What the hell was he doing on a troop commander's frequency? Keyes pushed his mike button, but was too astonished to transmit. Wilkerson didn't give him much time, anyway. The ADC overrode Keyes's wordless transmission and repeated his demand to know why the troop was standing by.

"Ace Five, this is Buckskin Six, I'm going to have the gunships move to perhaps intercept the column farther down the line. My scouts and I will displace farther north to find the tail end of this formation—to see how big it is before we attack it."

"Why not engage the Soviets now, hit them and run? Kill as many of the bastards in place as you can and, if you're outnumbered, fall back."

"This is Buckskin Six," Keyes responded. "Don't you want to scout the total numbers before we commit?"

"Buckskin, you heard what I want. Now let me tell you what I don't want—I don't want them to threaten the evacuation of Zahedan. Now start firing, mister, so we can buy some time for our troops on the ground. I've got a whole battalion waiting to back you up. You can retreat through their lines, and they'll get the Soviets off your ass. Behind them is a whole fucking brigade of Cobras. I'm behind you, son. You just open up and get this battle started."

"Buckskin Six, Wilco."

Keyes reluctantly gave a firing command to his platoon leaders. By now, more than fifty Hinds had crossed into the valley, and the lead Soviet craft had begun dipping over the next ridgeline. What's more, there seemed to be no letup in the flow of helicopters. Keyes looked out over the advancing lines. Indeed, it looked frightening as hell. Of course, none of this would have been so bad if he had been briefed to expect such numbers in the morning attack order. Obviously, Wilkerson had made some changes. Obviously, a general would have more updated information. Otherwise, there would be no other explanation for his directing troop operations.

The trio of sleek Black Eagles dispersed laterally, and thirteen Apaches, bristling with armament, hov-

ered up on line—two platoons of guns and the three
armed scouts. He called on the third platoon, dispersed with the rest of his scouts on a reconnaissance
to the west. He ordered them to come up and collect
in the rear of his attacking force. Wilkerson might have
plenty of forces behind him, but Keyes wanted to establish a little depth of his own by putting a line of
birds in reserve. He'd barely given the orders when he
heard the scratchy voice of the one-star countermand-
ing him.

"Negative," Wilkerson said. "Order the third platoon forward to bring the max firepower to bear,
Buckskin."

"This is Buckskin Six, I need somebody to cover
my tail. When they start coming after us, we need the
ability to leapfrog."

"Negative. Bring max firepower and they won't be
able to come after you right away. I already told you
I've got somebody covering your tail already."

Keyes opened his transmitter to protest, but Wilkerson again used his command override to drown him
out. "Start firing, mister."

Keyes bellowed angrily at his platoon leaders to engage.

The Apaches, spread out over a relatively narrow
two hundred meter front, hovered clear of their cover
at once, cutting loose at the Soviets with twenty-
millimeter cannon fire. Keyes himself fired with a vengeance, hoping by some miracle that Wilkerson's
Blackhawk might inadvertently fly into his gunsight.
Slaving his guns to his helmet sight, he picked out a
wave of three Hinds that had lined themselves up
broadside to him. The underbelly cannon turret slewed
violently to lock on to the spot the major was looking
at. The orange lighted reticle in front of his eyes covered the tail boom of the closest Soviet craft and began
blinking. Keyes squeezed off a burst of cannon fire,
simultaneously moving his head toward the front of
the craft, aiming higher than necessary. Half a second's firing delivered three hundred rounds with

armor-piercing rounds linked four-to-one with high-explosive bullets.

"Overkill,"he muttered as a pattern of twenty-millimeter explosions splattered across the side of the Hind. It dropped like a swatted fly and streaked across the desert floor in flames. Beyond the black-orange smear, the second Soviet bird dropped twenty feet of altitude and Keyes knew his overshot rounds had hit that craft and disabled it.

The third, most distant craft had seen the geysers of impacting rounds across the valley floor, and the Soviet pilot jinked away. Keyes gave the Hind a sweeping glance coupled with his pressure on the firing trigger. A bouquet of deadly diverging tracers took off in a pattern that covered the turning radius of the third helicopter as well as the damaged second one. Both exploded in the air, nearly at once.

Keyes hovered down into the cover of the gully and shifted fifty feet to acquire a new set of targets.

Seconds later, when he ascended, he saw the effect of his ambush on the Soviet formation had been both dramatic and instantaneous. The echelon of the advance broke up into scattered segments of individuals and pairs of enemy craft vacating the killing zone in panic.

Wilkerson, standing off at a distance, had seen it, too.

"We've stopped the bastards!" he shouted into the radios of his own Blackhawk airborne command center as the valley floor became dotted with burning helicopters of the enemy. The remainder had scattered to find cover. "I told you, Buckskin. I told you."

Keyes did not reply. In the first place, the humiliation of getting chewed out over the radio had not worn off. Secondly, he might have had to admit that Wilkerson was right—an asshole he might be, but he obviously knew what he was doing. He'd have to remember to pass this story along to Miles. Miles. He gave him a precious moment's thought and wished his buddy were here. Then he purged his mind of distractions and became engrossed in the excitement of the engagement.

The initial euphoria wore off within minutes with further reports of more and more Soviet helicopters. These began to maneuver, rather than to engage the Black Eagles and Apaches. Half drifted in a wide arc to the south, trying to encircle the American position. Those Hinds that had cleared the valley now returned to pin the Americans down.

At a distance of three miles or so, Keyes reported seeing yet another aerial river of Soviet helicopters bypassing this battlefield. He concluded that the Soviets most assuredly were enroute to relieve the tank column now under attack by Cobras and Kiowas.

Keyes barked the commands to get his helicopters disengaged from this contact. He hadn't heard a single report of one of his own taking fire, let alone getting shot down. However, he knew that couldn't last long with the superior numbers advancing.

Wilkerson had heard Keyes' order to withdraw. "Buckskin, can you hold for another ten minutes?" he asked over the major's command frequency.

"Hell no," came Keyes's reply. "I can't let them encircle us . . . goddammit, we barely have time to get clear as it is. We're out of here, Ace Five. Out."

Suddenly Wilkerson realized he had created a multitude of problems. It might be difficult for Keyes' troop to escape the open terrain if follow-on Hinds maneuvered to flank the gully. He ordered the promised backup battalion of attack helicopters and their scouts to pull out of reserve and meet the continuous wave of Soviets. Even as he gave the command, he knew it was a calculated risk. Those reserves had been positioned to support the defense of the airfield evacuation. Their secondary mission was to provide cover to the airlift of the defending airborne soldiers. He knew he'd put the battle against Soviet tanks in jeopardy, but now he was faced with losing unacceptable numbers of helicopters to the Hinds, too. Wilkerson hoped his calculated risk would pay off.

Within a half hour, the brigade commander had

heard from the commander of the reserve battalion Wilkerson had committed. "They've been pinned down also, Ace Five. What do you want us to do next?" he asked, his voice tinged in sarcasm, for there were too few alternatives left, and everybody, down to the most forward pilot, knew it.

Wilkerson chewed on his lip before he answered—with another question. "That depends on how many more Soviets are coming down the corridor."

He had his answer within the next ten minutes. Reports poured in, telling of similar formations of Soviet helicopters flying south. As the intelligence officer furiously posted the tactical map screen Wilkerson used in running his battle, it appeared there could be as many as two or three hundred attack helicopters moving in to do battle.

Wilkerson knew that such massive numbers meant his forces were in grave danger of being swamped in a tidal wave of fight helicopters. With the kind of numbers he was hearing, technological advantages meant nothing. As his guts began to lurch, he turned the battle back over to his brigade commanders. "Try to delay the Hinds until the airfield can be evacuated," he radioed to them. "Avoid decisive engagement, if possible."

The brigade commanders shot back at him with derisive questions: "Say what?" "How are we going to do that?" and statements: "Half my pilots report they're pinned down and already decisively engaged." "The other half are already running with the Soviets at their heels."

Wilkerson ordered the brigade radios tuned out while he called upon the Rapid Deployment Force command center asking for air support for his battle.

The response was that his battle was not the only action and that all air forces had already been committed to this theater. "First priority is a strategic strike scheduled farther west," the unemotional voice of the RDF operations officer told him.

The desperate Wilkerson exploded. "West? You've got to keep the Soviets away from Zahedan while the evacuation is underway. You've got to give us something before we lose any more helicopters. My brigade commanders are up to their asses in Hinds.''

Wilkerson recognized the call sign of the RDF commander himself, General Pickett. ''I understand your predicament, but there's nothing I can do right now, Ace Five. The air battle has shifted to the northern end of the Gulf. We have to take out the Davriaresh Dam. If we pull off our strikes against our target there, we'll have more chance of staving off the Soviets at Bandar Abbas than if we keep Zahedan. The Ospreys will be here by tomorrow and—''

''Tomorrow will be too late, goddammit,'' Wilkerson retorted, overriding the RDF commander's transmission, his mind swirling with the general's explanation. What the hell good were bashed dams going to do with all these Soviet gunships gunning down their backs? ''I need air support, and I need it now. I can't believe you're hitting fucking dams while—''

''General Wilkerson,'' said Pickett, overriding back, ''I don't have time to lecture you on the use of strategic air forces. You'll get any help I can give you, the rest is up to you.'' Then he broke contact.

Wilkerson had become desperate. His next command was to the brigade commander west of Zahedan. There, the older generations of helicopters, Cobras and Kiowa Scouts, were deeply engaged against armored forces. The superior mobility of these Soviet helicopters would soon tilt that battle's outcome the wrong way. Wilkerson ordered the brigade to release half the attack forces harassing Soviet tanks so they could be deployed in a last-ditch delaying line to slow the Soviet helicopter onslaught. About all he had left to hope for was the coming of night, which would give his commanders time to regroup.

Lieutenant Thomas Edwards was glad to be leaving the airfield proper, but the evacuation wasn't exactly what he had hoped for. He had expected a little consideration. After all, he had been among those in the first group to land. In the frenzy of packing people into planes and helicopters, though, he was ordered with the rest of his company to head out the north-eastern gate of the airfield, to march down the road to the nearest defensible position to await the tanks coming from that direction. In case the Cobras and Scouts were unable to head them off, he was going to have to emplace TOW missiles and employ his Collapsible Light Anti-tank Weapons, CLAWS, to throw up some last-minute defenses to gain time for the last of the transports and Blackhawks to lift soldiers out.

Farther east, in Afghanistan, a helicopter battle barely an hour old had already begun shifting in favor of the Soviets. Relief formations of Hind gunships—those that had bypassed the Black Eagle ambush—found the slower and outgunned Cobras and Kiowas easy prey. The Soviet tactic was simply to engage the American helicopters with leading attackers. The rest continued to maneuver southward and eastward, probing constantly for the flank of the American fighting positions, broadening the line of contact. Before long, the American helicopters were going to have to retreat or be flanked, leaving open the path to Zahedan.

The helicopters had out-maneuvered tanks at speeds of more than a hundred miles an hour, now they were similarly outmaneuvered by faster Soviet helicopters.

In terms of numbers, the Soviets had a decisive advantage. Wilkerson, who continued to eavesdrop on the battlefield reports, actually interjected several times to shout at the scouts and intelligence analysts to get their numbers straight, not believing the Soviets could have so many helicopters. "You must be counting them twice!" he shouted over the radio.

But soon it became apparent that the Soviets had committed nearly as many helicopters as they had tanks in this region. Where the hell did they come from? Wilkerson wanted to know.

"It don't matter!" shouted an irate, anonymous voice over the radio. Wilkerson sputtered, but had no reply.

Finally, there was the firepower. In terms of gunning, the American helicopters were equal to the Soviets. Neither had much success at firing area weapons like rockets at each other. Neither enjoyed much success firing the guided missiles through the air. For, as fast as they were, the guided missiles could be picked up and dodged by just jinking and moving laterally quickly and changing direction. Those who were forced to guide the missiles had difficulty keeping their sights on the target. Frequently the target simply ducked behind terrain and appeared somewhere else, leaving the gunner completely disoriented. Even when the gunner could maintain his laser spot or pin his sight reticle on the helicopter—even through violent maneuvers—the missile was not capable of receiving and reacting to the commands quickly enough to strike a target that moved four or five times at varying speeds or varying altitudes within a matter of seconds.

So it came down to basic air-to-air dogfighting with cannon fire. For this, the best tactic was to maneuver under cover of a hill or gully, pop up, fire off a burst at a target, and then disappear before fire could be returned.

As Wilkerson began receiving reports of helicopters being downed farther east, he became confused. Although he had perfected the division's system for keeping in touch with far-flung corners of a battlefield, he was still subject to human limitations in comprehending that data. He ordered Cobra gunships to shift across the battlefield to meet the latest threat.

The effects of his order were twofold—and neither effect was helpful to the American effort. In the first place, the Cobras and OH-58 Kiowas were not as well armed and well equipped as the Apache helicopters. Worst of all, they were slower than the Hinds. So, once in contact with the enemy, it would be difficult to disengage without covering fire from another source.

In the second place, the removal of the gunships that were facing the nearest Soviet tank threat put Zahedan's airfield evacuation in direct jeopardy.

"Ace Five, I thought I was supposed to remain on

the eastern battlefield to guard against tank attack," the brigade commander protested.

The frantic Wilkerson overrode his transmission. "If you don't respond now, we'll lose the airfield to enemy gunships. Do you want responsibility for that?"

After a long pause, the brigade commander answered, "Negative. But are you willing to take the responsibility of protecting my Cobra fleet? We're no match for Hineys, you know."

"I'll take the responsibility. You just get airborne and relieve this situation," Wilkerson ordered.

Another pause. Then the brigade commander said, "Wilco . . . uh, Ace Five, be advised, I'm going to make a full report of this maneuver to Ace Six and get his blessing on it."

Wilkerson did not respond.

Edwards was putting his men into fighting positions as high as he could along the slopes rising up toward Zahedan. The higher he was, the less chance the Soviets could raise their tank guns to take them on. Even better, he could fire his TOW missiles and CLAWS down into the tops of tanks, where there was the least armor.

When Edwards saw the helicopters pulling off from their own fighting positions around him, he was simply glad they would no longer be attracting enemy fire. After he had been around to a handful of his platoon's fighting positions, though, it occurred to him that they were trapped in these positions without an airlift. It would hardly be easy to run up these naked hills and escape over the top. There certainly was no going down toward the enemy tanks. Then he began to wonder about those helicopters again. Where had they gone? Were they refueling? Rearming? If so, they should have been back by now. Already the commanders in the Soviet T-80s and T-88s sensed that the helicopters weren't going to be pounding on them for a while and they took advantage of the lull to begin moving uphill.

The plan had been that the infantrymen would be a

defense of last resort against the Soviets, not used except in an emergency. Once the last transport aircraft was loaded at Zahedan, flights of Blackhawk UH-60s were to come down to protected landing positions and pick them up. They might get away from this battlefield without ever firing a shot. All of a sudden, though, without Cobras, Edwards started seeing an entirely different scenario. They had been left alone to face tanks.

He heard a strained voice over the radio giving commands to fire on the Soviet tanks as soon as the signal was given. The signal would be the firing of a TOW missile. The strained voice was his own. He cleared his throat angrily and repeated the order, this time with a calm, measured voice. He didn't feel calm, though. Or measured. He felt the continuous urge to pee. A roaring of tank engines accented the feeling.

A platoon of tanks, their hatches closed, crept up the hill, moving in file with a hundred meters between vehicles. The turrets were swiveling as tank commanders tried to recon through their gunsights.

Edwards knew those gunsights were not going to be effective. If the Soviets were going to do any good, they were going to have to climb out of their turrets and start firing the 12.7-millimeter machine guns mounted atop the turrets. Once they did that, they would be vulnerable to small-arms fire. Edwards began to feel different, a stirring of excitement that could almost be described as erotic. He was going to live the dream of every infantryman. He was going to be able to take on tanks—and he was going to enjoy a decisive advantage. He was going to be able to sit above them and knock them off one at a time. His only worry was that somebody else would knock out all the tanks before his platoon got the chance.

The steepness of the slope caused the road to form an almost complete one-hundred-eighty degree loop back toward itself. He could see six tanks in a column stretching out directly below him.

He shouted for Beach, his new weapons squad leader, "Come on, Greg, when are you—"

The distinctive whoosh of a TOW missile firing cut him off. He couldn't see its impact because it had been shot against the lead tank, which had already passed beyond his line of sight around the bend. Dammit, somebody had given the signal before he could get it out. No matter. It was time.

He spoke a soft command to his two other TOW crews, and they fired almost simultaneously. The range was about four hundred meters down the barren slope. Two tanks erupted in flames, one exploding in place, the other continuing to roll forward into the slope of the hill. A fourth TOW streaked off down the hill and sent a geyser of flame from the engine deck of yet another tank.

As the Soviet column stopped and bunched up, two tanks tried to force a passage around the flaming T-80s already killed. Edwards ordered another barrage and three more missiles killed those two. So far, every vehicle that had come into view had been blown apart, and now the road was blocked with flaming wreckage.

Quintana barked at Beach to take control of designating targets for the TOW crews. "You wasted two missiles on one tank in that last volley. We don't have them to piss away, kiddo." He flashed a pained grin as if to show he wasn't all that angry.

Edwards's men were jubilant at the destruction they had wrought, but not for long. The crumping of artillery from somewhere below prompted them to start digging for cover. "Shit, L.T.," Quintana crabbed, "if the goddamned Ruskies are going to start using artillery, this is going to become a fair fight."

Edwards chewed his lip before answering. "You reconned a foot trail up and over the top, Sarge?" His question held an edge of hopefulness that divulged that he had not.

Quintana smirked. "Good grunt always has a back way out, L.T. Just like goddamned gopher." He pointed to his left. "Ain't nothing directly behind us. If we tried going straight up, our asses'll be hanging in the breeze. Instead, we move laterally thataway. The hill curves around out of direct fire. Little gully goes up. It's steep, and it'll take longer, but by the time we have to use it, we won't be minding." His face creased into a smug smile as he waited for his due.

Edwards gave it to him. "Thanks for thinking of it, Sarge. You saved my butt." Quintana shrugged modestly and, embarrassed at the heaviness of the emotion in the moment, turned to bitch at a TOW crew that had selected a firing position too exposed to suit him.

Quintana turned back to Edwards and said, "I wouldn't want to be the last one holding this little fort." He punctuated his remark with a smirk.

Edwards grimaced, as if afraid to ask why.

Quintana told him anyhow, pointing directly up the steepest part of the slope. "Things'll be so hot, the only road out is going to be straight up thataway."

Before long, the sides of the hill were pocked with artillery rounds, leaving smoking divots on the earth and raining down shrapnel from the air bursts. The Soviets had not gotten the range yet, and the artillery was having as much effect on their observers. The poor terrain was preventing them from zeroing in for a final barrage. It was enough. Edwards's men were no longer ecstatically firing TOW missiles. With no further urging from Quintana, they were digging like badgers to protect themselves.

Edwards called a huddle with his squad leaders. "I know we've already accomplished our mission. We stalled the tank convoy."

"Come on, L.T., we kicked ass," said Umbreit.

"Quiet," Quintana ordered.

"Right. This is only temporary. There will be a response soon. They'll start bracketing their fire. If the artillery keeps up, there won't be a safe way to bring in helicopters to pull our butts out."

"L.T.'s right," said Quintana. "They ain't going to let us jump up and run across this hill, either. It's just going to be a matter of time before Soviet infantry starts moving up the road. They gonna try and make us pay, boys."

The thought of going head to head with infantry sobered everybody.

"Get back to your squads," Edwards ordered. "Keep digging in."

Umbreit said, "We gonna stay and fight?"

Edwards looked to Quintana for help with the answer. The platoon sergeant returned his gaze with a bland expression. Edwards smiled just as blandly and said, "What else have we got to do today? Until somebody pulls our asses out of here, our job is to bottle up the Soviets while they evacuate the airfield. Don't worry, they won't forget us—we're too important. Now get going."

Umbreit nodded. Edwards busied himself with folding his map so nobody could read self-doubt in his face. His noncoms ran bent over back to their squads. Except for Quintana. He paused, waiting for Edwards to look up. When the lieutenant finally did meet his eyes, Quintana paid him the highest of unspoken compliments a veteran sergeant can bestow upon a green officer, a wry grin and a quick wink. "Too important, eh, L.T.?"

Edwards had no time to respond, for by now three more tanks had advanced. They began bulldozing the burning hulks of two T-80s aside. The tanks slid over the edge of the ravine and tumbled down the slope. Again, tanks began moving forward. Behind them Edwards could see the heads of infantrymen bobbing up and down. He knew that the first gun crew to fire at those infantrymen was going to be the recipient of better-directed artillery or one hell of a lot of small-arms fire, but ordered Beach's gun crews to take them on, anyway. No matter the danger to his own platoon, he couldn't let them get clear. Then he ordered the remainder of his platoon to use machine guns and rifle fire to pin down the infantrymen—about twenty or so Red Army troops huddled in a knot behind the tanks.

Edwards called back to the company commander, requesting artillery to be fired into the valley. The captain's flat radio voice answered, "Negative artillery."

Edwards suppressed a sudden burst of emotion, trying to imitate his calm commander. "Six, this is two-six bravo, we're going to need that artillery to hold our position."

The company commander's voice rasped back at him, "Negative artillery. Only helicopter pilots can shoot artillery missions. Higher is afraid of grunts calling down friendly fire on top of helicopter moving around. See if you can get one of your supporting pilots to request it."

Edwards dropped the facade of flat emotions. "What helicopters?" he shouted back. "There haven't been any helicopters in this area for forty-five minutes." He yelled at his company commander, "If you don't get some artillery fire going, the Russians are going to be swarming the hills. Sooner or later, we're going to lose a hell of a lot of men. My men, goddammit."

"Wait, out," ordered the company commander. Edwards noticed a sudden note of concern in the captain's tone.

When word of Edwards's report reached Zahedan, Major General Little was incensed. He hollered for the brigade commander to report to him about the absence of Cobras on the main approach to Zahedan. "Colonel, are those men being left to hang out to dry?"

The brigade commander was apologetic but adamant. "General, we can't be two places at once. Ace Five ordered us about an hour ago to shift our Cobras to the battlefield in Afghanistan. I thought you knew."

"I didn't, goddammit."

"If you want, I can order them to get back here."

"You're goddamned right I want them back. And nobody but you or me is going to redeploy them. Got that?" The brigade commander smugly rogered that he did indeed understand.

Little then turned to Bernadino. "Stay behind and oversee the remainder of the airlift, General."

"There's only three battalions of very nervous paratroopers left here . . . that and the security detachment overlooking the road."

"They're supposed to loaded up on Blackhawks and flown into the hills. How the hell are they going to disengage now that the gunships are gone?"

Bernadino shrugged. "The last of the transports have taken off," she said. "The word from the Air Force and Navy fighters is that they'll be able to fly cover for no more than half an hour."

"Great," he said sourly. "Did you know Bayard was ordering brigades around, deviating from my directions?"

She shook her head. "Do you think we can get those troops off the hill?"

It was his turn to wag his head. "One way or another, Wilkerson owes me some damned explanations. Yesterday the brigade commanders complained he interfered. But this . . . this . . ."

They stood rooted to their spots on earth, two professionals in a vortex of chaos, a moment nearly as turbulent as the noise of dozens of helicopter turbines, chopping rotors, shouting men and women.

She broke the tension with a wooden salute.

He flapped his hand at his head and ran for his helicopter.


In Afghanistan, the helicopter battle was nearing a climactic and terrifying decision. More and more of the Hinds had funneled down from the north. As they came, they continued to slide southward until the Americans' fluid battle lines had been stretched practically to nonexistence. They had no choice but to pull away, withdrawing south in order to prevent themselves from being forced into pockets encircled by the Soviet helicopters.

The cost during this retirement action was dear. Because the Cobras had remained in contact with enemy helicopters, they had to fight every inch of the way, practically hovering backward across the battlefield. Only when completely masked by the terrain were they able to turn and dash toward another ravine or mound to seek protection, for any time their rotors stuck up anywhere along the horizon a Soviet missile was on the way. The only way to break lock with those missiles was to drop down and keep the rotors below their line of of sight for at least ten or fifteen seconds.

The missiles had been designed to counter this tactic, maintaining a flight attitude for five full seconds after losing lock with rotor blades. If the rotor blades again reappeared even momentarily within those five seconds, lock was restored. It took the Americans the loss of about thirteen Cobras, half a dozen OH-58s, and four more Apaches to figure out that one way to defeat the missiles was to hover high, permit radar lock-on, and then drop straight down into a covered position, forcing the missile to overcorrect a downward path. It was a delicate maneuver, this tactic of offering yourself to be shot at. Flight time of the missile was so fast that several helicopters were knocked down before they were able to drop out of sight.

In fact, the reports of helicopters being lost to enemy gunfire grew so numerous Wilkerson ordered his commanders to stop forwarding battle casualties over the radio—the reports were tying up the tactical necessities of maneuver and fire. Finally, all there was left to do was for Wilkerson to order his Apaches and Black Eagles to turn tail and dash into Pakistan, running as far as they could to get away from the Soviets. This worked fine for the Black Eagles and the Apaches, but the Cobras and OH-58s were sacrificed. They didn't have the airspeed or maneuverability to keep up.

Major P.B. Keyes punched up half a dozen preset radio frequencies to listen in on the progress of the battle elsewhere. No matter where his radio stopped, he recognized fear in the flat but quavering voice transmissions of Cobra and Kiowa commanders. The Soviets had routed them in several areas of the battlefield and were now chasing them, cutting American helicopters down from the rear.

"Goddammit!" he shouted into his cockpit. "Miles, where the hell are you?" He bit his lip. Despite his bitter frustration, of course, this had nothing at all to do with Miles. He and the Ospreys were on the way, moving as fast as the ships would fly, no doubt. If they were here, though, the Osprey battalion would be intercepting the Soviet gunships, stopping the slaughter. That was the Osprey mission.

Keyes and his company of Apaches and Black Eagle scouts had been lucky. They had extracted themselves after bloodying the Soviets farther north. He had rejected Wilkerson's recommendation to linger behind. By dashing ahead of the Hinds and passing through the lines of Cobras waiting in ambush, Keyes and his pilots had led the Soviets into a second bloodbath. Without losing a single bird, he had darted away from the battlefield with a head start the Soviets could never overcome.

Trouble was, the Soviets had collected themselves after the first two bloody encounters. Now they had the slower Cobras and Kiowas fleeing before them in disorder.

Keyes and his troop circled wide to the west until he found the kind of valley he wanted, one that was a quarter-mile wide and winding on a north-south course, yet did not peter out. Then he led his scouts and gunships north, racing parallel to the line of the bulk of fleeing American pilots, but in the opposite direction. Keyes was disgusted that he did not require a map to navigate but could orient by the towers of black smoke that rose from burning U.S. helicopters. He briefed his hasty plan in the air, and in ten minutes his pilots were ready to take up their positions for a new ambush that would provide some relief for the retreating American pilots.

Keyes split off with two other Black Eagles and a platoon of gunships, wending their way east along a gully to get into the path of retreat, forming the foot of an L-shaped ambush.

A second platoon of Apaches spaced themselves out a mile on a north-south line to become the ambush trigger and the long side of the L.

Keyes ordered the third platoon to disperse into the ravine, from which they could cover the retreat of either of the other platoons—from now on, he vowed, nobody in his command would have to run before the enemy without support of friendly fire.

Just seconds after giving the command for his element to land, the first of several disorganized flocks of American helicopters raced by and closely overhead. Keyes told his people to stay put and not show themselves to the enemy. From the reports he'd heard, he knew there might be Hinds mingled with the trailing elements of the friendlies, so he gave the order for the ambush to be sprung before all the Americans were by.

The line of Apaches on the flank of Soviet advance were to hover up out of the desert folds and fire in unison, their first objective to fill the air with explosive cannon fire, throwing up a curtain of ordnance that would check the tide. Secondarily, they were permitted to pick targets for aimed fire. Thirdly, Keyes had ordered them, "Get the hell out of Dodge. Don't wait around to count kills, and don't try hovering down and popping up elsewhere like a bunch of heroes. Shoot your goddamned wad and run. Any questions?" There had been none.

Now he waited as the concentration of enemy helicopters built up. When he suspected the the bulk of the Soviets had flown into the killing zone, Keyes commanded, "Now, goddammit, now!" springing his private counterattack.

Up through the wavy mirage of rising heat rose the string of Apaches, firing across the formations of Hinds. The Soviets' attention had been directed forward, their pilots mesmerized in the bloodlust of easy kills as they ran down the slower American craft. Suddenly, after knocking down one helpless enemy after another, their own helicopters had begun disintegrating in the air, tumbling to the earth in flames.

The first volley of cannon fire showered a formation back in the pack of Hinds, knocking down seven of them. The lead Soviets were not aware of the killing behind them at first, so they charged on, but those pilots strung out behind the killing zone reacted violently. They hauled back on their controls, bunching up, endangering following craft. Then, seeing the tracers flying across the front, they turned on the American ambush.

Keyes's trigger platoon used the next five seconds of Soviet confusion to advantage. Half the gunships directed aimed fire toward the front of the Soviet pack and the other half let loose into the Hinds bunching up behind. Half a dozen Soviet craft went down in flames. A similar number of pilots had to land their disabled craft. By the time a hail of answering fire had been directed at them, the Americans had dropped out of sight and begun their retreat.

Keyes heard the report he was listening for, "We're outta here, Buckskin Six, and they're hot on our ass. There must be a fucking million of 'em!"

Keyes grimaced, half in distaste for the worthlessness of the numerical report, half at the fear he was feeling for the safety of his pilots. His expression turned to a smile at the next fragment of news: "Nobody in our flock even got a scratch—not a damned one of us."

"Roger, good work," he replied, then gave the order for the second part of his strategy. His own group of armed helicopters, Apaches and Black Eagles alike, popped up to face the Soviet advance, which he hoped had turned its attention to the west, where the ambush was sprung.

He clenched his jaws hard as his scout hovered up, afraid he might get a face full of enemy craft. He did not. Instead, he saw what he had envisioned when he concocted this plan. Most of the Soviets, apparently bolstered by their earlier feasting on American gunships, had reacted by attacking the spot where his Apaches had sprung the ambush, turning to face the flanking fire directly, the most distant Hinds maneuvering to outflank their attackers. Keyes saw fewer than half a dozen enemy craft pointing his way—those were still chasing straggling American craft. "Fire!" he shouted, even as he squeezed off his own twenty-millimeter cannon, the gun aiming where he was looking, into the most dense part of the pack.

"Dammit," he whispered in awe over his radio.

This part of the ambush produced more kills in shorter time. The Soviets had bunched up into several swarms as racing helicopters from the north joined the stalled advance. In the confusion, throngs of Hinds tried to disperse so they could get clear of the pack and fire at the American positions, already vacated. Keyes' group hosed down the entire bunch from a new direction, adding to the Soviet disarray.

The first volley sent blossoms of fire exploding from no less than a dozen gunships. The Soviet pilots reacted by flinching away from the scattered detonations. At least three pairs of Hinds meshed blades and dropped to the desert floor. Pilots began landing their helicopters all over the new killing zone, either because of battle damage or because they found it had become unsafe to fly.

"We've stopped them, boys," shouted Keyes triumphantly. "We've broken the advance. Three more seconds, then let's get the hell out of here. Take the near targets next."

Keyes had assumed a huge calculated risk by shooting over the last of the straggling Cobras and Kiowas. However, he knew the most effective disruption would come from shooting into the greatest concentrations of Soviets. Now, although only seconds had passed, he turned his attention and his cannon on the Hinds nearest him, all within a quarter-mile. They had reacted instinctively to the sight of American gunships popping up in front of them, hauling back on their flight controls to stop, raising the noses of their helicopters, exposing their vulnerable bellies.

The first effect of this Soviet reaction allowed the escaping Americans their freedom. Next, the more cautious Apache pilots followed their own instincts to survive and disobeyed Keyes by shooting into the undersides of the Hinds before taking on more distant targets.

Had they kept racing into the faces of their attackers, the Soviet pilots might have shot by the line of ambushers safely. Now all of them had stopped, either to turn and run or to regroup and return fire. In the next seconds, all that Keyes could see were blown from the sky, killed by American pilots or by their own pack of attackers, now getting the range and shooting back at the second stage of the ambush.

"Get outta here!" Keyes commanded, banking his Black Eagle sharply to dash straight south. Just three miles away, his group was to pass through the platoons that had already moved to a secondary ambush site. From then on, they would leapfrog back, engaging the enemy at maximum range and running, buying time for themselves and the rest of the division to regroup. This would be an orderly, fighting retreat, inflicting damage on the enemy, making him more careful.

Keyes's neck tingled as he turned tail, waiting for the feel of rounds striking his craft. None came, and he dropped the Black Eagle well below the line of fire and accelerated. He looked left and right. Again, all of his ships had gotten off the first and second punches and survived. This was the only way to fight the bastards. He couldn't wait to shove his strategy up the line, contradicting that outdated inclination espoused by guys like Wilkerson, to attack, attack, attack, no matter what the odds.

"Give me your ammo status, Buckskin," he ordered. Already new concerns were forming. Sooner or later, he'd have to run more and shoot less. By then he hoped to have another ambush line arranged by somebody in his battalion so he could get clear for . . . a flash to his left interrupted his calculations. One of his Apaches tumbled and then skidded, breaking apart on the desert floor without burning. He saw broken men and aircraft parts bouncing on the dry ground.

As he began turning, he heard the report, "Six, this is Two-Six, we're being chased by a pair of Hinds that we must not have spotted. They're less than a half-mile back. They got my wingman!"

"Roger, contact. Everybody else keep running south."

The second platoon leader's voice came back, this time tinged with fear, "Six, they're both on my ass . . . *help!*"

Keyes laid his Black Eagle into a maximum bank, more than a hundred degrees, yanking the craft around, looking back and down at the earth. Both Soviet craft had ganged up on Two-Six, who was dodging and weaving, heading for a sharp cut in the earth that would give him cover.

Rolling back to level, Keyes kept his helmet sight on the nearest of the pair, waiting for the sight reticle to blink, telling him the gun had finally slewed far enough to catch up with his swiveling head, locking on and arming.

The Hinds, meanwhile, kept hosing down the desert floor, trying to bring down their quarry.

The reticle blinked as Keyes closed to within a hundred yards at more than two hundred knots. Even as he thought about squeezing the trigger, the cannon rattled the Black Eagle with vibrations.

Both Hinds blew at once.

Right in Keyes's face.

He yelped into the radio as he flew into the mushrooming ball of fire and broke into clear sky.

"You all right, Six?"

The voice of the second platoon leader cheered him—he had survived the attack, too. "Roger, I'm right behind—"

Keyes banked for a turn southward and felt the slop in the controls, then the hammering of a vibration. "I picked up a hit . . . debris from the explosion."

"I'm coming back, Six."

"Negative, keep heading south. This thing . . . is still . . . flyable," he grunted with the effort of controlling his damaged Black Eagle.

Even as he said the words, he struggled with the controls. The Black Eagle overreacted to every control touch, refusing to start into a bank for a full two seconds, then, once there, insisting on staying in a turn, trying to roll over on its back.

His ears filled up with the racket, the noise of the aircraft vibrating, the low RPM alarm. He saw the blinking FIRE light and felt his heart trying to jump out of his chest. Then his troop pilots began inquiring about him. "Shut the fuck up," he yelled, using his command override. "Keep going. You don't have time to pick me up. Stick to the plan, goddammit. I still have control. I'll put her down and hide out. Send out search and rescue when it's safe. See you later."

By now the Black Eagle had become barely manageable. Smoke began leaking into the cockpit through the air-conditioning vents. Now on a heading of south, his tail toward the enemy, his airspeed had dropped to fifty knots. He lifted the safety cover and punched his landing gear down, feeling a reassuring thump beneath his feet as the gear locked into place, and then he cut the engine and fuel switches.

The craft hit level and bounced off the desert floor at about ten knots, barely enough to register on the airspeed indicator. He finessed the controls trying to keep level for the second landing, which came nose-high. The tail dragged in the sand as Keyes stared at the empty late-afternoon sky; then, the horizon came into view and the nose settled down for good. Black smoke seeped over the cockpit from the rear as he reached up and popped the canopy and pulled on it—it wouldn't slide. He felt a moment of panic that he might be trapped and burned to death, but the emergency handles released the entire canopy and track assembly and he threw it overboard.

Smoke poured over him, renewing his fears. He fought his dread and unbuckled his safety belt. Then he remembered the fire extinguishers and pulled both handles, instantly replacing the hot black cloud with a cold, acrid white one. Grabbing at his helmet with one hand and fishing for a desert survival kit with the other, he stood up to jump to safety. Beneath his feet he felt the gun turret turning wildly in time with the motions of his helmet.

A shadow made him duck.

Keyes turned, standing in his seat and looked to the rear. Through the wisps of smoke and extinguisher chemistry rising from the engine compartment, he saw the awesome swarm of Hinds cresting the ridge, first singly and in pairs, then in bunches. Again and again, he ducked the enemy craft flying barely ten feet above his head.

He thought they might ignore him or count him as a kill and fly by in their chase, but one dropped its tail after it flew by, and banked into a turn. It was coming back for him, dropping out of sight into a ravine to double back.

He faced the front and dropped into his seat, repositioning the reticle of his helmet sight, calmly checking the firing sequence, arming his turret cannon.

When Keyes opened fire, fully half the Soviet fleet must have been to his front. The feel of the Black Eagle firing while parked surprised him with the severity of the vibrations. He'd never fought the craft in this mode, of course. The explosions of cannon fire striking a trio of Hinds actually made him flinch. He shot into another group and felt the concussions of more explosions. Then he looked to the spot on the horizon to the east where he expected the stalking Hind to appear.

He was off by a hundred yards. The sparkling of the Soviet gun turret out of the corner of his eye told him that, and he swiveled his head, trying to avoid ducking as still more Hinds flew over him. All the time, he kept his trigger depressed, knowing he'd have only the one sweep of his cannon to get the Hind before it got him.

Keyes didn't even have that. Before the stream of his tracers passed over the spot where the Hind had emerged, the ground around him erupted with gunfire, then an overflying enemy ship blew up, shot down by his own countryman and, finally, his Black Eagle erupted in a fireball.

# 13

The Ospreys had landed in formations of six on the flight deck aboard the carrier in the eastern Mediterranean. Navy crews had moved the aircraft out of sight below decks immediately for refueling and preventative maintenance. It was the battalion's first landing since an overnight stop at Fort Stewart, near Savannah, Georgia. In-flight, the Ospreys had been refueled by KC-135 tankers through the refueling nozzles that protruded out the right side of the fuselage. Each craft had also been fitted with an auxiliary fuel tank slung beneath its belly. Through the foresight of General Bernadino, the division had pre-positioned the most commonly needed spare parts and a detachment of technical personnel to go every inch of each bird while the crews rested. In addition, each Osprey had flown with extra maintenance crews and more parts. On this stopover, the unneeded extras—parts and people—would be exchanged for additional armament. On the upcoming leg of the flight, the Ospreys would be travelling combat-loaded, ready to fight upon arrival.

Nelson Miles gathered his staff and commanders around his map minutes after landing, using a steel maintenance table for his makeshift headquarters. He took inventory of the tired, but expectant faces. "I like what I see so far, ladies and gentlemen. Pass it along to your people. We've flown practically halfway around the globe without an incident of any kind—no maintenance problem, no radio indiscretions."

His group puffed up visibly at the compliment. Miles

smiled and said, "You're not hiding anything from me, are you?" The group relaxed, smiling, adapting to the laid-back demeanor of Miles's leadership. "I'm proud of you. There's a hell of a lot of work to do, and I'm not going to keep you in meetings."

He directed his exec to take the personnel and logistics officers aside and to put them to work on support functions. The intelligence officer, he sent looking for a Navy counterpart to get an update on the enemy situation in the battle zone. Because the Osprey battalion had been pared down in every staff function except maintenance, which was already fully occupied in swarming over the fleet, that left Miles with Blanks, his operations officer, and three company commanders.

These were probably the best leaders in aviation, he had come to realize, because of the unique structure of the Osprey battalion and the staggering size of its capability. Each company had ten Ospreys, three in each of three platoons, and the commander's ship. Depending on the mission and size of the area of operations, they flew in pairs and threes, the company headquarters becoming one of the fighting crews. The company had no administrative burden whatever—when its ten aircraft took off, everybody in the unit was on board performing a combat mission.

The remaining six Ospreys held the fighting staff of the battalion. Augmented by warrant officer pilots, the battalion commander and operations officer each directed a trio of Ospreys in combat.

Except for periodic maintenance requirements, the Osprey had no logistical umbilical cord to tie it down. It could be refueled and rearmed anywhere stocks could be positioned ahead of time. Miles thought of his fleet as an aviation parallel to a submarine wolfpack—give it a combat mission to kill enemy aircraft and get out of its way. He used the analogy to brief his commanders.

"So far, all I hear from theater is good news. First thing this morning, the division made contact with heavy concentrations of Soviets here . . . and here."

He pointed out the major battle areas in Afghanistan where the attack helicopters had stalled the tank advance on Zahedan. He gave them the numbers of kills and comparisons to losses, which cheered them, and added as much detail as he knew about conditions for flying. He reiterated the importance of holding Zahedan's airfield. Then he tossed in the clincher.

"Of course my intel is a few hours old, but no Soviet helicopters in the battle yet." He watched the expressions on the faces of his officers. "I know. I can't figure it out, either. All we can do is be grateful, I guess. Remember, this is a stale report. I expect more news later."

He briefed the status of the air war, still a tug-of-war between the two air forces, and he discussed logistics supports he'd received from General Bernadino.

"As soon as I get an update on the enemy situation, in particular, their helicopter deployment, I'll review our tactics with you. At the moment, we have no way of knowing whether the methods we used back in California will be effective in Iran. The tactics will be the last thing we discuss before we take off from this carrier for the final leg. Right now, each of you make sure you get a handle on all systems on every bird. Then get your people bedded down. We're off this tub at twilight."

Tired as he was, Miles felt buoyant about being so close to the combat theater. On the walk across the maintenance deck, he permitted himself the luxury of thinking about Julie and their last hours together. In a way, he owed a lot to the Osprey for the rekindling of their romance. Well, that didn't exactly make sense, he told himself. He'd been responsible for the tension between them because he'd pouted so much about being on division staff rather than in command. Once he'd gotten the Osprey battalion, regardless of how many hours of overtime he'd put in, he always found refreshment in her company, always tried to romance her. Did that make sense? he wondered. Should a man only permit himself to enjoy a civilized relationship with the woman he loved after he'd achieved his career goals? No, it didn't make sense, he decided. He vowed he'd keep that in mind when this was over. For starters, no matter how tired he felt after he finished his check of the battalion, he would write a letter to her. He'd leave it here for mailing from the carrier after takeoff.

Back at his Osprey, he found Sergeant Bachman directing the maintenance effort on the bird. In one hand, she waved the craft's logbook under the nose of a battalion maintenance technician. "How many goddamned times do I have to write up the leaking seals on these landing struts before you guys change them?"

The senior sergeant muttered, "It's within tolerance, Bachman."

"Your ass, Sarge, not in a desert environment it isn't." She looked up at the driver of a fueling vehicle as he connected his machine to a fueling port in the deck and approached the Osprey with a nozzle. "Hey, you . . . yeah, you. Have you ever refueled one of these things?" The sailor shook his head. "Don't you dare touch this damned bird until I show you how then." To the technician, she said, "We're changing the seals, Sarge. Today."

"It's a four-hour job, Joyce. You're never going to get any sleep once we start it."

She smirked at him. "Today, Sarge. You let me worry about my beauty sleep. Now what say you get the guys started while I show this squid how to refuel." She flipped the logbook at the maintenance sergeant and jogged over toward the sailor. On the way by Miles, she winked and smiled. He congratulated her for her attentiveness, and she stopped to murmur, "As long as you mention it, sir, you and Major Barger could do a better job of filling in the logbook before you un-ass the ship. I lose a good five minutes reading your handwriting and redoing the major's math. With all due respect, sir."

Miles knocked his heels together and laughed. "I'll straighten us both out. You'd better help that guy standing there with the fuel hose."

Inside the cockpit, Miles found Barger laboring with an eraser and pencil on several loose logbook pages. Barger cursed and looked up at his commander. Without a word, Miles stepped into the passageway between Raptor launch tubes and sidled back to the fighting compartment. There, he found his men engrossed in maintenance checks of computers, radios, target acquisition equipment, radars, and weapons.

Tryon gave him a short wave and kept reading off his technical checklist. Kopmeyer and Rush, engrossed in reading computer screens and instruments and responding by flipping switches, turning dials, and typing into their keyboards, answered the warrant officer in monosyllables, the shorthand they had developed for efficient combat communications. The two enlisted men didn't even notice their colonel. Miles, noticed them, however, working in the dank heat—the auxiliary power did not permit full operational checks to be run at the same time the air conditioning was on. He noticed that they remained intent on their duties, although he knew they must be as fully fatigued as he was. Nobody had whined about getting sleep or food or anything else. This crew had only one thing on their minds: getting their aircraft mission-ready. Miles shook his head imperceptibly, marveling at the professionalism and competence. They awed him.

He made his way forward, to find Barger still bent over the logbook pages. "I see Joyce talked to you about the logbook already."

Barger said, "Talk, hell. She chewed my ass. Better watch out, Colonel, she's looking to chew yours, too. Who's in charge of this goddamned bird anyhow?" He looked up, a bemused grin on his face.

"On the ground, she is, apparently. Wendell, I've never met a group of people like this. And it's not just on our Osprey. Every crew is cut from the same cloth. How did we get so lucky?"

Barger stacked his logbook forms on the instrument panel and said, "It isn't luck, Nelson. You know that as well as I do. First Joel, then you. You two were the first ones cut from the same cloth—thank goodness we didn't have to go through a major personality adaptation after you took command. The rest of us have our jobs, and we play off you. Give yourself credit. This is going to be one hell of a unit when it faces Soviets. I can't imagine anything that can stop us. Can you?''

A flash of gloom crossed Miles's mind in the mental picture of Wilkerson's face. ''No, Wendell,'' he lied, ''I can't think of anything that could mess with this battalion.'' Then he changed the subject. ''You want a cold one?''

Barger gulped. ''A cold beer? How in hell did you get . . . never mind how, the answer is yes.''

Miles gave him a secretive grin. ''Joyce showed me a spot near the air-conditioning compressor where a six-pack will fit. Before we left, I gave her a few bucks and some instructions to every crew chief in the battalion to requisition his or her favorite brews. When the chiefs are satisfied that each crew has finished up with assigned maintenance, they'll reward everybody before they turn in.''

Barger's face slackened. ''You mean I have to ask Joyce for a brew?''

Miles nodded. Without another word, Barger took down his stack of maintenance record cards and began poring over them again.

Later, with he and his crew assembled in the fighting compartment, Miles raised a can covered with beads of condensation and said, ''To you and the Osprey.''

''Kick ass, Osprey,'' said Bachman in solemn rejoinder.

''Kick ass,'' the others said in chorus before drinking.

Miles stood with his back to the passageway leading to the cockpit. He felt the Osprey rock as somebody climbed aboard. He raised his beer for another drink, but froze his arm halfway to his mouth. The expression on Barger's face told him of bad news before he looked. Over his shoulder he saw the drained face of Herman Blanks, who jerked his head toward the outside.

His first thought was fear that something had happened to Julie, but he dismissed that notion, unwilling to embrace it in any form. He followed Blanks to the hangar deck, feeling a horrible foreboding that he'd just experienced the last few hours of satisfaction, the last joyful time he would know for a long while.

"What's up, Herm?"

Blanks dragged a sleeve across his face. "Nelson, give me a second. The news is awful, and I don't know which of it to break first. I've been trying . . . Nelson, the Soviets have torn into our helicopter brigades with a vengeance. It looks like as much as half the division fleet has been flat wiped out."

"My God . . . how?"

"I don't know all the details. Just that there were so many Hind gunships they swarmed all over our guys. The Cobras have been hit the worst."

Miles breathed short, rapid breaths. "Herm, is there something else? Don't tell me P.B. is any part of this bad news." He saw Blanks sag, his lip trembling as he spoke the rest:

"Nelson, P.B. was shot down. He's missing. Presumed dead." His voice had turned to a whisper. "I'm sorry."

Blanks held out a sheaf of papers and left Miles standing. In shock, Miles glanced down. The sheaf was a computer printout. He held it up, letting it fall free, except for the top page. It was a list nearly as long as he was tall, a by-name listing of casualties, a third of them KIA. He saw name after name that he recognized. Then, in the listing of MIAs he found the verification he didn't want to see. "KEYES, PATRICIAN BOYD, MAJ."

Miles needed privacy. All his present feelings begged for privacy. He dared not double over and vomit in public, although he felt a sudden lurching of the beer warming in his gut. He would not fold up and cry, although his grief could not have been more deeply felt—P.B. Keyes was the brother he'd never had. He could fly into the mad rage that surged within him—he had vowed to bring the Ospreys over in time to protect Keyes and all the other helicopters, but had fallen short of fulfilling the promise. He wanted to explode. Barring that, to run off someplace to be alone. He dared not do either. He couldn't shriek in frustration that the goddamned Soviets would attack his brother pilots and destroy so many men and helicopters before he could get into the fray. Neither could he let the sadness get to him. For now his personal emotions took a back seat to the needs of his battalion.

He briefed his men and women, letting his anger show, but keeping his outrage in check. He affirmed the importance of keeping their professional demeanor, of entering the battle with cool efficiency instead of senseless revenge that might make them take dangerous risks. Everybody stayed somber throughout his briefing. There were no questions.

So, stiffening his spine, he strode off the hangar deck, demanding instructions from sailors until he found his way topside to a spot where nobody was nearby, a spot where he could face forward into the wind, letting the sea air dry the dampness welling in his eyes.

He slept fitfully, and arrived at the hangar even before Bachman. He fulfilled his promise to write to Julie, telling her of the loss of Keyes and of his love for her.

At the briefing of his commanders and staff, he reinforced the combat briefing with an affirmation of the tactics they would use. "Fly at night only. Pairs at least, trios at most. Wide dispersion. Support each other both by fire and electronic warfare capability. Everybody clear?"

Everybody was.

"One more thing," he said, "I have to repeat it. We may feel we have a score to settle with the Soviets because we all lost friends to the enemy. However, I'm telling you, no matter how much we hurt inside, we have our tactical mission, ladies and gentlemen. That comes first. The enemy is not fighting this on a personal level. You can't fight with your emotions, people. You have to use your head. Don't get reckless seeking revenge or something equally as useless. Is that understood?''

They all acknowledged that it was, indeed, understood, and Miles added, ''Let's get going, then. We have to get to Zahedan as soon as we possibly can.'' He dismissed them.

As he walked back to his own craft, though, he wondered if would ever be possible for him to engage an enemy craft without dedicating it to his closest friend in the world besides Julie.

General Amiri's attack into Khuzestan caught the Iranian defenses in disarray. Commanders in the province, preoccupied with news of fighting toward Baghdad, had begun shifting forces pulled from defensive positions, leaving skeletons of units in place. Protected behind mountains paralleling the border, mechanized units convoyed northwestward from Dezful toward the Baghdad-Tehran highway, either to defend against the expected Iraqi counterattacks there or to reinforce the early successes toward Baghdad.

The Iranians had reacted as Amiri had hoped they would, thinning border units to reinforce what they perceived as the main attack. At the very moment Bani-Sadr's lead tanks were being gassed, Amiri launched his lightning tank attack toward Dezful.

Four tank divisions and six motorized rifle divisions plunged into Iran's diluted defenses in northern Khuzestan. Avoiding forces in contact, his lead divisions bypassed resistance on the way toward fulfilling the dual mission of capturing Dezful airfield and strengthening the hold on the crucial Davriaresh Dam.

By the end of the first day's attack, the city of Dezful had been bombarded and bypassed by lead units. Now Iraqi tanks rumbled in strung-out columns down the road eastward from Dezful, racing across the narrow, dry plain between the mountains and the marshes in Khuzestan Province. The race was now to reach the Persian Gulf where the mountains nearly pinched down to the coast. That achieved, the Iranian province would be encircled. Reinforcements would have to filter down

from the north where Bani-Sadr was engaged—and
Amiri had left a blocking force west of Dezful to prevent that. Arabistan would be his.

Amiri felt fairly smug. Because he had kept pressure
on around Abadan and Shatt Al Arab, the Iranians in
contact there could hardly pull away to fight. Now his
only danger was that the circle would be too thinly
manned to withstand any concentrated and coordinated attack at any single point on its circumference.
For that reason, he had to finish up on those troublesome Iranians to the north around Baghdad. Then he
could bring other troops and strengthen what was going to be a fatal entrapment down here.

He could not feel too smug, though, for he knew
General Abolhassen Saddeq, the Iranian commander
of tank forces, simply would not roll over and give up
Khuzestan, and that Bani-Sadr was an able officer—
too damned able, for he'd nearly broken through
cleanly to threaten Baghdad, and that would have negated both the Soviet attack on Tabriz and his own
effort against Khuzestan. Luckily, Bani-Sadr would be
needed in the central battle—Amiri had ordered
enough pressure in the Baghdad counterattack to ensure it. The Soviets had reneged on their part of the
bargain by not following through to capture Tehran,
but still had tied down enough Iranians to allow Amiri's plan against Khuzestan to work.

Confidence, he told himself. He needed confidence.
He'd covered all the contingencies. The Iranians had
no air force left to threaten the dam, and Bani-Sadr
could not possibly get his units into the battle for Khuzestan.

Bani-Sadr's helicopter had circled Abu's retreating
tank force and landed in the midst of battle to leave
off a new tank commander and pick up the Ferret.

Once aboard the helicopter, Abu took the headset
proffered by a crew member and put it on.

"Well done, Colonel."

Abu studied Bani-Sadr's face to see whether the general might be mocking him again, whether he might

be adding the epithet, "cow." Bani-Sadr smiled genuinely, though, so Abu murmured a modest, "Thank you. I would have stayed, though. Why did you pick me up?"

"I was ordered to. We've both been directed to report to higher headquarters."

Abu looked puzzled for a moment, then realized his father must be behind such a command. He grew angry that Saddeq would interfere with his first combat encounter. He realized he no longer wanted to be protected. He had come into his own. On his own.

The anger vanished, however, after they landed and the helicopter swirled away. General Saddeq stood with his arms wide, though Abu kept his distance.

"If you were not contaminated," said Saddeq, wearing an exuberant grin, "I would embrace you, my son. Shower quickly and change into fresh clothing. We must be off to Bani-Sadr's new command."

Abu stayed rooted to the spot, a quizzical expression twisting his face. He looked to Bani-Sadr.

The squat, peppery Bani-Sadr explained: "I have been promoted and placed in command of the army defending Khuzestan Province . . . I should say, the forces responsible for wresting the province back from the invaders."

Abu cocked his head as if to say, "What does this have to do with me?"

Bani-Sadr said, "I have requested that you remain with me to command a tank battalion . . . if you accept such a command."

Stunned, Abu looked to Saddeq. "Father?"

The general nodded, and Abu ran to him, disregarding the chemical danger. They hugged for a long time. Both of them discarded their clothing and showered before boarding Saddeq's helicopter for the flight to Khuzestan Province.

They arrived in time to see the opening engagements between American and Soviet fighters in the sky. They monitored air force frequencies through their helicopter headsets, trying to determine the success of follow-on bombers, B-2s flying low level the length of

the Gulf to hit at the Davriaresh Dam. They cheered
when they heard the reports of, first the dam spouting
badly through a split, then of the gush of millions of
tons of water as it burst.

"This will flood the plains again," said Saddeq over
his helicopter's intercom. Many of Amiri's tanks will
be entrapped in mud. This water will split his command."

"For at least a month," added Bani-Sadr.

Abu laughed sardonically. "General Saddeq, take
us to our commands so we can finish these Iraqi invaders."

Saddeq smiled. "So you have been blooded and
wish to taste it again? Very well, but I hope you will
not be too terribly disappointed if I assign you to units
moving eastward. We will be using the Americans to
put pressure on the Iraqis for peace here."

"No!" said Abu. "Let us fight them. We can finish
them."

Bani-Sadr scowled at the Ferret. "Listen to your
father with respect, cow."

Chastened, Abu lowered his head.

Saddeq said, "The quicker we end the fighting with
the Iraqis, the better. It will mean we can avoid squan-
dering our tanks in a battle that can just as easily be
decided by diplomacy. It also means we can release
those tank forces to be sent eastward toward Zahedan.
There the Americans are in trouble. Here they have
saved our province—we must repay them in kind as
quickly as possible."

"What then, my general?" asked Abu.

"Already I have four divisions moving from Abadan, Ahvaz, and Esfahan. More will follow as fighting
ends here."

"Where will they be—"

"You may think you are a warrior," said Bani-Sadr,
"but you have a lot to learn about ordinary courtesy.
Be quiet and listen."

"We're going to encircle Bandar Abbas and delay
the Soviet advance against it. When that is secure, we
will move on to Zahedan."

General Amiri flew over the scene of the watery disaster in Khuzestan and ordered his helicopter back toward Iraq. He might as well make the personal report he'd been ordered to make to the president in Baghdad today. Nothing more of military value could be gained here. Rising water had inundated roads and turned the plains from dusty maneuver areas into swamps. It was not so bad that some tanks were trapped in mud—only a brigade or so had been bogged down. The crews had abandoned their vehicles already and had begun slogging their way out on foot through the waist-deep lake.

He arrived at Baghdad in a state of nervous agitation. "The worst part, excellency," he told the president, "is a force of a division and more that had advanced beyond the flooded areas. We can withdraw most of our army, but those forces are now trapped."

The president slumped deeply into his chair. When he spoke, it was softly, barely more than a murmur. "They will be bargaining chips, no?"

Amiri gulped. "Yes, excellency."

"It would seem we will be handing over the tanks and weapons of nearly a dozen divisions intact?"

Amiri nodded, finding no words that could mitigate the dimensions of the disaster. He began to feel as he had before, that there were security men waiting behind him to take him away.

"And I suppose the Iranians will simply take over those tanks and turn them eastward against the Soviets? Does this sound familiar, Amiri? Isn't this what happened before in Kuwait? Didn't you promise me it would never happen again to our proud army?"

Amiri didn't even nod this time.

The president sat up. "Well, that is the only bright spot in this affair then," he said, this time enunciating clearly. "The Soviets did not pull their part of the bargain. They did not drive on to Tehran. It is only fair that we provide part of the weaponry to be used against them."

The president bent over papers on his desk. Amiri

felt a growing sense of dread. His spine tingled as his mental image of the secret police force behind him had grown to a squad of a dozen. He chanced a glance over his shoulder, unwilling to believe armed men could approach him so silently. He was right.

Four men stood inside the doorway, their pistols drawn. They grabbed him roughly. Amiri refused to whimper. He glanced back at his president, who refused to look up from shuffling papers on his desk top.

After their commanding officer had been killed, the surviving gunships continued to gain time for the division's second brigade to regroup. The Buckskin troop passed safely through anti-aircraft defenses late in the afternoon with the loss of only five helicopters, including Keyes's. Wilkerson's last-ditch effort to stall the Soviets by stripping the airfield of gunship support, coupled with the intervention of Keyes's gunship troop, still might not have been enough to prevent a total catastrophe. General Pickett, however, ordered the fighters that had provided cover for the Davriaresh Dam strike to accompany a pair of B-2s north of Zahedan to expend their unused ordnance in a hasty strike at the helicopter pack. Although the kills were few—the Americans were driven off by Soviet fighters reacting to their feint—the maneuver forced the Soviets to halt their helicopter advance long enough for dark to fall. Still, by dusk, nearly half of the Cobras and Kiowas of the ACCD had been shot down. What was more, nearly a quarter of the Apache fleet had been destroyed or damaged. When the final count came in at day's end, Wilkerson's head-on aggressiveness had added up to a disaster barely mitigated by Keyes and his more effective hit-and-run tactics.

At Zahedan just before sundown, General Little joined a flight of Blackhawk helicopters landing to pull out the infantry company that had been held in position. The hasty plan was to direct gunship fire down on the road while Blackhawks landed behind the ridge hidden from the fighting. The infantrymen would withdraw from their fighting positions under the covering fire and escape via the lift helicopters into the mountains south of Zahedan.

When Lieutenant Edwards heard the order to prepare for evacuation, he whispered in relief, "Finally." Soviet fire from below had become far too accurate as the infantry had stopped trying to advance and took up covered sniper positions to harass the Americans. The tanks had begun moving again, and there was little Edwards's platoon could do to stop them now. Every time a TOW crew tried to acquire a tank, the Soviets raked them with rifle fire.

Edwards shouted for Quintana to get the word out to ready for withdrawal, "The gunships are coming," he said. Those within hearing cheered. Edwards felt giddy himself that they would be getting out of yet another tight spot. "On my command, get off as many TOW missiles as possible—less crap to carry. Then take everything that will still shoot and we'll get the hell out of here. Weapons squad first, then second and third squads. First squad last." His radio operator gave him a hopeful look. Edwards shook his head, and the man groaned. "We'll go out last."

Then they waited. All over the hillside, Edwards watched as other platoons from his own and other companies fired their last bursts and disengaged. He hated being last to pull out—it gave him the dreaded feeling of being left behind. "Where the hell are those goddamned gunships?" he growled. From beyond the crest of the hill, he heard the lift helicopters landing, then taking off with the first evacuees. He looked around him, and saw his men staring at him. "Goddammit," he yelled, "what the hell are you guys gawking at? You'd better be shooting down the hill." He snatched up his radio mike and hollered the question all his men wanted him to ask, "Where the fuck are those goddamned gunships?" He paused to listen for an answer, then looked up stunned and spoke to Quintana. "No gunships."

The grim platoon sergeant rolled over and shot a CLAW down the slope and followed it with a full magazine of automatic rifle fire. As Edwards's men unleashed bursts of their own covering fire, all over the hill, soldiers who had gotten the word they'd been left naked began climbing upward, many without showing an iota of discipline. Edwards kept yelling for his noncoms to maintain order. He crouched and ran laterally along his lines encouraging his soldiers, "Fire and move, men. Fire and move. Keep your heads. Protect your buddy's ass."

Even with the near panic, his platoon hit two more tanks. One merely threw a track on the downslope side, but the tank's driver never let up on the accelerator, and the tank whipped sharply left and drove into the chasm. The second tank, directly below them, erupted several times as its ammunition detonated in a series of explosions, throwing streams of fire. Edwards decided this was the time to pull out the remainder of his men. "Now!" he bellowed. "Get your asses out of here. Straight up." He pointed, showing them the way they already knew they must take.

The run for the top of the ridge became the longest, toughest hundred feet Edwards had ever travelled. Within only a dozen strides, his thighs had become inflamed, ready to give out on him. His lungs could not have burned worse if he'd been inhaling diesel exhaust. His combat pack doubled in weight, and his helmet pinched his throbbing head. He fell, scrambled to his feet, fell again. It took everything he had to step over stones the size of grapefruit, and repeatedly he lost his footing to gravel the size and shape of marbles. All the while, he felt a stinging sensation in his back, a tender spot growing bigger by the second, growing in rings as if he wore a target back there, the bulls-eye centered between his shoulder blades.

He screamed, half to encourage his gasping, struggling men, half to relieve the pressure accumulating in his chest. Somehow, his men took his outburst as incentive to make it to the top. As he neared the crest of the ridge, Edwards felt the concussion of explosions. He knew he was going to get it before he made it clear. The artillery was going to rain down again. But no! Quintana had turned the lead squads around.

They lay on top of the ridge, firing down at the Soviet infantry below. The concussions had been muzzle blasts in the face. He tumbled to safety over the crest of the hill. Some of his men lay down their weapons and exposed themselves to gunfire from below to grab the stragglers and haul them the last few yards to cover. Others began carrying and dragging their wounded companions toward the helicopters, which had parked a hundred yards farther down the slope, where the ground leveled out.

Edwards stopped a moment to herd stragglers. He grabbed the hand of a gut-shot private he didn't recognize and draped the man's arm over his shoulder, trying not to look at the thick drainage from a gash in his fatigue jacket, a six-inch-long exit wound at his kidney. The man shrieked in his ear, and Edwards tried to comfort him with words, although the smell from torn intestines was so foul he nearly vomited himself. On the stumbling way downward, he tried to record mental notes of the astonishing acts of courage he had seen so he could prepare commendations for bravery later. He couldn't wait to thank those who had lingered to save his life. He envisioned a time back in the States when he might buy beers for his troops and salute them. He felt a growing wind in his face. For a vanishing second, he was grateful for it blowing the stench of the wound away. Then he realized the helicopters were taking off. Still a dozen yards away, he saw that the Blackhawks were full—even overloaded—and that the struts were extending as the craft grew lighter. By the time he had stumbled the last few yards down the hill with the last group of men, the Blackhawks had lifted off.

He found breath to scream, but the rotor wash and noise of the engines and blades blew his words away. Dazed, he looked around. Four other men gesticulated at the sky and hollered obscenities he could not hear. The helicopters flew away, anyhow. Edwards felt the same panic the other men did, but when one man from the first squad pointed his rifle at the departing birds, he shoved the muzzle down with his free hand. A burst of fire stitched up the vacant landing zone.

The man yanked his rifle free and turned toward Edwards, his eyes wild and frenzied.

"Calm down, Corporal," said Edwards. "You might hurt one of the good guys. There'll be a ship coming back for us. Now let's take care of the wounded and redistribute ammunition in case they're delayed in sending a ship back here." He couldn't believe the calm in his own voice, a calm that utterly contrasted with the other man's hysteria, a calm belied by the emotions stampeding inside him—for one thing, his radio operator had found his way onto one of the birds, and the tiny group was without communications. In the corner of his eye, he saw the barrels of other rifles swing toward the corporal. "Don't you people dare point your guns at him. He's all right now. Right?"

Without waiting for a reply, Edwards lowered the wounded man from his shoulder to the ground, turning his back on the corporal with the murderous look. The bull's-eye tingled on his back again. This time he felt something—a touch. It was the corporal.

"God, L.T., I'm sorry. I went . . . crazy a second there when I saw them—"

"Forget it," said Edwards, barely controlling his impulse to gush his exhalation. "I felt like shooting the bastards down myself. Hell, I would have let you if so many of our guys weren't on board." He looked around. "Now. Whaddya say we get a perimeter organized in case those Soviet bastards come up here after us." As he tended to the wounded man, he became aware of the hushed composure among the men, then realized they were staring at him, whispering their astonishment. He heard words like "cool" and "calm" and "ballsy" and "ice water." If only they knew how close he had been to coming apart, too. It made him laugh as he bent over the awful stench of the wounded man, who had not uttered a sound since the run down the hill. "Fucking unbelievable," he heard behind him. Unbelievable. Exactly right. He didn't believe it himself.

* * *

When the last of the Blackhawks had taken off, Little received a frantic radio call that there was still a contingent of soldiers left, included at least one wounded man. When he heard this, he ordered his own pilot to drop in and pick up the remaining six soldiers. Once on the ground, he saw the relief on their faces as they scrambled in. He helped each one of them into the helicopter, grasping their hands, their arms, their uniforms, and pulling them in onto the deck. One man, a scruffy lieutenant, heaved an obviously dead man aboard and tumbled onto the cabin floor coming up face-to-face, screaming, "Where the fuck have you been, asshole?" spraying the general's face with spittle and rancid breath.

Little understood. In the strained, unshaven, oily, bloodied, grimy face, and in the smell of blood, he read the account of being left unprotected by gunships, then abandoned by lift helicopters. He smiled sheepishly as the lieutenant's face withdrew, gaining a broader perspective, twitching with the recognition of embroidered stars, eyes widening with a second of fear, then hardening as Edwards added a shouted, "Sir?"

"Sorry, son," Little said, and clapped the young officer on the shoulder.

As they lifted off, Little sighed in relief. It was as important to him that these six—five, now that the one had died—had been saved, as well as the battalions that had been airlifted from Zahedan earlier. He looked around at the men sitting on the deck of his helicopter. He felt extremely proud to be an American fighting man, one of these. These were the best that his country had to give and here they were fighting of all places, in Iran, for all reasons, to reverse the invasion of Iran. The men from the great Satan America playing savior to the Iranian Revolution. Imagine!

Now, if only he could find a reason for the reserve helicopter battalion being committed without his permission. The divisional operations officer had already answered his pointed inquiry by fingering General

Wilkerson. There must have been a reason for Wilkerson jeopardizing the evacuation, he thought. It had better have been a goddamned good reason.

The Soviet MI-24 pilot had been completely disoriented. His radar compass had been malfunctioning continually and he was unable to navigate except in gross terms on the magnetic compass on his dashboard. Losing contact with his flight in central Afghanistan, he had navigated on his own, following directions given over the radio by his commander. He was more than a hundred miles off course when he approached Zahedan and saw the scattering of American helicopters before him. Fearful as he was about being lost, he had been more fearful of missing out on the combat in Afghanistan. Now he saw his chance. Perhaps he might not even be reprimanded for getting lost.

Simultaneously he armed his missiles and picked out one of the Blackhawk helicopters. Eager to make his first kill, he let off a pair of missiles at a single craft just taking off, separated by a mile from the others. His cockpit radar confirmed slaving the missiles to the acquired rotor blades returns of the helicopter he recognized as a Blackhawk. He felt the missiles blown off with a tiny charge of the explosive bolt and then he saw them swish out before him, wriggling like fish until the rockets stabilized. They sent out streaming white smoke, accelerating faster and faster to twice the speed of sound. Even before the rocket motors had an opportunity to burn out, both missiles struck the rotor system of the Blackhawk. One had homed in on the main rotor blades and another had picked up the high frequency tail blades. Either would have been a killing shot. The explosions rocked the Blackhawk and made it first teeter, then spin around in slow motion and spiral downward. It caught its belly on a jagged boulder and split apart, rolling human bodies down on the ground, then toppled over into the ravine, bursting into flames.

On another day, the Soviet pilot might have fired his

cannons at the bodies sprawled on the mountaintop. But there were other helicopters to acquire. Feeling the erotic surge of his first combat kill, he planned to engage more of them—hell, all of them, he thought. As he chased them to the southwest, he saw the airfield below and knew this must be Zahedan. There were other helicopters down there, flights of them taking off heading south. What a rich area for him to fall into. No resistance. No gunships. He hesitated momentarily in deciding targets to acquire. There were so many choices!

He chose the men running around exposed on the airfield. He realized they must be demolitions teams preparing to crater the runway and sabotage the facilities. If he could prevent them from doing that, he might be a hero of the Fatherland. He slewed his gunship through the skies, hosing down the scattered pockets of men.

In his excitement, he failed to notice the white column of smoke, the trail of a Stinger shoulder-fired missile rising toward him. In the next second, his MI-24 exploded in the air, broke in half like a fiery egg and dumped the contents of the fuel tanks, flaming, streaming, down the runway.

Flying back to Karachi, Rita Bernadino was grateful for the cover of night. She directed the red beam of her flashlight over the map board haphazardly, even drunkenly, trying to study the tactical situation as best she could manage. She could barely see through the aching, blinding fog of her emotions. She needed to cry, but she did not dare. She knew she must compose herself, to take over command of the ACCD.

By now, she knew that the Blackhawk reported as being shot down by a Soviet gunship near Zahedan had been confirmed as that of Major General Steve Little's. There had been some seriously injured survivors, but they were all infantrymen. Among them had been a Lieutenant Edwards, who had survived well enough to walk away and rejoin his company. Edwards's report was eyewitness confirmation that could not be denied no matter how much one's emotions wanted to deny it. General Little, the division commander of the ACCD, had been cut nearly in two, his head severed, his blood . . . she could not handle the images conjured by the eyewitness report.

She was the senior officer. She would need to have Wilkerson remain in the field, since he was an experienced man, but she wanted to know why the hell Cobras had been pulled out of their fighting positions near Zahedan in the first place. Wilkerson would have a lot of questions to answer. This was not going to be a time to go head-hunting. She would have more than her hands full in taking over this division. Her mind did a turnaround. If that S.O.B had just pulled a stunt to get some of the glory that he'd missed out on in Desert Storm . . . she forced her mind to reverse directions again. This was no time to become preoccupied with anger at Wilkerson.

She found a clear space on the crew seat and stretched out across it and tried to sleep. Sleeping was impossible, but at least she could fake it. At least to cover her face and, under the guise of sleeping, she could try to cry to drain her grief away. She would need to have all of her emotions intact by tomorrow.

# 14

The moment Marshal Abramov arrived at the Zahedan airfield, he ordered a survey of the runways and servicing capabilities. By nightfall, despite the loss of half a dozen soldiers to mines and booby traps, he could report to Moscow the airfield would be fully operational within twenty-four hours—only a couple of craters and the wreckage of one of their own helicopters had marred the landing strip.

"I'm surprised," he told Mendenyev, who had arrived with the motorized rifle regiment that had come under helicopter attack. "Apparently, the Americans were so preoccupied with evacuating troops, they started preparing demolitions too late. Too concerned with safety, eh? Then our stray helicopter pilot catches them in the open. Such accidents are the ingredients that make me brilliant today. Tomorrow another imbecile of a pilot will destroy me, Major."

Mendenyev nodded hesitantly.

"You think we win these battles by our brilliance? No. Today, the Americans were unlucky. Tomorrow, it could be us. Whoever is lucky on the last day of battle is the winner, Aleksandr Mendenyev . . . but enough of an old general's philosophy, eh? You look exhausted, Major. The battle is less glorifying than fatiguing, eh? Are you surprised at war now that you are meeting it close enough to smell its breath?"

"Indeed, sir. I doubt I will ever be able to enjoy staff work as in the past, now that I have seen the destruction first-hand."

Abramov grimaced. Staring at the gritty tarmac remembering his own introduction to the reality of battle, he said, "War is not a philosophical entity. War is the smell of burning fuel and rusted, lifeless hulls of destroyed vehicles. War is charred, bloated bodies too horribly full of stench to regard as men or even former men. War is not a loss of respect for the living, Major. War is a loss of respect for the dead."

Mendenyev shuddered. "Every politician—no, every citizen should be made to march through the battlefield I saw today."

"It would be enough if every mother could see it," Abramov snorted. "They would force every politician to fall in line for peace. This is not the end of it for us, Major. We have other battles to attend to." He stamped his feet as if shaking off nonmilitary thoughts. "What can you tell me about the American helicopters you faced today?"

"They were deadly. Our vehicles were defenseless for far too long. Only when we controlled the panic and began returning a torrent of small-arms fire did the enemy pilots begin losing their concentration. Still, we lost many tanks and personnel carriers."

"And ZSU 23-4s. We lost most of our dedicated anti-aircraft capability early."

"In the first minutes," Mendenyev corrected. "The Americans clearly have a missile that homes on radar emissions. Only when the regimental commander realized this and ordered manual acquisition and firing did the losses return to an acceptable rate."

"Excellent observation. We will mandate manual firing until we have a specimen of the missile to analyze." Abramov wrote a note and ordered a runner to have it delivered to his commander of anti-aircraft forces. "What other observations have you to share?"

"Without the relief provided by our helicopters, it would have been wholesale slaughter. I expected the artillery to have an effect against American gunships. But they attacked artillery in the first volleys and left our tanks defenseless."

"Did you gain anything today?"

"Besides the appreciation that combat is horrifying? Yes. Helicopters rule the battlefield with their mobility. Tanks alone are no match for them. Even artillery can be neutralized."

Abramov wagged a finger. "Do not make the mistake of believing that anything you have seen today will apply to tomorrow's combat."

Mendenyev only stared ahead blankly.

"Major, did you have an opportunity to fill your second vial today?"

"Many opportunities, sir. The vial is empty still. When I fill it with blood, it will be my own."

"I understand. Come, let us hear the reports from the staff. Perhaps we can make some order of all this chaos."

In the briefing, Abramov received intelligence reports of masses of helicopters moving across from the Mediterranean from Europe, but the American helicopters already in Iran were bottled up by his own. These reinforcing helicopters were Apaches, designed to kill Soviet tanks. Now his tanks were rolling unimpeded through Iran, attacking on two axes: south to maintain contact with the retreating American infantry, and westward toward Bandar Abbas.

Following them to the west were eight motorized rifle divisions trekking across the Dasht-e Lut, the barren wasteland in the central part of eastern Iran. The road skirted the lower edge of that desert and then turned south at Kerman toward Bandar Abbas with the strategic aim of putting a choke-hold on the world's oil supply by shutting down the Strait of Hormuz.

After the meeting, Mendenyev approached Abramov.

"Moscow has finally relented in the matter of sending Mi-28s to you," he said.

Abramov harrumphed. "Only the three prototype helicopters and their test crews?"

Mendenyev nodded. "A new set of trials is being devised for the production models. They are now being delivered to elite aviation units." He raised his palms in a gesture of helplessness. "They promised that training would be expedited. Polomarchuk himself signed the dispatch.''

Abramov barked an obscenity. ''And how soon can we expect these production models? Did he promise that, too?''

The major's volume dropped as if he were ashamed to be relaying this information. ''Within sixty days. He promised.''

Abramov eyed him through slitted eyes. ''There is more. Spill it all.''

''The three Mi-28s now in transit come with restrictions . . . Polomarchuk. He insisted they not be allowed into battle in an offensive posture. They must be allowed to acclimate to the combat environment and learn the American capabilities, especially of their night-fighting tactics. The Mi-28 crews are to develop new tactics for training of units prior to arrival in the combat theater.''

Abramov snorted. ''What good is a mere trio of aircraft, anyhow? To me, power means superior numbers and the hammering of greater firepower. Let the Americans depend on technology. Superior numbers and an aggressive spirit will outfight technology every time, Aleksandr Mendenyev.''

Aboard the aircraft carrier *J.B. Bremner,* Rita Bernadino felt the emotional bands wrapping her soul begin to snap one at a time.

''General Pickett, what do you mean, I'm not going to be the commander of the ACCD?''

She'd known there was going to be trouble the instant she walked into the room. Pickett wouldn't meet her expectant eyes, but kept kept looking everywhere else in his war room. At the side of the general's desk stood Wilkerson, smiling with smug satisfaction. His division commander had been killed yet he seemed happy.

Bernadino knew what it meant. Wilkerson would be ''frocked'' and moved into command.

''General Bernadino, your support within the division has been long admired by Major General Little, rest his soul. You've been an invaluable asset to the success of the combat elements in the division and it's going to be necessary—for continuity's sake—that you remain in your present position.''

"No, General, it isn't going to be for continuity's sake that you're making this move. Let's discuss the real reason.'' She wasn't going to say what was on his mind. She'd been shut out of the "good old boys clique.'' In the past, their methods had been used to exclude women from plum positions—any excuse would do. Women hadn't even been seriously considered for command positions, that is, until a woman had become commander-in-chief of the armed forces and *she* had badgered the Congress to change their outdated attitudes toward women in uniform. Now, by any measure of logic, Bernadino was in line to command that division. Except now something had intervened. The good old boys network. Logic be damned.

"It's wartime, General Bernadino.''

"Bullshit.''

So she was going to play hardball. The general's eyes narrowed and his jaws knotted as he finally looked her in the face. "Listen, General, this is a war. This is not a goddamned place for social experiments to take place. We've got to have men who are combat experienced in order to prevent us from sacrificing helicopters and pilots to the enemy—''

"I call bullshit on that. If it hadn't been for General Wilkerson's so-called leadership on the battlefield—taking command in places where he had no business . . .'' Her gaze hardened accusingly as she looked at Wilkerson. "Let me be plain about this—if those helicopters hadn't been shifted away from the Zahedan airfield in the first place, endangering the evacuation of our soldiers there, we wouldn't be having this conversation. General Little was helping evacuate those troops''—she covered a catch in her throat with an angry cough—"and he was shot down because there were no attack helicopters to cover the evacuation.''

Wilkerson's eyes bulged as he glared at her. Pickett looked to Wilkerson, expecting a logical response.

"What the hell are you suggesting? Steve . . . General Little authorized me to commit those birds. Hell, if I hadn't, we'd have lost more of our gunships. Don't try tossing accusations around, General, unless you're ready to back them up."

"I'll give you accusations, Wilkerson. You undermined two brigade commanders yesterday, and they'll swear to it. You overcommitted an entire brigade without knowing or even trying to find out the full numbers of Soviet gunships in the attack. Caution would have been advised, but you chose—"

"Since when is it a crime to show a little balls on the battlefield?" Wilkerson shouted back.

Bernadino shrieked in reply, even as she did wishing she'd kept her composure. "It was a crime to throw good lives away recklessly by committing the Apaches without reconning. You compounded that crime by shifting older model gunships away from killing tanks to try to rectify the first mistake—"

"I had to—"

"It was a goddamned near tragedy to commit the reserve battalion and leave Zahedan defenseless."

"Like hell. It was good tactics. We lost a minimum of casualties, and that reserve battalion stopped the gunships."

"That's enough! Both of you," Pickett yelled. A yeoman burst into the general's office, a look of alarm on his face. Pickett waved him away. "Sit down. Now!

"I don't want to hear any more of this."

Bernadino opened her mouth, but thought better than to argue. She felt her anger taking the form of tears, and hardened her face to control the feeling. Control, she told herself. She had already taken the wrong approach, she knew, the woman's emotional outburst had been what they anticipated. She'd gain nothing by continuing, for turning on the waterworks would be what they expected.

Pickett turned to Wilkerson. "And you. Your tactics didn't save the day. Let me remind you that the tiny margin of relief you got came from naval and air force aviation dropping ordnance in the area of those Soviet helicopters. Let me put that another way, General Wilkerson. I had to risk the air battle to pull your ass out of the fire. I realize it's bad officership to second-guess a subordinate commander. And you can't be blamed for the Soviets massing their helicopters and attacking with hundreds of tanks. However, if you want to keep your command, you'd better show a little caution in the way you spend your capital. No more debacles. You hear?''

Wilkerson exhaled in relief. ''Yes, sir.'' He braced for a moment, then added, ''You know, none of this would have happened if the logistics people and that inexperienced battalion commander—what's his name? Miles?—could have gotten that Osprey unit over here. When are they coming again, General Bernadino?''

Bernadino saw Pickett grimace in disgust at Wilkerson's cheap shot. She sat there a long, tense moment, knowing that it would be useless to answer his bombast or to argue further—this discussion was over. She knew that insubordination in a dire military emergency like this would not fall on sympathetic ears at any level. She knew that she would have to gut this one out. She stood and said, ''Tomorrow at the latest.'' She saluted and wheeled, then strode out of the general's cabin. The only thing she felt she had intact was her dignity.

As she walked down the passageways and climbed the ladders to the top deck so she could catch a flight back to Karachi, though, she lost even that. It seemed as if half the carrier crew saw her break down and cry on the way back to her plane.

Lieutenant Colonel Nelson Miles only periodically glanced at the sight below. When he did look through his vision devices, the Khali Desert looked as trackless as the sea. His instruments told him they were nearing the horn of the Arabian Peninsula. In another hour, they would be clear of this desert. Then it would be across the Arabian Sea.

The Marines had landed! They were ashore at the

port of Chah Bahar on the Gulf of Oman, ordered to secure the airfield and port facilities there for future American supply and staging purposes. He knew that at least three more divisions were intended to enter the country there and move northward to support the beleaguered airmobile and light-infantry divisions that had abandoned Zahedan. If an armored or mechanized-infantry division could be mustered, it would land at Chah Bahar. He'd also heard the reports of Iranians sending armored divisions to threaten the Soviet advance.

And, in less than—he checked his watch—three hours, the entire Osprey battalion would be landing.

Only one of the birds had been left aboard the carrier, awaiting a rebuilt engine. Another one had been diverted to Ryadh, Saudia Arabia, with a hydraulics leakage. Thirty-two of the first thirty-six Ospreys manufactured had made the flight, and it looked as if all of them would soon be seeing combat.

"Take the controls, Wendell," said Miles, watching as Barger performed the switch—even at low level, Osprey would fly itself, maintaining a constant distance from the ground with terrain-following radar, but at less than a hundred feet, a pilot always kept hands on the controls to take over in an emergency.

Miles fiddled with routine checks that did not have to be made. He checked the automatic navigational screen against an aeronautical map and whatever features he could see. Of course, the computers were right. He checked his watch. Three minutes had elapsed. His nerves wouldn't last three minutes longer at this rate, let alone three hours, so he tried to occupy his mind with more composed thoughts, remembering Julie and their last hours together. That was not enough to remember, he thought. Theirs was a relationship cemented by continuity, not a series of incidents of high emotion like meeting, courting, sex, marriage, parting. Well, wasn't it? He tried finding the answer by remembering deeper into his past with her. No matter where he went into his past, though, P.B. Keyes kept showing up. He tried to dismiss his friend, not want to dwell on things like the recent death of somebody close—with the certainty of combat so near, that could be bad luck.

He shifted mental gears to his family—Julie, Christian. He remembered their parting, he hugging her so hard she had to beg him to let her breathe. For a long time, they stayed locked in their embrace while the car idled outside waiting to take him to the airfield. He'd felt a tug on his flight suit. Christian, his son, grabbed the Nomex fabric and fell backward, sitting hard.

The toddler had begun to cry. Miles had been grateful for a lighter moment to lessen the dark emotions of the good-bye with Julie. This was a moment none of the veterans had told him about.

When he picked the boy up, he saw the child was crying in earnest, heart-broken.

"My God," Miles had whispered, "he's not squawking because he fell down."

Julie had burst into tears. "He knows you're leaving."

"No," Miles said, clearing the emotion from his own throat. "How could he?"

The boy had fallen limply against his neck and clutched his ear as he sobbed. Somehow, Miles had realized, the boy did, indeed, know his father would be leaving—at least he'd picked up the deep emotional signals between his father and mother. Miles had made the handoff and kissed them both, tasting their tears. He had left hurriedly, hoping Kopmeyer, his driver to the airfield, wouldn't see the wetness in his own eyes.

Kop had seen it, of course. "Toughest good-bye I ever made, Colonel."

"Me, too, Kop. Me too." Remembering it now and feeling the loss of Keyes again, Miles wondered why it was that he'd ever spent so much of his career aspiring to combat. War was not about glory or gain, he realized. War was only about loss.

Even as he was preoccupied with the idea of loss, he heard the satellite-relay report from the RDF command. He was ordered to maintain listening silence—

not to reply. General Little, the report said, had been killed in action.

"No way," said Barger. "That's enemy propaganda."

Miles wanted to key his radio mike to respond to the message transmitted via airborne relay. He paused. There was that order to maintain radio silence. As if for emphasis, the RDF command center repeated it, telling them to stay quiet until they closed to within an hour of landing. Besides, Miles thought, what the hell could he say? He wanted to deny the report, to call the sender a liar—to repeat Barger's charge of propaganda. What an impression that would make. He could see the headline. Battalion commander suffers battle fatigue before engaging in battle.

He and Barger stared at each other. With this new death report, he felt somehow guilty. He had spouted so many negative remarks about the general because Little had chosen Parker over him to first command the battalion. But that was not his only reason for feeling guilty.

He did not feel the same extent of grief as he had in receiving the news of Keyes's death. He hadn't known Little all that well anyhow, so he shouldn't feel guilty about not grieving, either.

He felt bootsteps in the passageway and turned to see Sergeant Joyce Bachman's horrified face. Into the intercom she said, "Does this mean that asshole, Wilkerson, is going to be fucking with us?"

Miles didn't answer. Bachman's words stung him. Instead of feeling grief or sympathy over the news that Little had been killed, the first thought in his mind, too, had been that they would have to work for Wilkerson.

Lieutenant Edwards watched the sun setting like a fireball. All afternoon, he thought grimly, he had been watching other fireballs, those of American helicopters being shot out of the sky. The Soviets had been preying on any helicopter that tried to come in and evacuate the two divisions of airborne soldiers so they could regroup farther south. All day long, Mi-24 gunships had kept an aerial perimeter around this mountain overlooking Nazil. Fewer than a hundred Blackhawk sorties had succeeded in withdrawing safely. Nineteen had been shot down or had crashlanded on the slopes of the mountain. Consequently, Edwards' platoon was among the soldiers informed that the cost had been evaluated as too dear for continued daylight operations.

The air war was still a stand-off. The Soviets were unable to have much effect against ground troops with their strike aircraft. but the Americans were unable to conduct any worthwhile attacks against Soviet helicopters or tanks, either. Both sides were too preoccupied with the inconclusive struggle for air superiority.

Edwards finished talking into his radio handset, and turned to Quintana, who sat with his arms folded around his knees, his face resting on his forearms. "Platoon Daddy, pass along the word the evacuation is going to be postponed until after dark."

With a tired salute, Quintana acknowledged and scrubbed his face with his hands, dry massaging his perpetual grin, now grown weak. He was oblivious to the Soviet helicopters ringing the peak in wide orbits four miles away, virtually eliminating the possibility that any ground soldiers could move down to harass the armored convoys that continued to pour by, heading southward toward the sea.

Quintana held a heated meeting with his youthful but veteran squad leaders. When he returned, Edwards said, "Don't be too tough on them."

"Can't let them get down, L.T. Can't let them get the mistaken idea this war is over." The sergeant's eyes met the lieutenant's. "Can we, Lieutenant?" The remark was more a challenge than a question.

Edwards blinked. He turned to stare at the plume of dust that obliterated the horizon.

"Between you and me, Sergeant?"

"Between you and me, L.T."

"Our mission was to delay those armor forces in the

mountains. Know what they're doing now? They're bypassing us. We've been reduced to a pocket of resistance. Next will come the reduction of the pocket.''

Quintana's grin widened. ''Our platoon isn't going to give up. Right, L.T.?''

Edwards returned Quintana's grin with a weak smile. ''Right.'' Quintana saluted and left him alone.

Edwards rubbed his eyes, tracked with red lines from lack of sleep. Horrifying as it was, the battlefield was becoming monotony, being forced to move, or being left behind, all of which was interspersed with terrifying moments of combat.

Edwards watched the exhausted Quintana return half an hour later and squat close enough to growl in his ear. ''It's getting harder to keep these guys believing we're charmed, L.T.'' He held out his map. ''Look at this. Know what happens when the Russians reach Jabahar?''

''I know, Sarge. There aren't any mountains left.''

''What's next, Lieutenant?''

Edwards said, ''We wait. Tonight we get extracted again.''

''*If* we're extracted . . . then what?''

''Then I guess we stop being mountain fighters and turn into desert fighters,'' Edwards said, putting on a smirk.

''You know, L.T., I think these boys had the right idea.''

Edwards raised an eyebrow.

Quintana said, ''They said they'd follow you anywhere . . . even to hell. Good thing, too. Looks like that's where we're going.''

# BOOK IV

# EMBERS

# 15

General Bernadino attended the evening command briefing reluctantly. She couldn't avoid giving the bad news to the command group. The rate of combat effectiveness for maintenance purposes had declined twenty-five percent. The combination of Soviet kills against Cobras had reduced that fleet to less than forty percent. The Kiowa numbers were no better. Even with all of the modifications made to modernize these older craft, they had fared poorly.

The Apaches, which had redeemed themselves in Saudi Arabia, had sustained substantial losses as well, and now the combat effectiveness was around sixty percent. Only the post-Desert Storm Black Eagle scouts with their lethal firepower and stealth technology seemed to be capable of eluding Soviet radar-controlled missiles and guns.

She caught Wilkerson before the briefing. "Can I talk to you before we go in?"

"Oh, you. I haven't slept so good. Be quick about it. The staff is waiting."

"I want to talk to you about the maintenance availability, General. It's worse than ever . . ."

"For once, couldn't you just bring me solutions instead of problems? Our people been fighting day and night. You walk in here every day and disparage their jobs, including what your maintenance and logistics people are doing."

"Disparage? I agree with you, these folks have done Herculean work . . ."

''Then how about showing a little loyalty to them? While you're about it, how about a little loyalty to me, too?''

She paused to analyze his face to see if he was joking. His eyes, deep-set anyhow, seemed to have sunk even deeper. *He's worried sick,* she thought.

''We've got a battle to fight here,'' he said. He pulled aside the flap of the briefing tent and pointed at the map to show where countless red marks indicated Soviet positions. He pointed at the few blue markers that showed American soldiers virtually surrounded on the mountain to the northwest. ''I shouldn't have to tell you about the necessity to relieve those troops . . . to be able to regain the initiative and prevent the Soviets from using Zahedan airfield. They can't be allowed to launch fighter aircraft.''

''I don't need to be told . . .''

''That's our mission, General. You have to support it. You must make those helicopters capable of flying.'' He walked into the tent, leaving her standing outside.

As the intelligence officer briefed the friendly and enemy situation, she grew even more apprehensive. The initiative had been completely lost. The vaunted American fighting machine might lose most of the two divisions now huddled around Kuh-e-Taftan, a peak a mere hundred kilometers away. The RDF staff had surmised that the infantry up there would simply be contained as the Soviets drove toward the sea.

The next briefing officer was for a nighttime evacuation of the divisions. As before, the superior technology of the Blackhawk would allow them to fly at night, whereas the Soviets' fighting capability would be somewhat diminished.

That was true, Bernadino thought to herself. But now the encirclement of the two divisions was almost complete. ''Wait a minute,'' she said.

''Yes ma'am?'' the briefer said coolly.

Bernadino saw that the young captain had been told to expect her protest already. He was showing her he would not be ruffled. She saw his eyes flick a glance in Wilkerson's direction, and she looked over, catching the new division commander wearing a sneer. She continued anyhow. "The rules of the game have changed. In previous night redeployments, the infantry was always able to disengage. The division's lift helicopters always had clear flying lanes in and out of the night landing zones. There's no way to reach the American troops now without overflying Soviet positions."

Wilkerson spoke up. "What's your point, General Bernadino? I mean, so far you're talking about tactics, which is my business. What is your logistics point?"

"General Wilkerson, the combat availability of our helicopters is low . . . perilously low. Why didn't anyone consult logistics people about this plan?" It was one thing to fudge figures as Wilkerson had done at Fort Irwin, she was thinking, but the enemy here could not be fooled by papering over critical deficiencies.

"Even if there wasn't any enemy in the area, this would be a risky lift," she said, making a visible effort to control her emotions, "It will take dozens and dozens of sorties to get all of those soldiers out of there. The helicopters will have to overfly the Soviet positions again and again. Each time they're bound to lose more. We simply don't have the numbers to support such a mission."

Then Wilkerson stood up to show how he had anticipated such objections. "Our aim is as much to rescue those soldiers off the mountain as it is to draw the Soviet helicopters into combat at night. Because we have superior night-fighting capability, we'll be able to knock them out of the sky. We'll be drawing their helicopters into trying to prevent our airlift. When we do, we'll reduce the threat that's kept us from being able to stop those tanks. Once the tanks are out of the way—"

"Wait!" Bernadino cried, standing up. "We can wait for the Ospreys. They're within half a day away. They'll be here by tonight . . . by mid-day tomorrow at the latest. We can use those aircraft to neutralize the Soviet helicopters tomorrow night. We can even use them to provide cover as the Cobras and Apaches and Black Eagles kill some tanks, maybe to take out the air-defense batteries going up around that mountain. We can't afford to risk—''

"Precisely! You can't be sure the Ospreys will be here, can you?''

She didn't answer for a long moment. "Nothing is an absolute certainty—''

"Uh huh! Exactly, and we can't afford to risk the loss of two divisions of infantry on a hope—they're surrounded by more than six Soviet motorized rifle divisions. We just can't sit here hoping the Ospreys will arrive.''

She realized after a few seconds of the uneasy silence that nothing was to be gained by further argument. So she sat down. The rest of the briefing went on without interruption. Still there was an uneasiness in the room. At the end, the staff scattered, leaving the two general officers alone in the tent.

"You *dare* defy me in front of the staff?'' His face showed more than anger, and his voice was more pleading than accusing in tone.

"General,'' she said wearily, "it's not defiance to disagree. I'm sorry if I upset you. We both have the same objectives, you know.''

"In front of junior officers . . . never mind that now. Right now our mission is to get those troops out of there.''

"General Wilkerson. The fact that your plan cannot be supported by a dwindling logistical and maintenance capability is not something to be swept under the carpet like a dirty family secret. You can't make decent decisions without accurate input.''

An awkward pause followed. Wilkerson searched her face to see if she really meant to say he couldn't make decent decisions at all. Bernadino labored at keeping a neutral face so he couldn't see that was exactly what she meant.

"Listen, General Bern . . . Rita. I'm only human. I'm just as prone to making mistakes as anybody. I know I try too hard sometimes. You saw what happened aboard the *Bremner* with Pickett. He actually threatened to relieve me of this command in the same breath as he appointed me. I don't dare to screw up. Tell me, haven't you ever . . . even once in your life, haven't you made a mistake?''

She felt her heartbeat spike like a rimshot on a drum as she saw a picture of those EMI shields stacked up inside the hangar the evening before Joel Parker's crash. Was that what he was referring to? No. He simply had a pleading, vulnerable expression. He was asking for her help, something he'd never done before. She cocked her head and looked at him in an entirely new light. For a second, his guard had come down. He was telling her he was truly human, even a little intimidated by the magnitude of his new command. It was one thing to be running around boldly on the battlefield when the division commander had to take the blame for any divisional mistakes. It was quite another to be that division commander. She felt sympathy for him. Maybe she would be suffering the same lack of confidence now if Pickett had named her commander instead.

''Bayard. General Wilkerson. It's all right to have these feelings of uncertainty. I promise I'll do my best to help you keep this division from screwing up.'' She saw a momentary look of gratitude in his expression. ''That's why I'm recommending we wait for the Ospreys. I can make a radio call. I'll call Pickett's headquarters and get permission to break radio listening silence. I'll—''

''No!'' The moment of Wilkerson's vulnerability had passed. ''I won't wait. If I'm going to screw up, it won't be because of indecision. I've always been told in a crisis to do something, even if it's wrong.''

''General Wilkerson, they might only be little more than an hour away.''

''They'll have maintenance and refueling standdown.''

''Not for long, I assure you. It won't take but a few hours—''

''General Bernadino, we don't have hours. Thanks

for your counsel, but the evacuation begins in minutes.
I've made up my mind not to procrastinate. If Pickett
sees me equivocating—one minute it's on, the next it's
off—there's no telling—yes, there is . . . he'll fire me.
Is that what you''—he squinted hard at her for a second—''that is what you want, isn't it? You'd do anything for this command.''

''Don't be paranoid, Bayard.''

He strode away.

'General Wilkerson!'' she called after him. He had
gone.


Lieutenant Edwards pressed a button on the casing
of his watch to illuminate the dial.

A reflection of the light banked off Quintana's teeth
as he asked, ''What time is it, L.T.?''

''Nearly twenty-two-hundred.''

''I can't believe it. They've designated our platoon
to be lifted out first. I can't believe we're going to be
the first in line for anything good. I got a bad feeling
about this, L.T.''

Edwards lowered his face so his expression couldn't
be seen, although he realized it was too dark for the
revulsion to show. ''I'm never going to jump into a
helicopter again without remembering that major general.'' No, he'd never forget the takeoff, the explosion,
the helicopter somersaulting in the air. He'd never forget the fire, two of his men trapped inside the fuselage
screaming as the flames spread out preventing any
thought of a rescue. Sergeant Kluth and Terry Umbreit. Gone. The others wounded so seriously they
might not survive either. Edwards shuddered. He had
shoved his men aboard, deciding to wait with half a
dozen of his men to take the last helicopter out. He'd
sent them to fry. He'd never forget his last sight of
those two stars smoldering, burning toward the neck
of the corpse—the headless corpse, the blackened,
blistered body. The war certainly did not accord any
privileges to rank.

Now, hard as it was to believe, his platoon would
be the first one off this hill. Somebody had actually

calculated that his company had been in combat the longest. Somebody had realized that his troops ought to get a rest. So the first flight in would be for them. He knew one thing for sure. He wouldn't be the first one to jump aboard one of those damned helicopters.

For the tenth time since the sun had gone down, he felt the need to urinate. He was anxious, he'd decided. It certainly wasn't because he had drunk too much water. This damned country sucked the water out of the body as fast as it could be poured in, but today nobody was pouring much water in because of new rationing rules. He hoped he wouldn't piss his pants. Since the crash, he felt he was losing it.

"Listen, sir," said Quintana.

Edwards heard the rattling of blades against the air and shuddered again. "Helicopters coming," he said. "I'd almost rather they were Russian tanks. At least there's no mystery about whether they want to kill you or not."

For the dozenth time, he checked the filter on his flashlight. It was still there, still red, still illuminated. He'd be the one to signal for the lead helicopter. The lead Blackhawk would land to his beam. Two other helicopters would land behind. Then his platoon would be off. There would be a dash across the Soviet positions. Then they'd be out of here. The thought of it made him so anxious he wanted to urinate again.

He heard sporadic gunfire from the direction of those helicopter blades. Two explosions followed. SAMs? No, a flight of attack helicopters were suppressing the Soviet positions that had been firing at the utility birds. The noise of the blades grew louder, and although he knew the helicopters were closing in, he couldn't quite tell what direction they were coming from. Maybe that was why the damn things were able to survive so well flying at night.

He heard static on his radio, then the rasping voice of a pilot asking for him to illuminate. That meant that they were close. They certainly sounded close. Edwards stood up, pointing the flashlight toward the sky as vertically as he could, and then swung around, gradually lowering the angle on the beam until he was certain a helicopter might see him, but some sniper from below could not.

"Roger," said a rattling radio voice, "I have your marker."

Edwards took the hand mike and growled a code word into it.

The pilot responded with the words "Crestview Place." Three syllables. Edward flashed his light three times in reply.

"Roger, got it. Inbound . . ."

Edwards heard the rattle of distant gunfire, then somebody shouting across the helicopter intercom to the pilot. The words leaked over into the radio transmission. They were weak but unmistakable.

"Taking fire. We're taking fire, we're hit . . ."

Edwards gawked at his radio speaker as if he couldn't believe what he'd heard. Then he whirled to his men and shouted, "Hit the ground!"

Suddenly his platoon and all the other members of the division scheduled to go out in the first hour from this LZ were illuminated either standing, half-crouching, kneeling, or lying on the rubbled, sloping LZ. They were lit up by the explosion of a Blackhawk helicopter, an explosion that revealed a flight of three others within a hundred meters of Edwards's position, their tails lowered, their wheels stretching for the ground on final approach. Edwards saw four other helicopters that had been flanking the first flight at a distance of about three hundred meters. Two of those suddenly exploded as well. Then Edwards saw why. There was a hovering line of enemy helicopters aiming over the ridge from about a thousand meters away. The noise of missiles and cannon fire drowned out his own shouting. The rounds that had missed the helicopters were striking all around the LZ. Two more helicopters hit the ground and broke apart. One began burning, catching slowly like a piece of wet driftwood thrown on a fire.

"Take cover!" he shouted, though he needn't have. All around men were scurrying like rats in the light of burning helicopters seeking low ground or boulders big enough to duck behind.

Edwards found himself face down in a shallow depression downslope from one of the burning helicopters. He couldn't see much, but what he did see was the helicopter that he and part of his platoon should have been riding to safety was now settling into its flames, its ordnance and ammunition exploding. He saw the fuel begin flowing as a fiery stream ran in his direction, the dry ground soaking up the river of fire before it had gone more than twenty or thirty meters.

Edwards thought he heard men screaming, but he couldn't be sure. He couldn't be sure of anything. His senses had gone haywire in the cacophony of sight and sound. Explosions strobed the night, freezing panicked running men in herky-jerky motions, brightening widened eyes, exaggerating shadows of screaming mouths that could not be heard in the blasts, the roaring of fires, the shouts of pain and terror indistinguishable either from commands to get down or from pleas for help. Concussions from explosions pummeled his body, alternately pressing his flattened body into the rock ground, then shoving him roughly from side to side like an invisible surf yanking him about, now and then a nearby blast spanking him like a towel full of needles. His skin tingled from the heat on the side of burning helicopters and from the cold on the side away. His flesh crawled in fear. He could not stop himself from loosing a scream of terror, then a second in panic that he could not even hear the first, could barely even hear it tearing up his throat.

A while later, he realized the tumult had ended. The roar in his ears was of a white, fuzzy surf, as though he had conch shells clasped to both sides of his head. He found his hands hurt from clutching the earth. The light had grown eerie orange as the fuels, metals, and crews of the aircraft burned. His throat hurt from screaming. God, this morning a hero, and already a coward. He checked his pants. Dry. Thank goodness for that, at least.

The six helicopters burned for a long time. As far

as Edwards could tell, nobody had escaped from the
downed birds. Only one Blackhawk had wheeled and
dashed down the slope away from the LZ immediately
after the first explosion. In the confusion, Edwards
hadn't noticed whether it had been hit. So it might
have escaped. One bird. Six of seven Blackhawks shot
down. His ticket out of here burning down to a molten
pool of metal. He knew there wouldn't be anybody
coming back for him. He didn't know whether he could
muster the courage to board one of the flying death
traps if they did. For now, no matter what his men
thought of him or expected of him, he felt that he was
mere inches away from coming apart at the emotional
seams.

Bernadino listened to the combat reports, becoming
more ill by the minute. They could not be disguised
as anything less than yet another disaster. She grew
less ill and more outraged by the minute, until she
finally got up, put on her combat gear, and strode out
of the communications tent. No way was she going to
sit stewing about him—not while there was work to
do. There would be a hell of a lot to do once those lift
helicopters returned. If they returned. She should go
forward to a rearming area to check out returning gunships. She should make herself useful. Then again, she
knew the very presence of a general officer on site at
any forward location disrupted normal operations. It
was the very reason Wilkerson caused turmoil—always
trying to be omnipresent.

As she strode to her helicopter, she saw that the
crew was gathered around it, getting ready to bed down
for the night. They often got no more rest than she
did. They often were forced to catch naps between her
flights from Iran back to Pakistan and to many of the
forward areas often carrying supplies, ammunition, or
fuel either in the cabin or slung under her Blackhawk.

"Gentlemen,' '' she greeted them. Immediately,
they began to stir, getting ready to fly. So many times
she had placed such demands on them at odd hours

they responded automatically without protest or questioning. She climbed into the cabin and sat down.

Her pilot started to board behind her. "Where to, ma'am?"

"Back to Karachi—"

He suddenly whirled around and pointed toward the western horizon. "Hineys!" he shouted. "They've gotten through the air defenses."

The crew jumped for the cockpit and began the quickstart procedure.

"Wait!" she shouted. "How do you know? I can't see a thing."

"It's the sound. It's not like one of our own helicopters."

"Wait! Sit still! I recognize those sounds . . . It's . . . by God, it's the Ospreys."

She jumped out of the cabin and ran to the operations tent. By the time she got there, Miles was pushing aside the light trap to the operations tent door.

"Nelson, thank God you're here. Are your people rested? Are your birds ready to fly? Are you armed? What's your status?"

"Ma'am, Lieutenant Colonel Miles reporting . . ."

"Never mind that crap, Nelson, answer my questions."

"We've been trying to get in touch with you for the last hour. Apparently the radios are being jammed or we've got different frequencies or—"

"Goddammit, Nelson, never mind that. You're here. Is everybody here with you? You are here with the Ospreys, aren't you? How many birds did you bring with you?"

"We have thirty-two."

She abruptly demanded a full status report, and he gave it quickly, sensing that the urgency of her questions meant an immediate need for their deployment. He gave her the mechanical readiness and fuel status, items she would be interested in. He finished by saying, "We'll be ready to fly as soon as we recalibrate our navigation equipment and drop the auxiliary fuel pads off the belly mounts."

* * *

Miles had his plan before he briefed his commanders. Training at Fort Irwin had already prepared them for this kind of operation. He'd always insisted that the Ospreys use more or less independent battlefield tactics, flying in pairs and sometimes threes but no more than that. "Tonight, we're going to separate into three flights," he said to his assembled commanders, and Blanks and Barger. "The bulk of you—twenty aircraft in all, say, Charlie and Bravo companies—will remain on call on the ground near division headquarters." Those two commanders groaned at the idea of being left out. A second group of six he instructed to approach the mountain from the south as two attack units of three. "I'll be in a third group, two more attack units of three, standing off ten miles to the south. We'll observe the air battle, stay the hell out of the way, and be ready to react to the battlefield."

Less than thirty minutes later, he was there, able to watch what was taking place almost as if it were daylight. It was like viewing inside a video games gallery, watching the Soviet ground fire take out one American helicopter after another. Miles hoped that there weren't any ground soldiers aboard the three Blackhawks that he saw shot down.

After a quick orientation, he ordered his attacking group of six Ospreys to disperse in pairs and hit the Soviets from three different directions. As soon as the Ospreys reported their new positions, he gave the order. "You are free to engage." Within seconds, they'd begun launching the first Raptor missiles fired in anger. Seven Soviet helicopters raking divisional positions with cannon fire were batted down suddenly like June bugs in the bright flashes of Raptors exploding.

Miles watched the Soviet attack broken within the first five minutes. American helicopters that had been kept from their landing zones took off from the security of Saravan.

A pair of Soviet Hinds tried to flee across the mountain slope. Two Raptor missiles fired simultaneously. Seconds later, they lit up the battlefield with a brilliant white light. When the light had vanished, so had the pair of Hinds.

"Watch it," Miles commanded. "Talk to each other. Don't fire two missiles if one will do."

The Soviet flight commander saw his early successes suddenly reversed. Earlier, Soviet ground soldiers had reported the flight paths of American Blackhawks, and IR searchlights had illuminated the American landing zones. When the American helicopters flew into the killing zone, his gunners had been able to shoot the Blackhawks down as if it were daylight. Now he knew that many of his own helicopters must have been illuminated in much the same way. Even as he searched for possible explanations, a flight of three Hinds vanished in another flash of light, shot down in flames without even a report. Then the battlefield flickered irregularly for a quarter hour, each flash of light resulting in the loss of one of his command.

Damn, he realized, the total lost in the last fifteen minutes was seventeen Mi-24s—and those were only the ones he'd seen or had been reported. How many others had simply vanished? He tried a call on his regimental frequency. "What in hell is going on out there? Report! Report, dammit!"

Only a smattering of panicked voices replied. Had the Americans somehow laid a trap of their own? Had their infantry been armed with a new surface-to-air missile? Feeling sudden prickles of dread all over, he directed his crews, "Break contact! Break contact! Get the hell out of here!"

As they picked up a heading toward Zahedan, he felt chills creeping down his spine. He remembered the Patriot missiles from the War of Shame. Whatever weapons the Americans had used back there could very well be tracking them right now. After ten minutes, though, he was certain that his crews and aircraft were safe.

Miles's group of six birds had not even been engaged in the battle at the mountain—there wasn't enough maneuver room for all twelve Ospreys. Miles directed the group that had tasted blood to disengage and return to Saravan. "Disperse around the division area and begin preventive maintenance." His own group he ordered to dash ahead of the Soviets, out-flanking them. He decided they would wait for the Hinds in ambush as they approached Zahedan. With luck, they might break the back of the Soviet Hind fleet tonight.

He watched the formation of Hinds approaching the field for landing. With all the activity and noise on the field, now would be the time to slip in. Deciding to sample the quality of the opposing air defenses, he reorganized in the air, directing one other Osprey to stick with him on a firing pass. The four others he ordered to stay put, prepared to operate in pairs. He took the controls and lined himself up for the same approach path the Hinds had taken.

"Everything to the right of the centerline of the run-way is yours," he said to his wingman. "Left is mine."

"Roger."

Miles was halfway down the runway at Zahedan when he opened fire. He checked the airspeed indicator and saw that he was pressing two hundred knots. He fired his cannons forward blindly, just clearing a path for him to overfly. Almost every burst of gunfire rewarded him with a secondary explosion as he over-flew a formation Hind-D helicopters hovering in re-vetments in a row.

He could hear Tryon reporting and engaging targets with the Raptor missiles. He thought he heard him say that three MiG-29s had been struck, but he wasn't sure because he had to concentrate on flying and shooting. Besides, there was this urgent shouting voice leaking through his earphones on a receiver set that he hadn't even selected.

His copilot touched him on the shoulder, but Miles shrugged him off. "Keep your damned eyes on the road, Barger. Keep checking the instruments. Be pre-pared to take the controls."

"Colonel Miles, it's the general," the copilot said grimly.

"Tell her we're kicking ass, buddy."

"Nelson, dammit, it's not Bernadino, it's Wilkerson. The goddamned division commander is yelling to talk to you right damned now."

Without taking his eyes off the windscreen display, Miles instructed the copilot to switch his receiver so that he could listen. Immediately he was sorry that he had. The voice of Major General Bayard Wilkerson screamed at him.

". . . who gave you authority? Break off the engagement! Get your tails back here! I want to talk to you *now*, Miles."

Miles tried to roger the transmission, but the general kept shouting.

"Override the sonofabitch," he told his copilot. He felt a rap on his elbow, indicating it had been done. "General, I can't disengage right now. I've got my hands full on Zahedan, over."

"Don't you dare override me, Colonel. We're trying to manage a disaster by evacuating troops, and you're off on an independent mission."

"But General, we're killing Hinds by the fistful—"

Wilkerson overrode him. "The mission is to evacuate the infantry, mister. You're endangering two whole divisions by being there. Put your Ospreys back on security around that mountain. Once you've done that, get your butt back here to headquarters. Is that understood?"

"General, we've got enough Ospreys to do both mission—"

Again the override. "Now!"

"Wilco," Miles growled into the radio. He punched up a radio change and gave the direction Wilkerson had ordered. Then he jerked his Osprey angrily back toward the airfield and ordered Tryon to launch another pair of Raptors before breaking off the engagement.

A white flash behind them was followed by a tattoo of secondary explosions. Tryon whooped into the intercom, "We hit a string of parked Hineys. Must be near a rearming point . . . shit, look at it blow."

Miles could not enjoy the fireworks. He knew they might have inflicted even more damage. He ordered Blanks to situate the remaining five Ospreys so they could protect Blackhawks lifting troops off the mountain. Then he said to Barger, "Technically, we've done what he wanted. Now let's go back and see what the sonofabitch wants."

Barger snorted. "You gotta ask? He wants to chew your ass, Colonel."

Miles and his wing Osprey made a low-level break to the west and he plotted a course to return by a roundabout way to the division headquarters. As his adrenaline began to settle down, and the anger passed, he began to worry that he actually had done something wrong. Didn't he have permission to make this attack? Did he lose anybody? Was he supposed to be somewhere else?

All he knew for certain was that they had just been called off an attack that could have netted them dozens more kills. Another thing he knew—Wilkerson was one pissed-off major general. Too goddamned bad.

The intensity of General Wilkerson's rage had diminished in the thirty minutes it took for Miles to appear at the operations headquarters. When Miles entered the headquarters, he was immediately taken by stern staffers to face the division commander. Miles was astonished that Wilkerson had lost ten pounds since the last time he had seen him in the states. That weight loss was made even more dramatic by the gauntness in his jowls that now seemed to practically slide off his face. Wilkerson's eyes had sunk deeper than ever into his head, making him look sorrowful.

"Colonel, I hope you have one hell of a fine excuse for risking that evacuation without my specific orders."

"General Wilkerson . . . sir . . . when I arrived, General Bernadino met me. She told me about the battle action around the mountain. She indicated that we had soldiers trapped there and I took some of my battalion out to do what we could—''

''Without *my* orders.''

''But, General . . . sir . . . I received orders from . . . a general officer. I was in no position to refuse those orders. Besides, we drove away the Soviet helicopters.''

''Are you questioning my orders, Lieutenant Colonel Miles?'' Wilkerson's tone had softened.

''No, sir.'' He looked to Bernadino, and she nodded almost imperceptibly. ''I might have misunderstood your priorities at first, but they are perfectly clear now.'' The effort of being civil made Miles aware of his pulse throbbing in his temples.

Wilkerson responded with an indulgent smile. ''No harm done, I suppose. At least you didn't lose any of the Ospreys. And, fortunately for you, the evacuation is progressing without a hitch. In fact, General Pickett has congratulated me . . . the division. Tomorrow, we go after the Soviet tanks with every Apache, Black Eagle, and Cobra we can muster. The Ospreys will stand off and wait for the Soviet attack helicopters to react. Then you will take them and jump the Soviets at a respectable standoff distance and get rid of those infernal Hineys once and for all. Then it will go back to the way it was the first day. Then it will be a turkey shoot. We're going to destroy the Soviet armored forces where they sit.''

''General Wilkerson, if I may say so . . . I could take part of my fleet back there and take out maybe a hundred Hinds on that airfield. They're everywhere. The advantages over the Soviets are almost doubled or tripled when we use our night-fighting technology.''

Wilkerson squinted at Miles. ''I appreciate your offer, but if you don't mind, I'd rather use you as the division reserve so I can get the most out of other helicopters killing tanks. We're a little depleted in that department, if you haven't heard, and I don't need you to start running this war for me.''

''Sir, with all due respect,'' said Miles, ''the Osprey was designed for more than convoy escort.''

''Don't give me that 'due respect' shit, Miles. You have your orders.''

Miles didn't know what to say, so he did not say anything. He wanted to curse Wilkerson for being so damned pig-headed. He gritted his teeth and looked at Bernadino. She shook her head, so he kept his mouth shut.

# 16

Abramov stood outside surveying the damage on Zahedan airfield. Although the sun had begun to rise, bringing on another blazing day, he felt a clammy crawling on the back of his neck that slithered up into his scalp. In a few minutes, he would receive the detailed battle damage reports that he had ordered. He had wanted to see with his own eyes, too. What he saw was awesome destruction.

He felt a presence at his shoulder. "Aleksandr Mendenyev," he said, "One pass! Whatever attacked this airfield had done so in a single pass. What could do that? The damned stealth fighter?"

"I too have assessed the airfield, Comrade Marshal. Not every area of the airfield was attacked. The stealth fighter did not use this kind of weaponry in Iraq. This is different from those so-called smart weapons. Wherever it was . . . whatever it attacked, it caused ninety-percent destruction."

"No misses to speak of. Fortunately, there had been only half a dozen fighters stationed on the field. More are due today. I am to establish this airfield with enough anti-aircraft protection and to put the skies under the umbrella of our own fighter cover. Then the complexion of the battle here will change. We have to win this battle today. If I have to undergo another night like last night . . ." His voice trailed off.

"You have a briefing, sir. I'll see if I can find anything to help out."

Abramov clapped a hand on the shoulder of the man

who had been sent to spy on him. He searched Mendenyev's face: he was hiding no secrets now—instead, the younger man was looking at him with respect. In a way, Abramov felt sorry for him. Eventually, Mendenyev would have to answer to Moscow, and loyalty to him would do the young man no good with those jackals.

Abramov turned and hurried toward the briefing room. He listened to the reports of battle damage glumly. He had hoped to hear that his personal assessment was an inaccurate glimpse. Not so. Everywhere the strike had been focused, it had been unleashed with accuracy.

Abramov then heard from the commander of airdefense weapons. The officer was nervous, more so when Abramov sat up in his chair and narrowed his eyes. "So tell me," Abramov asked sternly, "what was this weapon that struck the airfield last night? Was it similar to anything that devastated Iraqi tank regiments in the last American war?"

"No, Comrade Marshal. These weapons from last night seem to have been fired at nearly ground level. It was as though infantry soldiers had deployed the weapons that had struck last night. And . . . we did not acquire them with radar."

"Helicopters, then?" Abramov asked, leaning forward to stand up. Everyone suddenly stiffened, for they now knew he was in a dangerous mood. Indeed, Abramov stood up and stalked across the room to the tactical map table. Waving his hand across it, he cried: "Look at this! By any measure, we have won this battle in Iran. We have achieved air parity with the Americans, and the Iranians have nothing left in the air to challenge us. In the northwest, we have completely surrounded Tabriz and the oil fields. Along the eastern border, the Iraquis have completely tied up the Iranian army until the last few days. Our way is clear to drive the Americans into the sea to drown like kittens. One would look at this map and assume that this war is over."

The staff shrank back in their chairs as Abramov took a deep breath.

"This war is not over," he shouted. "The Americans could change the complexion of this war even without a major engagement if they have the kind of weapon that could do the devastation that you have seen on this airfield in a single pass!" Abramov smacked his fist against the map table, upsetting half the markers meticulously laid out by his staff.

"I want to know what in the hell the Americans have used to make that strike. Was it a strategic weapon? If so, I must advise Moscow so we might consider countering it with strategic weapons of our own. Where were they based? Should we send long-range strike aircraft after this weapon? Were these space weapons? I want to know. Somebody tell me—"

Abramov heard a disturbance at the back of the room and turned to see Mendenyev elbow a younger man, whose hand rose reluctantly.

Abramov acknowledged the hand by barking, "What?"

The timid junior staff officer cleared his throat. "Comrade Marshal—"

"Speak up!" Abramov cried, even as his eyebrows rose in curiosity. Mendenyev had dragged the youngster to the staff meeting from a field position with his troops. His clothes were disheveled and dirty. His trousers and boots were filthy from the mud. Where had the young fool found mud in this desert, anyhow?

"Comrade Marshal, I was out with my men on patrol last night when the attack occurred. We had been watching through our binoculars as our helicopters returned from battle when I saw a . . . a craft—I am an intelligence officer, you see, so you know that what I say next—"

"Out with it, man." Abramov motioned, as if pulling the words from the officer's mouth. His tone was more interested than harsh.

"It was a craft common to the American services, the Marines, the Navy and the Army. It was thought to be used only for carrying high-ranking officers and for carrying platoon-size forces. Its biggest threat to us was thought to be when the American Navy used it for anti-submarine operations. We saw three such aircraft flying last night just before the strike.''

"What are these aircraft? Are they helicopters? Are they airplanes? What would anti-submarine aircraft be doing here?" Abramov threw his arms out in supplication. "Did these craft land ground forces?"

The young officer cleared his throat. "Comrade Marshal, they are capable of hovering like helicopters and flying like airplanes. They have rotors on their wings which become propellers in forward flight and the wings can rotate toward the vertical so that the propellers become rotors. Last night they were flying as helicopters. We did not see them fire at the airfield, but the strikes in the distance would seem to indicate that the airfield was hit shortly after those hovercraft flew over us. I don't see how they could have had time to insert saboteurs, inflict their damage, and pick up all traces of ground troops.''

Abramov whirled on the air-defense commander. "What sort of radar indications have you not told us about?"

The commander, already shaken, tossed a hateful glance at the young intelligence officer, then stood up on shaky legs. "Comrade Marshal, the only radar returns we received last night were of ordinary helicopters hovering at the distant perimeter of our airfield. None fired in our direction. None flew over—"

"Something flew over. Soldiers on the ground reported that. Something blew up our goddamned—"

The young intelligence officer raised his hand again, like a reluctant child in classroom. Abramov had already acquired a healthy respect for this officer simply because he was not afraid to get his boots dirty. How many of his staff officers would have risked their own hides on infantry patrol?

Abramov nodded toward the young officer.

"We brought back what we believe to be a working transmitter which perhaps could account for the signals our radar received.''

"Tell me more," Abramov said gently.

"The construction of the aircraft would almost certainly prevent any radar returns from the rotors. When the aircraft hovered, its horizontal profile of the blades was covered by a tapered ring that certainly was designed to defeat radar. I have studied such things in electronics school, Comrade Marshal—"

Abramov waved his hand, a signal to tell the young man to proceed with his report rather than to lay out his credentials.

"There were others of these devices, but as our soldiers approached them and touched them, they exploded. They were apparently constructed to avoid being taken." He pointed at a shiny cylindrical tube with a black ball at one end and a point at the other. The staff shrunk away from the device.

"Don't worry, comrades, we have had this device examined by our demolition engineers. The self-destruction charge has been removed, but the rest of the device is intact. We have examined it as much as we were able and find that it emits a signal which appears on our radar as the return from helicopter blades. Many of these were fired upon and destroyed by our anti-aircraft weapons."

The air-defense officer, feeling vindicated, seemed to relax. He stopped shuddering and looked at the young intelligence officer in a more favorable light.

There was a long pause. Abramov had suddenly grown thoughtful and calm. He began pacing the room as if oblivious to anyone else in the room. For their part, the staff sat expectantly, not daring to say a word.

Finally, Abramov asked the young officer, "Who approached this device after other soldiers had been killed?

The officer lowered his eyes and whispered, "It was I, sir."

Nodding, Abramov regarded the young officer. "You have seen this craft? And you are certain that it was those craft which fired these . . . transmitters into the ground to deceive our radars?"

The young officer nodded. "That is affirmative, Comrade Marshal."

Reassured, Abramov began issuing new directives. All battle plans were to be adjusted immediately. All air priorities were to orient on one mission. "The demon aircraft has to be found and destroyed," he said. "Do that before all else." He eyed his staff, letting his command sink in during the pause. "Any questions?" There were none.

The coming of daylight was a relief. Now Abramov's army would not have to rely on electronic gadgetry. He'd always believed that in battle a commander must rely on his own eyes. By day he might see this demon bird for himself, and what he could see, he could kill.

Nelson Miles stood stiffly, leaning forward into Wilkerson's argument. "You're my reserve for today's operation, Colonel. You're the only flexibility we have after we commit our helicopters against those tanks. I'm keeping those on a short leash, mister. No more of your damned independent operations. This is supposed to be a team effort, Miles. There's no room for mavericks."

Again Miles grew angry. Had one of his peers made such a remark, there would have been a fist fight on the spot. With Wilkerson, he could only grit his teeth. Against Bernadino's advice, he was having trouble holding his tongue.

Miles said, "General Wilkerson, the Ospreys can handle any threat the Soviets throw out. They'll make a great reserve at night."

"Don't lecture me, Colonel. I know the Osprey's capabilities."

"All I'm saying, sir, is that the key to their success is darkness. The stealth qualities and deception technology built into the Osprey prevents Soviet radar from picking them up."

"I said—"

"Dammit, General, Osprey's potential will be virtually useless as a daylight reserve. They'll be visible to enemy gunners. Any damned Ivan with a rifle could spot one and punch holes in it.''

''Are we going through this again? I thought I told you the decision had been made. Don't you have any sense of imagination? What about your loyalty? I have read the book you yourself wrote.'' He tossed a thick manual of Osprey doctrine on the table.

''Turn to Appendix E, why don't you?'' Wilkerson said.

Miles jaws clenched shut. ''I don't have to, General. I wrote it. It's the chapter on emergency combat operations—''

''Daytime fighting, if I remember correctly.''

''*Emergency* daytime fighting. The reason that chapter was made an appendix instead of a regular chapter. In the next edition of that manual, daytime fighting is going to be declared an *extreme* emer—''

Wilkerson sneered at him. ''Next edition? We don't have time to wait for the presses, now do we? Tell you what, I'm declaring a daytime emergency, Colonel. Time for you to salute and step out.''

''General Wilkerson, last night you insisted my birds pull convoy escort, and they did. Today's a different ball game. They're too vulnerable for daylight employment.'' He turned and pleaded his case with Bernadino, his eyes begging for her support. ''Tell him, General.''

Wilkerson turned to Bernadino. ''Yes, tell him, General. Give him the status of our attack fleet. Tell him our fighting availability is so low we can't kill tanks unless we use every damned gunship that can fly. We can't protect them without the Ospreys.''

Bernadino was distracted with her own thoughts. Miles sighed in relief when she said, ''I have to agree with Colonel Miles. We'd be better off waiting until dark before using the Ospreys.''

Wilkerson stared at her in disbelief. ''Surely, you're not contradicting me, too. Fine, maybe I've been a little too democratic in seeking advice from the both of you before deciding on my battle plan. All right, here's the way it is. I've listened to your suggestions for employing or for not employing the Ospreys. I have the division's top logistics officer's opinion as well as the Osprey battalion commander's. But my decision is made. Discussion is done. Time to support the plan." Wilkerson spun on his heel and walked away, leaving both of them staring at each other.

Miles saluted and said, "I'm on the way to brief my officers. What shall I tell them, General Bernadino? That we're fighting naked in broad daylight?"

She shrugged helplessly. "Go back and follow orders to the best of your ability. I . . . have to check on something. Colonel, I'm going to do something I've never dreamed of doing. I'm going to check discreetly with the general's staff to see why they approved such a cockeyed plan to use those birds during the day. Meanwhile . . . until I get back to you, think of a way of . . . conserving your resources in a day battle. Stall until you hear from me."

He stared at her, comprehending fully what she was telling him.

"Nelson," she said, "I would never drag you into anything that wasn't fully above board unless—"

"Don't say another word, General Bernadino. Don't say anything either of us will have to admit to or lie about later. I'm going to conserve my precious resources. You get hold of the general's RDF staff."

She smiled gratefully and flicked a salute at him. Then she went off to check behind her division commander's back to find out whether he'd been arrogant enough to deploy Ospreys in his daytime battle plan— declaring a so-called emergency—against massed Soviet forces without informing higher headquarters.

The first condition of Wilkerson's battle plan was fulfilled. The Soviets had massed their tanks and armored vehicles for an attack on the thin American lines southwest of Khash. Wilkerson overheard word on the radio that the lead defenses of the American infantry had been overrun by Soviet tanks. He tuned in to the frequency of the battalion in contact. He grew sanguine at hearing the numbers of tanks that had overrun the American positions.

"Now," he ordered the division operations officer. "Now get those Cobras out there and hit those tanks with flanking fire. Have the Apaches standing by."

Wilkerson's plan was simple. Cobras on the south-eastern flank of the armored columns were to strike and then withdrew through the Apaches, which were to make a second strike. If there was no Soviet response by their anti-helicopter Hinds, then the sequence was to be repeated. First the Cobras then the Apaches would strike at a different part of the column.

Miles, sitting in his cockpit, heard his command to join the attack directly from the division commander's mouth: "Fire up your Ospreys. I want them deployed in force in Zone Juliet. All available firepower, understand?"

Miles studied his large-scale map in disbelief. Zone Juliet was small enough to be covered by a trio off Osprey, four at most. All his craft at once would seem like fish in a rain barrel. He decided to try one last attempt at reason. Reluctantly, he keyed his radio mike. "General, it's much better to leave them dispersed and to attack in ones and twos. It does us no good to concentrate them. It only makes them more vulnerable. A single Osprey is able to deliver the firepower of an entire battalion—"

Wilkerson shouted over the air, "You just don't get it, do you? You just don't think that you ought to be taking orders, do you? You think because you've been handed the command of these Ospreys, you ought to be in charge, don't you? Well, there's always somebody else who can do your job, Miles. If you don't get moving, I'll relieve you and move on down the line of officers in that battalion until I find somebody who will fight. Got that?"

Miles gulped down a retort. There was no point in resisting any longer. The best way to protect his men was to command them as best he could, better than anyone else could. He would be forced to other measures. The idea of somebody else trying to pull off this risky plan gave him the shudders worse than if he took it on himself.

He would have to adjust his battle plan. Somehow he had to concoct a scheme to save his Ospreys from ruin. He called for a meeting of his commanders, and Blanks, his operations officer.

"Gentlemen, this is a meeting for listening, not talking," he told them. They squinted at him. "We're going to have to fight by day, against all my advice to the contrary. So I'm taking matters into my own hands and using my own emergency tactics. First, I'm under the impression that there's some sort of maintenance virus running rampant through your aircraft. That's true, isn't it?"

His last sentence was no question. He stated it in a way that demanded an affirmative response.

"Yessir?" they all replied.

"I understand that three Ospreys from each company will have to be grounded for daylight hours for maintenance repairs." He looked at Blanks. "And yours, Major Herman, from headquarters section."

Blanks answered, "That's right, Colonel," and the company commanders followed his lead with a "Yessir" in unison.

"Fine. Do the best you can to get these birds up and flyable no later than sundown but no earlier than darkness. Got it?" They nodded to indicate they did.

"Great, then in today's battle, those who do go out and fight, make sure we try to avoid shooting missiles or cannons directly to the front. Try to engage the Soviet helicopters at distances of a mile or more, even if that means shooting laterally. That way, we'll all have responsibility for protecting our brothers and have less chance of being spotted by Ivans right off our noses."

They rogered.

"Another thing. We'll set the birds on the ground and try to fight without raising dust clouds. It might help us if the Ivans don't have any movement to spot. Anything else you come up with by way of good ideas, let me know about."

Miles dismissed the commanders. Blanks looked at him squarely and said, "One part of this plan I don't like."

"You don't want to be left behind."

"Correctomundo."

"You have to say I ordered it. Now that you have some time to kill, make a memo for record. Address it to Bernadino and Wilkerson to cover your ass."

"No fucking way, Nelson."

"Herm, there isn't time to argue. If Wilkerson court martials my butt, I want you to be in the clear so you can take over, got it? No arguments."

Blanks lowered his gaze and scuffed at the ground with the toe of his boot. "I get it, Nelson." He raised a formal salute. "Good luck, my friend. You're going to need it. If the Ivans don't get you, the goddamned general will."

Edwards's platoon had come under the heaviest barrage of the entire campaign. First came the artillery. Air bursts sent shrapnel shrieking through the air. Mixed in were delayed-fuse projectiles that penetrated the ground before exploding, sending shock waves through the earth and collapsing the sides of nearby fighting positions. Around Edwards's positions, the artillery seemed like one continuous roar, with only the distance of the guns providing any variation in the howls. All the soldiers could do was hunker down inside the fighting positions and cower.

Edwards found his senses almost useless. The exploding rounds deafened him so he could not even hear the squawking from his platoon radio receiver. Only when someone very nearby yelled was he able to hear anything, but even then he was hardly able to understand what was being shouted. Just as frightening was the inability to see. When he dared to look out from the sandbags that held up the overhead cover, he could not see for the dust raised by the explosions and sent swirling by the wind. The concussions raised instantaneous dust, fogging in his senses in an impenetrable clamor.

Fifteen minutes into the barrage, Edwards began to feel a new sense of dread. This fusillade did not seem to be rolling by or diminishing as with a preparatory artillery attack. No, the dust continued to filter in, threatening to suffocate him. The smell of the explosives had accumulated, so he and his men were gagging. Already, his radio telephone operator had puked, his nausea caused as much by burnt cordite as by fear.

Finally, he was growing panicky as the earth continued to shake. Would he be buried alive here in this godforsaken region? More and more the earth trembled, shaking him loose of his senses. His mind began playing awful tricks on him. There! Soviet tanks! He heard them rolling through his position.

But no! The earth shivered again as more artillery rounds struck and he was certain that it was only an increase in the intensity of the barrage.

Even as he argued with himself, he knew he must take a look outside to try to get some grasp on the reality of the situation.

Edwards pawed at the sifting sand that had begun to pile up around the firing port just in front of his face. As he did so, he realized he was hearing other sounds. There was the snapping of small-arms fire, he realized with a panic. The ground *was* shivering with much more than the erratic pounding of artillery. *My God, they were advancing!* He'd been paralyzed by fear, simply lying in a hole waiting to be overrun by Soviets?

He swept armloads of sand into the fighting position, pouring it down the front of his shirt and into his belt, piling it up around his ankles trying to get a clear view of what was happening outside. As he did so, a vague shadow passed over, eclipsing the irregular rectangle of light that he had excavated. A tank! A Soviet tank was passing by. Its right track had almost run directly over the top of their fighting position. The Soviets were advancing buttoned up, rolling through their positions. Once again he was in the midst of a Soviet army, only this time they had all the escape routes covered. They were going to end this once and for all.

Today, all this fighting was going to end for Thomas Edwards. This he knew for certain. He also knew something worse—he was going to die a coward.

Abramov watched from a distance, barely able to see for all the dust raised by the tanks and the continual pounding of the artillery. He should have been concerned for the American demon birds, but his first fear was for Mendenyev, who had insisted on riding in the front ranks of their attack helicopters to be Abramov's eyes on the battlefield.

Intermittent reports from forward observers told him that lead troops had encountered the first of the defensive positions and had begun rolling through without resistance. Abramov shrugged at these. That part of the attack was simply a ploy to draw out an escalation of defenses from the Americans. He expected the anti-tank helicopters to show themselves first. Then he would counter with his own anti-helicopter defenses, the Mi-24s, now hidden five miles to his rear with engines idling. They would pursue the American helicopters. Pressure, pressure, pressure. It was the only thing that worked. It was the difference between his army and the Iraqis one war ago. Abramov needed pressure to force out whatever secret weapons had caused the destruction at Zahedan last night. Then he would unveil his own trap.

"Lift the artillery," he ordered, looking over the top of his field glasses. "Shoot only after the sighting of American helicopters, and only on my order. I want air bursts."

Abramov's artillery commander looked at him incredulously. "We are lifting fires?" he asked. "What about covering the movement of our own tanks and helicopters?"

"They are on their own. Lift your fires."

The artillery officer hesitated a moment longer. "We are sacrificing tanks and men, Comrade Marshal."

"Yes," he said. "Perhaps it is a sacrifice of men

and tanks, but it is one I am willing to make if we can see those damned birds.''

The artillery officer had not given the order.

''Lift it now,'' Abramov ordered. ''Only if we see them can we kill them.'' The artillery commander ran to a radio to give the commands.

Abramov bit his lip. He felt as reluctant as the artillery commander. But he had to do it. This was to be one of the moments of truth in his battle.

A pair of OH-58 Kiowa pilots first sighted the Soviet tanks. The pilots found a safe place behind a ridge to touch down and observe through the awkward-looking periscope and target acquisition device that rested atop their rotor system. By positioning themselves below the horizon, their rotor blades did not create a radar signature. From there, using their maps as reference, they guided a patched-together company of Cobras— there were only twenty-three left from the entire brigade—to turn northward at a point where the entire column of helicopters could then turn their weapons at once toward the west and be able to fire one or two volleys before escaping en masse. Everybody understood perfectly that they would not wait around to seek new firing positions. The Cobras would fire and run, passing through the faster Apaches. The pilots grew increasingly busy as more and more scouts worked up along different axes to assist in observing and in designating targets with their own lasers. In all, only a dozen Kiowas had survived, and each would be able to designate two targets. As the scouts looked over the ridge, though, and saw the advancing columns of tanks, the reaction of all of them was the same. ''Shit! How many tanks do they have?''

Even through the rising clouds of dust, it was evident that hundreds of tanks pressed forward into the pass to break through American ground forces. The infantry wouldn't be able to hold them back. The helicopters weren't going to make a dent in this advance.

The lead Cobras reported they had traveled about a

mile since it had turned northward. The trail Cobra reported it was approaching the turning point.

The scout pilot directed the twenty-three helicopters to turn west to flank the linear, rising dust cloud. "Fire on command," he ordered. "Then get the hell out of here!"

Lieutenant Edwards had recovered somewhat, for the firing of artillery had slackened. Tanks still thundered by, and one had even run over the edge of his platoon command post, knocking a couple hundred of pounds of gravel into the hole. Little firing was going on outside. Edwards realized that the Soviet tankers must have been driving through this area buttoned up to protect themselves from their own artillery. They might not even know that they were in the middle of the American fighting positions. Cautiously he looked out the firing port in front of him and saw a convoy of personnel carriers approaching. He suddenly felt calm, despite the increased danger. He might still die today, but he felt sure it wouldn't be as a coward, after all. He would die all right. But fighting.

Edwards made a quick radio report to his company commander. Then he switched down to his platoon frequency and ordered his gunners to take on the infantry vehicles first, then to turn their tubes in the opposite direction and see if they could inflict any damage on the rear of the Soviet tanks. No option looked particularly good right now, but he decided he might be able to start a firefight that might get the Soviet tanks and infantry shooting back and forth at each other.

Edwards burrowed through the constricted exit trench to fire his own Collapsible Light Anti-tank Weapon. The CLAW had been developed in the 1990s as the lightest, smallest anti-tank weapon on the battlefield, and one man could carry four rockets and a fifth in its firing tube.

Edwards rolled clear of the bunker so the rocket's minimal back blast would be deflected upward, then aimed at the first Soviet personnel carrier. As he ex-

posed himself, a chill ran up his spine. A big chill.
He could feel a Soviet tank turret turning around, preparing to fire at that bull's-eye on his back.

He fought off the feeling, took aim, squeezed the
trigger. A blast like a firecracker blew the rocket out
of its tube ten feet, simultaneously lighting the rocket
motor. Then, at a safe distance the rocket lashed out
at a thousand feet a second, faster than a bullet. Immediately after firing, he switched ends, shook the
sand off a second rocket and stuffed it into the tube.
When he turned, all he saw was the rear end of a tank.
It hadn't spotted him. He fired a second rocket, catching the tank in the ring between the turret and the hull.
The tank exploded and the turret separated, lifting high
on one side as ammunition inside began blowing, then
toppling over and landing upside down on the ground.

Edwards had hardly fired when he heard other explosions. Had the rest of his men come out to fire at
the tanks? Everywhere he looked, Soviet vehicles were
being blown up. Marveling at how accurate the firing
was, he looked around to congratulate them. He saw
nobody.

How could that be? One after another of the Soviet
tanks and carriers blew up violently, as if every single
CLAW had hit as vital a spot on the tanks as his had.
He heard a singing as an artillery round flew over his
head and ducked his face into the sand. Then he realized it wasn't artillery after all. And it wasn't
CLAWS. There were logs about the size of fence posts
flying across the earth from ten to twenty feet above
the ground. Then he realized that the Soviet tanks were
under fire by larger weapons.

Helicopters! Helicopters must be firing Hellfires and
TOWs.

He turned back toward the Soviet personnel carriers
and saw two more go up in orange-black explosions.
Then, looking down toward the city through a clear
spot, he saw a flock of Soviet helicopters coming his
way. He realized that the Soviets were now counterattacking with their own helicopters. This battlefield
had grown too busy, too noisy, too deadly for him, so

he belly-crawled down his trench and flopped like a fish into the bottom of his fighting position. Below, his men looked at him in amazement, as if they were astonished to see him return alive.

Beach said, "Lieutenant, how many hits did you get out there? It sounds like you busted up the whole goddamned Russian army."

Giddy, Edwards laughed and said, "No, there's a helluva goddamned war going on outside there now, and it's bigger than any of us now."

The moment the scout pilots spotted Soviet Hinds in the distance, they began shouting for the Cobras to scatter. About half of them immediately broke off their firing engagements, even before the missiles they were designating had made it all the way to their targets. These pilots had already been chased by the Soviet Hinds. They weren't about to allow them to get too close again. The remainder of the pilots decided to stick around and guide their missiles on to impact.

The Kiowa pilots were five hundred meters farther away from the advancing Hinds, but they too had been routed by the Soviets often enough in the past and they wanted no part of them now. One by one they began breaking contact, cutting loose their laser guidance of Hellfire missiles and the wire-guided TOWs, letting them fly off ballistically toward the battlefield. The lead scout broadcast a warning:

"Snake elements, Snake elements, you've got bandits at twelve o'clock . . . and one o'clock and two o'clock on a direct heading for your position. Suggest you break off and depart due west. I say again, you've got bandits closing fast! Break it off! Break it off!"

Captain Sean Elliott was the last one to see a pair of Cobras still engaged. It wasn't bravery, he decided. In his opinion, the pilots were idiots who would never see another day. Disgustedly, he took the controls from his copilot and turned his craft around, wheeling and pivoting at the same time, then sprinted across the open area, hoping that he could get to the next ridge line before the Hinds began firing after him. There, the Cobras and the Black Eagle scouts would be putting up another line of defense. Beyond them would be the Ospreys. If he could make it to that ridge, perhaps he and his copilot would survive. A big if.

Edwards had stuck his head up to get another first-hand report for his men. He saw the American helicopters turn tail. Then he spied a tank rolling directly toward them. The tank was going to run over their position, perhaps falling down into the hole they had dug, probably crushing them. Frantically, he raised the tube of his CLAW to the firing port. It hardly mattered whether he died from being squashed or suffocated or fried. The only difference now was whether he could take out a Soviet tank before he died.

The shadow looming outside the slit grew darker until it shut out the smoky, cloudy sky. By the time Edwards had gone through his firing sequence to the point where he could flick the safety latch off the CLAW, the top of the bunker began to crush down on them, pinching in from the edges. The tank driver had exactly centered his vehicle across the fighting position. Neither track would fall into the hole with them, but they did smash the edges of the walls to either side. Now they were trapped inside. Edwards couldn't fire at this close range. If he were to hit the tank and punch through its underbelly, he might destroy it. It would remain over their fighting position, baking them like potatoes in a bed of coals.

Suddenly the tank stopped. The ceiling of the fighting position shook and began caving in again. Edwards realized that the tank was backing off. They had probably been discovered. Or else the tank had high-centered on the fighting position. In either case, it was backing up, giving Edwards a second chance.

He set his CLAW aside and began pawing frantically at the dirt. So much had fallen that he had to stoop over as he scooped more and more into the hole. "Help me," he shouted at his team. "Help me get a firing port clear."

"Lieutenant, you can't fire that damn thing in here."

"Help me, goddammit. If I *don't* fire this thing in here, you're going to get a 120-millimeter projectile firing in here."

The three men inside the bunker began pawing with him widening the hole quickly until Edwards could shove his arms through with the CLAW. It wasn't enough. They renewed scrabbling furiously.

As they did, they could see the tank backing away, see the gun turret swiveling, see the enormous bore of the cannon coming around. One man began whining, but the others just grunted louder as they desperately tore at the dirt. Finally, the turret stopped swinging. Seeing it lower, all of the men swore. In another moment, though, they gained new hope. Although the cannon had been depressed all the way, the tank was too close to fire into the hole. They heard the engine rev and the sprockets grind as the tank pulled back farther.

"Enough!" Hurriedly Edwards grabbed the CLAW and batted it a couple of times to knock the dirt out of it. He held the tube at arm's length and pointed himself toward the hole as though he were a projectile himself. "Grab my legs. Lift me up and shove me through that hole as hard as you can. I'll try to get clear before I shoot. Hurry up, dammit! Hurry up!"

They needed no encouragement. The men grabbed him and began shoving him through the hole. Edwards felt his arm and the CLAW had come clear of the bunker. His shoulders had gotten wedged.

"Push!" he screamed.

His men had pushed him as far as they could. He tried moving an elbow and shifting one shoulder higher than the other so that it would work. He tried squirming. He gained another inch or two, but needed more. He exhaled, feeling a sudden panic as if he was going to suffocate in this hole.

Meanwhile, his frenzied men were shoving against his buttocks. As one hand crammed his testes against his crotch, his knees buckled, and they no longer had his legs to use as a ramrod. All the while, he screamed, unaware that they could not hear a thing with his body muffling his voice. So Edwards did the only thing that he could think to do. He began kicking. He felt a shin bone striking something hard, probably somebody's head.

Then he also saw the lowering of the cannon. He was looking right into the cyclopic eye of a 120-millimeter tube.

The CLAW! He had to fire first!

If the Soviet tank commander fired first, Edwards knew he was dead, even if the bastard missed. The blast alone would tear his head off. As he held out the CLAW, he could not wrestle its rear end clear of the tunnel. That meant some of the blast would be directed upward into the top of the tunnel, practically into his face.

Ironically, Edwards found himself in the philosophical position he had hoped he would find at the moment of his death. Raised a Catholic, he'd always wondered if he would have the opportunity for a last-second repentance.

Here it was. He grunted half a prayer, begging forgiveness from a God that he had never felt particularly close to. He squeezed the grip of the firing mechanism.

His last sensation was that he had suddenly been pricked with a million tiny needles that both stung him and penetrated to the core of his body. He realized that he'd been deafened and burnt. He knew he was dying. Then he knew no more.

# 17

The lead Soviet Hind pilots made wide detours around the rising smoke and dust columns of the tanks, not wanting to lose sight of the ground. At last their commanders had ordered them to engage the enemy head-on during the day. The tactics for this exercise had been practiced many times in the foothills of the Ural Mountains, but this would be the first opportunity for these pilots to use them on the battlefield.

These pilots were brimming with confidence. In past engagements, it was true, they had been required to stand off and remain under cover and use their superior numbers of direct-fire weapons to pick off American helicopters as they moved back and forth across the battlefield, but that tactic had proven immensely successful. Improved radars had been slaved to the firing turrets on the Mi-24 fleet. The radars were designed to pick up returns from helicopter rotor blades or propellers. Once this weapon was on full automatic and directed toward a likely avenue of American helicopter approach, the radar would pick up the returns, instantaneously direct the guns onto the target, and begin firing without a command from the pilot. The only safeguard was a three-second delay where a message flashed on the windscreen of the helicopter. The pilot could interrupt the firing sequence if he felt the target could be a deception or if one of his own helicopters had flown into the path. Otherwise, the gun would begin firing without further command.

The magnificence of this weapon system was that

man and machine could combine their capabilities to
fire on the move more effectively as a team than either
could alone. A pilot could hover with his guns clear
of the terrain and simply make pedal turns back and
forth in the general direction of targets. The automated
guns could acquire and shoot down as many as three
targets in twelve seconds. Once it had locked on, it
continued firing bursts, dispersing cannon fire out to
a maximum spread of a thousand meters, sufficient to
counter all but the fastest lateral movement. This
weapons system permitted the plots to give almost their
full attention to flying at high speeds across the battlefield toward the Americans. Whereas U.S. pilots
might have to stop and aim their weapons or divide
their attention in the cockpit between fighting and flying, the Soviet pilots simply had to worry about flying
and about not permitting their brother pilots to be en-
veloped in the radar scan out in front of them.

"Today we smash those that escaped yesterday's attack," a Soviet pilot in the first echelon said to his
copilot as they advanced across the battlefield at 150
knots.

A pair of warrant officer Cobra pilots named Crider
and Earlywine had lingered for the additional time required to continue guiding their TOW missiles and
Hellfires onto Soviet tanks and personnel carriers. The
seconds lost were precious ones for them and the other
eight Cobras that hung around, for their rotor blades
provided excellent radar returns for the advancing
Hinds.

The Hinds' initial bursts took out three Cobras. Two
of these had already begun turning away and thus had
presented an even larger rotor return. A third was hit
head-on, as four rounds struck the mast, the rotor
head, the transmission, and the cockpit. Three other
Cobras broke off their attacks and within ten seconds
were dashing across the low ground, temporarily hidden by higher terrain. Still, half a dozen Cobra pilots
continued to hold position and watch their missiles

plow into five T-80 tanks and BRDMs among the American fighting positions.

A chorus of shouts went up over the air. Then six Cobras turned for their dash back through the secondary line of defenses. As they turned, one erupted into a ball of orange flames and scattered flaming debris down the slope where he had been firing just moments ago. Three other Cobra pilots cut loose with twenty-millimeter cannon fire from their nose turrets as they were sweeping around and turning to leave. Out of the formation of Mi-24s sweeping across the ground like airborne tanks, one lost power and dropped down. It rose up momentarily, but seconds later began weaving, its rotor system flying apart, flinging its blades in a wide arc that struck a second Mi-24. Two streaks of flame skidded across the battlefield as the Hinds plummeted to the ground. The remaining Mi-24s pressed the attack, and three more Cobras were shot down.

The last Cobra to break contact was the one piloted by Crider and Earlywine. Reluctant to miss their first combat kills, they had been the last to disengage from acquired targets.

"He's backing," said Crider, the gunner, who was maintaining his reticle on the tank turret, guiding the Hellfire missile streaking barely ten feet above the ground. "He's backing up, as if he's trying to avoid us, but I got a lock on the bastard. We're going to get him."

"Better hurry up," said Earlywine, his pilot. "I think we're already sticking around here too long. Everyone else is busting the hell out of here." The moment they saw their tank erupt in a cloud of smoke, dust, and flames, Earlywine dropped the collective. Below the level of the slope, the helicopter plunged. He turned their craft to dash across the two thousand meters to the next ridge, beyond which the Apaches and Black Eagles waited. As he started his run, he and Crider saw to their dismay that only two other Cobras were ahead of them. Less than a thousand meters behind and closing were the Soviet Hinds. Even as they watched, they saw the last pair of Cobras knocked from the sky, rolling to earth and beginning to burn in the sand.

"I ain't a rocket scientist, but it ain't safe going across that open space," Earlywine cried.

Crider cleared his throat over the intercom. "What are we going to do, then?"

"I dunno." As Earlywine jerked back on the cyclic, raising the nose of the Cobra, he lowered collective pitch, watching outside so that the tail stinger did not hit the slope. Simultaneously, he began sliding toward the left. Gradually the Cobra began to settle toward the bottom of a ravine. He moved forward carefully, settling deeper and deeper, until the ravine's sides were barely wider than the disk described by the main rotor blades. In front of them, the gully widened out and flattened into the valley where the other Cobra pilots had met their deaths. The lead Hinds had continued fanning out and attacking toward the ridge in pursuit of the Kiowas. In this final attack, every Cobra but those in maintenance had been destroyed or damaged. Except one. The lone flyable survivor, in the hands of Earlywine, now hovered in a naked gully behind the first wave of Soviet attackers.

Suddenly two Hinds disintegrated in flames and joined the burning American helicopters on the floor of the desert. All across the line of attacking Hinds, gunfire opened up and several explosions erupted from the far side of the slope. The Apaches had opened fire from the ridgeline.

Both warrant officers suddenly ducked as a shadow flew over them from the rear. Their helicopter ducked as well, for an instant later the downwash of the Hind lowered them several feet deeper. Half a foot more and the main rotor blades would have been slapping the gully. Both men reacted the same way, pulling mightily on their collectives at the same time to counteract the downward blast. Ahead of them, nearly one hundred meters away now, a Soviet Hind had begun bucking and turning back, its pilot finally realizing he had overflown a Cobra.

As the Hind wheeled about, Earlywine shouted, "The twenty is armed."

Crider flipped up the protective cover of his trigger and squeezed off a hundred plus rounds as quickly as he could crook his finger. Feeling the vibrating buzz of the Vulcan cannon as the barrels rotated beneath, Crider walked the stream of tracers as a gardener guides a jet of water from a spray nozzle. The rounds stitched up the side of the Soviet helicopter before he could get completely around, and the Hind broke apart in a fiery explosion.

"Let's go!" shouted Earlywine. There was little else to do. In seconds, they had been trapped behind enemy lines. If they stayed here, they would certainly be discovered as more Soviet helicopters pushed forward. So they took off flying behind a flight of four Mi-24s. Crider acquired the trail craft and began shooting. The Hind's tail rotor disintegrated. The Soviet helicopter hit the ground, rolling before it broke apart.

"Conserve your ammunition," cautioned Earlywine.

"Roger. I'll try to give them each a little burst. If you'd pull some airspeed out of this hog, I might be able to catch up and do even better."

"Don't worry about that, asshole. The only way we're going to catch up with these guys is with twenty-millimeter slugs. They're flying top speed and we're eating their dust right now."

Crider squeezed off another burst at a second Hind. He squealed over the intercom as it, too, disintegrated, spinning sideways out of control and began rolling in a fiery ball in the sky, then began rolling across the desert floor.

He picked up a third helicopter in his gunsights and squeezed off a third burst.

The attacking Soviet pilots had no idea their brothers were being shot down from the rear, because they continued to focus all their attention forward. The Cobra had soon expended all its ammunition and was left with nothing but a few white phosphorus rockets used for marking targets. So all the pair of warrants could do now was dash for safety.

Behind them, a third wave of Soviet helicopters came on, and two of their gunships picked up the lone Cobra as it knocked down the last of its five kills. Both slaved their guns to automatic and watched in awful fascination as their radars picked up the returns from their own helicopters as well. They shot down two of their own before the guns slewed to the Cobra. Enraged and horrified, both gun crews took manual control of the weapon system and fired at once, expending far more ammunition than was necessary to make this kill. Even after the Cobra exploded and then scattered across the desert floor, the two angry Hind crews kept firing into the wreckage, not stopping until they had passed through its burning column of smoke.

Miles, with one of his radio sets tuned in to the Cobra attacks soon realized from what he deciphered from the fragmentary reports, that there were no Cobras left. Next would come the Apaches. Would the next step be the disintegration of the Ospreys? He knew for certain if he were required to remain concentrated with his aircraft the way Wilkerson demanded, he was going to be in as much trouble as the commander of those Cobras.

The radio crackled, and the raspy voice of Wilkerson rattled off his eardrums. "Osprey nine seven, we're not going to wait as long as I initially intended. Our Apache elements are now in contact. Begin moving forward. Mass your fire at a line just behind the deployment of the Apaches as soon as they're clear, over."

"Wilco," Miles acknowledged bitterly. What kind of plan was this? He had to cram all twenty-two of his aircraft into Zone Juliet, a goose-egg space barely more than a mile long, barely a half mile behind the Apache line. The plan was to let the Apaches slide through and start taking on the Hinds.

At least there hadn't been any Soviet artillery fire reported yet. Miles passed along his interpretation of

Wilkerson's orders and began assembling his Ospreys.
Six would do on the first line. Two to four hundred
meters behind them, he would station six more and so
on, until he had dispersed his precious birds as much
as he could manage without directly disobeying Wilkerson's orders. He spotted his birds on the console
video screen and began chewing on his lip.

Barger said, "Damn, that's a lot of Ospreys in such
a tight spot."

"You're damned right, Wendell." Miles snatched at
his radio mike and ordered the last four craft in his
formation to break free of the confines of Zone Juliet
and stand off ten miles away as a reserve force. When
he saw the lighted dots creeping toward the edge of
his screen he began feeling a little better. But not too
much better, for eighteen Ospreys were still three to
four times the craft needed for this area. "And goddammit," he cursed, expressing his frustrations over
the intercom, "there shouldn't be any of us out here
by day at all."

Hearing the radio report of the Mi-24s engaging the
Apaches, Abramov looked around the control center
to make sure his artillery commander stood at his
shoulder. This battle was coming to its decision point.
Any time now, he should he hearing the code word
from Mendenyev.

For his own part, Abramov had also made sure that
the frontal aviation commander was standing by. The
Soviet air force was assuming that the air war would
remain a standoff for perhaps another week at most.
Once the airfield at Zahedan was fully operational,
they expected to achieve air superiority over the entire
southern part of Iran. They would also be capable of
extending that superiority deep into Afghanistan and
Pakistan, if necessary.

But Abramov had given orders that a good part of
today's assets would be dedicated toward support of
his helicopters and tanks. Already he had decided he
wouldn't be using Zahedan for stationing fighters any-

how. He had ordered preparations for a shift to an alternate air base, Kerman.

Zahedan would be used for another purpose.

The Apaches and Black Eagle Scouts enjoyed great success against the first wave of Hinds sweeping across the open. Most of the leading line of attackers had been shot down. Still, American losses were staggering. Fully one in three sustained some sort of hit and, although US helicopters had been heavily armored, one in five was either shot down or forced to land because of some damage to the rotors or airframe. Even a kill ratio of three to one was going to decimate the American defenders. And soon. A second wave of Hinds approached the Apaches' line of defense just as fast as the first, and in the distance American scouts reported seeing even more helicopters coming over the horizon. That meant that within minutes their position here was going to be untenable. The scouts began calling off the Apaches. Just as quickly, they began disengaging themselves and retreating. Now, these pilots thought skeptically, the so-called miracle weapon, the Osprey, had to save the day in its second combat test as it had saved the night in its first.

Gliding into the second echelon of his Ospreys, Miles grimaced at seeing so many of them so close together. The most he had ever expected to see at one time in combat was four at most, and at night at that. Most of his planning had been to fight his command from an electronic map board.

When the Apaches and Black Eagles fell back, each pilot was to switch transponder code to indicate his retreat. In this way, the Ospreys could keep track of them. In all, there were five different codes designated for the battle today. One electronic code was for contact with the enemy, another was for departing from the present position to pass through the lines of the Ospreys. A third was to indicate distress. A fourth was for resupply of ammunition fuel and the last to be a declaration of a tactical emergency deemed to be capable of effecting the entire battlefield.

One by one, then in groups of twos and threes, the Apaches and Black Eagles began breaking off and dashing toward the rear.

Miles slid out of his cockpit seat and wormed his way through the narrow passageway into the fighting compartment so that he could get a look at what was happening. When the Osprey was fighting, he had to be at the controls, but he could better track what was happening if he had access to the maps and scopes in the cabin compartment.

He passed Joyce Bachman, who smiled wanly. He asked for a brief report, although he knew what the response would be. "A-OK, Colonel. Weapons up, airframe up. I'm ready for battle."

"You do a hell of a job, Sergeant. Keep it up."

He walked back into the WEW and looked down at the array showing the positioning of the light dots on the scope that represented each of his Ospreys. It practically took his breath away to see them so closely clustered together. Ordinarily, the array would be on a scale of one to half a million. Here the map scale was one to twenty-five thousand, and even at that it seemed as if all the Osprey lights were touching one another. The array so alarmed him that he grabbed a radio hand mike and issued a brisk command, "Be ready to disperse upon my order." Hell with Wilkerson.

Each of his Ospreys had been ordered to seek the lowest ground possible: in the bottom of stream beds and gullies and behind outcropping of rocks from the desert floor. Each had been instructed to get in as close to the ground as possible, even to land if they could do so and stay in position on ground with a flat pitch to avoid raising dust and giving away their positions.

Miles knew the Ospreys would be just as invisible to radar during the day as at night, but he wanted to be positive that there were no visual pickups by Soviet gunners for as long as possible. He looked at his watch. Fifteen hundred. If they could only hold out for a few more hours, then he could at last breathe easier, for at night they would be practically invulnerable to anything the Soviets could come up with.

The major in command of the first echelon of Ospreys saw the Soviet helicopters as they came over the hills a half mile to his front. Of the Ospreys under his command, four had found areas level enough to land on. Ahead of each was complete cover, and the crews were able to see by raising their periscopes above their cockpits to the maximum of ten feet. All the same, they would not stay hidden from somebody on the flank or from above. If their gunfire was not accurate enough to stop this first wave, they might well be overrun because of sheer numbers and the speed of the onslaught. Once the Ospreys had to take off, they would be as vulnerable as any other aircraft on the battlefield. Before the last of the Apaches could escape, several of them were shot down. Scenting even more kills, three Hinds swooped over the ridges a kilometer away and continued to close the gap to the Apaches.

Because the Soviets were flying at high speeds and low altitude, they had their attention directed forward. They would not see the blast of a missile or the backblast of a gun coming from the periphery. Miles again cautioned his pilots and gunners, "Final reminder—avoid firing directly at targets to your front."

The engagement began when the right-flank Osprey picked up the close formation of three Hinds pursuing a Black Eagle scout. The Osprey pilot saw the chase but had to wait for the indication it would be safe to fire without endangering the American bird. No matter. The Black Eagle wobbled in the air and skidded into the ground, flopping like a Frisbee. The Osprey pilot responded instantly, commanding his gunnery officer. "Fire! Get those three bastards."

The Osprey fuselage thumped as a firing port opened up and a Raptor missile was pumped skyward by a launch blast of compressed air. The Raptor spurted to a height of fifty feet, then the missile motor ignited, and the weapon streaked across the sky, accelerating within a half second to Mach two.

The four-foot-long Raptor blew up in the faces of the Soviet pilots. The Raptor's body, titanium steel serrated in long bands and crosshatched, blew apart into pellets.

None of the Soviet flight crews saw the wisp of white smoke that the Raptor left across the sky. All they saw was a brilliant white flash, and their worlds disintegrated as the titanium pellets shattered glass, penetrated armor, blew engines, and mangled human flesh. All three Soviet helicopters—a formation fifty yards across—went down, struck by the fragments of a single missile. The pilots cresting the ridge right after them reported the shootdowns, but nobody had seen the source of the fire.

Seven more Hinds crossed on the mile-long front. Within ten seconds, six of them blew into fiery balls, downed in the flash of brilliant white light. The seventh helicopter wheeled and raced back over the horizon, its pilot yelping into his radio mike as he did.

What he said was unintelligible to those that heard it, for a split second later his own helicopter disintegrated as well.

Mendenyev, riding in a jumpseat in the following wave of MI-24s, heard the yelp and knew he was about to encounter what Abramov was concerned about.

"Move forward," he ordered his pilot. He switched to Abramov's radio frequency and reported, "We're losing our attack helicopters in clusters."

Abramov himself came on the radio. "Should you be sending the code word yet?"

"No, let me move forward and see the battlefield.

Seconds later, his Hind crested the hill in a wave with ten other gunships. He saw a dozen pyres of flaming wreckage on the ground, then four more Hinds disappeared into the white strobes of light, rupturing into flames and streaking blackly across the desert floor.

What kind of weapon could have devastated these forces so swiftly? he wondered, suddenly afraid. He still hadn't seen the deadly weapon, but he knew enough from its effects to shout the code word Abramov had given him.

"Gordeyev!" he yelled into his radio repeatedly. "Turn back," he shouted at his pilots without waiting for a response from higher headquarters. As the MI-24s wheeled back over the ridge, he ran off a quick summary of the numbers of downed craft and relayed the coordinates of where most had been hit. He spoke fast, fearing that at any second he, too, might be uttering his own final words. His voice was, indeed, cut short by a brilliant bolt in the sky. The ground before him went white with extraordinary long, crisp shadows. The shadow of the MI-24 lurched as he felt a violent kick in the pants.

Mendenyev saw the pilot and copilot fighting their controls, heard them cursing fiercely. He felt the impact as the helicopter's belly banged the ground on the slant. It rocked, teetered, then continued rolling. He saw the blades striking the ground outside. He felt the craft begin tearing itself apart. He closed his eyes and screamed the code word again, although he knew by the deadness in his headset that the radio had already been silenced.

General Bayard Wilkerson heard the news from the battle front and reacted with glee. The report that more than three dozen Soviet helicopters had been struck down in barely a minute's fighting completely vindicated his boldness in using the Ospreys during the day. Immediately, he ordered the situation report to be relayed to the Rapid Deployment Force commander, saying that the Soviet helicopter attack had been blunted and that his Ospreys were preparing to counterattack.

To Wilkerson's delight, the RDF commander himself responded to his report, asking for Wilkerson to personally speak on the radio.

Wilkerson was aglow when he picked up the handset and spoke into it. "This is Ace Six," he growled into the radio mike, ready to receive the general's personal congratulations.

"Ace Six, this is Seahawk seven-niner. I'm inbound to your location. I want to meet you personally. Furthermore, I'm directing you not to commit the Osprey birds to any further combat. I repeat, I want you to withhold those birds from action. If they are now engaged, I want you to have them break it off."

"This is Ace Six . . . those elements are already committed. They've stopped the enemy in his tracks. It's the perfect opportunity to pound on him."

"This is Seven-Niner. I say again, do not commit those elements to any further combat. Break it off immediately. Get them the hell out of contact. Now!"

Wilkerson dropped the hand mike onto the radio set. He walked away, his face drained of color, his jaws so tight that his jowls almost lifted out of their permanent sag.

"That goddamned Miles . . . he's behind this . . . somehow . . ." He whirled and ordered the chief of staff to immediately have his Apache helicopter standing by for him to leave and go to the front. "Get Miles up on the horn. I want to talk to him. He's out of a job. No, goddammit, he's out of the Army."

"General, don't you want me to uh . . . tell Miles to pull those Ospreys back? Like the general wanted?"

"I'll take care of that. You just get the damned Apache warmed up and waiting for me at operating RPM."

"Yes, sir. What about meeting the RDF commander?"

Wilkerson stormed out of the command headquarters without answering.

Even if Wilkerson had immediately relayed Pickett's order, Miles would not have been able to disperse his Ospreys before the first artillery rounds began falling.

Simultaneously, radio reports began crackling from different spots within the irregular rectangle occupied by the Ospreys. They all indicated the same thing: the artillery was blanketing a wide area, rolling forward like a tidal wave. Miles didn't need radio reports to tell him that. He could see the eruptions of black smoke and dust surging toward his aircraft positions.

His first impulse was to yell an alarm. He held back. The last thing his pilots needed was to hear a panicked command that might incite them to flee. He collected himself and spoke in measured tones. "If you're not in the path of the oncoming barrage, stay put. Prepare to cover the withdrawal of other elements. If you're exposed to the artillery fire, disperse immediately to the rear and flanks. Make sure to engage every possible target before you cut and run. Keep their heads down. Good luck." He ordered the Ospreys at the rearmost files to turn tail and immediately depart the battle zone. Wilkerson be damned. He had to save what Ospreys he could.

Even before he had finished speaking, the intensity of the artillery fire redoubled. It was like a spring rain shower developing into a tempestuous hail storm. Except in this case, the hailstones were lethal artillery rounds. Some hit the ground, but most rounds had been preset to burst at about a hundred meters above the earth. That way they rained down shrapnel onto the broad surfaces of the Osprey fuselage and spanked into the propeller blades facing upward.

Miles' reaction was immediate and urgent. "Disperse! Watch out for your wingmen, but get the hell out of here!"

The Hinds from the third Soviet attack wave hovered up and eased forward as the first artillery rounds began to strike. Suddenly they saw the flock of odd aircraft rise up out of nowhere, turn broadside, show their tails and flee from the battle zone. After a few seconds of stunned silence, radios sparked to life as pilots made their reports. Among these was the revelation that their radar was unable to lock on to these strange new craft.

The Soviet aviation colonel in command of the fourth wave took control of the radio airwaves and told everybody to shut up. He restored order by directing his pilots to take manual control of their cannons and to begin directing fire visually. The colonel surveyed the wreckage of the earlier waves of attack helicopters. Ahead of him, a mangled MI-24 had broken apart and flattened out like a dropped melon. He saw a soldier crawling from the debris. As he hovered forward, his mind temporarily distracted from the battle, he read the tall number on the helicopter. He knew his counterpart, the commander of the preceding wave, had flown it. He thought the colonel, his friend, might have survived. He hovered near to pick him up, knowing he'd risk court-martial for delaying the attack. He dropped his landing gear and set his craft down to pick up the survivor. When the man was hauled aboard, he instantly regretted his decision. The man was not an aviator, let alone his friend. It was a goddamned staff officer, a major—Abramov's man.

Minutes later, the first wave of fighters from Zahedan arrived on station. Below them, they saw the sparkling of artillery rounds, the dust, and the smoke from the latest bombardment. Their instructions had been to immediately begin strafing and firing runs, shooting indiscriminately into the entire area, trying to pick up any moving target, especially helicopters or other aircraft that might be flying within or near the area of bombardment. Their orders instructed them not to worry about picking up point targets, locking on with anti-aircraft missiles, or using heat seekers. The first strategy was to simply fill the air with gunfire and hope that the rounds would be falling in enough volume to have an effect. Follow-on waves of Soviet fighters were armed with both heat-seekers and radar-guided missiles, set to operate on frequencies returned from rotating blades or propellers. They were to rely on their transponder codes to sort out the Soviet helicopters from the enemy birds. But if they couldn't distinguish, the orders were to shoot first and sort them out on the ground later.

Miles received word that the rear two files of Ospreys had gotten clear and were flying scattered in all directions, but that only gave him a few seconds of relief, for what was happening within the umbrella of the Soviet artillery fire was disastrous. One Osprey had already exploded. Three Osprey crews reported being grounded by severe airframe damage. Since they were capable of continuing to fight, the crews reported they would try to hold off any advance by the Soviet helicopters while the flyable birds tried to escape the lethal artillery fire.

The ingenious feature of the Osprey's gunnery radar was its burst capability. In a millisecond of a powerful radiating emission, the radar was capable of painting and receiving returns, analyzing, and directing computer operations to fire. All this took place within two to three milliseconds, far faster than any human could react. Even inside the Osprey, data was processed so quickly by on-board computers that human beings were constantly seconds behind the reports generated for them.

The downed Ospreys immediately locked their weapon systems on Soviet helicopters appearing on the ridge line. Launching in pairs from the three Ospreys on the ground, six Raptor missiles at a time streaked toward the horizon and exploded. Four Hinds vanished in white strobes of light and subsequent explosions. Farther down the hill, three more Hinds dropped to the ground as shrapnel splattered airframes and blades, cutting the invisible strings that kept the craft aloft.

The Soviet colonel at the controls of his helicopter divided his attention between hovering and the major he'd pulled from the wreckage. Mendenyev was his name.

"You want me to hover up and look only, not to attack?"

Mendenyev, holding his throbbing head between his hands, murmured into the microphone. "Yes. That weapon is extremely deadly. It is essential that we report on it."

"Why then, Major, don't we kill it and then our analysts will have all day to examine it?"

Mendenyev struggled as pain hammered his head and rattled through his chest with every breath. He could not even raise his voice to shout. It would do him no good to provoke the senior officer, thick-headed as he was. He reached deep inside for sycophancy he'd almost forgotten since he'd joined Abramov. "Colonel, you certainly should attack it. But first, let us report to Marshal Abramov some details about its appearance and method of fighting. He will want you to kill it, I am sure."

The mention of Abramov persuaded the colonel. He popped over the ridgeline for two or three seconds, dropped down, and moved laterally for another look. In these visual snapshots, he saw one explosion a half mile ahead and knew that at least one of the American aircraft had been struck. But for all the firing, he knew they were going to have to do better. Three of his own helicopters behind the ridge were struck. He heard reports that others were hit.

"What now, Maj—"

He saw that the major had collapsed on the deck of the gunship. He ordered his crew chief to render first aid and made his report to Abramov's headquarters. Then he ordered the Mi-24s from the fourth wave to move forward. In an astonishing display of power, two hundred aircraft appeared at once above the hill. Directing his helicopters to use the much-faster automated firing system, the colonel gave a command to begin firing indiscriminately across the entire front. Whether the enemy had radar decoys, as he had been briefed, or not, they could not escape a storm of blanket fire at such a close range.

The Soviet crews opened fire at one time across the front, sending a virtual wall of tracers and explosive rounds into the battlefield. The colonel was well pleased with this tactic he had developed on the spot. The three violent explosions that answered the torrent of cannon-fire were so enormous that they could not have been artillery rounds but must have been these American aircraft blowing.

Then a flickering of those infernal white lights on

either side of his helicopter indicated to him that the enemy was still answering fire. He shouted into his radio, ordering the helicopters to drop behind covered positions again.

Abramov began hearing the reports of the American devil birds being spotted. He growled an anxious, muted cheer every time he heard a new report of one of the craft being downed.

His outlook had suddenly brightened. The numbers of kills were still small in comparison to his losses, but at least his pilots were discovering the enemy was neither invisible nor invulnerable. To top off that news was the word that Mendenyev, the major who had been sent along to spy on him, had survived the afternoon's battle and was being flown back to his headquarters for medical attention. He'd earlier heard the major had been killed. Now he'd been found alive. Abramov was less surprised by that news than by the fact that he'd found himself gladdened by it.


Among all the engine indications and gunnery systems Miles had to monitor—not to mention helping to fly the aircraft and monitor radios from both Ospreys and higher headquarters—came the agitated voice of Tryon from the rear: "Fast movers twelve o'clock high. I got six, no, seven, no, eight returns."

Without keying his mike in answer, Miles began cursing to no one in particular. The noise, the confusion, the tension—they were almost more than a single human being could handle at one time.

"Take 'em on," he said into the intercom. "Take on the bandits with Raptors. For the moment, forget about the Hinds."

In the next second, another radio voice boomed in his ear. The company commander who had escaped the Soviet artillery bombardment with two other Ospreys told him he had acquired the MiG-29s. "We'll be taking them on ourselves," said Blanks.

Miles, almost feeling self-conscious about it, thanked the trio. "I'll continue painting them with my radar. I'm in the shit anyhow, so there's no reason for you to light yourselves up before you fire.''

In the midst of all the confusion, the last thing that Miles wanted to hear was Wilkerson's voice calling him. Miles impatiently snapped, ''Ace Six, whaddya need?''

''This is Ace Six, disperse your elements and disengage. Meet me back at my location for a consultation.''

Miles barked a ''Roger.'' It was all that he could do to keep from howling, *Now you want us to disperse? You fucking idiot!* He kept his calm, though.

A half-dozen Raptor missiles streaked off into the sky toward the incoming MiGs. Tryon reported the firing and shut off his radar. Miles instinctively looked upward and saw the wisps of white trailing the rocket motors. The explosions that followed seconds later were like the snapping of flash bulbs in his face. They were followed by three black, oily streaks of Soviet fighters across the sky. More white streaks indicated a second firing had been computed before Miles's radar shut down. A second wave of Raptors were on the way. Four more black streaks followed the speckling of flash bulbs in the sky. Seven of the eight attackers had already been shot down, but Miles was not in the least capable of enjoying the moment because Kop, his radar operator, immediately came on to report another burst transmission indicating a flight of at least two dozen more aircraft approaching.

''From what direction,'' Miles demanded in exasperation.

''From the south. I got a friendly transponder code response. It looks like the Navy is sending in the cavalry. We've got our fighters coming in to meet theirs coming from the north. We've got a standoff, Colonel. We've got . . .''

''Okay, cut it off. Let's get down to business here.''

General Pickett stomped across the pebbly ground surrounding Wilkerson's headquarters. Wilkerson marched out to meet him briskly, brimming with good news to report. As many as thirty to fifty Soviet helicopters had been downed. Sure, he had lost some Cobras, and maybe even a few Ospreys. But they were kicking ass on the Soviets. All the same, Wilkerson knew something was wrong. Why would the general, with all the fleet and aircraft and communications out there in the Arabian Sea, be coming in to check on the land battle? Maybe he'd be moving ashore to establish a land headquarters now. Maybe he needed to use the divisional communications as an interim command post until his own could be installed. Maybe . . .

Bad news. Emerging from the general's helicopter was Bernadino.

When the RDF commander approached, Wilkerson stopped and threw up a salute.

"Never mind that, General." Pickett put his hands on his hips. "Did you get those Ospreys disengaged?" Before Wilkerson could answer, he snapped, "Why the hell were you deploying them during the day, anyhow?"

Wilkerson shrugged and opened his mouth to answer.

"Doesn't matter anyhow, General."

As Bernadino approached, he noticed that she looked triumphant. Why the hell was she with the general in the first place?

"General, I can't afford to stay here very long. I've got to get back to my command center aboard ship and get ready to establish a land command and control site. You're coming with me. I'm leaving the division in the hands of General Bernadino here. I understand you're a genius with setting up command systems. You're going to oversee mine."

"I don't understand—"

"All right, General, let's discuss the matter that's on your mind. Why wasn't I informed about your plan to use the Ospreys today? You've jeopardized them and the entire war with your deployment of those birds in the daytime. In mass formation, no less!" Pickett's taut lips barely moved as he struggled to maintain his composure.

Wilkerson whined, "Miles didn't tell me—''

Pickett's head pecked forward, his expression one of exaggerated astonishment that Wilkerson would be blaming his decision on a subordinate.

Wilkerson read the look and changed his tack. "I wanted a victory. This is an emergency situation that demanded emergency measures."

"If it's an emergency, it's one of your own making."

Wilkerson huffed, switching to yet another strategy. "Look, General Pickett, with all due respect, I can't fight this division if you're going to micromanage from the top. This isn't Vietnam again, is it?"

Pickett guffawed, barking in Wilkerson's face. "Don't lecture me, pal. Where were you in Desert Storm? Those Ospreys are a strategic weapon and I've got a string on their deployment, General. It's in the plan. Always has been."

"Steve Little didn't—"

Bernadino gasped. Pickett waved a hand to put an end to the discussion. "Oh, shut the hell up, General." Pickett grabbed Wilkerson's shoulder with one hand as his other balled into a fist. Wilkerson cringed. Pickett slapped his subordinate on the back. "You're too valuable to be up here, man. I need you to set up my land command post." As he spoke, Pickett wiped off the hand that had touched Wilkerson. "I'm placing you under supervision of the chief of staff. He's a Marine lieutenant general." he said, finally gaining control of his anger. "You can tell your story to the Marines."

# 18

Miles first saw the shadows sweeping from the west out of the setting sun. Then he saw the ridge line above begin sparkling as explosive rounds began raking the countryside. American AV-8D Harriers and F-14 Tomcats were strafing.

Cluster bomblets began a staccato tap dance across the horizon. Wave after wave of fighters and fighter bombers began attacking along a two- to three-mile line ahead of the Ospreys. The effect was instantaneous relief from the cannon fire. Miles shouted over the command frequency, "Now! Everybody move. Get the hell out of here."

He commanded everybody to rally to predetermined locations that would once again give the aircraft the safety of being dispersed at least a kilometer apart. "Get those birds under camouflage," he ordered.

When he heard radio reports from his pilots that all that were capable of flying had departed the area of artillery bombardment safely, he allowed himself a sigh of relief. Even that relief was short-lived. He remembered his downed aircraft, and called back to division headquarters to request Blackhawks and Apaches be sent in to recover any of his surviving aircrews.

He completed his report on a low note. "We'll require an assessment of the battle damage to our craft. I'm unsure of the losses at this time, but they may be substantial."

He paused. "We probably should destroy the

downed Ospreys so they don't fall into Soviet hands. All sorts of new technologies are in those birds.''

"You needn't worry about that, Colonel," said the voice of General Bernadino. "I understand the importance of that operation and I'm perfectly capable of directing it from my position. For now, you worry about assessing the combat capabilities of your surviving aircraft. We're going to need those in operation as quickly as possible. Tonight. I want to meet with you personally back at this headquarters as soon as you're able to make your assessment."

"Roger, ma'am," Miles said, puzzled. General Bernadino in command? He suddenly felt a hell of a lot better.

The lower the sun fell, the more depressed Marshal Abramov became. Although his commanders back from the battle site reported shooting down at least half a dozen of the new American aircraft, that was small comfort. Half a dozen could hardly have a significant effect on the Americans' new weapon. And at what cost! As the figures continued to mount, he determined that today's action had cost him more than eighty tanks and armored vehicles and the loss of a significant number of soldiers. Worst of all, though, he had suffered the loss of a hundred and twelve helicopters either completely destroyed or battle-damaged to the extent that it would take at least two or three weeks to repair them. That was much too long! Tomorrow, he would lose more tanks to the American helicopters because he had fewer Mi-24s to protect the T80s and 88s.

His imperative was to have destroyed all those American aircraft as a fighting force by the end of the day. Now that night had fallen and his soldiers could no longer see them to shoot them down, there was no telling what damage they would cause.

It gave him little comfort that he still had more than one hundred and fifty helicopter gunships and three lousy Mi-28s capable of taking on the depleted American helicopter force. At the rate of today's losses, that was barely more than a day's fighting. Abramov could only hope that he had pushed enough of his tank fighting force forward to have completely eliminated the combat effectiveness of the American infantry. Maybe, just maybe, enough of the conventional American helicopters—Apaches and Cobras—had been destroyed, so that they would no longer be able to hammer away at his fighting divisions. After all, he had nearly ten reinforcement divisions moving south within a day's march of Zahedan. He had the freedom to send those forces directly into battle to follow up today's costly successes. Or he might send them toward the interior to help the push toward Bandar Abbas. He needed a surprise, a new front, something that would confuse the Americans. He needed to go for Bandar Abbas, to win that city quickly. He called for his staff to put a new plan into action.

The only consolation for the day's effort was that Mendenyev had been returned, wounded but very much alive. Before he retired to his cot for a fitful rest, Abramov visited the medical ward where Mendenyev had been admitted with broken ribs, a damaged knee, and a concussion. He felt relieved to see the major sleeping under sedation. He felt a moment's disappointment for the younger man that he had not been wounded seriously enough to be evacuated. Unless the direction of this battle were to change suddenly and decisively, Mendenyev would have a task before him much more difficult than anything he'd seen in his life.

When he heard the damage and casualty report from the afternoon's fighting, Miles felt his knees buckle. Five Ospreys destroyed. Eleven damaged seriously enough so that they could not be restored to fighting capability until major components had been received from the States. In some cases, those components would have to be manufactured from scratch. At best, four of the eleven might be rebuilt from parts cannibalized from one to the other. But even at that, it could take a major maintenance effort, something that Rita Bernadino was willing to undertake, but which he knew would almost certainly be too late. Another four Ospreys had been lightly damaged but would be useless for battle for the next day or two. That certainly eliminated them from fighting tonight.

"So, Nelson," said Bernadino, "that means that half the force you brought over was effectively wiped out in today's battle. My maintenance experience tells me we'll have to ground two or three more for the night just as a matter of course. You've got maybe a dozen birds to take out tonight and see what you can do."

"It's just a damned lucky thing that those fighters were able to throw down enough ordnance so we could get clear of that artillery," Miles said.

"Don't be so modest, Nelson. You saved a good part of the fleet just by sending some back and by dispersing the rest. No telling what might have happened if you followed that man's orders to the letter."

He smiled, basking in her compliment for a second. Then he took a deep breath. "We still have a lot of firepower, General." He walked across the headquarters and poured some coffee into his canteen cup. "No telling the kinds of problems we're going to start developing when we just run into routine maintenance problems. We dare not create the same problems that arose during intensive training back at Fort Irwin. I don't think we should allow that to happen to us here. We have to do two things. First, we have to do as much fighting as possible when we have the birds flyable. Second, when they're not flying—that is, during the day—we have to get as much maintenance done as possible."

"You leave the logistics end of this to me, Nelson. If there's one thing I know how to do, it's control the support and maintenance functions of this division."

Two hours later, Miles was in the air again, flying northwestward. As exhausted as he was, he felt a great deal of relief in knowing that he was going to be allowed to command his Osprey fleet without meddling from the weenies at division headquarters. Bernadino had assured him of that.

His mission was vital. First, he was to attack the airfield at Zahedan. There, he was to knock out air defenses, Soviet fighters, and refueling and maintenance facilities, in that order. A second mission, of equal importance, was to seek and destroy all of the Soviet gunships that he could in a night of fighting, while the Ospreys had the advantage of darkness. "No telling how many of these critical nights will be left in the life of this war," Bernadino had told him.

Tomorrow, the division's patched-up fleet of Apaches and Scouts were going to do what they did best. They were going to be taking on Soviet tanks and armored vehicles, trying again to blunt the Soviet advance toward the sea coast. If those forces could be neutralized long enough, the infantry troops would be airlifted to safety and be reinforced by fresh troops, the Marines that had landed at the seaport city. Only in that way would the port be denied the Soviets.

In the meantime, the RDF commander was struggling with the problem of the additional Soviet divisions moving down from Mashhad and expected at Zahedan within a day or two. He had nothing capable of stopping those divisions once they arrived. That did not even take into account the fourteen or so motorized and tank divisions marching south of Kerman toward Bandar Abbas. On that front, the Soviets faced no resistance at all. The Americans needed a miracle.

Abramov frantically hurried about the Zahedan airfield, giving orders and making corrections to earlier instructions. Now that it was night, he felt as if he'd been severely handicapped. The Americans with their weapon system now had such an enormous advantage because they couldn't be seen. However many of those devil birds he had struck down today, it wasn't enough. Not until every single one of those bastards was destroyed could he feel comfortable. Plus, he needed one of them for his engineers to examine. Otherwise, they posed an enormous danger to the Soviet Union.

If such technology should be turned into offensive, deep-strike systems, the Fatherland might be in as precarious a position as after World War II, when the Americans had the hydrogen bomb and the Soviets did not.

He had ordered his headquarters moved yet again, for the second time in twelve hours. Now he wanted it at least thirty kilometers away from Zahedan.

He ordered all fighters off the airfield and sent them to Kerman, directing that nobody could land there until after dark and well after the last pass of the US reconnaissance satellite. To help provide security, he directed the Mi-28s be moved there as well and to rove the airfield all night long. Surely Moscow would not object to using the precious craft to secure even more valuable planes, the fighters who would be called upon to win the conventional battle in the days to come.

Then he directed his full attention to Zahedan, where he hoped to draw in the deadly American craft and inflict another blow this very night. The Americans were in effect controlling this airfield because they had denied its use to his air forces. Every battle-damaged helicopter incapable of flying he ordered to be pushed into parking spots on the airfield in a simulated formation. They were to be bait to encourage the Americans to make another strike.

He then ordered all flyable helicopters to be dispersed, again no closer than thirty kilometers to Zahedan. He also instructed that no aircraft could come closer than two hundred meters to another. Of course, this caused enormous security problems for his aviation forces commanders. That was better than having them all destroyed in single passes by the devil bird.

In order to establish a semblance of night defense for the airfield, Abramov ordered that soldiers from two complete infantry divisions encircle the airfield with hundreds of individual listening posts. Every spotlight and searchlight had been collected, and fully half his air-defense weapon systems had been brought in from his combat divisions. Throughout the evening, bulldozers raised piles of sand so that truck headlights pointed into the sky. Upon the sounding of the general alarm, all these lights were going to be turned on, turning night into day and giving him back the advantage enjoyed today. Then he would destroy those birds.

As he flew ever closer to Zahedan, Miles continued to be nagged by the raw intelligence reports provided via afternoon satellite photography. No Soviet fighters had been spotted at Zahedan or Kerman airfields. Why not? Could the Red Air Force still base out of the southern Soviet Union, subjecting themselves to the disadvantages of the great distances from the Soviet border to the current battlefields? If true, the fact that enemy commanders were denying themselves those two airfields meant that the Ospreys were already having a significant effect on the outcome of this battle.

No, he told himself. As much as he wanted to believe it, that couldn't be right. The Soviets were going to have to have a forward airfield. That field would likely be Zahedan, the objective that both armies and air forces had struggled for. Miles knew he would have to strike Zahedan.

His strategy had not changed from last night's. He planned to send a flight of three on a raid across the airfield, taking out all fighters and helicopters possible. A second flight of two would remain at a distance observing. Once air-defense sites were picked up, a second wave of attacking Ospreys would strike the SAM sites.

Suddenly he was startled by the crackling in his ears. He realized that his radios and intercom had been silent for a long time and that he had become immersed in his thoughts on determining what it was that nagged him so much about tonight's plan.

"Osprey lead, this is one-six, we are at our departure line ready for the assault over."

"Roger. Stand by."

Miles studied the dashboard clock. If it was correct, within the next minute or so two B-2 bombers would be sweeping over the airfield at supersonic speeds, leaving bombs, bomblets and cratering charges to destroy the runway and taxi-ways.

Even as Miles was thinking about it, the horizon lit up abruptly.

"Holy shit!" The exclamation over the air came from the first wave of Ospreys. "The place looks like a drive-in movie just let out."

Miles raced forward to the last ridge line providing cover and elevated his periscope to its maximum height. What he saw startled him. The B-2s had hit a fuel supply point and started a fire there and that added to the brightness of the sky and two or three helicopters parked in a formation of about twenty had begun burning. But after the initial explosions of the bombs and the cluster bomblets left by the B-2s, the airfield was lit up even more by the searchlights and headlights arranged by Abramov.

Streaks of fire from half a dozen SAM sites scratched at the night sky. Miles gritted his teeth, hoping the missiles would not lock on the bombers. A violent pair of explosions dashed his hopes as the sky illuminated even brighter with burning B-2s. Tracer fire from machine guns and anti-aircraft guns snaked across the sky like streams of water from a fire hose.

"Holy shit," Miles said. It would be suicide to risk an attack now, as ridiculous as Wilkerson's plan to use the Ospreys during the day. If Miles needed a clincher to call off the attack, it was the dazzling display of tracers shot up into the air, covering a mile perimeter around the airfield.

The Soviet strategy was obvious: to fill the air so full of gunfire it would be impossible for the Ospreys to get off the field once they attacked.

Miles had to laugh. The Soviets were *that* scared. The Ospreys had made *that* much of an impression. Such a primitive strategy might have worked had he been the first over the field instead of the bombers.

He surveyed the airfield using maximum magnification available in his periscope. The bombers had been extraordinarily effective in their pass. Not only had they damaged a good part of the runway but they had also apparently inflicted damage to every Soviet helicopter in sight. Wait! Were the B-2s that good? Or had the Soviet commander parked damaged helicopters on the airfield to draw such an attack from the Ospreys?

Although the range was nearly five miles, Miles instructed the three other Ospreys in his flight to select the most active anti-aircraft guns and aim two Raptor missiles apiece so they would burst above their targets like artillery fire. Miles decided there was no harm in making the Soviets believe that the Ospreys were even more invisible than they thought.

Eight Raptor missiles blew clear of their firing tubes in the Ospreys' fuselage. Their rocket motors ignited as they streaked off toward the airfield. The Ospreys turned, lowering their periscopes, and dashed away before there could be answering fire. In the distance, the horizon lit up again with eight white flashes. Then the field lit up again as small-arms fire and new lights began waving around over the airfield.

Miles smiled. Not only would the attacks keep the Soviets up all night, but their fear of the Ospreys would minimize the likelihood they would bring MiGs in, even if the runway could be repaired. By simple process of elimination, he knew this was not the field enemy air forces would be using.

His satisfaction over messing with the Soviet minds was short-lived.

The remainder of his battalion had scattered to search the terrain for Soviet helicopter positions and area refueling and rearming points. Their mission had been to reduce the number of Hinds so that the remaining Black Eagle scouts and Apaches could attack Soviet armor.

Within minutes of the encounter at Zahedan airfield, Miles began receiving reports from other aircraft commanders. Their problem was not a dearth of targets at all. Indeed, the Red Army had scattered so many trucks, tanks and personnel carriers among the helicopters that any shot fired would yield a hit of some kind. No, their problem was that no Soviet aircraft were flying. None. Thus the only aircraft aloft had to be Americans. So the Ospreys reported that they could barely fly more than a mile in any direction without receiving ground fire of some kind. This caused them to be bouncing around Iran like pinballs.

If Soviet soldiers were firing up in the air at the slightest sound, sooner or later, the odds would catch up to Miles's aircraft. He remembered the night in the desert in Fort Irwin when he'd introduced Kop to the birds—if he and the sergeant been firing at sounds with automatic rifles, they very likely could have brought down the test Osprey themselves. He knew he didn't have the aircraft numbers to sustain the potential losses. So he instructed his aircraft commanders to call off the random searches. "Just engage targets that can be positively identified as Soviet helicopters, command sites, or major refueling sites," he instructed them. "Rendezvous back at Saravan within the hour," he growled, striving to keep the disappointment out of his voice.

"Dammit," he cursed to his copilot. What good was his battalion if they could not use their night-fighting capabilities? The Soviets had adapted a primitive strategy to balance the Osprey's night-fighting technology. Fighting by day was out. He needed a countermove or he wouldn't be able to fight the Osprey at all.

Three hours later, as he eyed his exhausted command gathered for a strategy session, he still had not found his answer. On the positive side, his aircraft commanders reported a strike on a Soviet command headquarters. Furthermore, they had confirmed at least seventeen other kills on parked Soviet helicopters and had fired on at least twice as many more positions that might have been camouflaged helicopters.

On the negative side, a grim executive officer, Ron Burns reported, "Three more Ospreys battle-damaged. One crashed and burned immediately. The entire crew's presumed dead. Search and Rescue hasn't been able to get to the crash site yet."

Miles wanted to ask the names of the crew members, but he did not. Too many of his men and women had been killed today, and he didn't want to hear names of the people he'd grown to respect in his brief time as commander. He needed to harden himself. So he gulped back his emotions and said flatly, "What's the extent of battle damage?"

"They landed under their own power. Near as I can tell, they're shot up badly enough so they won't be available for at least seventy-two hours—*if* they can be recovered from the battlefield tonight with the operation ongoing. Otherwise, they might have to be destroyed in place."

Miles grimaced. "Only as a last resort, Ron. Only to keep them out of Soviet hands, okay?" His executive officer nodded. Miles inhaled deeply and glanced at his watch. "Twenty-three-hundred hours. So, what do we have available for the rest of the night? I've got to have a new strategy. This flying around waiting for every Ivan snuffy with a rifle to shoot us down is a bunch of nonsense. Even at the rate of seventeen of theirs killed to one of ours, we'll be out of birds first."

"You'll have six definite for tonight. A fifty-fifty chance maintenance will get a half dozen more up in time for missions before dawn."

"Plan on the six then. Let's make sure we get a max maintenance effort on everything we can before tomorrow night's missions . . ." He left unspoken the words, *if there is a tomorrow night.* "I've got to talk to the boss and get her ideas about pulling some kind of worthwhile combat mission out of our hats for tonight. You debrief the aircraft commanders. Put together enough crews for each of our flyables. Then get them to a stand-down for a couple hours. Tell them to be ready to launch when I get back."

When he was still more than fifty kilometers away from Kerman, Miles took his flight of three Ospreys off in a new direction toward the northwest. He would approach through the mountain passes north of the airfield. He needed every advantage, and it was possible that the Soviets would be less likely to expect an attack from that direction.

In his tactical briefing, he'd kept the mission simple. One trio of Ospreys, commanded by him, would recon Kerman. The other, led by Blanks, he sent north to recon Birjand, halfway between Masshad and Zahedan. He'd recommended the plan to General Bernadino. She approved it immediately. "Better to be flying around in Ivan's rear area than up here where anybody with a rifle might bring you down."

As the Osprey flight approached Kerman, they received more and more radar sweeps from the airfield. More and more they adjusted their course to a circuitous approach to the field. So far, none of the radars had been able to pick up the Ospreys, but Miles ordered at least three kilometers' distance between his birds. Outside, the night was black, but with his night-vision instrumentation, he could see plain as if it were a cloudy day. Now he felt he had the advantage. His birds had been dispersed. His electronics gave him the power to detect the enemy well beyond the range of sight. This was the way it was supposed to be.

His copilot spoke to him on a private intercom circuit: "What do you suppose all those radars mean? MiGs, or what?"

"You know, Barger, I'm starting to get the feeling they mean this war is going to be won or lost right here."

Major Herman Blanks had been flying parallel to the highway looking for night resupply convoys or temporary supply depots along the way. So far, nothing. At Birjand, however, he stumbled onto a sign.

The airfield proper was barren of any air defenses. There were no supply or maintenance activities. As they approached, Blanks saw a huge transport lifting off, heading north. At first he considered shooting it down, but something else on the airfield caused him to interrupt the Raptor firing sequence. On the ground, stacked in a neat row, were six Hind-D helicopters. A ripe little plum, he thought, and more dangerous to the effort because they could threaten the anti-tank helicopters.

"Right wing, be prepared to make an assault and take out half a dozen enemy vultures, over."

"Copy assault to take out a six-pack."

"Wait . . ."

Blanks watched as a swarm of men approached the helicopters and immediately began preparing them for flight. Blades were extended and bolted into place as tie-down and mooring gear was removed. Besides the many men working on the craft, another bunch twice as large stood by, as if ready to help out.

They were preparing the ships to fly, Blanks realized. Why would they do that, he wondered, when the rest of the Soviet fleet had been grounded tonight? Why wouldn't they be moved into a hangar, hidden from U. S. recon flights and satellites?

His right wing in the flight of three gave another call, "You want me to hit them now or are you going to wait until they get airborne? I recommend doing it now where we could take out some maintenance people at the same time. Besides, it will take fewer missiles to get them now—"

"Wait. Dammit, stand by. I'm thinking."

"Copy thinking" came the impatient reply.

Why did the Russians only have six helicopters on this airfield? Blanks asked himself. Why all those maintenance people here? They were stumbling over each other for the sake of a half-dozen Hinds. It would be funny if . . . Christ, it could only mean that there was a staging area near here. He decided to wait and see where these six went. The more he thought about it . . . sure, they'd learned enough from Desert Storm. They wouldn't be putting these birds into hangars. Even hardened hangars could be struck by smart bombs. No, they'd be dispersing them.

Miles and his flight of three closed to within ten miles of the Kerman airfield. Miles's craft was shooting through a rocky gorge when he got a scare big enough to make him flinch. Suddenly, a huge silhouette filled his windscreen, passing through the slice of the sky he could see from inside the ravine walls. It disappeared so quickly, he thought it might have been an illusion of a dragon's head. With the recoil, he jerked his controls, nearly flying the Osprey into the wall of the gorge. He righted the craft and cursed into the cabin. He slowed the Osprey to a hover before anybody spoke.

"Christ, what was that?" yelped his copilot.

"I don't know. Fast mover?"

A cry from Kop came through the intercom. Another came over the radio. The electronics of two Ospreys had confirmed a sighting of two Soviet fighters.

"MiG-31s," reported Kop.

"Damned Russians are serious now," said Barger, the copilot.

"Obviously, they were on final to Kerman. They're flying down the valley between the mountains. In MiG-31s. I've never heard of them being out of Russia before."

Again the windscreen view darkened as a second pair of fighters crossed the sky, flaps down, landing gear extended.

"What do we do now?" asked one of his wingmen.

"We'll wait." He ordered the two commanders dispersed at mile intervals. It was a long wait. At one- to two-minute intervals for the next hour and a half, pairs of Soviet fighters and attack bombers continued to stream down the invisible chute of the approach path to Kerman.

"What's it mean, sir?" asked Barger.

"It means something is up, partner. We're just going to have to stay here until they've all put down and then we'll just have to stir up the pot around here."

The six-pack of Hind-Ds began flying westward from Birjand, and the Ospreys' secure radio nets came alive with chatter. Because their positions were exactly due west of the airfield, the Hinds had taken off right at them. Blanks' wingmen requested permission to fire.

Blanks refused. "We're spread out enough. If you need to, slide sideways to get out of their way. I'm going to set it down here and hope they miss flying directly over. If a single one of them falls out of formation toward me, I expect some help immediately."

"Copy help."

Blanks set his Osprey down and shut off the electrical switches that lit up instruments and armament in the cockpit, cutting off any glow, however slight. Besides, he didn't need low-light television to be able to see the Hinds. They were silhouetted against the black skyline and flying directly at him less than three hundred meters away now. Blanks heard his copilot whisper, "Bastards."

His weapons officer in the back calmly informed him that he was ready to fire if necessary. He added, "These guys are so close, the Raptors are barely going to have an opportunity to arm themselves before they're on us. Be advised that we might even be hit by their wreckage if we do have to strike them."

Blanks whispered into his mike, "Roger." Then, "Why am I whispering? If any one of them deviates from its flight path, I'm going to punch out of here and fly directly underneath them toward the airfield. You be prepared to acquire and shoot at them from my rear. Just get the round off. The flash from the Raptor detonation should buy us a little bit of time, even if you don't hit them. Which you probably won't."

"Don't worry, boss. If they burn your tail, we'll get even."

Blanks didn't have time to answer the verbal jab. He cringed as the Hinds passed over. He kept an eye on the IR screen, watching the string of dots maintain formation as they flew well past. His hands tensed on the controls, ready to jerk the Osprey into the air and weave across the sky. In ten seconds, though, he relaxed. He visualized the Soviet pilots engrossed with their instruments and maps, navigating to their night assembly area. He remembered how often he had taken off preoccupied. Nobody ever suspected trouble until they'd flown a while. He tucked it away in his mental inventory of lessons learned.

His Osprey rose from the desert floor, and his loose

formation followed the Soviet six-pack of Hind-Ds westward, then northward. Well west of Birjand, and not far from Kerman, the Soviets entered a shallow, winding gulch that weaved for several miles ahead into the floor of a larger valley. Here countless dry stream-beds snaked through the terrain like the veins of a leaf, and every one of them had become sheltered parking places for Soviet attack helicopters.

"Chrissakes, it's a staging area. No wonder the damned things were so few and far between down there around Zahedan."

"Damn," whispered his copilot. "I count fifty of the damned things just in the first mile or two. Gives me the willies."

"Give you the willies?" said Blanks. "Imagine what it'd do to those gun pilots . . . what's left of them. C'mon, you oughta be happy we get to wipe up the countryside with these bastards."

"Oh yeah? Where the hell're the SAM sites? You don't think Ivan would park these babies out here without protection, do you?"

"Hmmmmm, that is a problem, ain't it? But just suppose . . ." Blanks paused, formulating his thoughts. "Just suppose the bastards laid in all their anti-air at Zahedan just to suck us in, which they nearly did, and what's the first thing they always do for something important?"

"They always set up a raft of SAM batteries and guns."

"Exactly. Our recon birds and satellites find the SAMs, then they go looking for the pot at the end of the rainbow. But what if this time they didn't use SAMs just because they didn't want us snooping? Suppose they figured that using mobile heliports like this would be the best choice? Just stay on the spot until the satellite flies over. Then, before the data can be analyzed and a strike mounted, they move on."

"Okay, Sherlock, if you're wrong, we're dead. If you've deduced a new Ivan tactic, what do we do next?"

"We report this little old bonanza to the boss. Then we brutalize the Slavic barbarians."

When Miles heard the faint, crackling report from Blanks, he felt as if a giant puzzle piece had fallen into place. Clearly, the Soviets had done more than just move their helicopters out of danger. They were marshaling them for an offensive. The tank divisions had closed to within a hundred-fifty miles of Bandar Abbas on the Strait of Hormuz. Now the fighters flying across his windscreen to Kerman had been moved up to support the offensive.

He shared his intelligence and ideas over the radio with Bernadino at division headquarters.

"So far I agree with you, Nelson," she said. "But I'm nervous about committing just three birds against so much massed air power. They must have a curtain of anti-aircraft fire ready to protect that airfield. We'd better wait a while to see if I can get some more Ospreys up to you and Blanks."

"We may not have the time," Miles insisted. "The Soviets surely don't plan to let those craft sit here all day tomorrow. They brought them forward to use them. In the morning. This is no time to get cautious. If we can't use them tonight, we sure as hell can't use them tomorrow. Look what—"

He paused. Look what Wilkerson caused today. He didn't say it.

Bernadino said, "I'm checking with higher to see if we can get air strikes, Colonel. I'd feel a whole lot better if we—"

Miles interrupted with his tactical radio override: "No time to wait for the chain of command to work, General. No time for staff weenies to analyze the risk. We've got the bastards concentrated in one spot. There's only two things that could make a decisive difference this very moment. One is a nuke, and you'll never get permission for a first strike. The other is right here and now with two flights of this damned bird. Over."

She came back at him brusquely, "Get on with it,

then, Colonel. I'll inform higher. Be ready to pull off if I give you the word. Good luck, Miles.''

The Osprey attacks commenced simultaneously more than two hundred miles apart. The strategy was the same for both.

Miles and his flight of three accelerated out of the gorge where they had been hiding. When the last reported clear, Miles directed them to turn to a final approach heading toward Kerman. The moment he had clearance, he shot a Javelin radar emitter into the ground and set it to begin activating in two minutes. By then the attack would have gone off from north to south, and they'd be clear.

Before they'd covered half the distance to the field, an excited call came from the center Osprey, who'd been assigned the job of killing anything close to the runway and of responding to any kind of air cover.

''We've got a radar lock-on from above. Maybe they've got a high-flying air cap on this field.''

''No, it's not anything at altitude.'' It was Kop's voice on the intercom.

''What, then?'' Miles demanded over the radio so both would hear. So far they'd only encountered ground radars that could not detect the Osprey's improved stealth characteristics. Sooner or later he knew an airborne platform looking down on his rotors might pick up and classify returns. Now the question would be whether the Osprey's Electronic Counter Measures system would be as effective as its weapons system had proven. But what was the source of the radar? He couldn't watch his scopes because he and Barger were too busy flying the craft as it screamed along over the rugged surface of the earth on the approach to Kerman.

''Is it from a MiG?'' he asked. The later versions of Soviet fighters had the all-weather, look-down, shoot-down capability to acquire and attack targets on their own without assistance from an attack surveillance radar site. They would be the more difficult problem.

"No, it's an early warning platform . . . something equivalent to our AWACS . . . the way I read the radar frequency from the second Osprey."

"Wrong," Kop said impatiently. "The band is right, but I just planted a Javelin, and there's no return from altitude. Something is painting us from one of these mountains. Something down here on the deck with us. Something stationary or . . . something hovering!"

The battle command center interrupted excitedly, "Fighters launching from Kerman. Six on the roll in pairs."

"Hit the fighters, then the platform," Miles ordered. What did it matter what the hell was painting them and from where? The response needed this very second was to send a Raptor up the damned radar signal right back to its transmitter. "Hit 'em fast and hard and now, dammit!" he shrieked.

The Soviet colonel had spent his career in helicopters, mostly the Mi-24 attack models, and when the new Mi-28 had been developed, he had been assigned as the commandant of the training school for all Mi-28 pilots and crews. At the time, he thought the army was putting him out to pasture, but now he was the leader of the three prototype Mi-28s suddenly posted to Iran. When they were deployed in numbers, he had no doubt he'd get the command.

Now he hovered behind a ridge line five miles southwest of Kerman airfield watching the sleek black shadows ghosting across the surface of the earth. They would not stay on the screen of his ambient light collecting device. The American devil birds seemed either to absorb or reflect light in exactly the same intensity as the background. These craft were some type of technological chameleons.

The radar returns came from the colonel's front line Mi-28, stationed on a ridgeline closer to the field. The pilot's instructions had been to use radar only long enough to acquire and fire upon a target. Or, in the case of imminent attack, to paint the entire valley continuously until an enemy craft had responded in some way. Either the devil birds did not cause a radar return or his other pilot had simply gotten careless.

The colonel marveled, comparing what he was seeing to an image of a manta ray he'd once seen on an undersea pleasure dive. He remembered then that it was easier to see the shadow of the fish on the sea floor than it was to pick up the actual animal in the water. Then it occurred to him that he was seeing more shadow than aircraft tonight. That was it! The Americans could make the aircraft blend visually with its surrounding, but they could not control its night shadow.

He knew his number-one craft was acting like a beacon, attracting the attention of receivers. He decided not to call off the pilot. He calculated that the shape of the craft he'd seen in the brief glimpses would not permit a permanent lock by any radar homing device. Almost automatically, he'd assumed the night shadows possessed some kind of superior infrared suppression because no hot spots showed up on his passive devices.

He asked for a video replay of the recording made in his night-vision devices of the last minute. When the proper moment on screen matched the image in his memory, the colonel stopped the replay and examined the fuzzy screen image.

Good enough, he thought. One of the craft had flown onto the shadow of another of the planes. The colonel could make out the enemy quite clearly. He studied the fuselage, the wings, the rotors with their protective shrouds. The light-colored spot beneath the craft seemed to fog over the shadow beneath the bird. It was a hot spot. So, the night shadow was ducting its exhaust downward at the earth, avoiding any IR homing weapons from above.

He smiled. An attack plan was forming in his mind. He knew how he might ambush this night shadow.

Major Blanks used the same kind of strategy as Miles to direct his three Ospreys against the array of attack helicopters that lay before him. "Like a goddamned picnic,'' he remarked over the radio as he and Miles had discussed tactics.

As three of the Ospreys swept across the five-mile long staging area they could see, the weapons officer in each one directed a firing sequence. Burst radar returns could instantly be identified by computer and targeted within three seconds, and humans would make the firing decisions. The difficulty with the attack was the low-level runs over the washboard terrain. Only a few targets could be illuminated at a time, and then only for a few seconds. Of course. After all, that was the point of dispersion in any case.

The radar returns were intermittent. The IR signatures were mostly cold except for dozens of trucks and the small engines of power generators running. So, each weapons officer concentrated on his television monitor, which gave him the capability to view nearly 360 degrees. With an electronic stylus, the weapons officer in Blanks' Osprey designated his targets manually by pressing the tip of the instrument to the screen each time he identified a target.

As soon as the firing began, he realized this tactic wasn't going to work very well, either. The automatic cat-eyelids that detected and diminished the effect of flash white-outs on the screen soon began to blink his screen. Things were moving too fast for him to be effective.

''Why the hell ain't we shooting?'' Blanks demanded.

''We're too fast and too low . . .''

''Can't stop in the middle of this shit,'' said Blanks. The Osprey vibrated as the twenty-millimeter shuddered, firing at targets in the flight path of the Osprey.

''The terrain is protecting these things.''

''Turn loose the computer,'' Blanks ordered.

Even the automatic acquisition capability of the computer was stymied by the terrain. The IR kept showing a preference for examining the hotter signatures of truck engines and generators. The ground kept hiding parts of the fuselage or other components of the helicopters, making it difficult for the radars to form a complete picture to recognize.

By the time the first run by three Ospreys was complete, Blanks knew the attack hadn't been nearly as successful as it should have been. There hadn't been enough firing, enough flashes from the Raptors, enough secondary fires. The cannons had been the most effective weapons, which meant the Ospreys hadn't been effective enough.

One after another, his aircraft commanders reported clear.

"Ammunition status," Blanks barked.

One by one, the commanders told him they had eighty percent or more Raptors left unfired but that nearly fifty percent of cannon fire had been expended.

"Haul it around," he ordered.

"Want another run?" asked one commander.

Blanks saw the intermittent fires of burning Hinds. "Naw, we can't do that again. Hell, I don't know what the hell—"

Suddenly he felt the thumping of the Osprey's fuselage, which he recognized as a Raptor firing

"What's going on?" he demanded of the weapons officer.

"Sorry, Major, I left the computer on free-fire, I—"

"Never mind being sorry . . . *Keerist* . . ."

The battlefield in front of them was suddenly illuminated by the flashing of Raptors detonating. His weapons officer hadn't been alone in forgetting to shut off the target acquisition computer. As Soviet pilots scrambled to launch, firing up their engines and setting their rotor blades into motion, the Ospreys finally had identifiable targets.

In groups of two to six, the Soviets tried to take off from helicopter parking areas over a ten-square-mile area.

"Christ, I didn't know it was that big," Blanks murmured.

As quickly as the Hinds broke clear of cover, Rap-

tors thumped free of their launch tubes and sent them
back to the earth in flames.

"Boys, take manual control of those firing systems.
Find the biggest groups to fire on. We're going to have
to maintain some kind of firing discipline or we'll be
out of missiles before we're out of targets. Keep moving, boys. Don't let your ass get shot down by some
rifleman who sees you in the middle of one of those
flashes."

Miles's flight of three didn't have nearly the target
acquisition difficulties Blanks experienced. His centerline Osprey fired upon the radar transmitter and at
the first pair of MiG-31s rolling out to a nearly vertical
takeoff climb simultaneously.

The first blast occurred in front of the lead pair of
MiGs. An instant later, the sky twinkled at an altitude
of two thousand feet, and two streaks of fire began
falling toward the Gulf.

Miles heard a report that the Osprey was engaging
the other Soviet fighters trying to take off, but his own
attention by now was riveted to his sector of the airfield. It was difficult to believe the enemy had concentrated this many craft in one spot. Obviously, the
Soviets had planned their major attack for today—
perhaps only an hour or two away.

He saw line after line of parked craft being refueled
and checked for flight. The entire paved area of the
airfield was filled with fighters and fighter-bombers.
Even nonpaved areas had been used. Other craft were
being towed behind airfield tractors and trucks to get
them clear of taxi and takeoff lanes. No question about
it, the Soviets had intended to make a powerful thrust
this day, to end this war once and for all before the
United States could get properly mobilized.

Miles saw the sparkling of twenty-millimeter HE on
the other side of the runway, and he cut loose with this
own into the heaviest concentration of fighters. The
effect was immediate and spectacular. Hardly a round
went wasted, as he could see men scattering and the
fires sprouting from the explosions of his twenties.

Secondary explosions forced him to weave, changing his flight path dramatically. But no matter. Wherever he pointed the Osprey's nose, he pulled the firing trigger and hit more aircraft. Finally, he just decided to hold it down and to sway back and forth with the cyclic control, sprinkling deadly tungsten bullets and intermittent high explosives across the airfield. In less than ten seconds, they were by.

"Holy Christ!" "Did you see that?" "Three in one goddamned burst," his pilots cried as they reported enemy battle damage.

"Skip the damage assessment," Miles ordered. "Keep your eyes open for—"

His sentence was cut off by the alarm sounding in his ears. They'd been acquired by J-band radar, and already a missile had fired into the radar's locked-on beam.

"SAM sequence!" he shouted into the radio and intercom at once. But Kopmeyer was ahead of him. He felt a kick in the pants as the flare dispenser shot off a trio of hot devices to attract any IR-seeking missiles. Then a Javelin transmitter ejected to send a juicy rotor blade signal to attract a radar lock-on.

Miles jinked right hard, then left, to present the edge of his protected rotor disc, trying to break lock for just the instant required so the missile could reacquire the transmitter.

He felt a concussion followed by a buffeting explosion behind him. They'd just about bought it.

"Lock still!" Kop shouted.

"Goddamn, it's coming in from above. One of the MiGs must have gotten away clean . . . Yes! Contact at two thousand meters to the . . ."

"Shoot the bastard. SAM sequence again," Miles yelled.

"It's not a SAM! Goddammit, it's not a MiG, either. It's practically stationary."

"Who cares? Shoot the bastard! Blow the somebitch—" Miles flipped on the tail-gun television and saw an image he recognized instantly. "It's a goddamned helicopter. Oh, shit, the goddamned Russians have a new night-fighter down here, too.''

The Soviet colonel watched the devastation in amazement. How could three damned American aircraft cause so much destruction in so short a time?

First had been the pair of fighters blown apart as they climbed. Second, nearly simultaneously, his number-one craft, the one who used his radar transmitter for the group, had vanished in a blast of white light. Abramov had been correct in his assessment. These were truly devil birds.

''Ignore the signal on the ground south of the airfield,'' he shouted into his radio mike for the benefit of his number-two pilot. He knew from Abramov's thorough briefing that the enemy could jab spiked transmitters into the earth to send decoy signals that simulated the blades of a flying helicopter. ''Shut down your radar transmitters. Don't use them. Use only passive infrared and gunfire. Acquire visually if you can. Try to get below . . .''

Even as he spoke, the center devil bird banked hard left into an impossibly hard turn. Again, he watched in awe.

But he had no time for gawking. The belly of the craft had been presented to him. He saw a pair of white-hot marks show up on his IR sensor screen. Instantly, the firing sequence was executed by his onboard computer. Instinctively, he snapped the trigger.

From five miles away, his Aphid-generation air-to-air missile, a version adapted and down-sized from his country's fighters, streaked on its way. Once the missile was slaved by the mother computer, the job was practically done. The computer had already solved an impact point, calculating the target turn, bank, speed, and direction, comparing that to the Mi-28s own movement data and figuring in the missile data and wind, temperature, and humidity factors. Up to the instant the missile launched, the solution changed a dozen times every half-second as the computer updated. In flight, the missile's on-board computer—not as sophisticated, but still deadly accurate—continued updating data as long as the nose retained lock on the target. If the target should break lock, the missile would stay on the last path computed and detonate at its latest calculated destination. It might reacquire and recompute simple adjustments if the original target presented itself—its thermal image had been "finger-printed" by the missile. But it would not be jerked off course by any decoy device like a hot burning flare, no matter how attractive the thermal image.

The colonel saw with satisfaction that his wingman had fired a second missile within two beats of his own firing.

Miles stabbed at his fire control screen in an attempt to launch a Raptor at the target streaking across the terrain a few miles away.

"Interrupt!" hollered Tryon from the WEW.

Miles started to scream at his weapons officer, but stopped the eruption as he realized what would happen if he fired at the Soviet missile. He saw his number two abruptly change course, and he caught the ignition of a Raptor missile. His heart clutched between beats as a second missile screamed toward the Osprey.

The Raptor exploded within half a second of motor ignition, blowing the first Soviet missile in place. The Osprey would have taken no more than a shower of shrapnel and a healthy blow from concussion, both probably survivable. The second missile detonated within fifty feet of the Osprey and knocked it to the ground. Hard. Miles watched the bird break up and scatter across the rubbled terrain.

He knew he shouldn't have been gawking. He should have been firing.

Fortunately, Tryon did not fall victim to the same distractions. He'd interrupted Miles's firing sequence, which would have intercepted the Soviet missile with a Raptor at the same rough coordinate as the Osprey and contributed to the shootdown. Now, Tryon had punched off a pair of Raptors in the direction of the Soviet helicopters that had fired on them.

Miles hauled the Osprey over on its side and pointed his craft back at the airfield.

"Watch my tail," he ordered over the radio so both Tryon and the other surviving Osprey could hear.

He felt the rat-a-tat rattling of the flare dispenser working. Then two Raptor tubes thumped, sending off a response to the Soviet ambushers.

"What're you firing at?" he said.

"Just shooting blind," Tryon answered. "Trying a new tactic. I computed the reverse course on those missiles and threw out a couple Raptors as something to preoccupy whatever's out there."

"They're Soviet helicopters, and I don't remember seeing anything like them anywhere in the intelligence books. They must be new. Leave them to our wing. We're going back after fast-movers. We've got to shoot the goddamned kitchen sink at those MiGs. We have to finish this job before they get those fighters off. Then we can take on the Russian helicopters."

His instructions were met with silence. Not so much as a grunt came over the intercom. Don't save a thing, he had said. Maybe that was a little extreme. *Jesus, don't make me such a damned cornball,* he said half-aloud.

"Save a pair of Raptors for the Russian helicopters once we mop up the airfield."

The "rogers" came over the intercom as one.

The Soviets had sent trucks onto the runway to push aircraft wreckage off in order to make way for the surviving MiGs to fly away. Already three pairs had begun rolling for takeoff. The first pair had begun rotating skyward, their afterburners kicking in to expedite the blast-off in streaks of exhaust fires.

Miles felt the Osprey thump twice, then twice more, then twice again. He glanced at his fire-control screen to see where the missiles had been shot.

A pair were rising to intercept the two MiGs shooting nearly vertically toward the heavens. Brilliant, Tryon, he thought. The two had split into different takeoff trajectories, and a single Raptor would not have downed them both. The third and fourth missiles, however, had been allocated to the pairs of MiGs rolling down the runway practically wingtip to wingtip. The final two missiles had been aimed at two different spots on the airport taxiways where the Soviet fighters had concentrated in greatest numbers.

Six was the maximum number of engagements the computer could handle, so Miles looked for a spot he could attack to complement the damage until the next half-dozen firings could be programmed.

He yanked the Osprey over on its side and flew across the runway centerline, accelerating to get clear. When the MiGs blew, their wreckage would keep its momentum down the runway. Just as he crossed over, the Raptors began detonating rapid fire.

But by then he was fully engrossed in his own engagement. He touched the trigger on his control stick and sprayed down a line of parked craft, mostly Su-26 fighter bombers. Instantly he was aware of a dozen simultaneous sensations.

The Osprey thumped anew as another six-pack of Raptors was launched at a new set of targets. By now, the firing duties were being carried out by the computer, he was sure, and Tryon was making corrections to ensure the missiles would be dispersed for maximum effect.

In front of him, aircraft ordnance and fuel began erupting in a chain of fiery explosions as his HE rounds scattered destruction. He kept jinking right and left to avoid overflying explosions that might bring him down.

He saw a SAM emplacement and tapped his firing trigger in time to hit one or possibly two of the six missile emplacements. But he had to curse himself for missing the radar van at the center of the formation. In his headset, he heard the radar lock on the Osprey intermittently.

A swarm of the rounds that had missed the SAM site disappeared into a dark spot on the edge of the airfield, then the ground lit up in a huge fireball.

"POL dump," said Barger unnecessarily as the fuel burned yellow-white, flickering in and out of black, oily clouds.

As he rolled back for another run, Miles felt his craft shudder rhythmically as another series of Raptors was launched.

The airfield came into view. Nowhere was a spot not burning or exploding.

"Colonel, I had to take the Raptors off auto-fire. They want to start shooting at targets we've already engaged."

"Take the buildings, starting with the hangars. Maybe they've got something parked inside there for—"

"Roger buildings."

The Osprey's fuselage thumped twice.

"Let me have it a second, Colonel."

Miles felt Barger's touch on the controls and released the Osprey to him. As Miles shook out his cramping arms, Barger pulled the aircraft around, continuing the turn Miles had begun. "We'd better not overfly again. It's just like broad daylight out there. We're liable to have some damned rifleman take us out."

Miles remembered the afternoon and the folly Wilkerson had perpetrated on the Osprey battalion. He mashed his floor radio mike button to talk to his wingman, but before he could even ask the question about the progress against the newest Soviet helicopter, he heard the word that freezes the heart of any pilot.

"Mayday," the voice of his wingman reported calmly. "Mayday, Mayday."

Miles saw the Osprey break up in the air, sliced to ribbons by tracer fire from below, and ripped by the explosions of at least one, possibly two missiles. "Get out of this light, Barger. Off the airfield. Now! We've got to find the bastard that's shooting at us."

He felt his stomach lurching, the vision of that exploding Osprey forever burned into his memory. Somewhere in the contents of wreckage spilling from that aircraft were the bodies of his soldiers. He gulped back his emotions, knowing he could not afford to be distracted now, fearing that he would be overcome later.

* * *

The Soviet colonel had seen the belly of the second devil bird just as he had seen the first. He punched off an IR-seeking missile and accelerated to two-hundred-fifty knots to try to catch up to the American craft.

The enemy bird was faster. It turned its tail and jinked hard left, and the IR signature disappeared. The missile kept tracking its last solution, flying a divergent course. When the missile detonated, the colonel thought it was a clean miss. Then he saw the American craft wobble and slow down dramatically. The pilot was looking for a place to put down safely.

The Soviet Mi-28 began closing fast. He saw flames begin sprouting from beneath the tail section of the fuselage of the devil bird.

The craft touched down and bounced a couple times less than a quarter mile away, lost in a cloud of smoke and dust. He'd seen his wingman erupt in a flash of white. He didn't dare risk that the devil bird could engage him with one of those damned missiles. He loosed a string of gunfire at the smoking craft. It blew, and the colonel pulled up, immediately looking for the last of the three craft.

Of course, he'd been aware of the explosions and fires from the direction of the airfield. But now he was able to see for the first time what had happened. What he saw made him feel fully inferior.

"Bastards," he muttered, although the curse was more in astonishment than anger. He'd seen the continual stream of fighters, bombers, and supply transports landing for the day's massive operation. For hours nonstop, the planes had touched down and hurried off the strip to make way for the next craft. In all, more than a hundred fighters and bombers of all kinds had put down. Now he could not pinpoint a single area of parking or maintenance where fires were not raging, where explosions were not painting the skies.

All of this from three aircraft? he wondered. How so?

A sliver of black on the horizon seemed to be a mirage at first, perhaps a shimmering cloud of fire drifting across the sky. Then the image broadened. He realized that he was watching the third devil craft banking away from him at four miles, presenting the belly. Again.

He called for backup, giving the position of the American craft. It was a blind call, and he was surprised when the commander of Mi-24s told him he had escaped the destruction on the airfield with four of his craft.

"Where the hell are you?"

"Standing off to the south, waiting for . . . instructions."

"Instructions, hell, you damned coward!" The colonel composed himself, and said, "I'm giving you instructions now. Fly to the west of the airfield. Look for a strange craft—an airplane that can fly like a helicopter. When you see it, fire everything you have until it is destroyed."

"Yes, sir."

"Don't use your radar or automatic fire control," the colonel warned. "Use the goddamned eyes in your goddamned fool head." The colonel caught another glimpse of the Osprey. He glanced at his screen and saw a firing solution had already been computed while he was giving his instructions. He punched his firing trigger once, then twice, and saw a pair of IR seekers stretch out before him, ignoring the burning fires on the airfield in preference for the flying enemy craft that had already been distinguished by the Mi-28s computer.

For a second, Miles had relaxed.

Then he heard Kop shriek.

"Soviet helicopter just fired on us," Kop yelled. "Shit! Twice!"

Miles shot a glance at the fire-control screen. Even as he felt his last pair of Raptors launched, he knew they weren't going to be doing any good. Tryon had made his first mistake of the evening . . . of his life, as far as Miles knew.

But a mistake it was. The severe banking attitude of

the Osprey had offered the belly and the exhaust ports to the Soviet gunner. Worse yet, the Raptors had been punched from the top of the Osprey, which was facing away. The Raptors would have to kick over and arc back a full hundred and eighty degrees before they could get off. That would take fractions of seconds. Probably too long a time.

Miles hit the exhaust switch, instantly flipping the channel that would divert heat out the top of the Osprey—on the side away from the enemy. That might help if the missiles were heat-seekers.

Then he grabbed the controls away from Barger without a warning and flipped level. Then he jinked hard left, and hit the exhaust switch again, diverting gases out the bottom again, now that he had turned the belly away from the attacker.

The Soviet colonel watched the maneuver and wondered how the crew and craft could handle such violent aerobatics. He knew the American heads must be banging off the bulkheads of that aircraft, just as he knew his pair of missiles were going to miss as they continued to fly on a phantom solution to the devil bird's previous flight path. They continually arced toward the northeast as the American began flying west.

His missiles exploded, and within seconds a pair of brilliant flashes indicated American missiles had detonated in the same general area. That handful of seconds was a lost period of history.

But now the colonel had one hell of an advantage. Now the fires of the airfield would be the destruction of the very American devil bird that had started those fires. For now he could see the craft as plainly as if in daylight.

The colonel touched his computer screen, manually indicating a firing solution for the receding target. He punched off a pair of ballistic missiles that would bring down the American if he made no violent changes in course. Then the colonel launched another pair of IR seekers on the same trajectory, with newly updated data. If the devil bird did maneuver—and if that maneuver did present an IR image, even a momentary one, it would be fatal.

Finally, he accelerated until he felt the Mi-28 hit full throttle. His finger ached, poised over his firing trigger, ready to loose a stream of thirty-millimeter cannon fire to back up the missiles.

Miles' heart jumped as Kop sounded the insistent electronic wailing of the SAM alarm.

"Only it ain't a SAM," he heard Tryon say. "It's a pair . . . make that two pair of air-to-air missiles."

"No Raptors ready to fire yet," Barger said, giving voice to what Miles already knew.

"I'm working it," came the frantic voice of Joyce Bachman.

"And I'm going aft to help," Kop added.

Miles felt a stinging in his skin as alarm sent an overdose of adrenaline into his circulatory system. The tone in Barger's voice sounded like resignation. Joyce Bachman struggled in the passageway, trying to assist the automatic reloader in replenishing a firing tube with a pair of Raptor reloads. Kopmeyer threw a shoulder into the reload and, bracing himself in the tunnel, helped with final connections and firing preparations.

Miles knew there might not be time to spend waiting for Raptors to come up. "Compute the back course, Tryon. Give it to me on screen. We've got to do something about that Soviet night-fighter."

Miles looked down and saw the solution as a straight line on his own screen even before Tryon opened his mouth.

He jerked the Osprey hard left and accelerated, feeling the thrust force him back into the seat.

"Shit, Colonel, I just picked up four more blips. They're Hinds lifting off from south of the airfield. Heading our way."

A pair of explosions behind him kicked the Osprey ahead another notch in airspeed. Miles glanced down.

"We're still okay," said Barger, interpreting the engine and flight instruments before Miles looked at them. "Right engine oil fluctuating but in the green."

"Raptors up," Bachman shouted in triumph.

"Great work, Joyce," Miles whooped. "Fire them up, Tryon."

"Colonel?" The instant he heard the tone in his weapons officer's voice, Miles knew there was trouble. He glanced at his own weapons status panel and saw the problem before Tryon reported it.

"Colonel, that last blast has rattled the target acquisition computer. It's picking up a hundred targets instead of the four or five we need to identify."

"For chrissakes, stop explaining the problem and fix it," Miles barked, regretting his rudeness under pressure.

"Roger."

Miles didn't even have time for an apology. He slammed the stick to the right, aligning the Osprey with the line Tryon had placed on his screen. He reached out and flipped up his screen selector so he could watch backward through the tail gun's camera. He saw the fuzzy image of a helicopter in the distance. He gripped his firing trigger and a blossoming stream of tracers flew out to form a cloud that obliterated the Soviet craft in an orange flash.

"Got him!"

The victory cries of his crew was lost in the concussion of another pair of explosions so close together they might have been one.

Then the Osprey's control stick nearly flew out of his hand, slapping forward in the cockpit. Miles marveled at the sudden boot in the ass he felt. He saw the earth tumbling below him, then above him as Osprey tried to roll onto its back. A sudden flash blanked out his vision. He blinked, trying to regain his sight, but realized the blindness came from a blow to his head. A flow of blood down his forehead confirmed it. His side of the windshield had shattered. Momentarily, he felt a hot rush of anger that one of his wingmen had not taken out the helicopter earlier. Then he knew he could only be angry with himself for not checking the sky, for trusting somebody else while he was engaged in blowing away parked aircraft and fleeing Soviet maintenance crews. Besides, those people had paid with their lives. The emotion surged up, and he shoved it back down. It fought its way back up again.

In a flicker of memory, he saw Julie's face, and Christian's. Enraged, he growled at himself for allowing himself to believe he was finished. He knew he should not be looking for somebody to blame, not even himself. He was not ready to die, dammit. There was his crew, his command, the division. They all depended on him and these Ospreys to check the Soviets. *Only The Game Fish Swims Upstream.* And there were his wife and son. Goddammit, he couldn't die—he wouldn't. *Only The Game Fish Swims Upstream.*

He couldn't see the ground, but his altimeter told him it was still flying up at them.

"We've lost the night-vision system. Is the altimeter accurate? Can you see to call out the altitude?"

"Barely. A hundred feet," Barger said, his voice breaking.

"Engine status," he yelled.

"Left in the green but oil pressure is dropping in the right," Barger responded, "and we must have serious airframe damage," he added, looking out his door window.

"Computer damage," Tryon called from the rear.

"Eighty feet and dropping through."

The Osprey whipped itself left, then continued pulling back right. Miles corrected, overcorrected, and tried to find the proper touch to balance the sloppiness in his flight controls. The cold night wind streamed across his face. At least it blew the blood flow across his forehead, directing the trickles back into his ears.

"It's trying to spin right and nose into the ground," he said, grunting with the effort of fighting the controls. "See if you can see anything out there on the wing."

Barger pressed his face harder against his door window. "Holy shit! The wing is bent up and locked in a half-hover, half-flight mode. Fifty feet, Colonel. Do you want the gear down?''

"No, I think the ground is too rough. We'll go in on the belly.''

Miles glanced out to the left for a second and saw the rotor disk responding to his control movements. "The left side is free. That's why everything is so wobbly. I'm going to try to match the left rotor and wing with the right. He rotated the wing up and nosed forward. Immediately, the Osprey stopped pulling right, and the nose stabilized, but the craft kept dropping.''

"Twenty feet—no, less than that . . . ten!''

"Never mind, I see the ground.'' Squinting through the wind blast and the tears it brought to his eyes, Miles picked out a spot for a landing. It would never work, though, because the ground was uneven, strewn with boulders. He decided to try one more strategy before they were fully committed to a controlled crash. He tweaked up the throttle with the governor control button, adding power to the rotor-props.

"Oil pressure in the right engine is still dropping.''

"Mayday!'' Miles hollered, "Mayday, Blanks, Mayday.''

The extra RPMs he got from the governor control button were enough to put the Osprey into a gentle climb, pulling him clear of the boulders. He climbed straight out, looking for more suitable ground, feeling momentarily sheepish for calling Mayday, but there was no time for being embarrassed—that would come later when he got a ribbing over beers at the club. That's more like it, he thought, thinking of survival.

Thinking of survival, he remembered the report of four Hinds just before they'd been hit.

"Tryon, do you have the computers back yet?'' Of course he didn't, Miles thought, otherwise, he'd be able to see his screens. After the longest seconds he'd ever lived, he asked, "What's our altitude, Wendell? I can't see below us anymore, thank goodness.''

"We've got maybe a hundred feet again.''

"Great!''

"The right engine is in the red. It's going to conk out or start burning, Colonel. Want me to shut it down."

Miles grunted. "No way. It won't fly on one engine in half a hover. We'll never get enough airspeed back." He tried turning the Osprey gently, as if to test his own conclusion. The craft bucked up, then nosed down and began pulling right again immediately. He felt an immediate loss of altitude as his belly rose against the pull of gravity. He returned the controls to neutral, and the Osprey righted itself. However, the nose had turned about ten degrees to the right, toward the airfield, now less than a mile away.

"Colonel, I know you've got your hands full already, but what about those four Hinds?" Barger asked tentatively.

"Hah!" Miles barked into his intercom, "we've got them right where we want them."

He felt Barger's eyes on him, the major trying to decide whether his colonel had gone over the edge. Miles, formulating his plan now, didn't have time to feel self-conscious or to explain. "Check on our computers and weapons systems," he said.

Barger went to work on getting a report. "EW down," Kop reported. "All we have is one radio and the intercom."

"Computers dead—navigation, fire control—everything," said Tryon.

"Raptors out of commission," said Rush.

"What about the guns?"

"Wait . . . the entire automated firing system is computerized, so . . . you've got manual firing ability with the cannons. But you can't see to the rear, so you've only got the front. Can you maneuver to shoot it?"

Miles responded by making a course correction to line the Osprey up with a taxi lane on the airfield. The craft fishtailed through the sky and dropped twenty feet of altitude. He got it back over the next few seconds with another tweaking of RPM. "There's your answer. Wendell, I'm going to try to set it down. Can you see those Hinds to the south?''

Barger pressed his nose to his door window glass. ''Oh shit!'' he replied to the question. For Miles, it was answer enough.

Blanks had heard the distress call that included his own name. He recognized Miles's voice and felt his heart clunk a couple times before racing ahead, juiced by the adrenaline of his own situation. The Soviets had not yet recovered enough to threaten his flight of four. They kept cranking up their helicopters, trying to take off in formations. The Raptors kept cracking white and deadly over their heads.

''What's the ammo status? I want to kill every damned Hiney here.''

His weapons officer responded, ''We aren't going to be around for the last helicopter, Major. Our ammunition isn't going to hold out that long.''

Blanks did a quick mental calculation. By his count, they'd brought down or set fire to more than fifty and perhaps damaged as many as a hundred helicopters altogether. Each Osprey had started with twenty Raptors, and used up far too many ineffectively in the first pass. After that, hardly any was wasted. Still, each of his three other commanders had reported they were down to one or two of the missiles. Each had resorted to using their twenties against single birds and pairs. Only three or more helicopters in a group could warrant the expenditure of a Raptor.

Finally, the Soviets stopped trying to pull off the ground.

''Maybe they've run out of pilots or birds,'' Blanks opined over the radio.

''Don't matter,'' said one of his commanders. ''I'm expended. Empty. Out. Request permission to cut and run.''

''Roger. We're only an hour before first light. Let's rendezvous later. Get the hell out of here.''

The Ospreys scattered to fly by prearranged, widely dispersed routes to refuel and rearm.

As they whirled to depart, Blanks' weapons officer reported a flight of three Hinds taking off.

"Any Raptors left?"

"One, sir."

"Engage them then."

"Copy . . . no, can't, we're too close, too damned close—goddamn, they're right below us!"

The pilots of the Hind rose up beneath Blanks's Osprey, the main rotor blades of the lead Soviet screwing upward through the air toward the fuselage of the American craft.

"Pull up! Pull *up!*" screamed the weapons officer.

Reacting to the terror in the shriek more than the words, Blanks hauled up on his collective pitch, pulling the Osprey into a violent climb that pressed him into his seat with the G-force.

"Not enough!" cried the weapons officer. "More, more!"

"No more left," Blanks grunted with the effort of pulling his pitch lever against the stops. "Fire a Javelin. Now! Don't ask questions, just fire a—"

He felt the thump and saw the ground bathed in a sudden orange glow as the pole of the Javelin shot downward from the belly of the Osprey, penetrating the humpback Hind's engine compartment a scant thirty feet below. In the next instant, the Javelin was struck by the main rotor blades. The Hind disintegrated, its blades and other debris slung laterally, starting a chain reaction of explosions and blade-slinging among the other Soviet craft. The crash destroyed all three Hinds.

Blanks nosed his Osprey over and sprinted away from the battlefield, directing his crew to rearm his Raptor tubes, pointing out a rendezvous spot for the next mission.

"What the hell is our next mission?" called one of his other pilots in alarm. "Haven't we done enough for one night? Do we have to win the whole goddamned war by ourselves?"

"No, goddammit!" Blanks bellowed. "You heard the Mayday from Kerman, didn't you? We've got

downed pilots there. One of them is Colonel Miles.
Do you think for one goddamned minute that Nelson
Miles would call it a night if he thought one of us was
out there helpless?''

There was a long silence, then a muffled, ''Sorry,
boss.''

Miles's Osprey hit the tarmac with fifty knots of airspeed, dropping the last ten feet to the taxiway by cutting back throttle and hollering for his crew to brace
themselves.

Barger still had his forehead pressed to the side,
bouncing off the window glass. ''They've spotted us,''
he said. ''They're coming our way! They're—'' He
ducked away from the glass, too startled to finish his
sentence. The explosive cannon rounds tearing up the
taxiway in front of the Osprey completed his report,
anyway.

''Hold on!'' Miles grunted. He stood on his brakes,
then hit right rudder, sharply turning the Osprey on
the tarmac. He felt the craft sliding left and heard the
screeching of tires.

''Cannon armed,'' came the call from the rear.

Miles kept the engines revving faster than taxi RPM,
holding the Osprey with the brakes. He used his toes
to wiggle the bird's tail until he saw three Hinds pass
back and forth in the hole in his windshield. He
crammed down on the cannon trigger.

Nothing. ''They won't fire!'' Miles shouted.

All three Soviet helicopters, two miles away and
closing, twinkled on each side of their fuselages.

Barger gargled an incoherent curse and squirmed in
his seat, adding his body English to the Osprey's
movement, trying to avoid being hit.

Rush's panicked voice came over the intercom. ''The
electrical doors in front of the cannon won't open. I
can't get the manual crank to turn, either. It's jammed
by a wrinkle in the fuselage''

''Pull the stealth door bypass breaker, Wendell.''

''Huh?'' Barger cringed as a spray of explosions rose
up in front of them. They could hear and feel the re-

sulting shower of shrapnel fragments raining off the aircraft's skin.

"Pull it, dammit! We'll bypass the cutoff circuit."

Barger fumbled with the overhead circuit breaker panel. Miles kept his finger on the cannon trigger the whole time, his hand aching from squeezing it so hard.

"Got it—"

The Osprey vibrated heavily as its wing-mounted twenty-millimeter cannon belched fire, blasting away the stealth doors, scattering burning embers of graphite composition fragments. A stream of tracers reached out half a mile, then burning out a half mile beyond.

Barger hollered a cheer.

Miles pedaled with his toes, sprinkling the sky as he directed the stream of cannon fire by wriggling the Osprey fuselage. The vibrations from the sputtering engine on the right wing gave a wide dispersal pattern to the bursts.

Two of the Hinds flew right into the stream seconds apart. Both flashed and disappeared. The third Soviet gunship banked sharply away. Miles pressed down hard on the right rudder pedal. The aircraft pirouetted, dragging rubber on the tarmac because the brakes were still on. The tracers swept the dim horizon below the Hind, missing.

"Shit, you can't get any elevation," Barger said.

"Like hell I can't," Miles growled, adding takeoff power and releasing the brakes. The Osprey leapt ten feet into the air, nose high. He squeezed off another long burst, and this time, the third Soviet gunship blotted up the cloud of red sparklers and burst into streaks of fire.

"I can't see the fourth one . . . oh, shit! we've got an engine fire," Barger yelled.

Miles fought the controls, trying to regain a level landing attitude. He never made it, because the right engine seized suddenly, showering the sky with sparks, while the craft was still at ten feet. Miles dropped the collective to level out the bird, but he was too late. The Osprey landed right wing first, its rotor-disk ring striking the bare earth just off the taxiway, the rotor-

props disintegrating against the bent metal. The craft
bounced. Squealing, crunching metal sounds from below told them the landing gear had collapsed. The Osprey began grinding away at the earth, corkscrewing
on its broken gear, the tip of the right wing as a pivot
point, heavy black smoke pouring from the engine,
flames pouring lazily into a burning pool of oil and
fuel beneath the wing.

Miles feathered the left rotor, chopped the throttle
and cut the engines, bringing the craft to a chattering
halt.

"There it is . . . the fourth Hind," Barger
screamed. He pointed to the right front quarter. Miles
squeezed off another burst of cannon fire, which went
streaming aimlessly into the deepest, blackest part of
the sky. Nowhere near the craft bearing down on them.

"Get everybody out of here!" he shouted. "You
people in back, get out—get away from the bird. Scatter, hear me?"

In frustration, he squeezed the trigger again. The
guns fired for three seconds more, then quit, out of
ammunition. He could hear the barrels rotating use-
lessly.

"You get out, too, Colonel," Joyce Bachman ordered. She reached around him and unsnapped his
safety harness. "Come on with us. There won't be
any bullshit about the colonel going down with his
ship—"

"Wait! Did you see that little streak of light across
the sky? I think I saw—"

The sky flickered in a sudden, brilliant burst of
white, a strobe light going off in his face. The Soviet
attack helicopter vanished.

"That was a Raptor. Blanks is here," Bachman
whispered.

Miles's communications helmet crackled, but no
sound came through. "Get a signal flare out and—"
He saw an Osprey suddenly take shape in the orange
glow of burning Soviet craft at the other end of the
airfield. Its gear was down for landing. "—never mind,
they're coming in to pull our asses out."

Three of Blanks's Ospreys circled the airfield, mopping up on the destruction with cannon fire and protecting the extraction of Miles's crew. When they were aloft, Miles remembered one important detail. "You have to destroy the bird on the ground. Can't let the bad guys get our technology."

Blanks and his wingman made the run, firing cannons until the Osprey's little fire burst into larger flames and then exploded into one fireball. Miles, a bandage pressed to his wounded forehead, stood between Blanks and his copilot, watching in distress as his craft erupted.

Blanks put the Osprey into a steep bank. As they wheeled to fly by the pillar of fire, Miles tossed his flaming bird a forlorn salute.

# Epilogue

"What time is it in Iran?" Dudov asked glumly.

"It is six in the morning."

"What is the assessment at this hour?"

Zuyenko said, "Nearly ninety percent of the fighters and bombers at Kerman. And more than eighty percent of the Gulf attack helicopter fleet west of Birjand . . . and all three Mi-28 helicopters. Our secret weapon has been defeated by theirs."

"What does Abramov have to say for himself?"

"He recommends we send an overture for peace. Without air cover, he says his tanks will be defenseless."

"He is right. The Americans have begun hitting our tank forces outside of Bandar Abbas with their anti-tank helicopters. We have no air force within range to retaliate. Their own bombers have now virtual freedom to attack our columns. The damned Iranians will be attacking us there before day's end. We should never have allowed the Mi-28s into the battle, should never have turned them over to Abramov."

"Still, we have their two airborne divisions held hostage on the mountains near Khash," offered Zuyenko.

"A trade-off, I assure you—our tanks for their infantry." He sighed heavily. "They will trade, I am sure. I have requested a telephone conference with the American housewife who calls herself president."

"No!" Zuyenko said, only half adamant. His face

darkened, ''That goddamned Abramov. Shall we bring him home for trial?''

Dudov clenched his jaws. ''He cannot come home. Get Mendenyev for me. I have a personal message for the major.''

Mendenyev felt as if he'd been paralyzed from the inside out as he limped into the command headquarters, which had grown silent as staff officers wandered the rooms aimlessly. He found Abramov sitting bent over, his huge, shaggy head lowered.

''Aleksandr Mendenyev,'' the marshal said in a low voice without looking up. ''Should you be out of the clinic?''

''I have spoken to Moscow. Comrade Dudov.'' Mendenyev gasped for air.

''Did he tell you I have offered a surrender to the Americans and Iranians?''

''Yes.''

Abramov looked up, his craggy face more rugged than ever. He raised an eyebrow in mock surprise. ''You have dressed in your parade uniform?''

Mendenyev flapped his arms gingerly, wincing at the pain in his chest, the tightness of his tunic over the heavily bandaged ribs.

''Why so formal?'' asked Abramov. Then his face showed a dawning of understanding. ''Ah . . .'' He raised a hand. ''Never mind the charade. I know why you look so ill. Welcome to the world of reality, Major. Dudov has told you I cannot return alive to Moscow.''

Mendenyev nodded.

''He has ordered you to kill me?''

Mendenyev's eyes dropped.

''I will make it easy for you, Major.'' Abramov stood up and opened his arms wide. Mendenyev's hand flinched toward his holster, but then he let it fall empty to his side.

''Comrade Marshal, if you were to draw your pistol and shoot me first—''

Abramov burst into harsh laughter. ''That's the

trouble with zealots. They are too eager to sacrifice their lives for their causes, even when the causes have been revealed as frauds."

The bewildered Mendenyev said, "You would not fight me? You would want me to kill you?"

"That's two questions. The answer to both is no. I will not fight you. I do not want you to kill me. I have been in contact with the American general who commands the aircraft that defeated ours. It is a woman. Can you imagine? I am going to surrender to . . . well, that is no matter, eh?"

"Dudov does not want a surrender yet. The terms haven't been fully negotiated. He has ordered me to prevent that."

"You know better, Aleksandr Mendenyev. Those devil craft will strike again, perhaps tonight. Then his bargaining position will be worsened."

Mendenyev's jaws tightened.

Abramov shrugged. "You have your orders then, Major. You are an excellent officer. I would want you in my command even if you had not been forced upon me. Then, I will never have a command again. You see, I am going to defect, to seek asylum with the Americans. They will not wish to grant it at first. But I think I can make a case that my life is endangered as a political dissident, don't you? My position as a former insider at the Kremlin will make me a tempting morsel, wouldn't you say?" Abramov stood up. "I have a helicopter waiting. You'll excuse me."

Mendenyev drew his pistol. He did not point it at Abramov, and the marshal only glanced at him before offering his back. Abramov adjusted his own holster and started toward the door.

"Wait," barked Mendenyev.

Abramov stopped but he did not turn. "I cannot stop you from doing what you must, Aleksandr Mendenyev. I will not. Do you remember those vials I gave you?"

Mendenyev choked on his answer. "Yes."

"After you do your duty . . . fill one of them with

my blood. I'd be honored if you would remember me in that way.''

Mendenyev raised his pistol, then lowered it.

"No! I will not fill the vial with your blood."

Abramov slumped. He laughed harshly. "You know, my son, that is more painful than the idea you would shoot me. At least the killing is in obedience to orders." He began walking again. "In one way or another, this is farewell, Aleksandr Mendenyev."

"No!"

Abramov cringed, tensing his back for the bullet, but he kept walking.

Mendenyev tossed down the pistol and limped toward his commander on his heavily bandaged ankle. "Wait. I will go with you . . . if you will permit me, Comrade Marshal."

Standing on the aircraft carrier's deck in the brilliant day, Miles felt dreamy, even narcotized by the sun. His forehead throbbed, the stitches and swelling seemingly pulling his eyebrows up into his hairline. He had to keep reminding himself that the almost imperceptible swaying he felt was not dizziness, but the carrier absorbing the gentle swell of the Persian Gulf.

He felt a touch on his shoulder and turned his head to see the two stars on Major General Rita Bernadino's helmet. "Nelson, General Pickett is almost ready. Look at them," she said, pointing to the collection of men and women assembled before the Osprey parked on the deck.

"I wish everybody in the battalion could be here," he said.

"They have to rest in case we need them tonight—" She caught the look in his face. "I'm sorry. You meant the ones who were lost in action yesterday and last night." She inhaled deeply. "It's surreal, isn't it? All that blood and destruction just a few hours in the past, just a short flight into the future if the Soviets don't honor the surrender."

He shook his head, catching himself as he swayed a little. "It bothers me to be honoring some of our heroes with medals the same day we're sending the others back home in body bags.''

"Try not to think about that. Think about the price they paid in terms of the results they earned for their country. Because we still have a third of our original Osprey fleet—and the Soviets don't know how many birds that is, anyhow—they don't dare even launch their gunships up at night—by day, for that matter. If you could say anything positive about the stunt that Wilkerson pulled, it would be that the Soviets now think the Osprey is just as effective by day as it is at night. They're feeling paralyzed for the moment. The politicians in Washington know the score, and they're pressing for a quick accord. The Soviets are going to have to trade all those divisions in eastern Iran for a complete withdrawal from Tabriz. Nelson, I think we're going to get out of here with few or no more lives lost." She shook his shoulder, and he winced. "Nelson, we've won. We've pulled off another Desert Storm, this time against the Soviets. Do you know what that means in terms of world peace?''

"You're right, of course. The big picture is one of total victory. It's the little details, the loss of men and women . . . you know, lots of people whose names we know and those we'll never know.''

She nodded and stood silently by his side until she saw a hand signal from one of the Navy's master chief petty officers. "It's time," she said. "You'd better take command of your formation.''

Miles stiffened himself, placing the thoughts of his wife and son to the spot in his mind from where he could recall them when he needed a lift, he marched across the deck and saluted Major Herman Blanks, who took his position beside the first rank of Osprey pilots and crew chiefs to be honored.

Next, General Pickett stood before him, congratulating him, pinning the purple heart and a medal for bravery to his flight suit. Miles heard only snatches of the citation: "—withering fire—" "—determined enemy—" "—strategic implications—" "—instrumental to victory.''

Miles, who had always tried to keep to the tough-guy image accorded him because of his height and bulk, didn't feel tough at all. He felt awed in the aftermath of his first combat experiences. All his career he had trained for the action that had been crammed into a combat career lasting less than twenty-four hours. He remembered all the hours he'd spent whining to Julie about being late for Vietnam, about not getting into Desert Storm at all. It now seemed like the rantings of a spoiled brat. Anybody who had seen what he had would never beg to repeat the experience, the horrors. He knew he would never beg to get into a battle again. He wondered if he could ever even answer a call to arms—tonight, if that would be required of him because the Soviets broke the cease-fire or something. He wondered if these thoughts meant that, after all the years he'd wanted the test of battle, he'd found himself wanting in the courage department. He remembered getting the news of the loss of P.B. Keyes, the sight of every Osprey he'd seen shot up, every bird that had crashed, every crew member that had been scattered over the rubbled earth with the debris of aircraft wreckage, the—

"—Colonel Miles?" the general's voice startled him.

"Yes, sir," he said, realizing he'd just been asked to accompany Bernadino as she got in step beside the general.

The ceremony was starkly simple. In turn, the general stood before every Osprey crewman, each looking awkwardly at a spot on the general's uniform while the citation for bravery was read. The general then pinned on the medals, shook hands, and moved to repeat the sequence a step to the right. Bernadino and Miles followed, shaking each crewman's hand. By the third presentation, Miles was finally standing in front of somebody: Blanks.

Miles didn't stare at a spot on the uniform of his operations officer. He stared into his eyes, into the return gaze. Then he understood. This too, was a combat veteran—of two wars now. He'd never heard any bravado from men like Blanks. He'd only heard the big talk from guys like Wilkerson—and even himself—men, who'd never been there. Blanks had known the terrors of fighting, and he'd stayed on to answer the call a second time. Blanks didn't see himself as hero because he did his duty, and he was no coward just because he might have been too afraid to beg for combat.

Miles was grateful for men and women with the unadorned courage of Blanks. Because of them, he knew the answer to his momentary quandary—when the next call to battle came, he would answer it by fighting again, for them. Besides, this man had saved his life. He broke the gaze and looked down at his own chest. Then he pulled off the Distinguished Flying Cross Medal and pinned it to the chest of his operations officer, making a total of two decorations with "V" devices for valor.

Blanks answered with a modest smile, showing that he understood.

"Thanks," Miles said, gripping hard in the handshake. Then he moved on to the next pilot, then to the other men and women in turn. The one word was all he said to each of them. They each seemingly understood his feelings, perhaps valuing his gratitude as much as the decorations they wore.

The firing on the mountain overlooking Khash had unaccountably stopped. Inside the dank, smelly cavern, the men seemed to sense it all at once.

"Damn, L.T.," said Quinlan, baring his teeth, "seems like the war is done."

Edwards sat up. "Speak up, I can't hear." His ears still rang from the explosion in his face, and the back of his head still stung where his hair had been burnt off, but he had survived the explosion of the Soviet tank. The tank round had not cooked off in the breech as he lay there, the gun pointed down the length of his spine.

"Is it day or night?" Edwards asked.

Nobody knew. The firing port had been packed with dirt and the men had decided it was safer to stay underground, hoping they would not be discovered by Soviet infantry, wondering how long the air would hold out.

Plenty of traffic had moved by. But nobody had molested their hiding spot.

Now they dug out a spot of daylight, pulling dust and gravel into the hole.

"I gotta take a leak," said Edwards.

"Stop yelling, Lieutenant. Piss in the corner over there like everybody else."

Edwards hadn't heard, because the ringing in his ears was too persistent. He stepped up to the firing port and stuck his head out. Again. The back of his scalp scraped against the dirt, and the pain made him swear. Then, he said, "Hey, the bastards are gone. There ain't no Russians out here. The only guys out here are all GIs and . . . shit, there's a bunch of Iranians piling out of a helicopter." He pronounced it, "Eye-rain-ians."

When he had assembled the ragged remnants of his platoon, Edwards introduced himself to a pair of Iranians watching the Americans dig out. One was a slight man with a narrow hatchet face. His nose and lips protruded like the muzzle of some animal, Edwards thought, a weasel. The other was a bulldog of a man.

"I'm Lieutenant Thomas Edwards, Savannah, Georgia," he shouted over the roaring in his ears, extending his hand to the weasel-like Iranian.

"Pleasure is to meet you, Lieutenant Georgia. This is General Bani-Sadr, and I am Colonel Abu al-Batt," said the Iranian in halting English. "My countrymen call me Abu the Ferret. We have come to thank you . . . and to take back our country. We have many tanks coming. Don't try to stay here."

Edwards saw the stern look that accompanied the threat. His first inclination was to flatten the pointed nose. Instead, he laughed and clapped the Iranian on the shoulder. "Don't worry about that. I just want to go home. You take your country and put it where the sun never shines."

"What is this American cow laughing about?" Bani-Sadr demanded in his own language.

Abu, feeling superior to his boss in the important new role of translator, tried out the phrase in English first, "At his home, the sun never shines?" then repeated it to Bani-Sadr in his own language and more assertively.

"Tell him he has been in combat too long," Bani-Sadr growled. Abu snarled the translation at Edwards.

Edwards repeated Abu's exchange to his troops, and before long, all the Americans lay gasping for breath, laughing and writhing in the dirt.

## About the Author

Born in Philadelphia in 1946, Lieutenant Colonel
J. V. Smith, Jr., obtained a B.A. in political sci-
ence from the University of South Carolina and an
M.S. in journalism from the University of Kansas.
The Army drafted him in 1966.
After two tours in Vietnam (one in tanks, the other
as a helicopter pilot), he began a successful career
within the ranks, and, later, as a journalist. Jim is
married to Susan, with whom he has had four children, and lives in Fishers, Indiana.